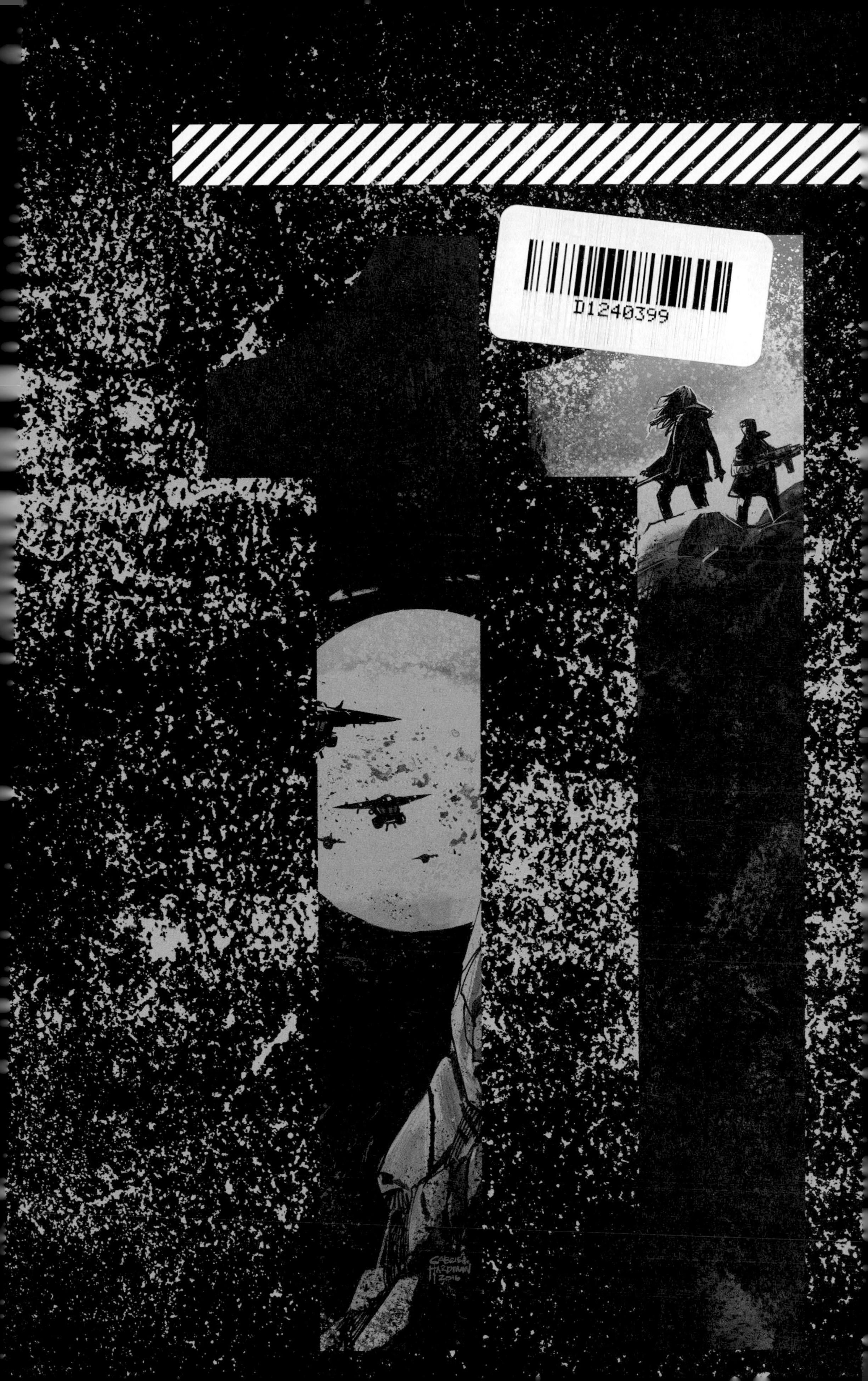

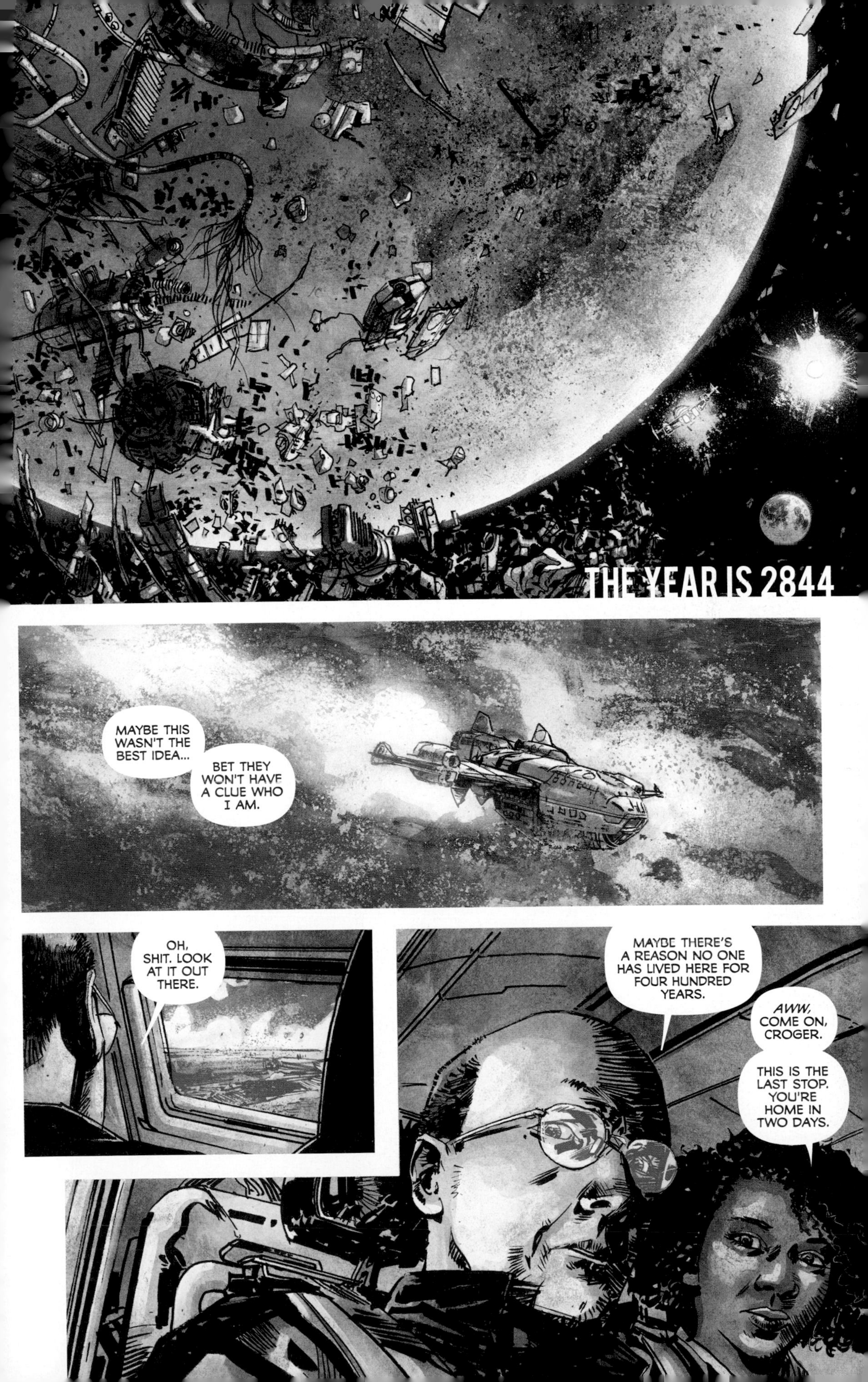

THE YEAR IS 2844
MAYBE THIS WASN'T THE BEST IDEA...
BET THEY WON'T HAVE A CLUE WHO I AM.
OH, SHIT. LOOK AT IT OUT THERE.
MAYBE THERE'S A REASON NO ONE HAS LIVED HERE FOR FOUR HUNDRED YEARS.
AWW, COME ON, CROGER.
THIS IS THE LAST STOP. YOU'RE HOME IN TWO DAYS.

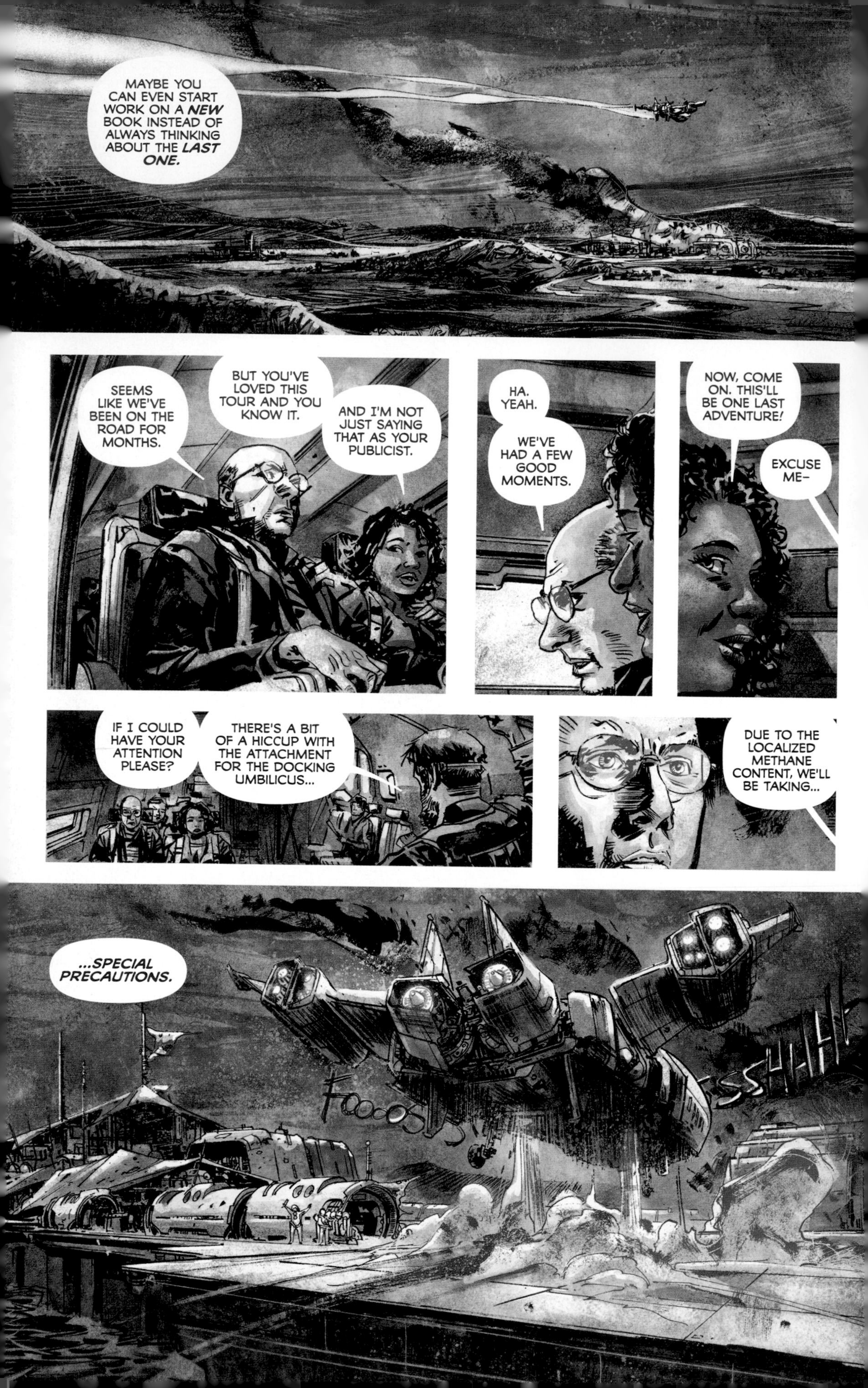
MAYBE YOU CAN EVEN START WORK ON A *NEW* BOOK INSTEAD OF ALWAYS THINKING ABOUT THE *LAST ONE.*
SEEMS LIKE WE'VE BEEN ON THE ROAD FOR MONTHS.
BUT YOU'VE LOVED THIS TOUR AND YOU KNOW IT.
AND I'M NOT JUST SAYING THAT AS YOUR PUBLICIST.
HA. YEAH.
WE'VE HAD A FEW GOOD MOMENTS.
NOW, COME ON. THIS'LL BE ONE LAST ADVENTURE!
EXCUSE ME–
IF I COULD HAVE YOUR ATTENTION PLEASE?
THERE'S A BIT OF A HICCUP WITH THE ATTACHMENT FOR THE DOCKING UMBILICUS...
DUE TO THE LOCALIZED METHANE CONTENT, WE'LL BE TAKING...
...SPECIAL PRECAUTIONS.
FOOOOS
SSHHH

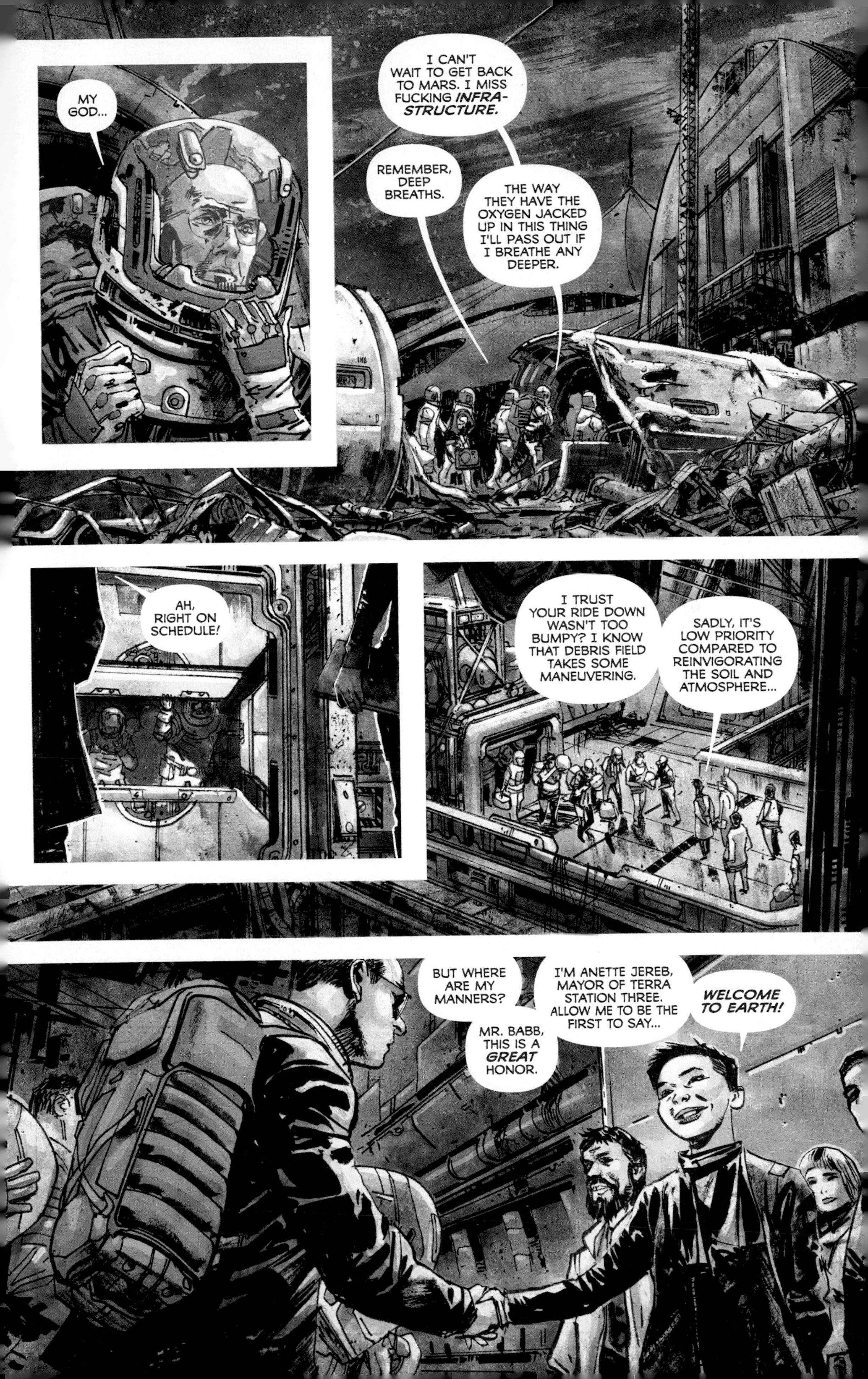
MY GOD...
I CAN'T WAIT TO GET BACK TO MARS. I MISS FUCKING *INFRA-STRUCTURE.*
REMEMBER, DEEP BREATHS.
THE WAY THEY HAVE THE OXYGEN JACKED UP IN THIS THING I'LL PASS OUT IF I BREATHE ANY DEEPER.
AH, RIGHT ON SCHEDULE!
I TRUST YOUR RIDE DOWN WASN'T TOO BUMPY? I KNOW THAT DEBRIS FIELD TAKES SOME MANEUVERING.
SADLY, IT'S LOW PRIORITY COMPARED TO REINVIGORATING THE SOIL AND ATMOSPHERE...
BUT WHERE ARE MY MANNERS?
MR. BABB, THIS IS A *GREAT* HONOR.
I'M ANETTE JEREB, MAYOR OF TERRA STATION THREE. ALLOW ME TO BE THE FIRST TO SAY...
WELCOME TO EARTH!

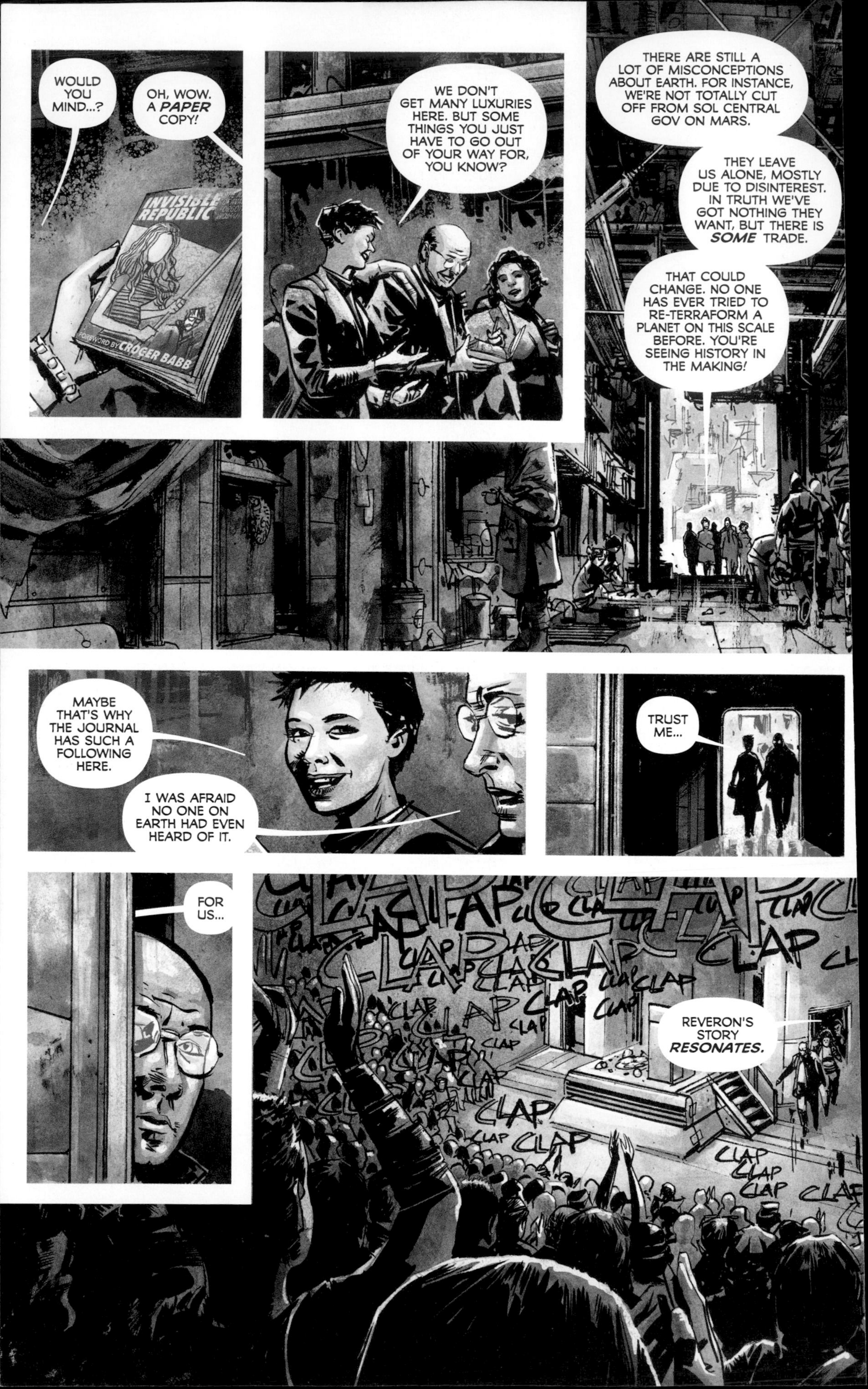
WOULD YOU MIND...?
OH, WOW. A PAPER COPY!
INVISIBLE REPUBLIC
FOREWORD BY CROGER BABB
WE DON'T GET MANY LUXURIES HERE. BUT SOME THINGS YOU JUST HAVE TO GO OUT OF YOUR WAY FOR, YOU KNOW?
THERE ARE STILL A LOT OF MISCONCEPTIONS ABOUT EARTH. FOR INSTANCE, WE'RE NOT TOTALLY CUT OFF FROM SOL CENTRAL GOV ON MARS.
THEY LEAVE US ALONE, MOSTLY DUE TO DISINTEREST. IN TRUTH WE'VE GOT NOTHING THEY WANT, BUT THERE IS SOME TRADE.
THAT COULD CHANGE. NO ONE HAS EVER TRIED TO RE-TERRAFORM A PLANET ON THIS SCALE BEFORE. YOU'RE SEEING HISTORY IN THE MAKING!
MAYBE THAT'S WHY THE JOURNAL HAS SUCH A FOLLOWING HERE.
I WAS AFRAID NO ONE ON EARTH HAD EVEN HEARD OF IT.
TRUST ME...
FOR US...
CLAP CLAP CLAP
REVERON'S STORY RESONATES.
CLAP CLAP CLAP

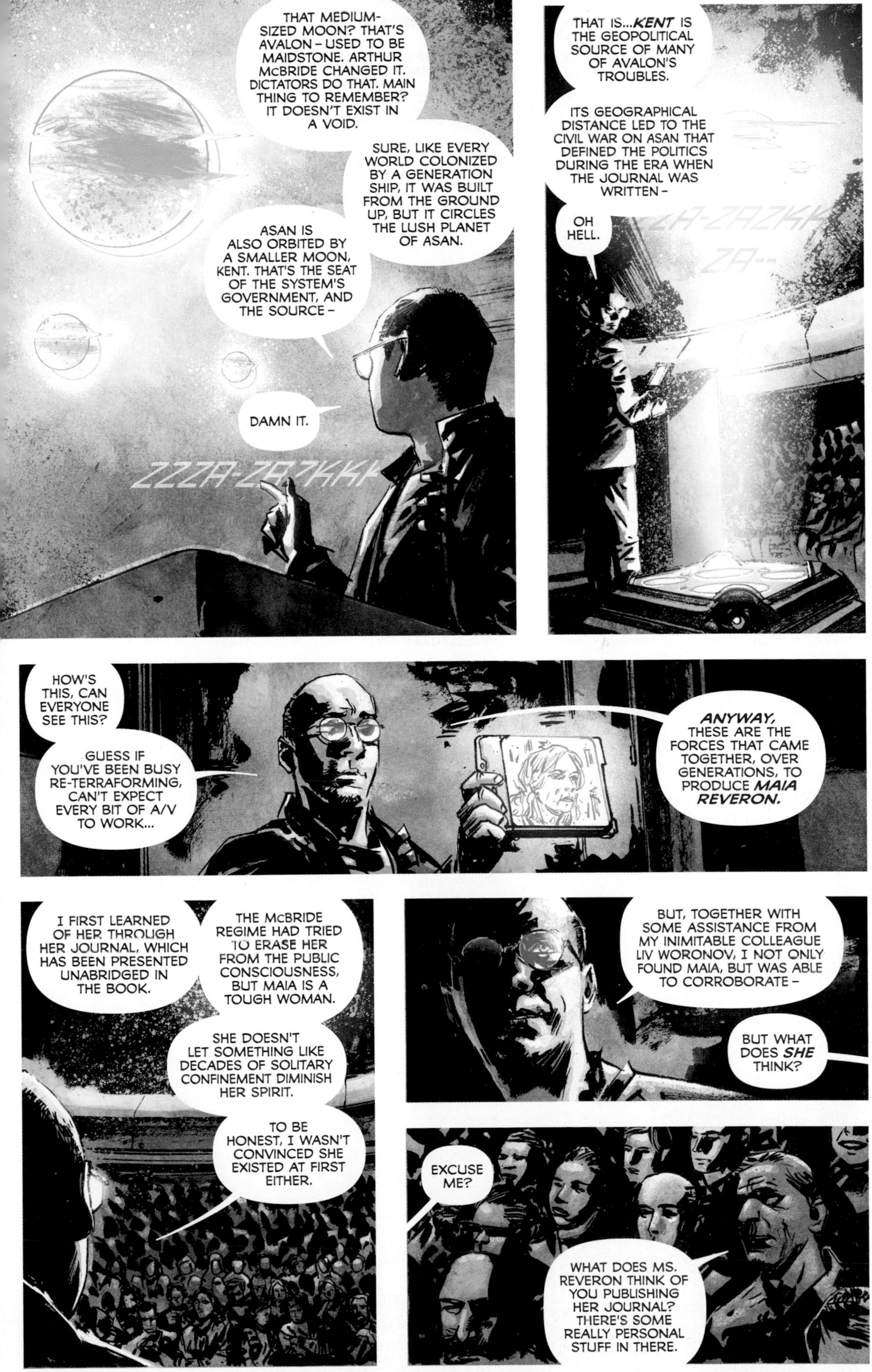
THAT MEDIUM-SIZED MOON? THAT'S AVALON – USED TO BE MAIDSTONE. ARTHUR McBRIDE CHANGED IT. DICTATORS DO THAT. MAIN THING TO REMEMBER? IT DOESN'T EXIST IN A VOID.
SURE, LIKE EVERY WORLD COLONIZED BY A GENERATION SHIP, IT WAS BUILT FROM THE GROUND UP, BUT IT CIRCLES THE LUSH PLANET OF ASAN.
ASAN IS ALSO ORBITED BY A SMALLER MOON, KENT. THAT'S THE SEAT OF THE SYSTEM'S GOVERNMENT, AND THE SOURCE –
DAMN IT.
ZZZA-ZAZKKK
THAT IS...*KENT* IS THE GEOPOLITICAL SOURCE OF MANY OF AVALON'S TROUBLES.
ITS GEOGRAPHICAL DISTANCE LED TO THE CIVIL WAR ON ASAN THAT DEFINED THE POLITICS DURING THE ERA WHEN THE JOURNAL WAS WRITTEN –
OH HELL.
ZZA-ZAZKK ZA--
HOW'S THIS, CAN EVERYONE SEE THIS?
GUESS IF YOU'VE BEEN BUSY RE-TERRAFORMING, CAN'T EXPECT EVERY BIT OF A/V TO WORK...
ANYWAY, THESE ARE THE FORCES THAT CAME TOGETHER, OVER GENERATIONS, TO PRODUCE ***MAIA REVERON.***
I FIRST LEARNED OF HER THROUGH HER JOURNAL, WHICH HAS BEEN PRESENTED UNABRIDGED IN THE BOOK.
THE McBRIDE REGIME HAD TRIED TO ERASE HER FROM THE PUBLIC CONSCIOUSNESS, BUT MAIA IS A TOUGH WOMAN.
SHE DOESN'T LET SOMETHING LIKE DECADES OF SOLITARY CONFINEMENT DIMINISH HER SPIRIT.
TO BE HONEST, I WASN'T CONVINCED SHE EXISTED AT FIRST EITHER.
BUT, TOGETHER WITH SOME ASSISTANCE FROM MY INIMITABLE COLLEAGUE LIV WORONOV, I NOT ONLY FOUND MAIA, BUT WAS ABLE TO CORROBORATE –
BUT WHAT DOES *SHE* THINK?
EXCUSE ME?
WHAT DOES MS. REVERON THINK OF YOU PUBLISHING HER JOURNAL? THERE'S SOME REALLY PERSONAL STUFF IN THERE.

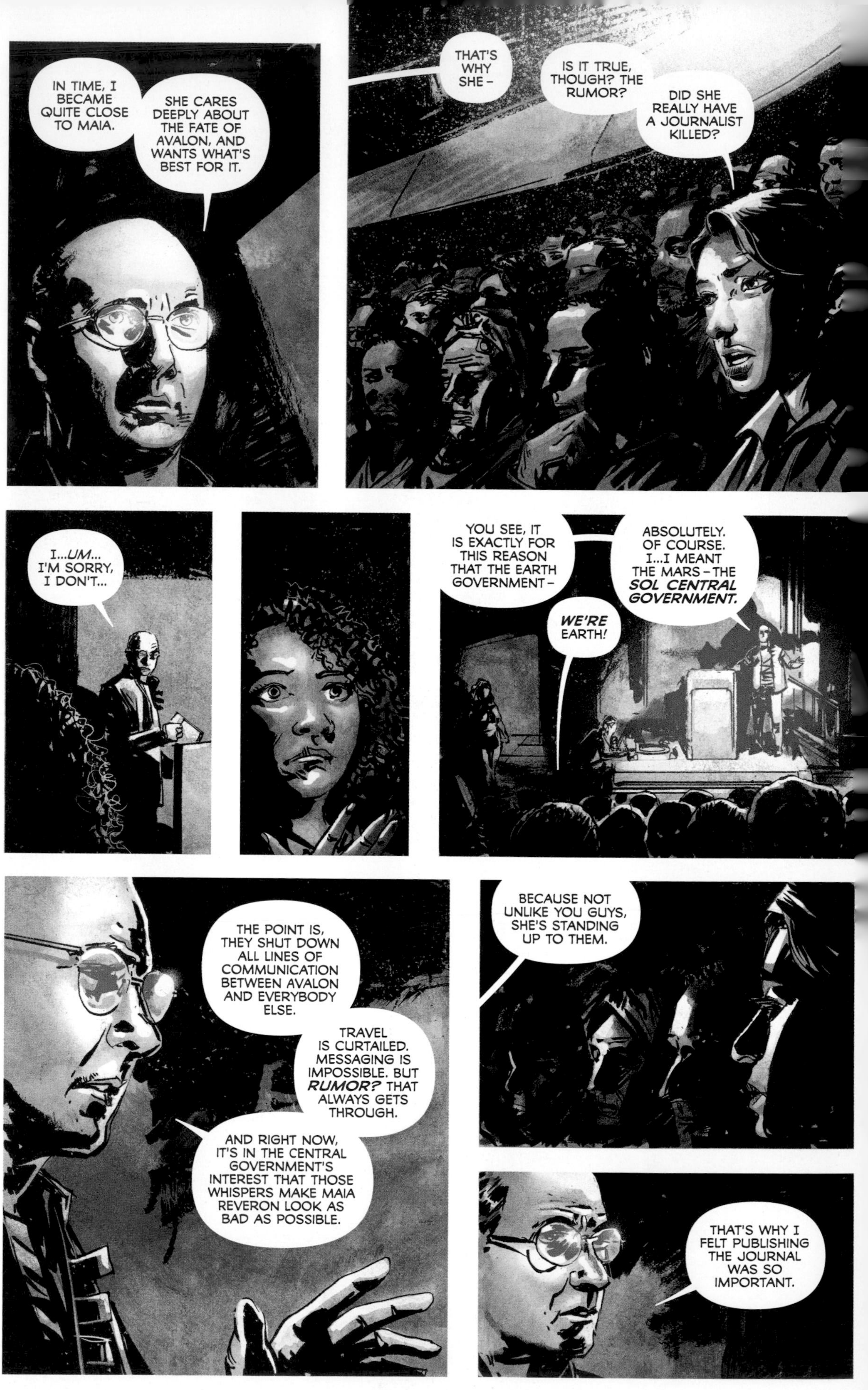
IN TIME, I BECAME QUITE CLOSE TO MAIA.
SHE CARES DEEPLY ABOUT THE FATE OF AVALON, AND WANTS WHAT'S BEST FOR IT.
THAT'S WHY SHE –
IS IT TRUE, THOUGH? THE RUMOR?
DID SHE REALLY HAVE A JOURNALIST KILLED?
I...*UM*... I'M SORRY, I DON'T...
YOU SEE, IT IS EXACTLY FOR THIS REASON THAT THE EARTH GOVERNMENT –
WE'RE EARTH!
ABSOLUTELY. OF COURSE. I...I MEANT THE MARS – THE ***SOL CENTRAL GOVERNMENT.***
THE POINT IS, THEY SHUT DOWN ALL LINES OF COMMUNICATION BETWEEN AVALON AND EVERYBODY ELSE.
TRAVEL IS CURTAILED. MESSAGING IS IMPOSSIBLE. BUT ***RUMOR?*** THAT ALWAYS GETS THROUGH.
AND RIGHT NOW, IT'S IN THE CENTRAL GOVERNMENT'S INTEREST THAT THOSE WHISPERS MAKE MAIA REVERON LOOK AS BAD AS POSSIBLE.
BECAUSE NOT UNLIKE YOU GUYS, SHE'S STANDING UP TO THEM.
THAT'S WHY I FELT PUBLISHING THE JOURNAL WAS SO IMPORTANT.

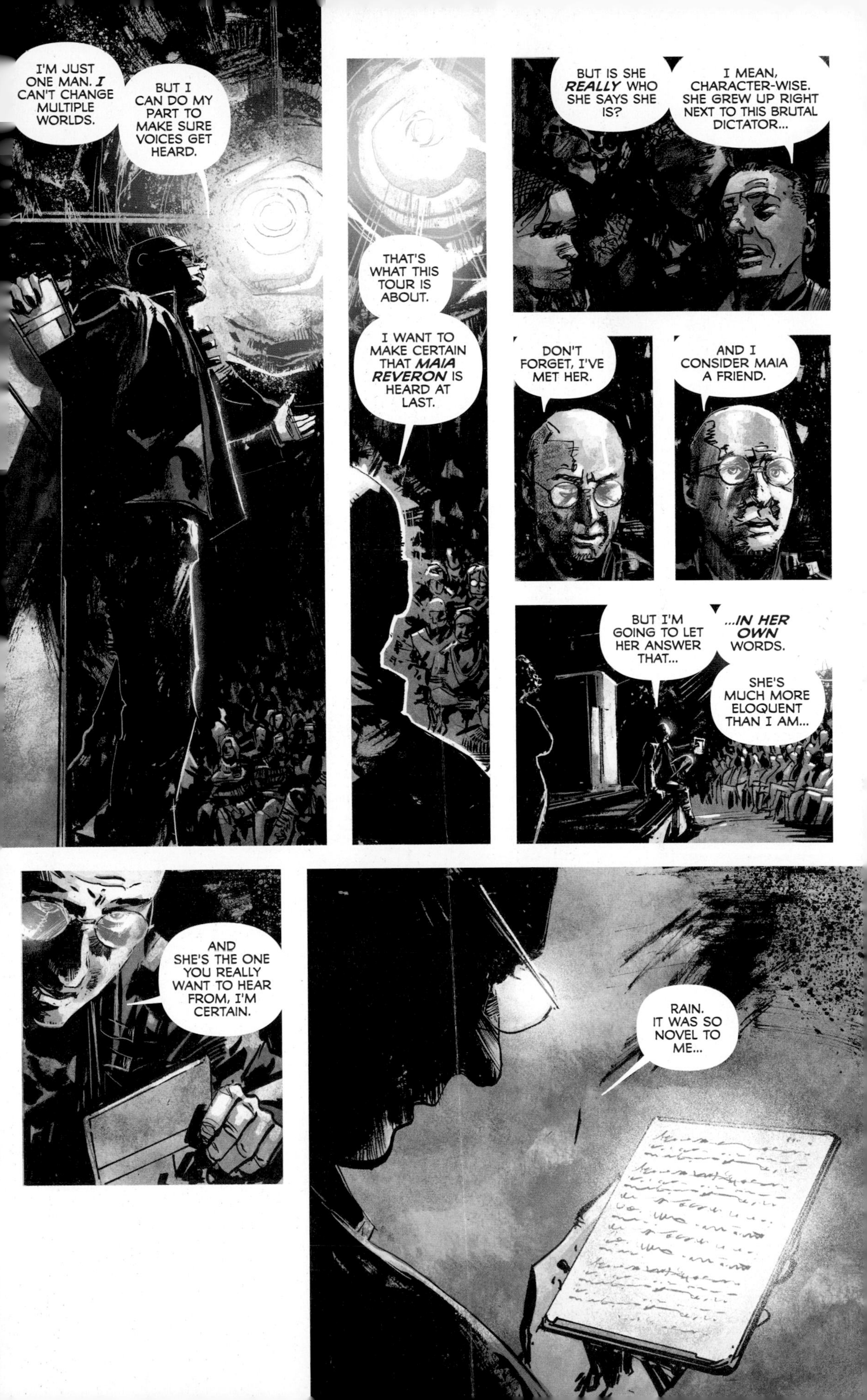
I'M JUST ONE MAN. *I* CAN'T CHANGE MULTIPLE WORLDS.
BUT I CAN DO MY PART TO MAKE SURE VOICES GET HEARD.
THAT'S WHAT THIS TOUR IS ABOUT.
I WANT TO MAKE CERTAIN THAT ***MAIA REVERON*** IS HEARD AT LAST.
BUT IS SHE ***REALLY*** WHO SHE SAYS SHE IS?
I MEAN, CHARACTER-WISE. SHE GREW UP RIGHT NEXT TO THIS BRUTAL DICTATOR...
DON'T FORGET, I'VE MET HER.
AND I CONSIDER MAIA A FRIEND.
BUT I'M GOING TO LET HER ANSWER THAT...
...***IN HER OWN*** WORDS.
SHE'S MUCH MORE ELOQUENT THAN I AM...
AND SHE'S THE ONE YOU REALLY WANT TO HEAR FROM, I'M CERTAIN.
RAIN. IT WAS SO NOVEL TO ME...

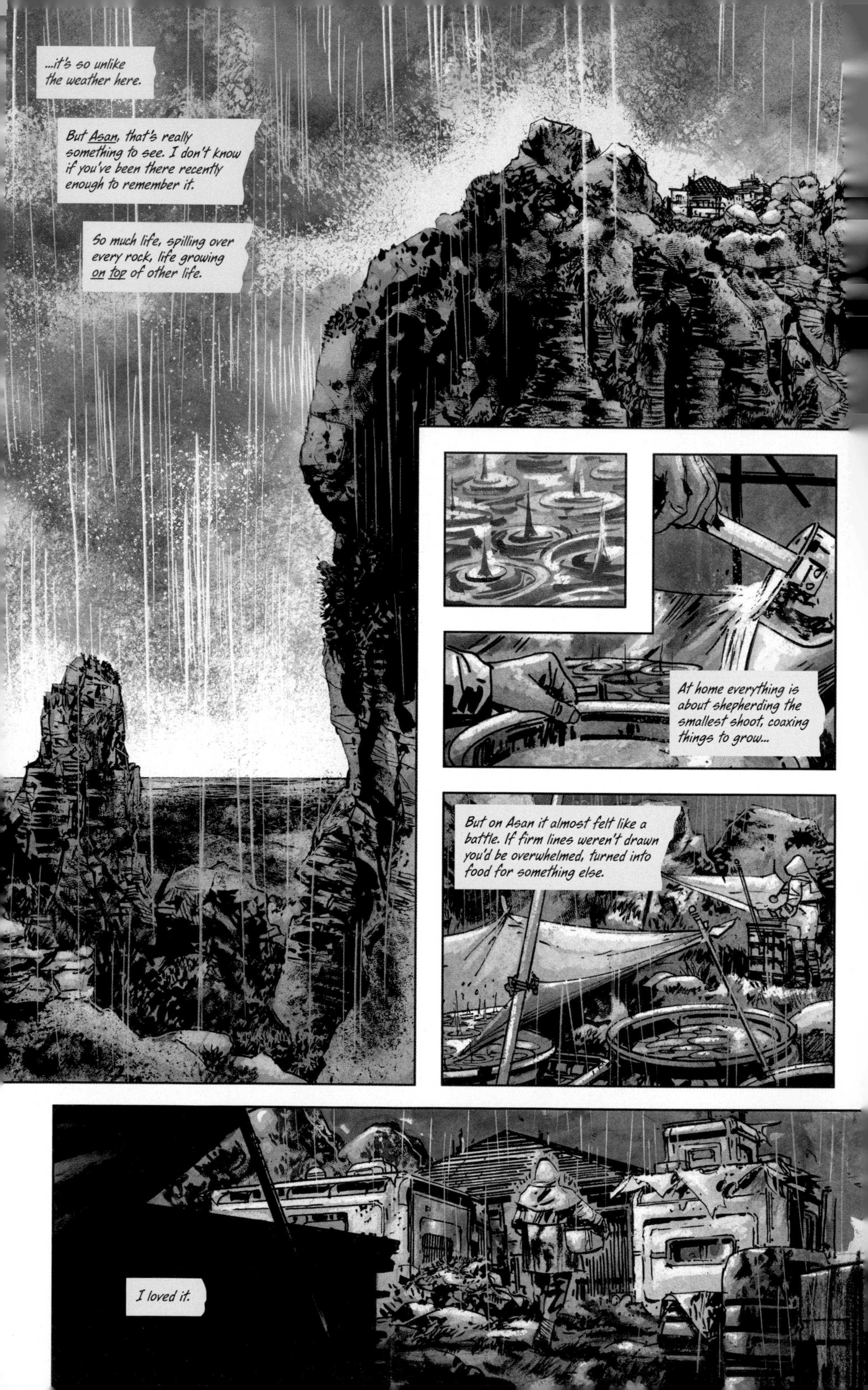
...it's so unlike the weather here.
But Asan, that's really something to see. I don't know if you've been there recently enough to remember it.
So much life, spilling over every rock, life growing on top of other life.
At home everything is about shepherding the smallest shoot, coaxing things to grow...
But on Asan it almost felt like a battle. If firm lines weren't drawn you'd be overwhelmed, turned into food for something else.
I loved it.

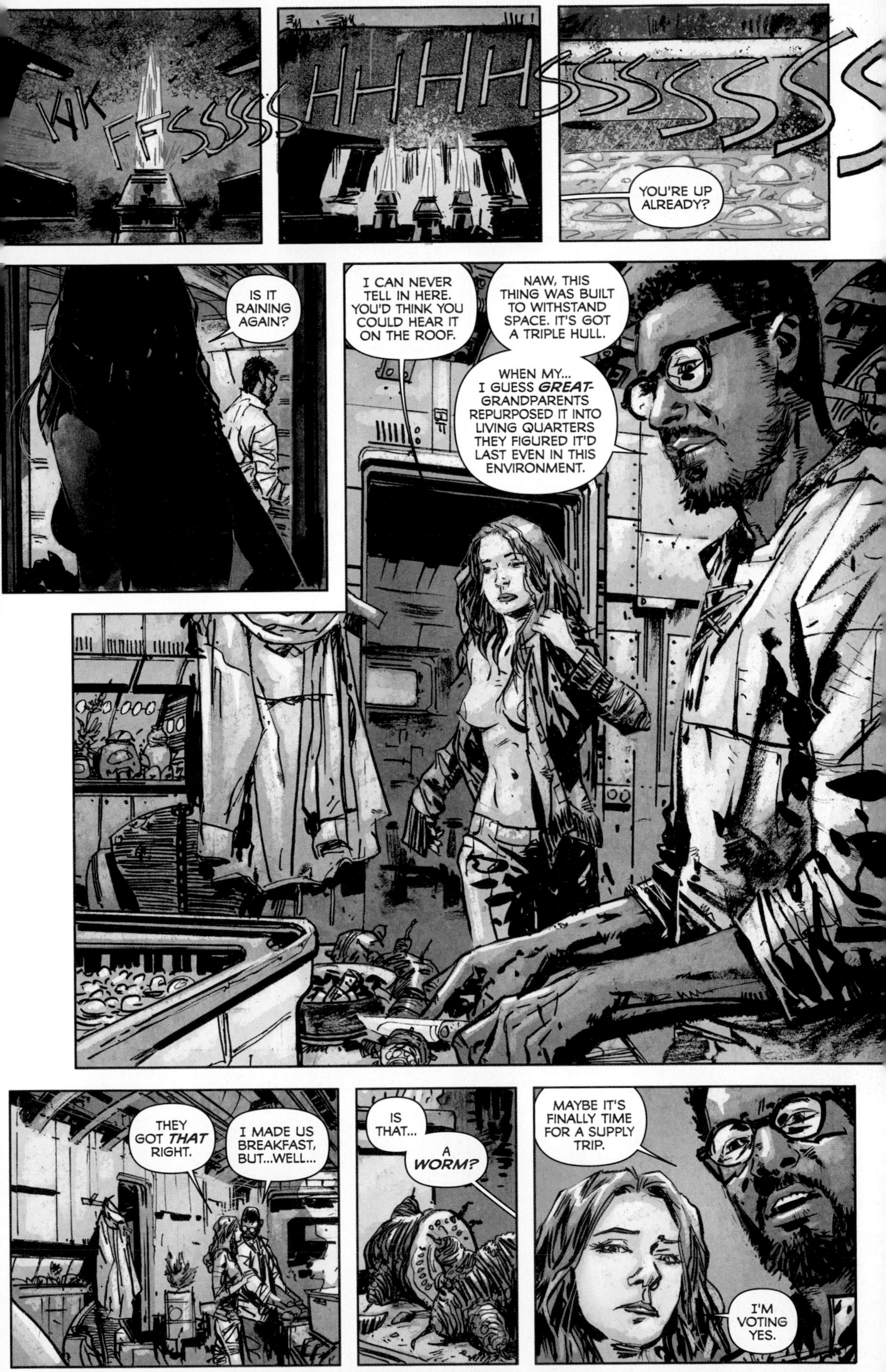
KAK
FFSSSSSHHHHHSSSSSSS
YOU'RE UP ALREADY?
IS IT RAINING AGAIN?
I CAN NEVER TELL IN HERE. YOU'D THINK YOU COULD HEAR IT ON THE ROOF.
NAW, THIS THING WAS BUILT TO WITHSTAND SPACE. IT'S GOT A TRIPLE HULL.
WHEN MY... I GUESS GREAT-GRANDPARENTS REPURPOSED IT INTO LIVING QUARTERS THEY FIGURED IT'D LAST EVEN IN THIS ENVIRONMENT.
THEY GOT THAT RIGHT.
I MADE US BREAKFAST, BUT...WELL...
IS THAT...
A WORM?
MAYBE IT'S FINALLY TIME FOR A SUPPLY TRIP.
I'M VOTING YES.

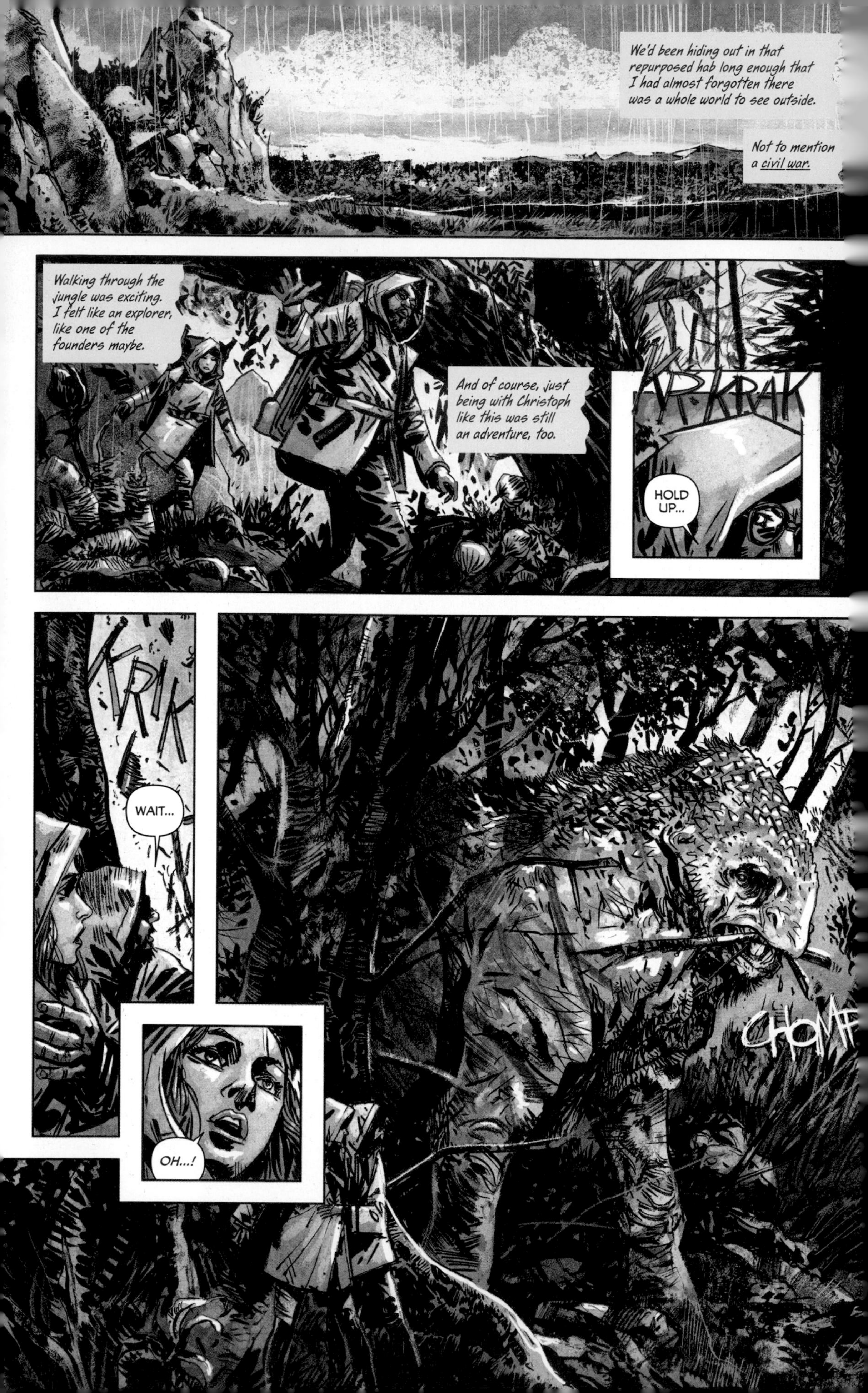

We'd been hiding out in that repurposed hab long enough that I had almost forgotten there was a whole world to see outside.
Not to mention a civil war.
Walking through the jungle was exciting. I felt like an explorer, like one of the founders maybe.
And of course, just being with Christoph like this was still an adventure, too.
KRAK
HOLD UP...
KRIK
WAIT...
OH...!
CHOMP

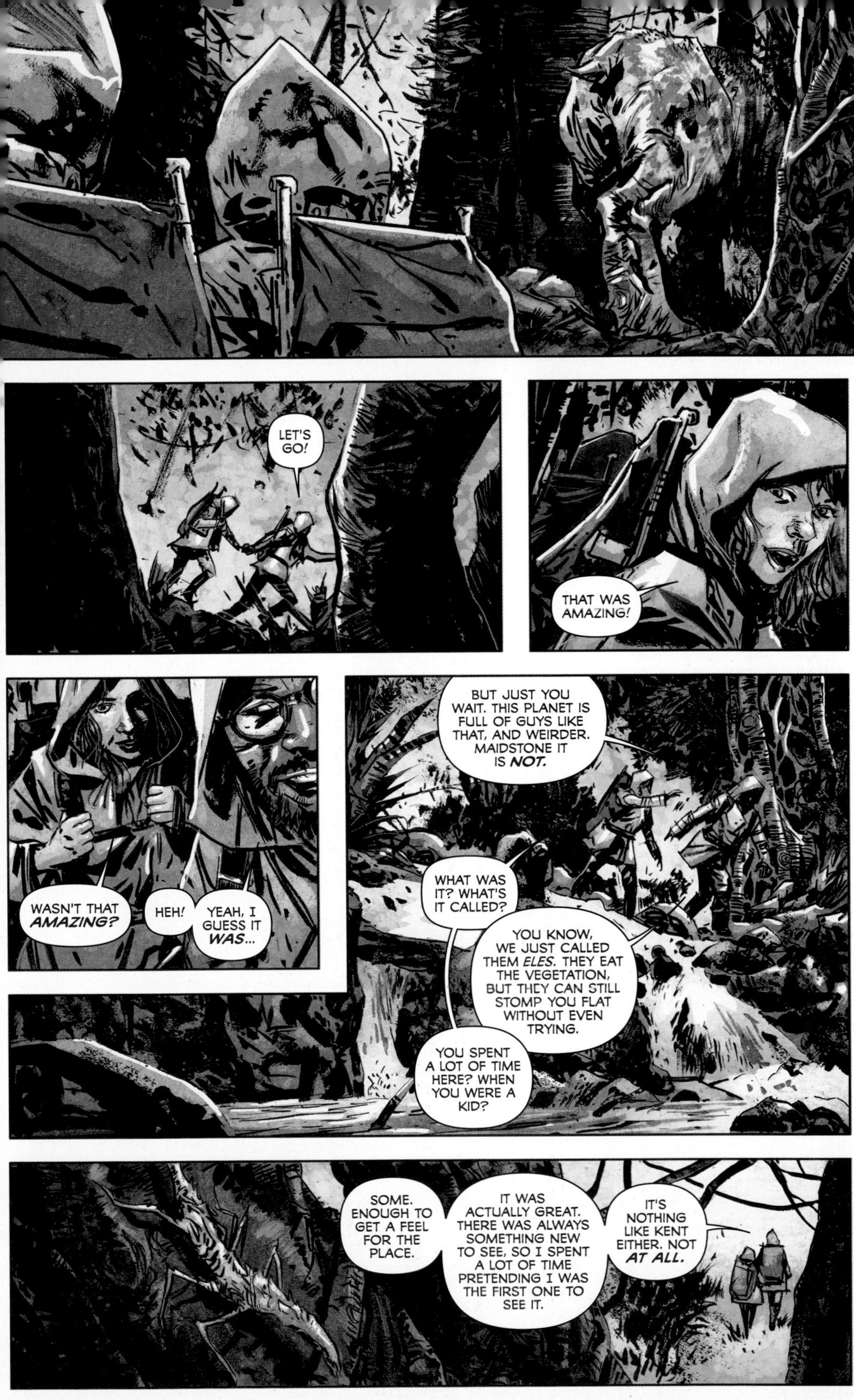
LET'S GO!
THAT WAS AMAZING!
WASN'T THAT AMAZING?
HEH!
YEAH, I GUESS IT WAS...
BUT JUST YOU WAIT. THIS PLANET IS FULL OF GUYS LIKE THAT, AND WEIRDER. MAIDSTONE IT IS NOT.
WHAT WAS IT? WHAT'S IT CALLED?
YOU KNOW, WE JUST CALLED THEM ELES. THEY EAT THE VEGETATION, BUT THEY CAN STILL STOMP YOU FLAT WITHOUT EVEN TRYING.
YOU SPENT A LOT OF TIME HERE? WHEN YOU WERE A KID?
SOME. ENOUGH TO GET A FEEL FOR THE PLACE.
IT WAS ACTUALLY GREAT. THERE WAS ALWAYS SOMETHING NEW TO SEE, SO I SPENT A LOT OF TIME PRETENDING I WAS THE FIRST ONE TO SEE IT.
IT'S NOTHING LIKE KENT EITHER. NOT AT ALL.

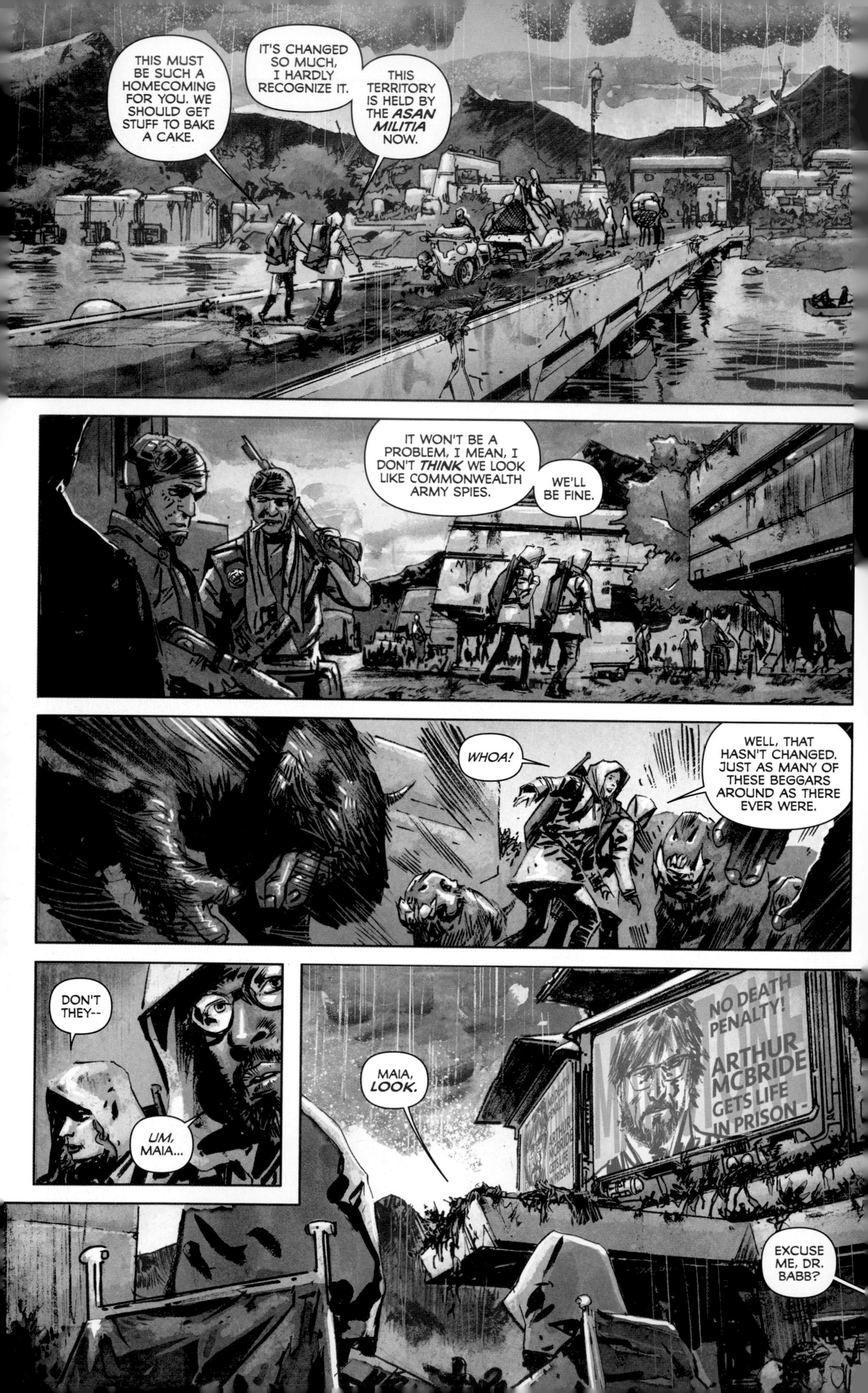
THIS MUST BE SUCH A HOMECOMING FOR YOU. WE SHOULD GET STUFF TO BAKE A CAKE.
IT'S CHANGED SO MUCH, I HARDLY RECOGNIZE IT.
THIS TERRITORY IS HELD BY THE ASAN MILITIA NOW.
IT WON'T BE A PROBLEM, I MEAN, I DON'T THINK WE LOOK LIKE COMMONWEALTH ARMY SPIES.
WE'LL BE FINE.
WHOA!
WELL, THAT HASN'T CHANGED. JUST AS MANY OF THESE BEGGARS AROUND AS THERE EVER WERE.
DON'T THEY--
UM, MAIA...
MAIA, LOOK.
NO DEATH PENALTY!
ARTHUR MCBRIDE GETS LIFE IN PRISON -
NO DEATH PENALTY
ARTHUR MCBRIDE GETS LIFE IN PRISON
EXCUSE ME, DR. BABB?

PLEASE, CALL ME *"MISTER."* THE DOCTORATE IS ONLY HONORARY.

OKAY, *MR.* BABB...

WHAT ABOUT THE FACT THAT REVERON IS THE ONE TELLING HER STORY? *OF COURSE* SHE'S GOING TO PUT *HERSELF* IN A GOOD LIGHT.

HOW COULD YOU EVER FACT-CHECK THIS PART? IT'S NOT LIKE YOU CAN ASK THOSE ANIMALS...

OKAY, WE'RE DONE. LET'S WRAP THIS UP.

ALL RIGHT, LET'S GIVE CROGER BABB A BIG TERRA STATION THREE THANK YOU!

CLAP CLAP CLAP

CLAP CLAP CLAP CLAP CLAP CLAP

NO JOKE, CROGER...

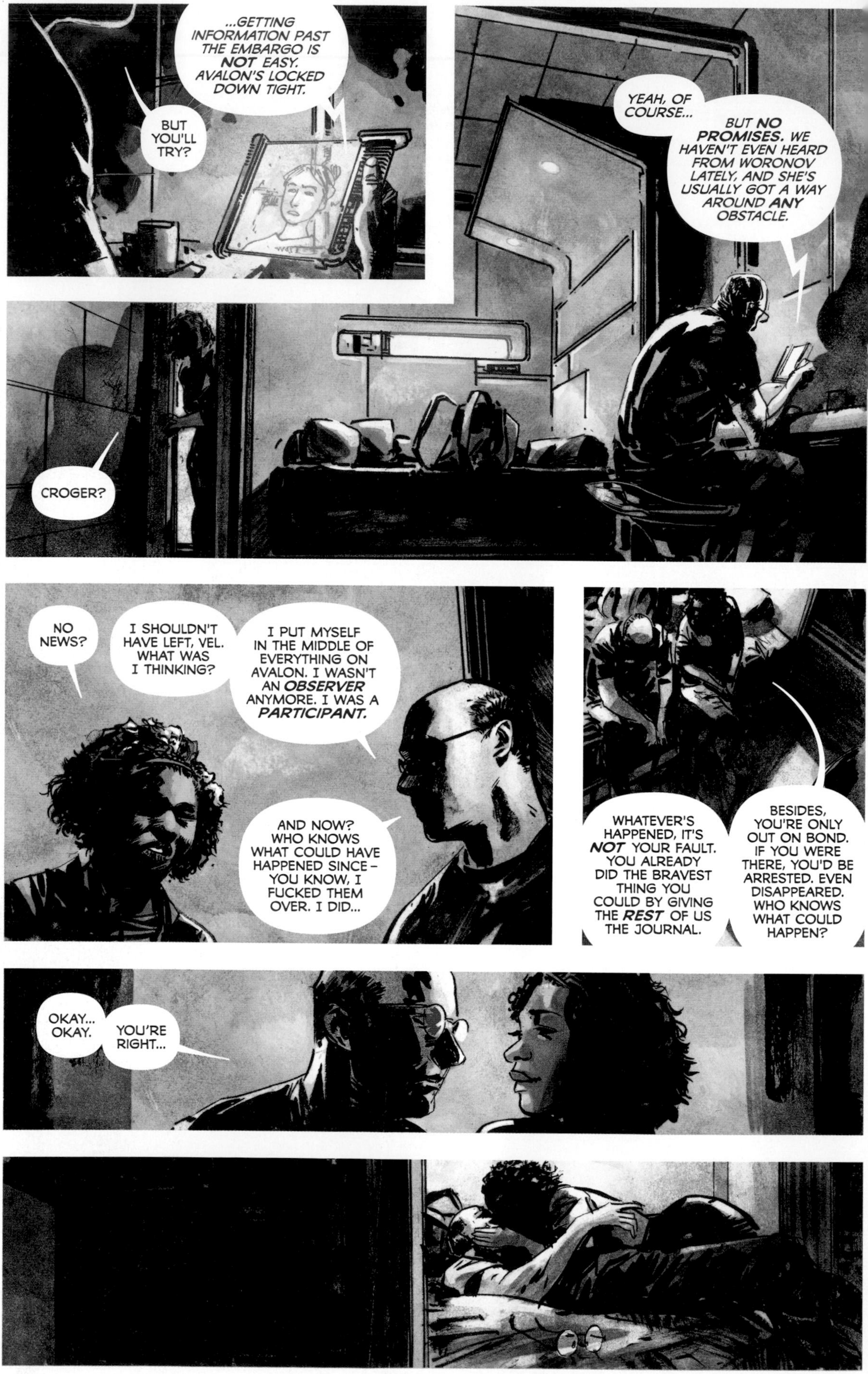
...GETTING INFORMATION PAST THE EMBARGO IS NOT EASY. AVALON'S LOCKED DOWN TIGHT.
BUT YOU'LL TRY?
YEAH, OF COURSE...
BUT NO PROMISES. WE HAVEN'T EVEN HEARD FROM WORONOV LATELY, AND SHE'S USUALLY GOT A WAY AROUND ANY OBSTACLE.
CROGER?
NO NEWS?
I SHOULDN'T HAVE LEFT, VEL. WHAT WAS I THINKING?
I PUT MYSELF IN THE MIDDLE OF EVERYTHING ON AVALON. I WASN'T AN OBSERVER ANYMORE. I WAS A PARTICIPANT.
AND NOW? WHO KNOWS WHAT COULD HAVE HAPPENED SINCE – YOU KNOW, I FUCKED THEM OVER. I DID...
WHATEVER'S HAPPENED, IT'S NOT YOUR FAULT. YOU ALREADY DID THE BRAVEST THING YOU COULD BY GIVING THE REST OF US THE JOURNAL.
BESIDES, YOU'RE ONLY OUT ON BOND. IF YOU WERE THERE, YOU'D BE ARRESTED. EVEN DISAPPEARED. WHO KNOWS WHAT COULD HAPPEN?
OKAY... OKAY.
YOU'RE RIGHT...

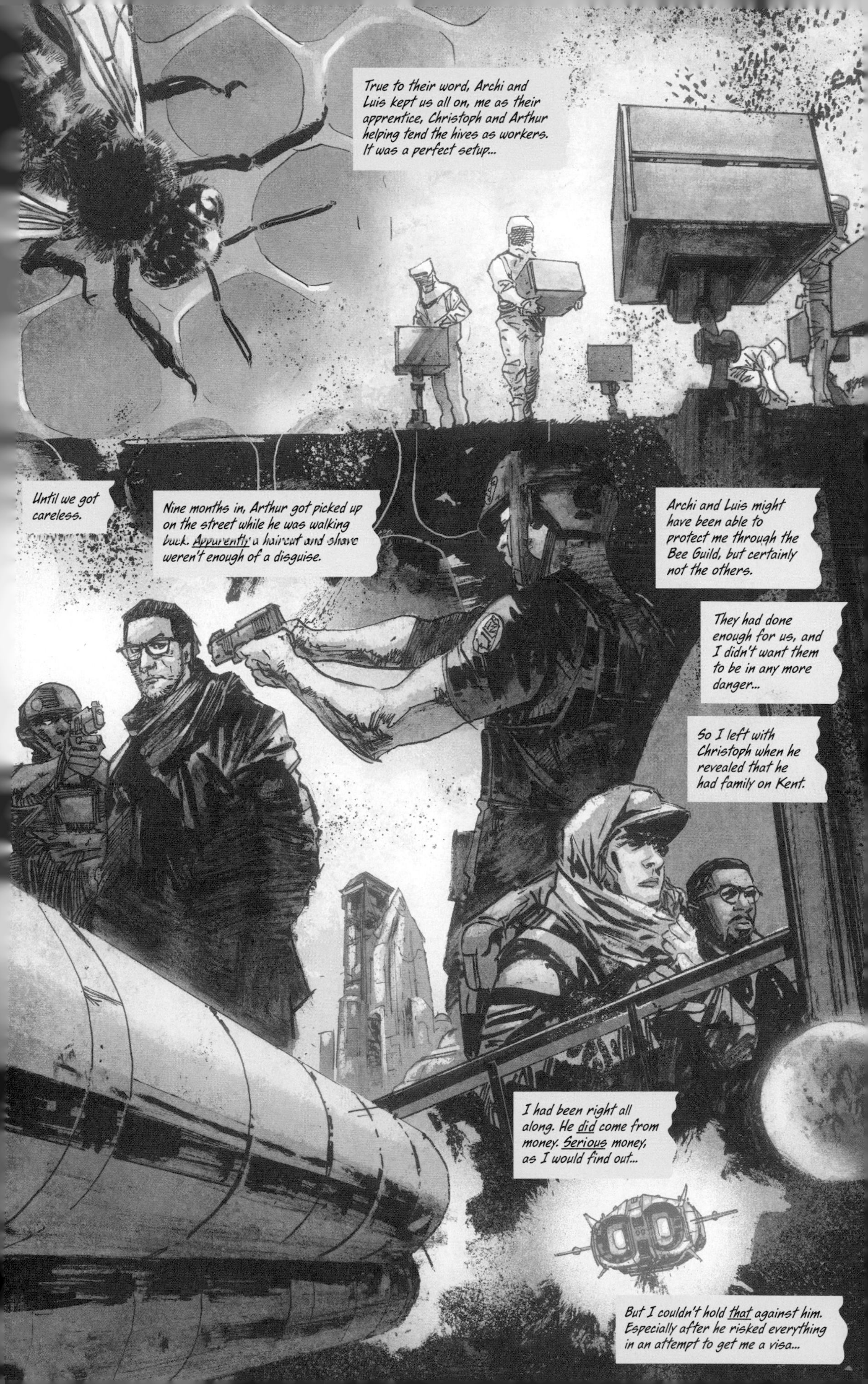
True to their word, Archi and Luis kept us all on, me as their apprentice, Christoph and Arthur helping tend the hives as workers. It was a perfect setup...
Until we got careless.
Nine months in, Arthur got picked up on the street while he was walking back. Apparently a haircut and shave weren't enough of a disguise.
Archi and Luis might have been able to protect me through the Bee Guild, but certainly not the others.
They had done enough for us, and I didn't want them to be in any more danger...
So I left with Christoph when he revealed that he had family on Kent.
I had been right all along. He did come from money. Serious money, as I would find out...
But I couldn't hold that against him. Especially after he risked everything in an attempt to get me a visa...

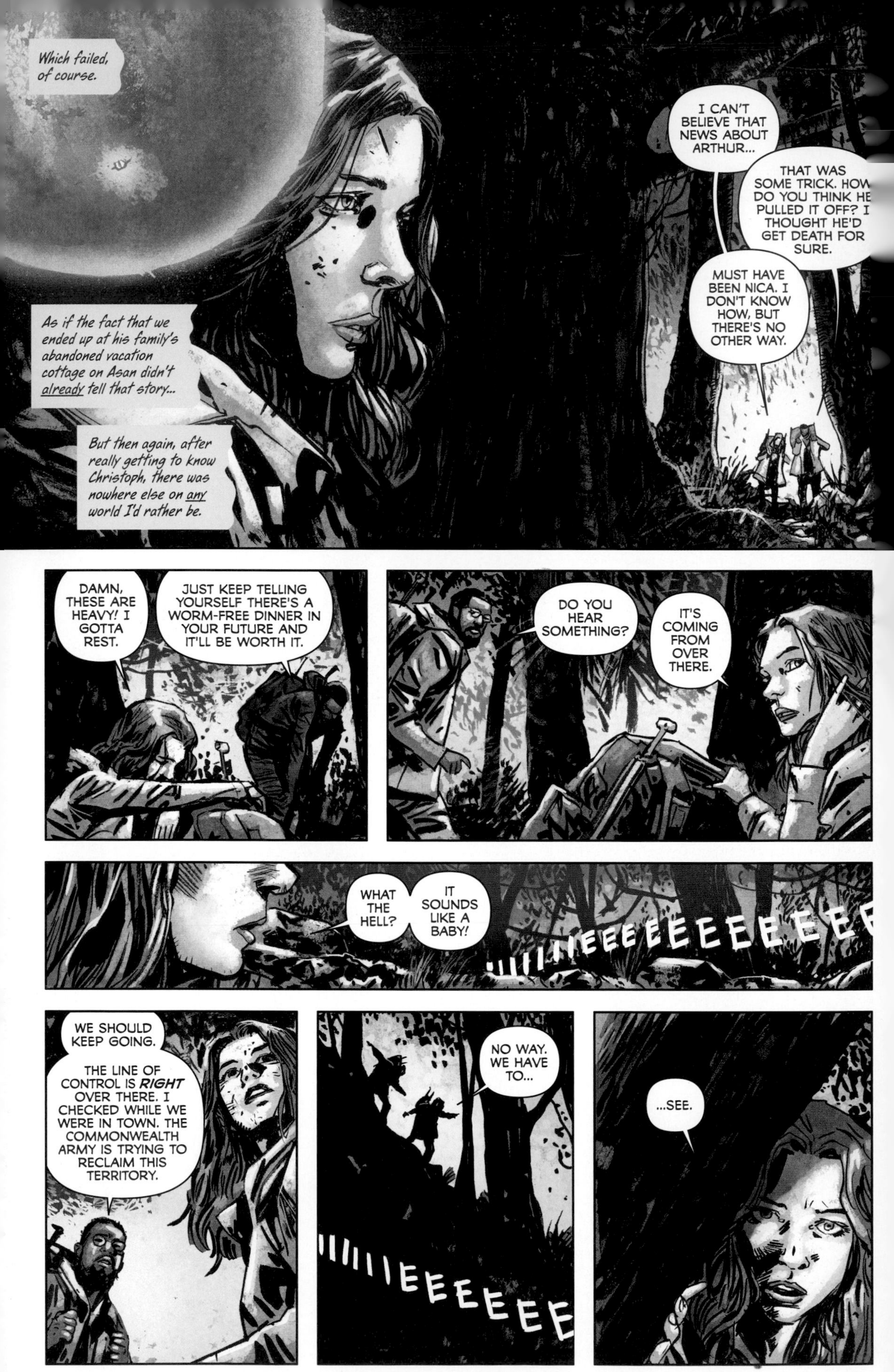
Which failed, of course.
As if the fact that we ended up at his family's abandoned vacation cottage on Asan didn't already tell that story...
But then again, after really getting to know Christoph, there was nowhere else on any world I'd rather be.
I CAN'T BELIEVE THAT NEWS ABOUT ARTHUR...
THAT WAS SOME TRICK. HOW DO YOU THINK HE PULLED IT OFF? I THOUGHT HE'D GET DEATH FOR SURE.
MUST HAVE BEEN NICA. I DON'T KNOW HOW, BUT THERE'S NO OTHER WAY.
DAMN, THESE ARE HEAVY! I GOTTA REST.
JUST KEEP TELLING YOURSELF THERE'S A WORM-FREE DINNER IN YOUR FUTURE AND IT'LL BE WORTH IT.
DO YOU HEAR SOMETHING?
IT'S COMING FROM OVER THERE.
WHAT THE HELL?
IT SOUNDS LIKE A BABY!
IIIIIEEEEEEEEEEE
WE SHOULD KEEP GOING.
THE LINE OF CONTROL IS RIGHT OVER THERE. I CHECKED WHILE WE WERE IN TOWN. THE COMMONWEALTH ARMY IS TRYING TO RECLAIM THIS TERRITORY.
NO WAY. WE HAVE TO...
IIIIIEEEEEEE
...SEE.

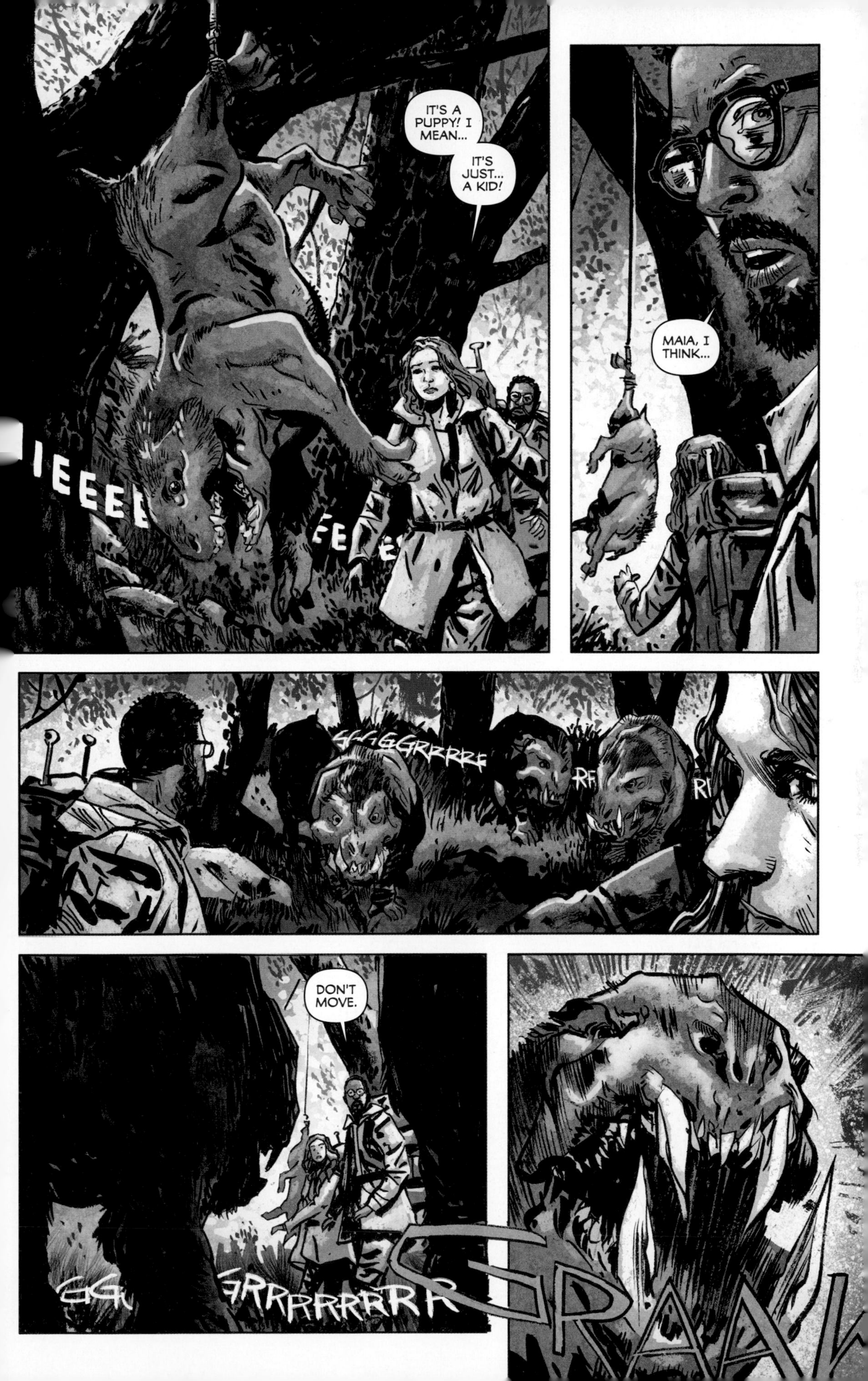
IEEEE
EEE
IT'S A PUPPY! I MEAN...
IT'S JUST... A KID!
MAIA, I THINK...
GGGGRRRRR
RR
RR
DON'T MOVE.
GGGRRRRRRRRR
GRAAA

COME ON!

NO, WE HAVE TO DO *SOMETHING.* IT'S SUFFERING.

HUH?

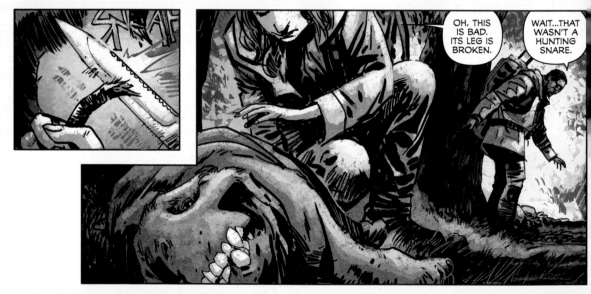

OH, THIS IS BAD. ITS LEG IS BROKEN.

WAIT...THAT WASN'T A HUNTING SNARE.

THIS IS A BOOBY TRAP. MEANT FOR *PEOPLE.*

CREE

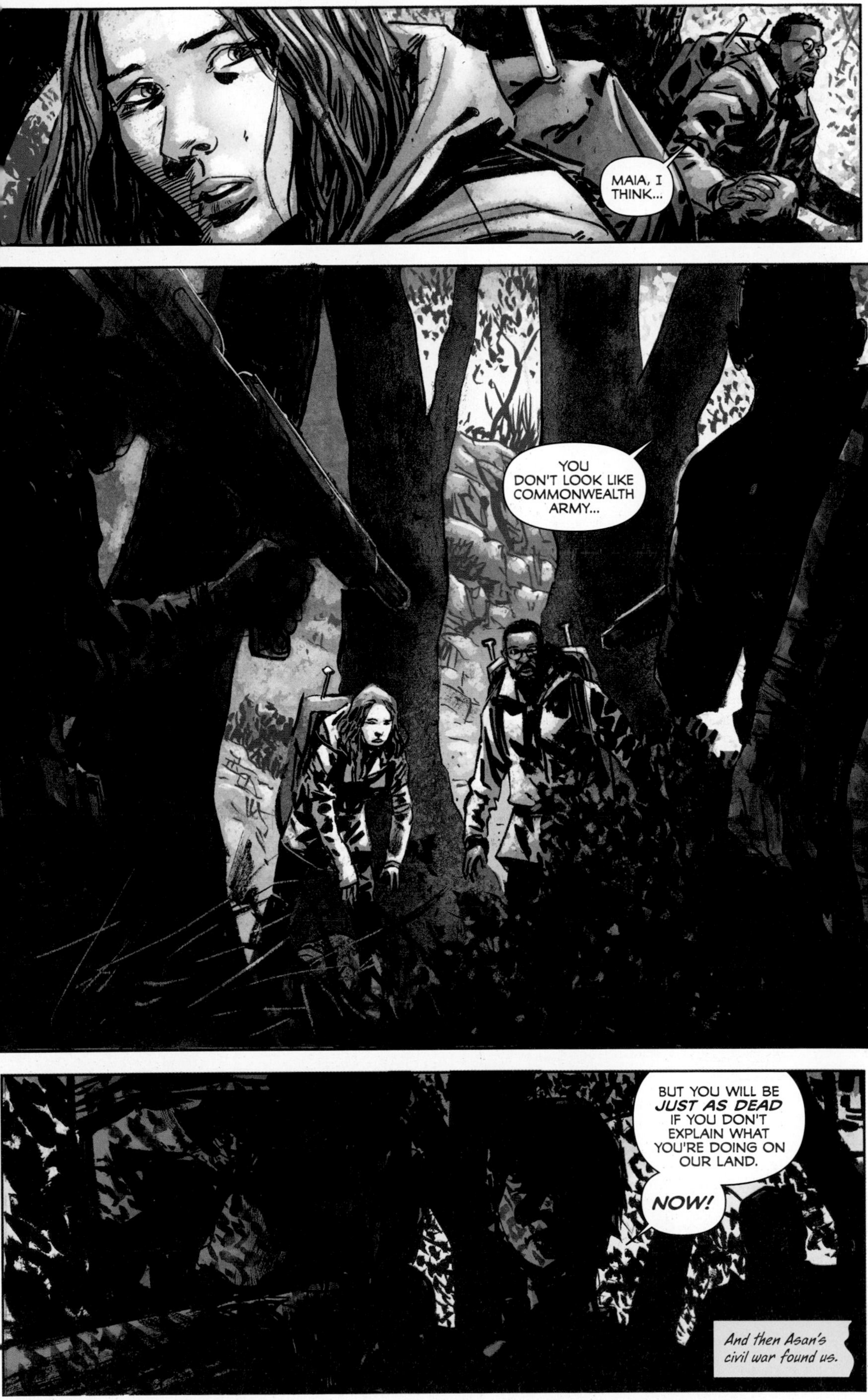
MAIA, I THINK...
YOU DON'T LOOK LIKE COMMONWEALTH ARMY...
BUT YOU WILL BE JUST AS DEAD IF YOU DON'T EXPLAIN WHAT YOU'RE DOING ON OUR LAND.
NOW!
And then Asan's civil war found us.

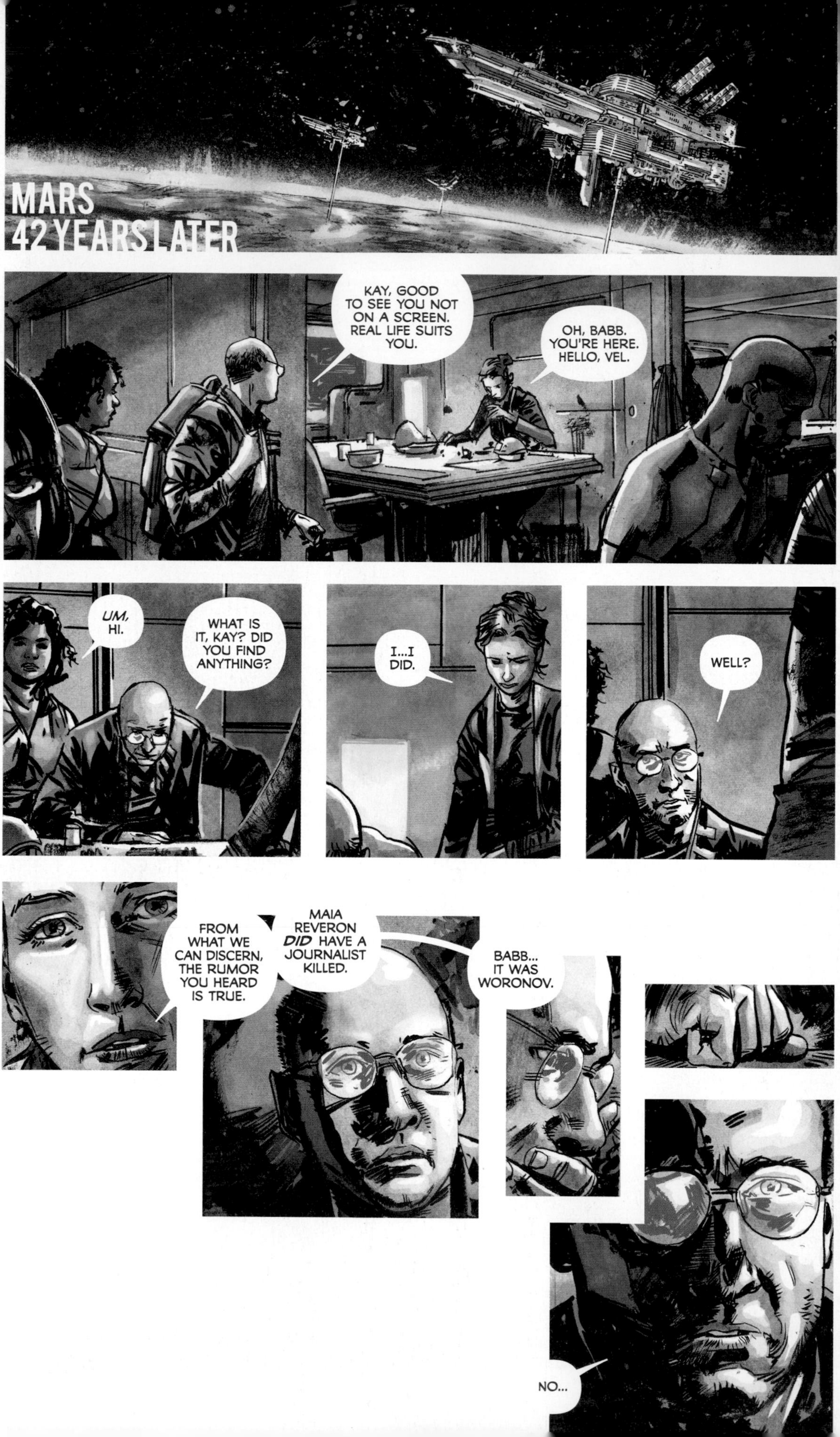
MARS
42 YEARS LATER
KAY, GOOD TO SEE YOU NOT ON A SCREEN. REAL LIFE SUITS YOU.
OH, BABB. YOU'RE HERE. HELLO, VEL.
UM, HI.
WHAT IS IT, KAY? DID YOU FIND ANYTHING?
I...I DID.
WELL?
FROM WHAT WE CAN DISCERN, THE RUMOR YOU HEARD IS TRUE.
MAIA REVERON DID HAVE A JOURNALIST KILLED.
BABB... IT WAS WORONOV.
NO...

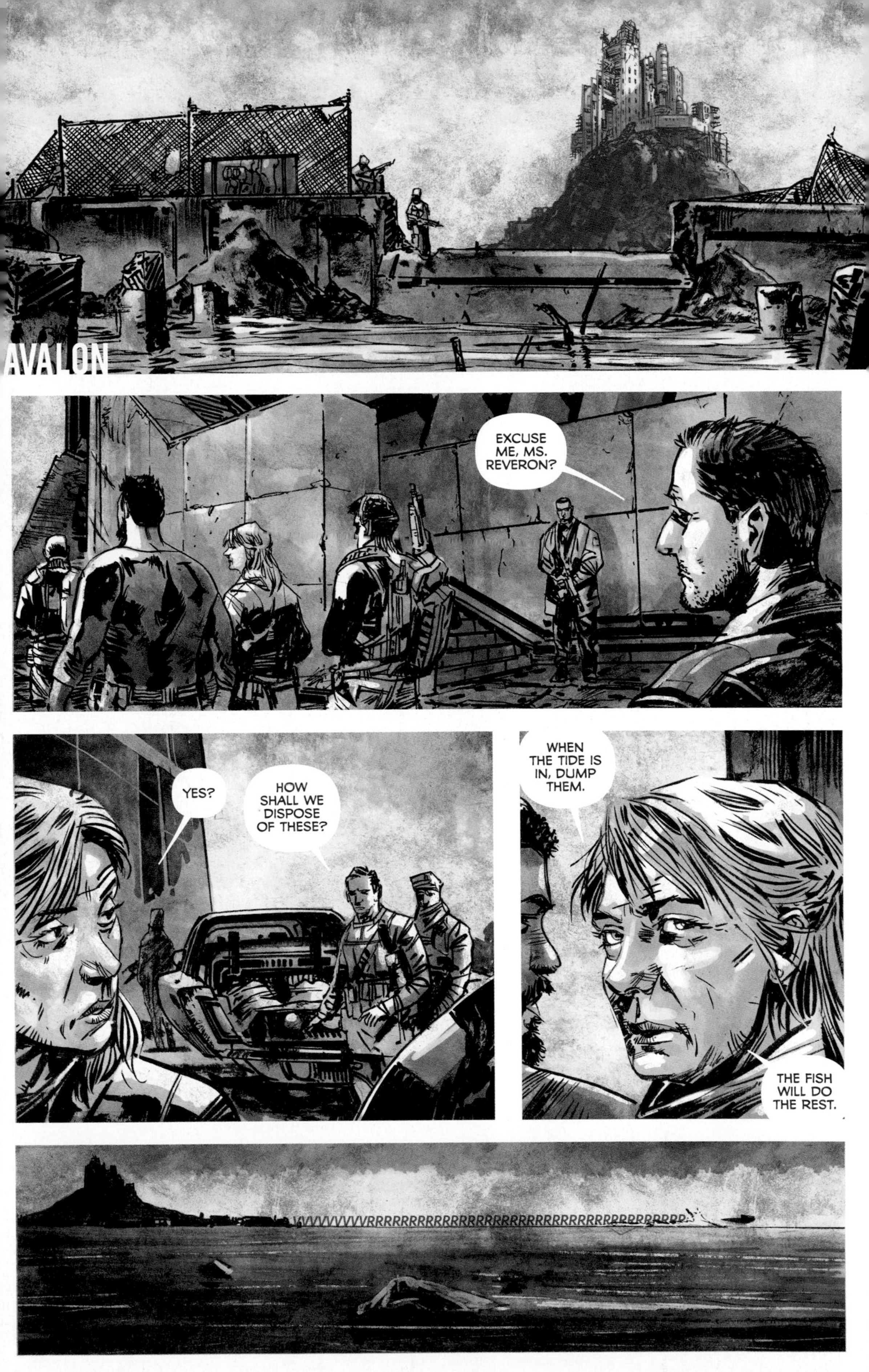
AVALON
EXCUSE ME, MS. REVERON?
YES?
HOW SHALL WE DISPOSE OF THESE?
WHEN THE TIDE IS IN, DUMP THEM.
THE FISH WILL DO THE REST.
VVVVVVVVVRRRRRRRRRRRRRRRRRRRRRRRRRRRRRRRRRRRRRR

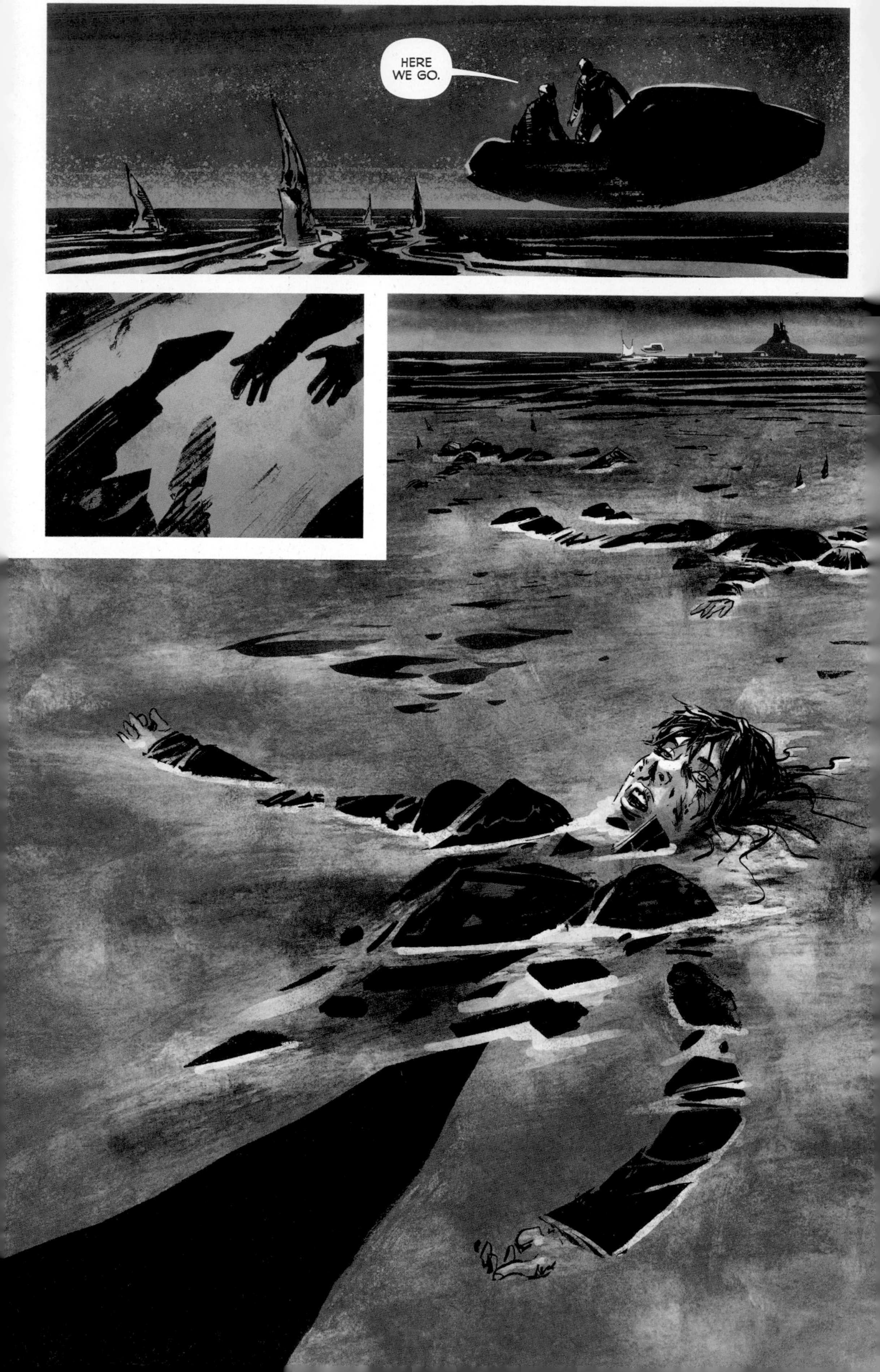
HERE WE GO.

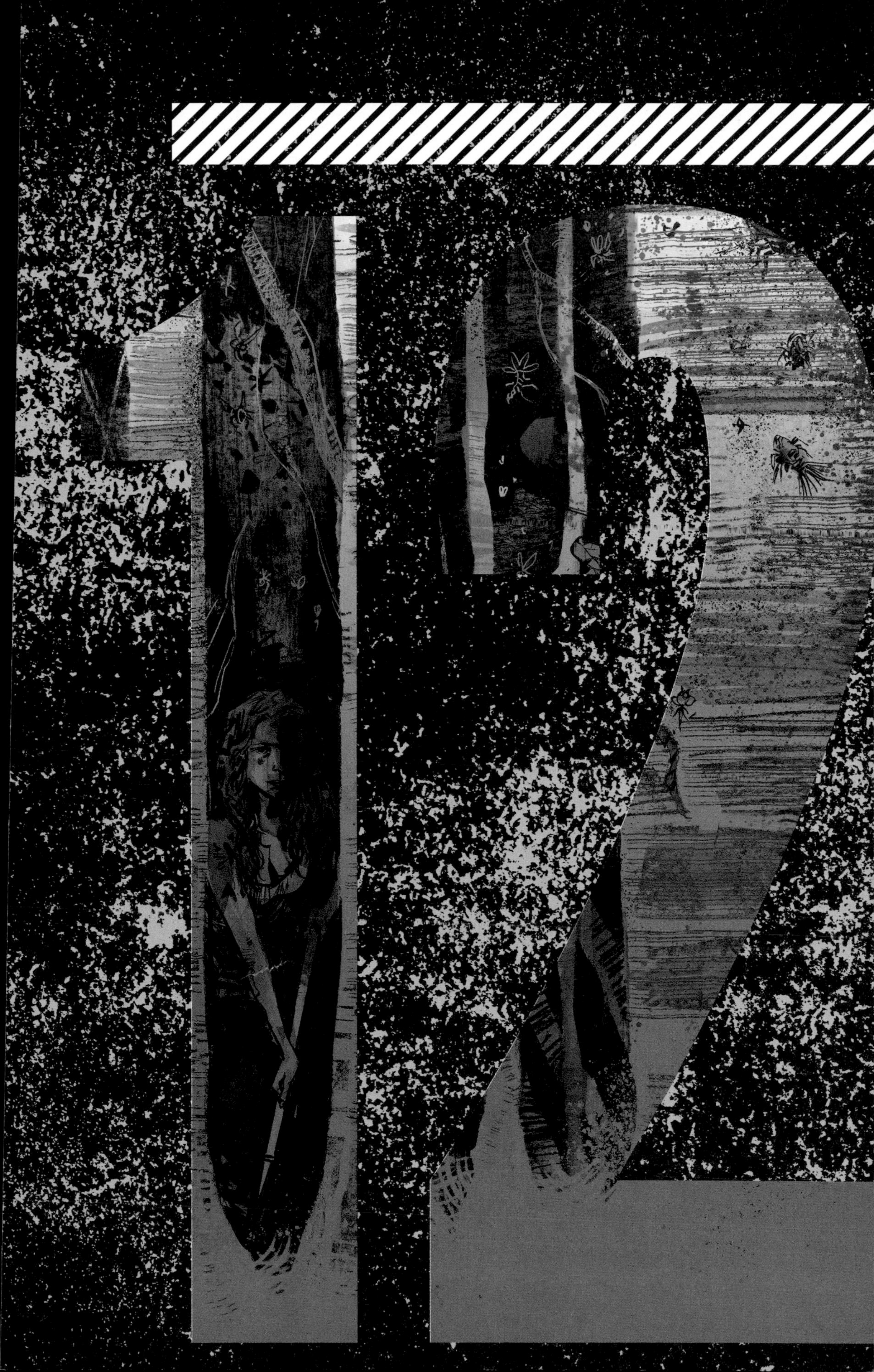
12

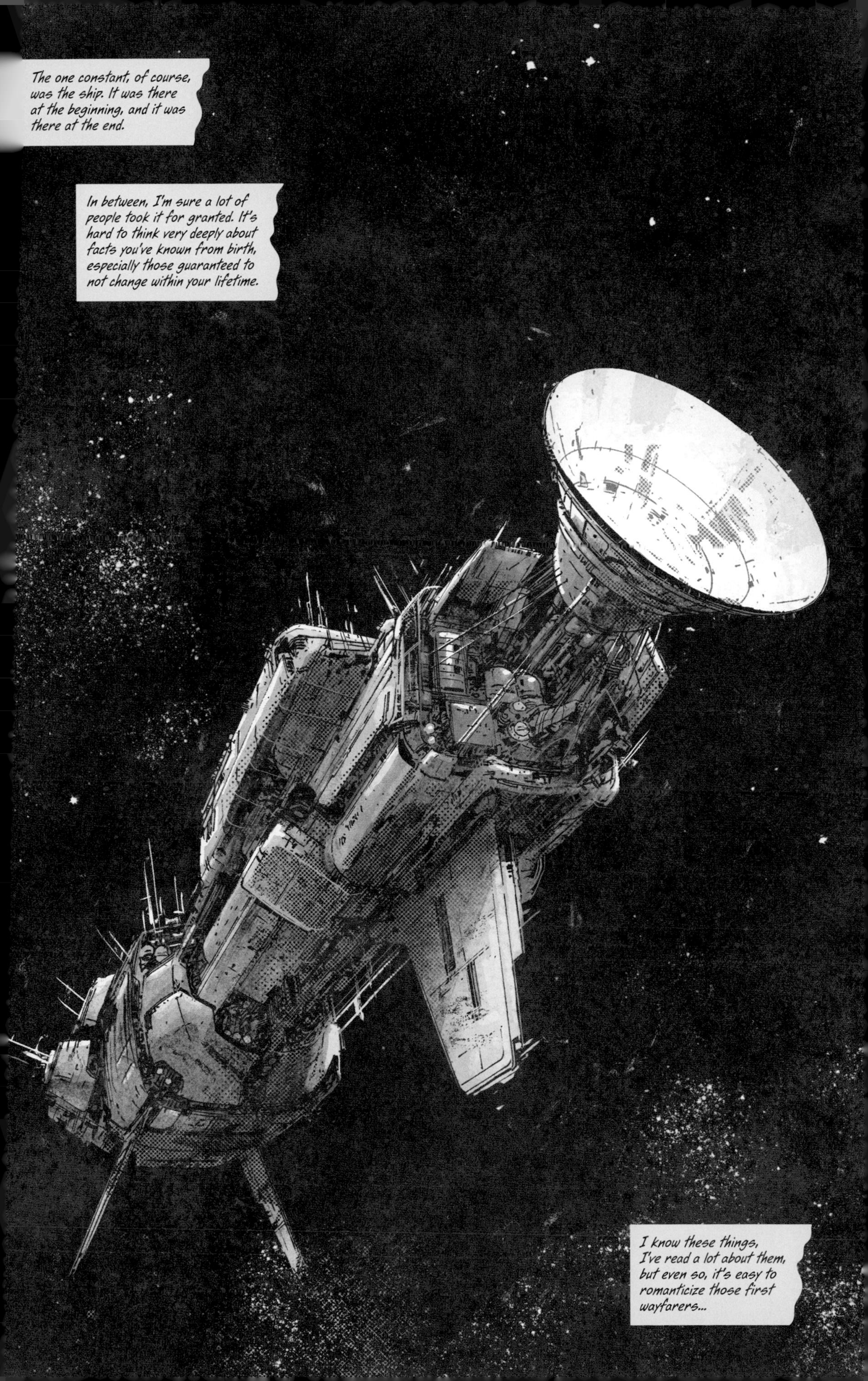
The one constant, of course, was the ship. It was there at the beginning, and it was there at the end.
In between, I'm sure a lot of people took it for granted. It's hard to think very deeply about facts you've known from birth, especially those guaranteed to not change within your lifetime.
I know these things, I've read a lot about them, but even so, it's easy to romanticize those first wayfarers...

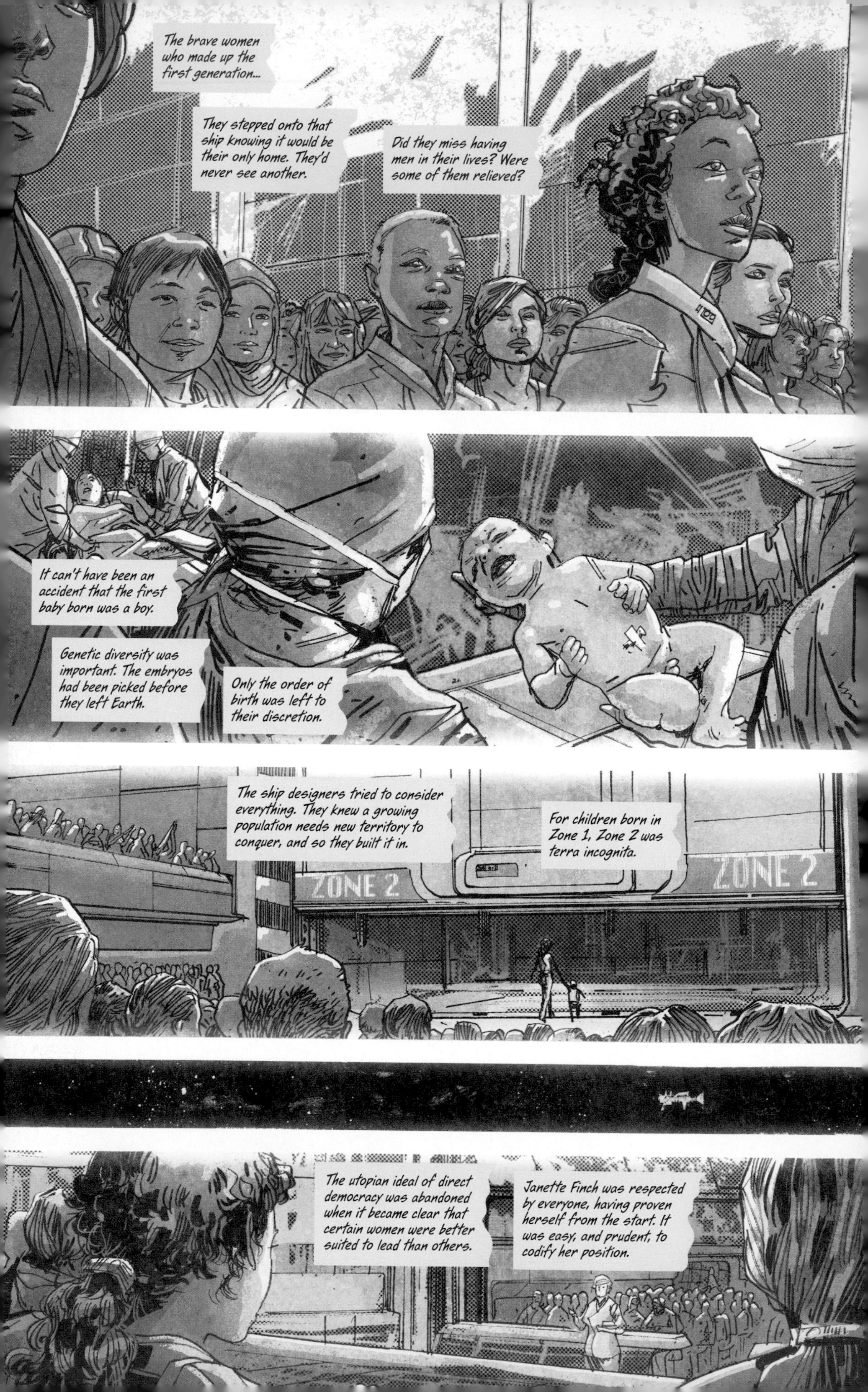
The brave women who made up the first generation...
They stepped onto that ship knowing it would be their only home. They'd never see another.
Did they miss having men in their lives? Were some of them relieved?
It can't have been an accident that the first baby born was a boy.
Genetic diversity was important. The embryos had been picked before they left Earth.
Only the order of birth was left to their discretion.
The ship designers tried to consider everything. They knew a growing population needs new territory to conquer, and so they built it in.
For children born in Zone 1, Zone 2 was terra incognita.
ZONE 2
ZONE 2
The utopian ideal of direct democracy was abandoned when it became clear that certain women were better suited to lead than others.
Janette Finch was respected by everyone, having proven herself from the start. It was easy, and prudent, to codify her position.

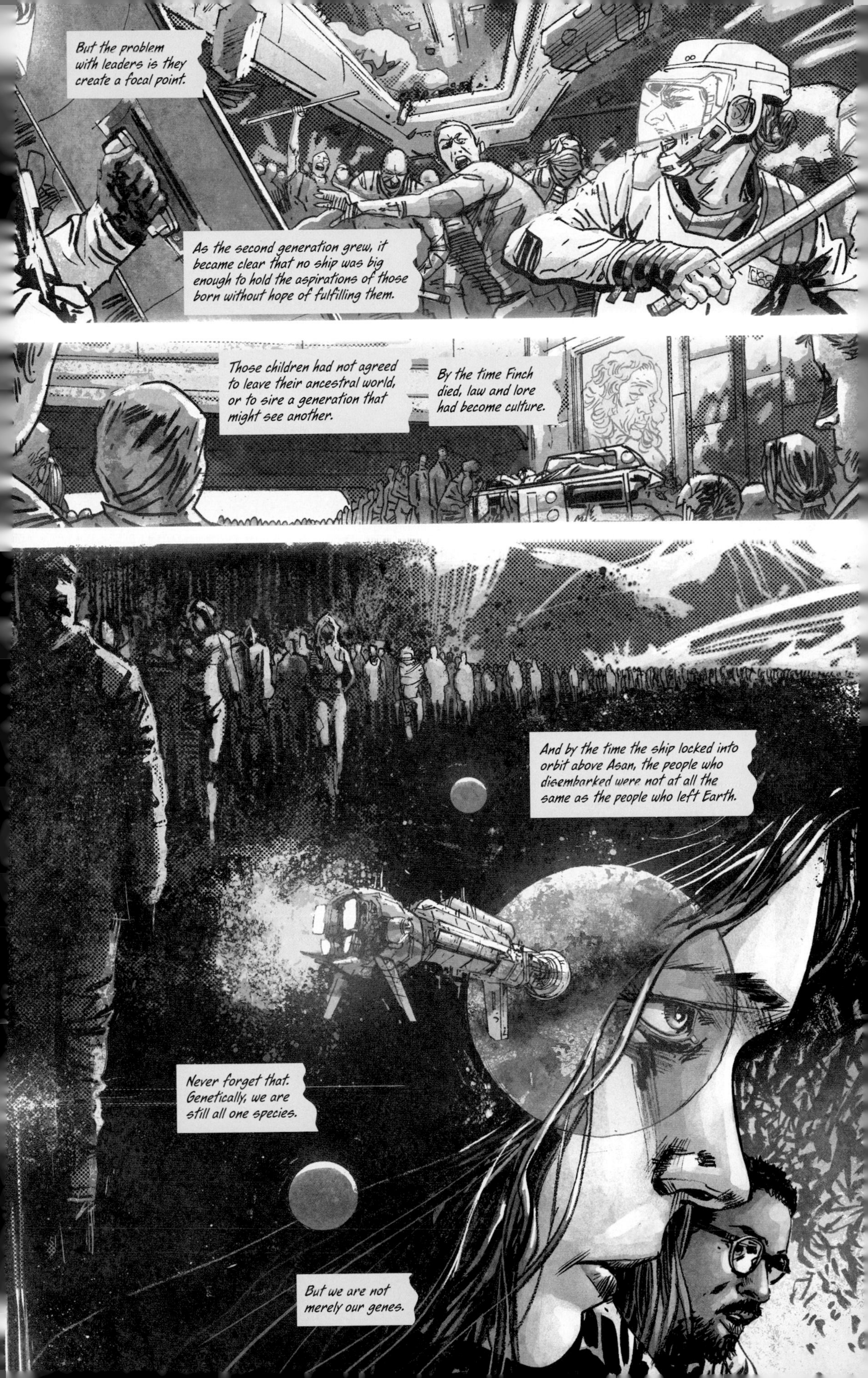
But the problem with leaders is they create a focal point.
As the second generation grew, it became clear that no ship was big enough to hold the aspirations of those born without hope of fulfilling them.
Those children had not agreed to leave their ancestral world, or to sire a generation that might see another.
By the time Finch died, law and lore had become culture.
And by the time the ship locked into orbit above Asan, the people who disembarked were not at all the same as the people who left Earth.
Never forget that. Genetically, we are still all one species.
But we are not merely our genes.

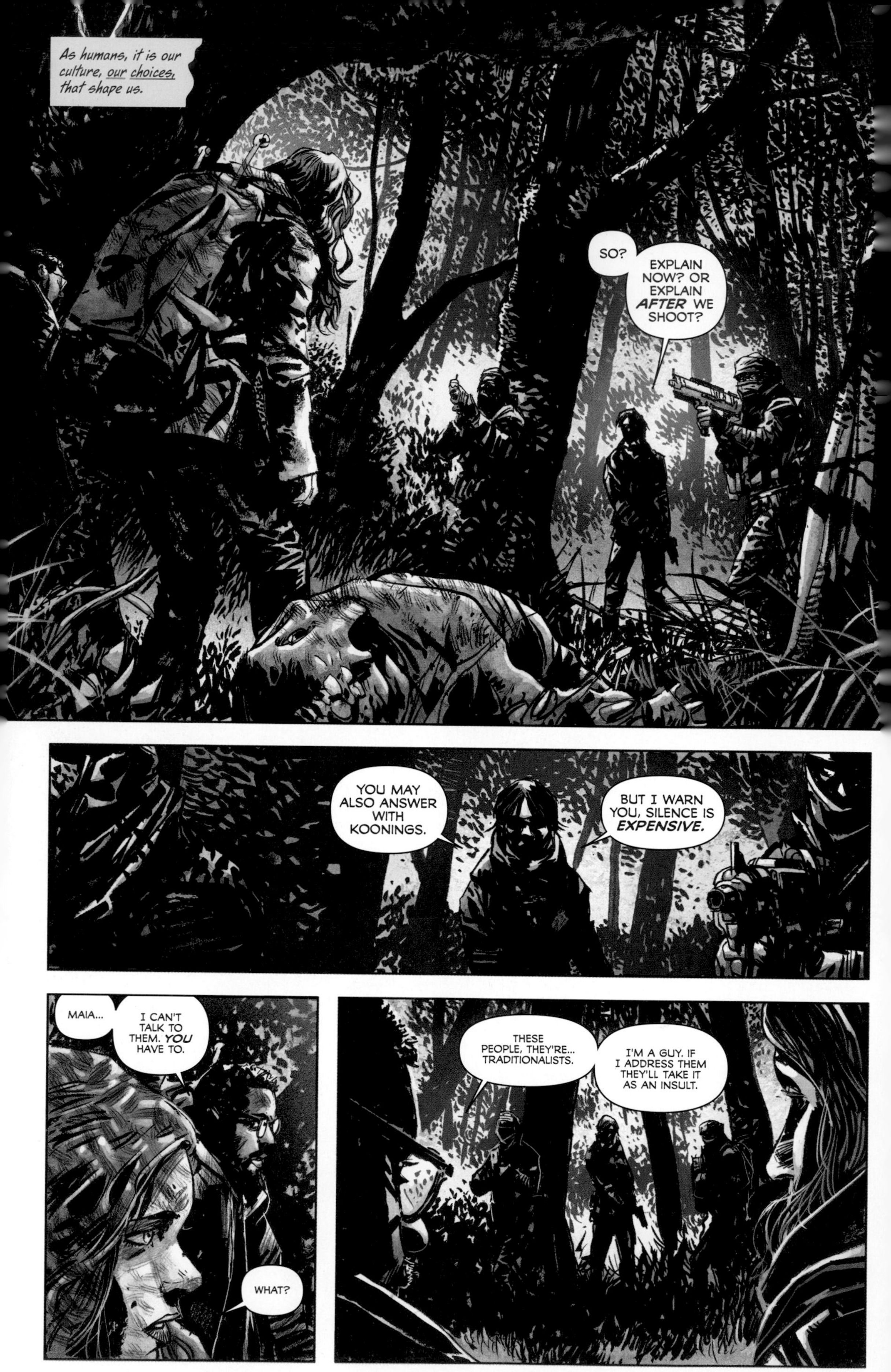

As humans, it is our culture, our choices, that shape us.
SO?
EXPLAIN NOW? OR EXPLAIN AFTER WE SHOOT?
YOU MAY ALSO ANSWER WITH KOONINGS.
BUT I WARN YOU, SILENCE IS EXPENSIVE.
MAIA...
I CAN'T TALK TO THEM. YOU HAVE TO.
WHAT?
THESE PEOPLE, THEY'RE... TRADITIONALISTS.
I'M A GUY. IF I ADDRESS THEM THEY'LL TAKE IT AS AN INSULT.

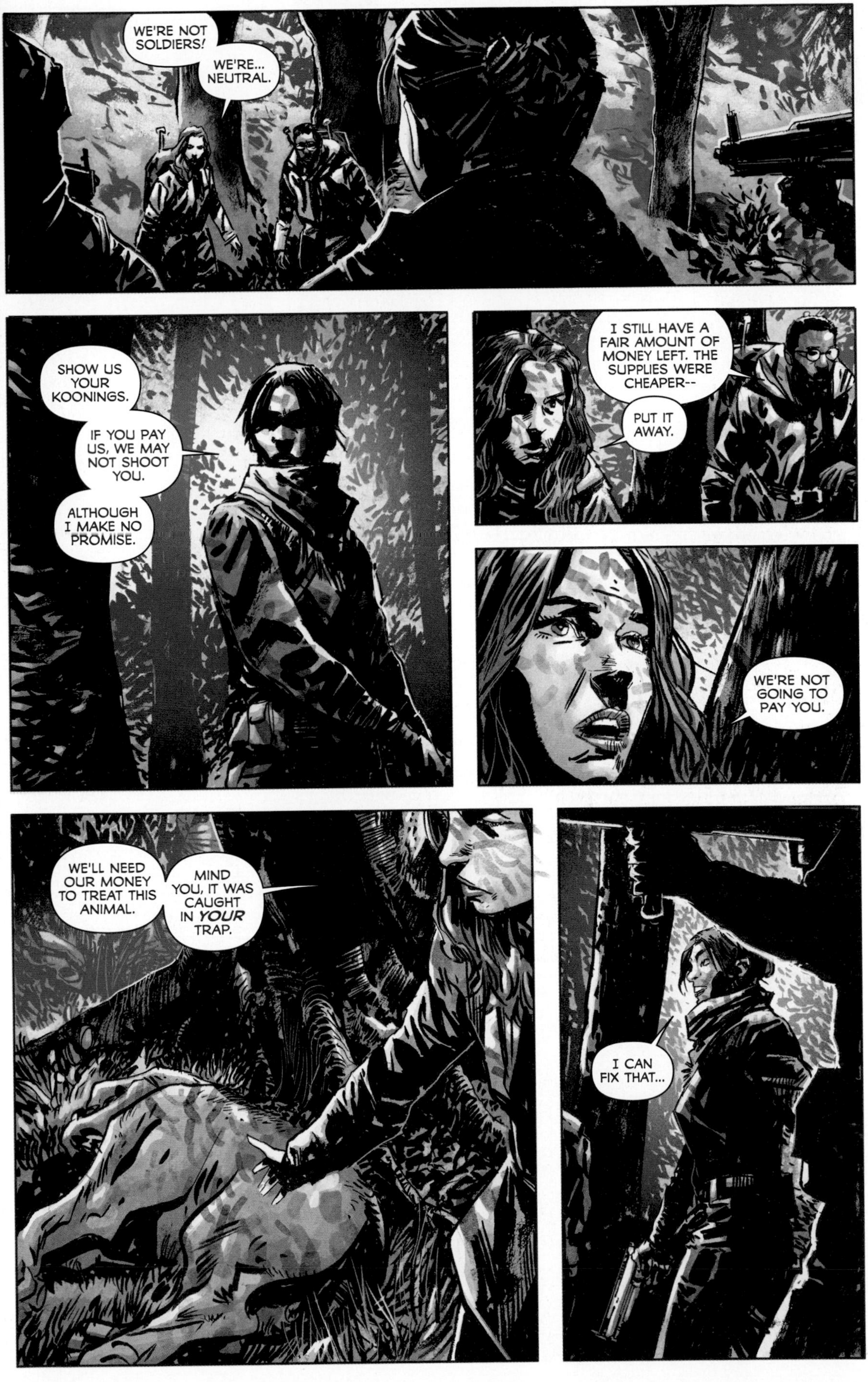
WE'RE NOT SOLDIERS!
WE'RE... NEUTRAL.
SHOW US YOUR KOONINGS.
IF YOU PAY US, WE MAY NOT SHOOT YOU.
ALTHOUGH I MAKE NO PROMISE.
I STILL HAVE A FAIR AMOUNT OF MONEY LEFT. THE SUPPLIES WERE CHEAPER--
PUT IT AWAY.
WE'RE NOT GOING TO PAY YOU.
WE'LL NEED OUR MONEY TO TREAT THIS ANIMAL.
MIND YOU, IT WAS CAUGHT IN *YOUR* TRAP.
I CAN FIX THAT...

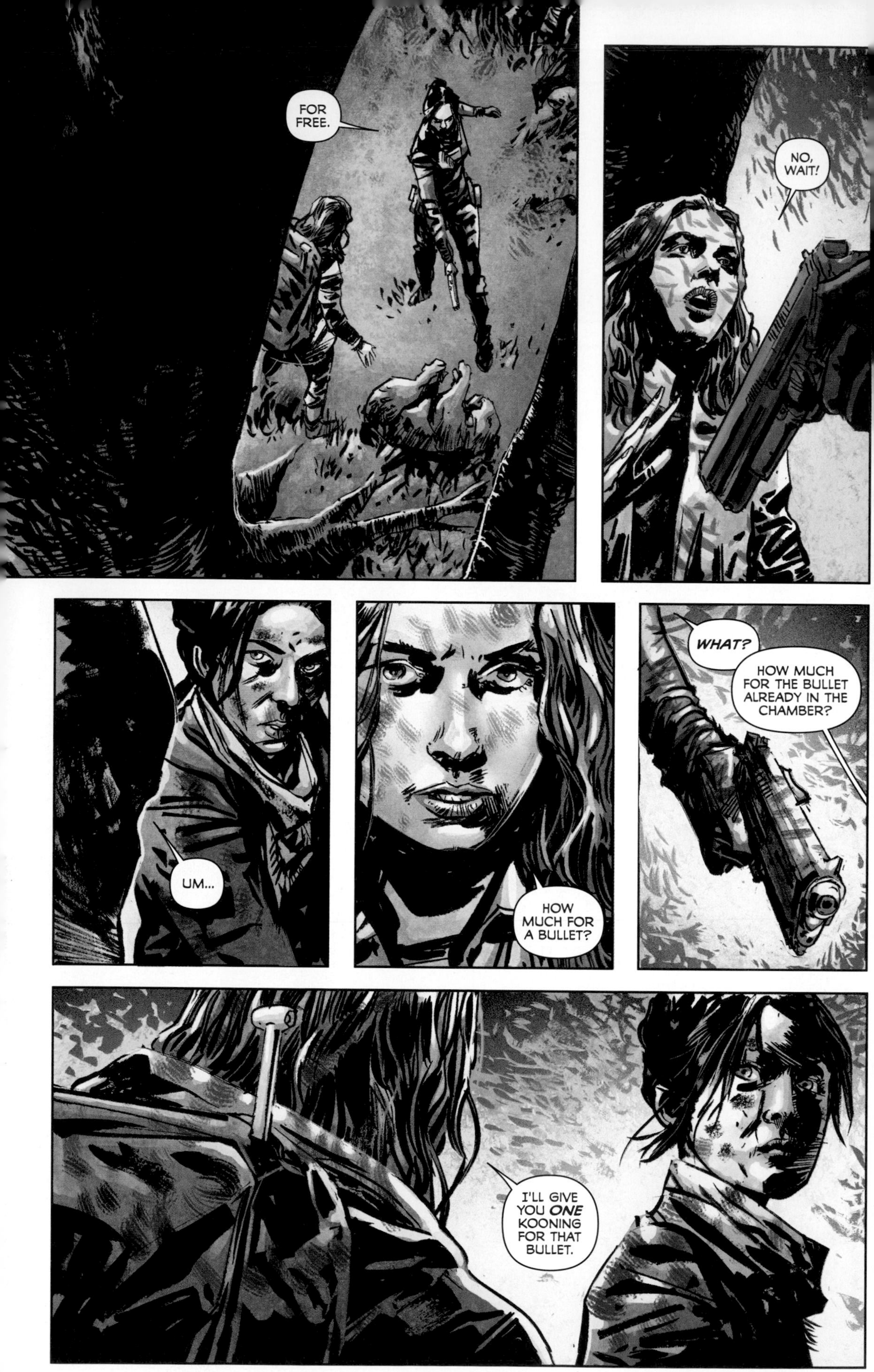
FOR FREE.
NO, WAIT!
UM...
HOW MUCH FOR A BULLET?
WHAT?
HOW MUCH FOR THE BULLET ALREADY IN THE CHAMBER?
I'LL GIVE YOU ONE KOONING FOR THAT BULLET.

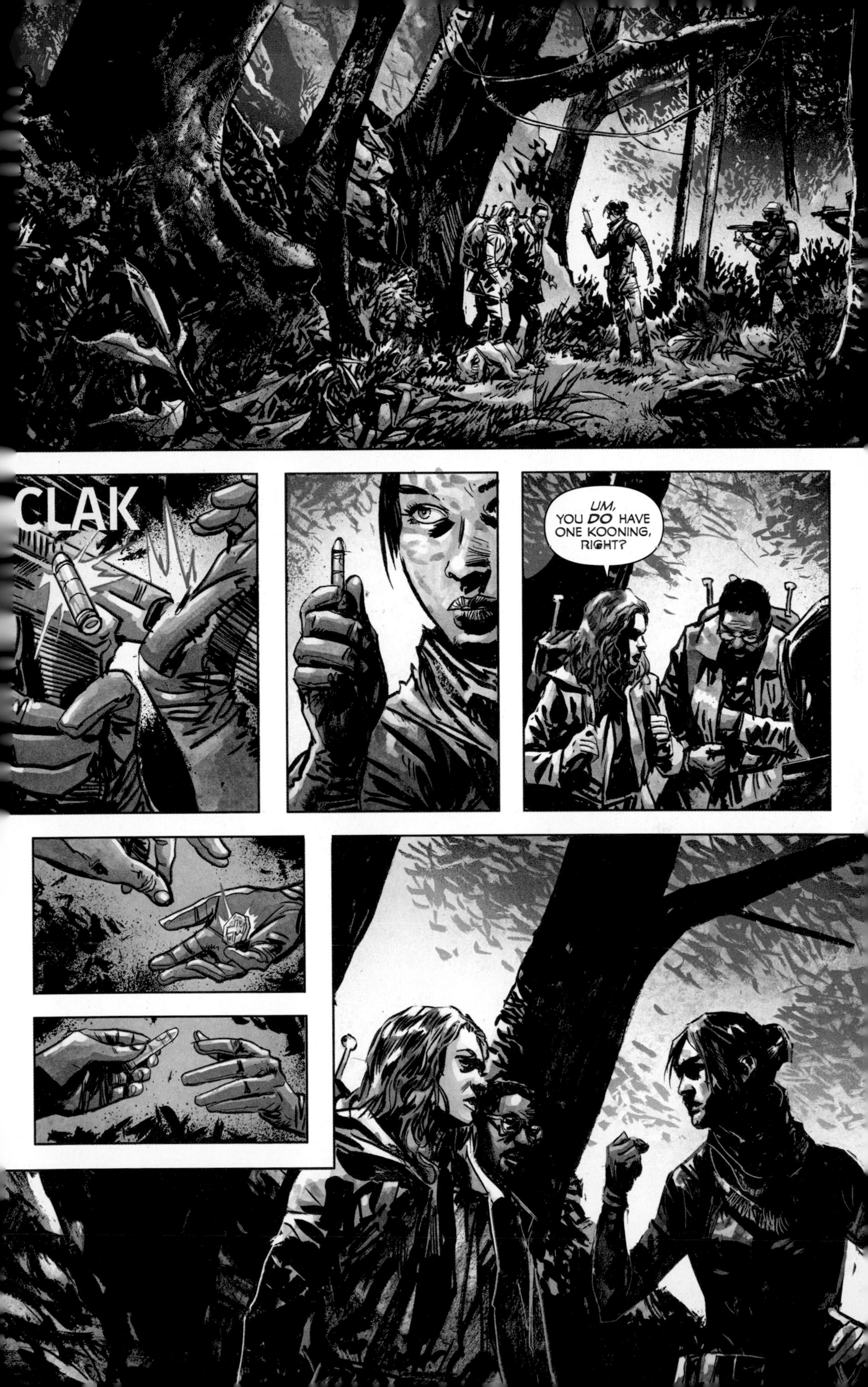
CLAK
UM, YOU DO HAVE ONE KOONING, RIGHT?

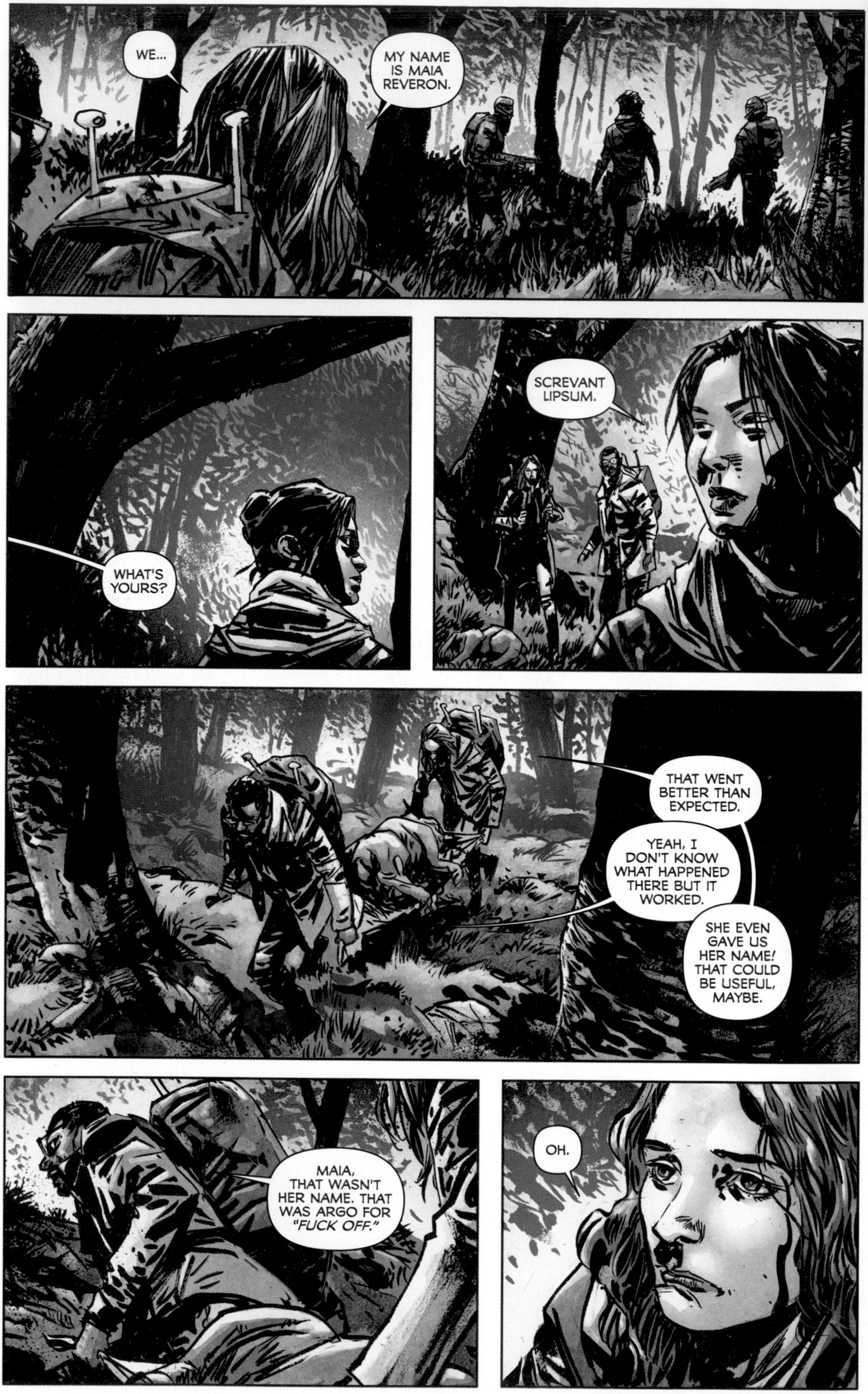
WE...
MY NAME IS MAIA REVERON.
WHAT'S YOURS?
SCREVANT LIPSUM.
THAT WENT BETTER THAN EXPECTED.
YEAH, I DON'T KNOW WHAT HAPPENED THERE BUT IT WORKED.
SHE EVEN GAVE US HER NAME! THAT COULD BE USEFUL, MAYBE.
MAIA, THAT WASN'T HER NAME. THAT WAS ARGO FOR "FUCK OFF."
OH.

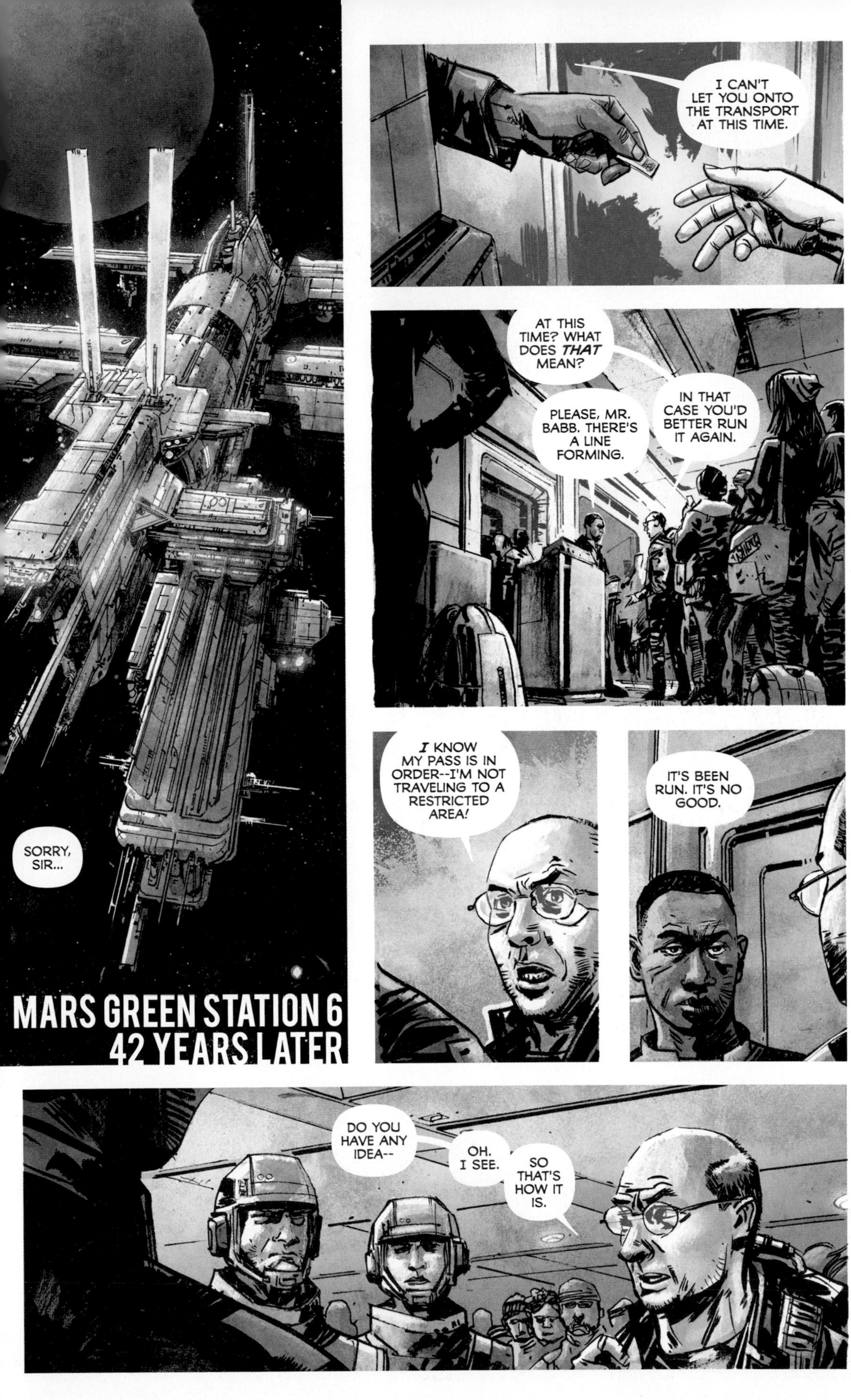
SORRY, SIR...
MARS GREEN STATION 6
42 YEARS LATER
I CAN'T LET YOU ONTO THE TRANSPORT AT THIS TIME.
AT THIS TIME? WHAT DOES THAT MEAN?
IN THAT CASE YOU'D BETTER RUN IT AGAIN.
PLEASE, MR. BABB. THERE'S A LINE FORMING.
I KNOW MY PASS IS IN ORDER--I'M NOT TRAVELING TO A RESTRICTED AREA!
IT'S BEEN RUN. IT'S NO GOOD.
DO YOU HAVE ANY IDEA--
OH. I SEE.
SO THAT'S HOW IT IS.

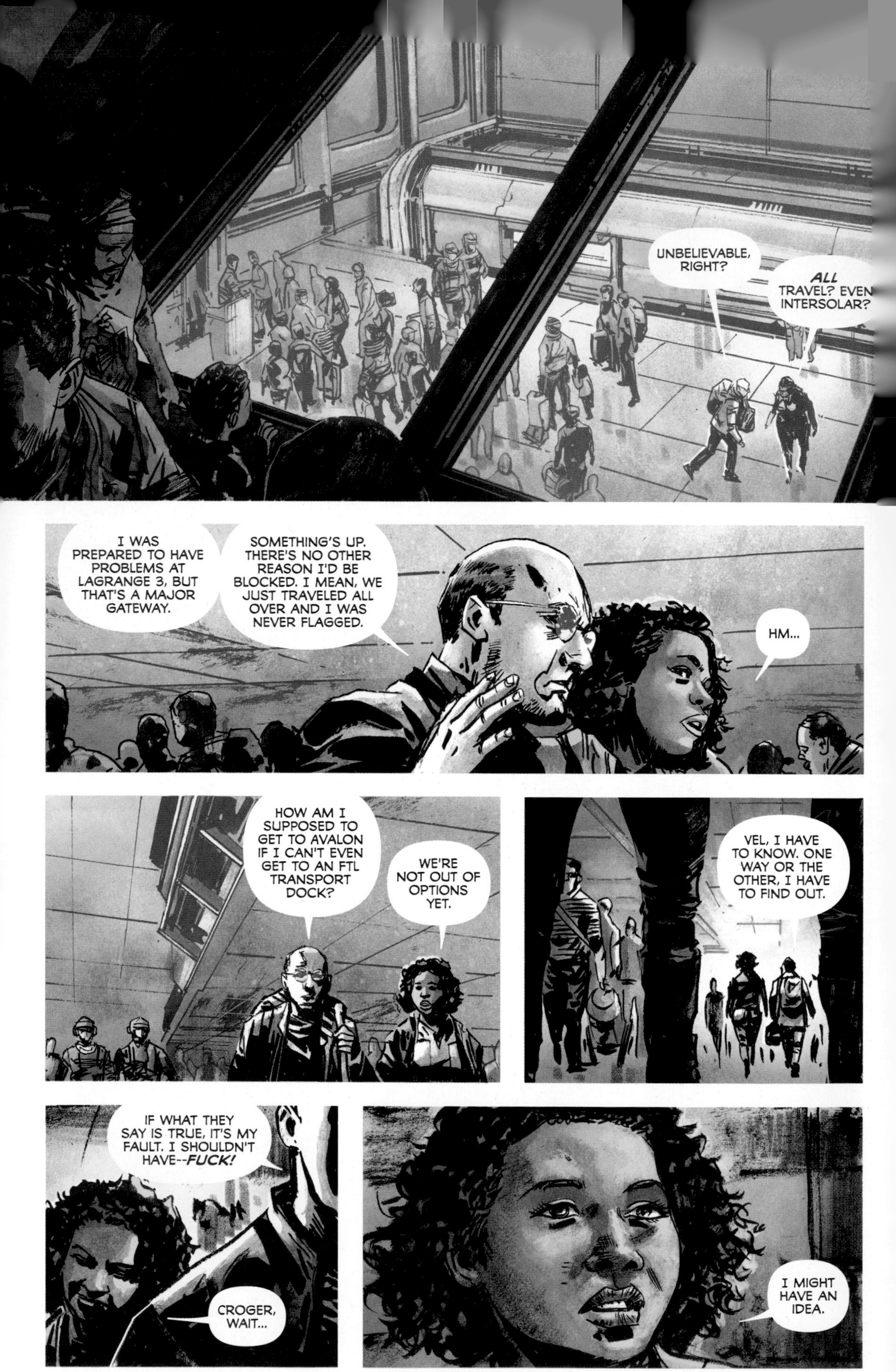
UNBELIEVABLE, RIGHT?
ALL TRAVEL? EVEN INTERSOLAR?
I WAS PREPARED TO HAVE PROBLEMS AT LAGRANGE 3, BUT THAT'S A MAJOR GATEWAY.
SOMETHING'S UP. THERE'S NO OTHER REASON I'D BE BLOCKED. I MEAN, WE JUST TRAVELED ALL OVER AND I WAS NEVER FLAGGED.
HM...
HOW AM I SUPPOSED TO GET TO AVALON IF I CAN'T EVEN GET TO AN FTL TRANSPORT DOCK?
WE'RE NOT OUT OF OPTIONS YET.
VEL, I HAVE TO KNOW. ONE WAY OR THE OTHER, I HAVE TO FIND OUT.
IF WHAT THEY SAY IS TRUE, IT'S MY FAULT. I SHOULDN'T HAVE--FUCK!
CROGER, WAIT...
I MIGHT HAVE AN IDEA.

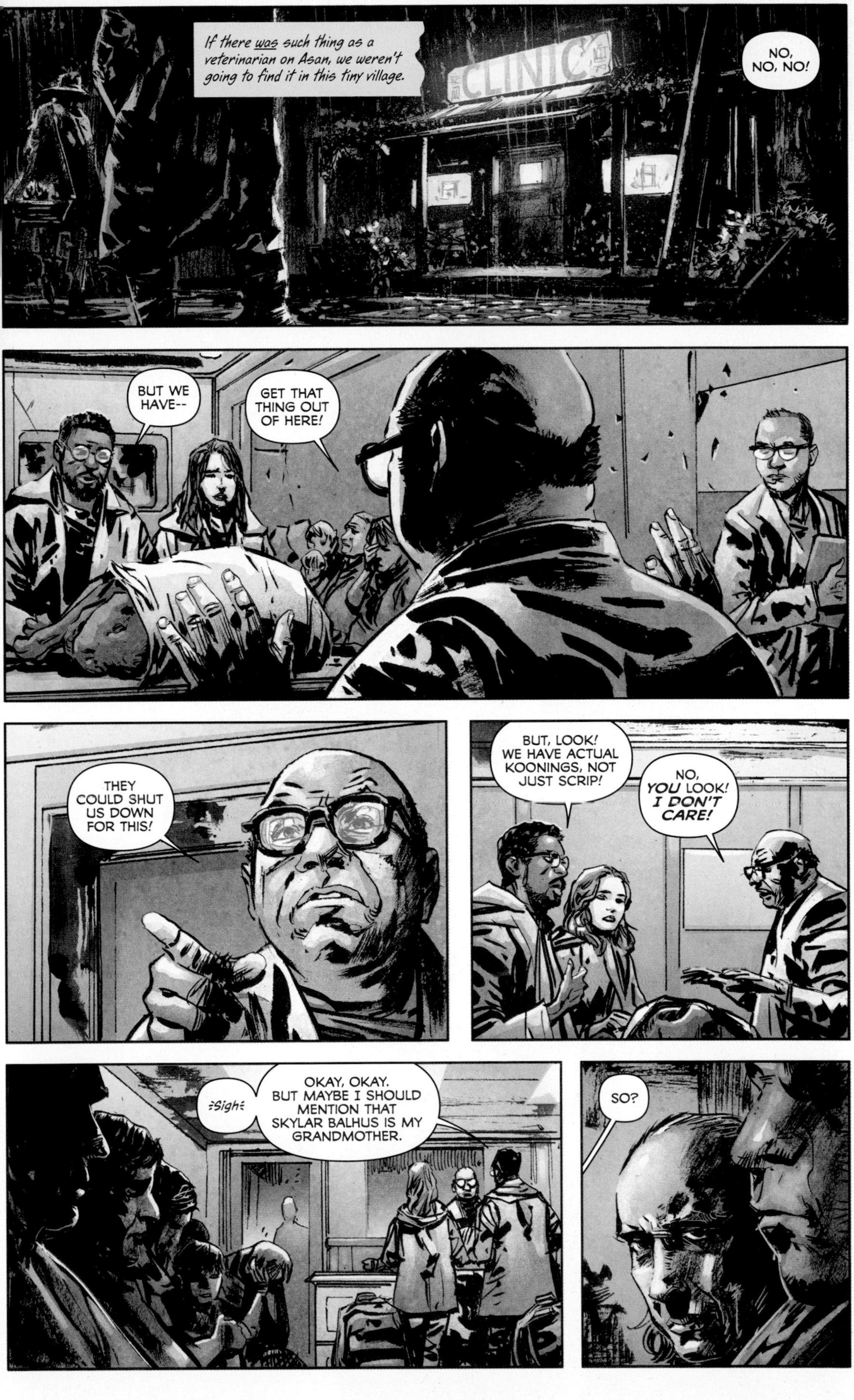
If there was such thing as a veterinarian on Asan, we weren't going to find it in this tiny village.
CLINIC
NO, NO, NO!
BUT WE HAVE--
GET THAT THING OUT OF HERE!
THEY COULD SHUT US DOWN FOR THIS!
BUT, LOOK! WE HAVE ACTUAL KOONINGS, NOT JUST SCRIP!
NO, YOU LOOK! I DON'T CARE!
Sigh
OKAY, OKAY. BUT MAYBE I SHOULD MENTION THAT SKYLAR BALHUS IS MY GRANDMOTHER.
SO?

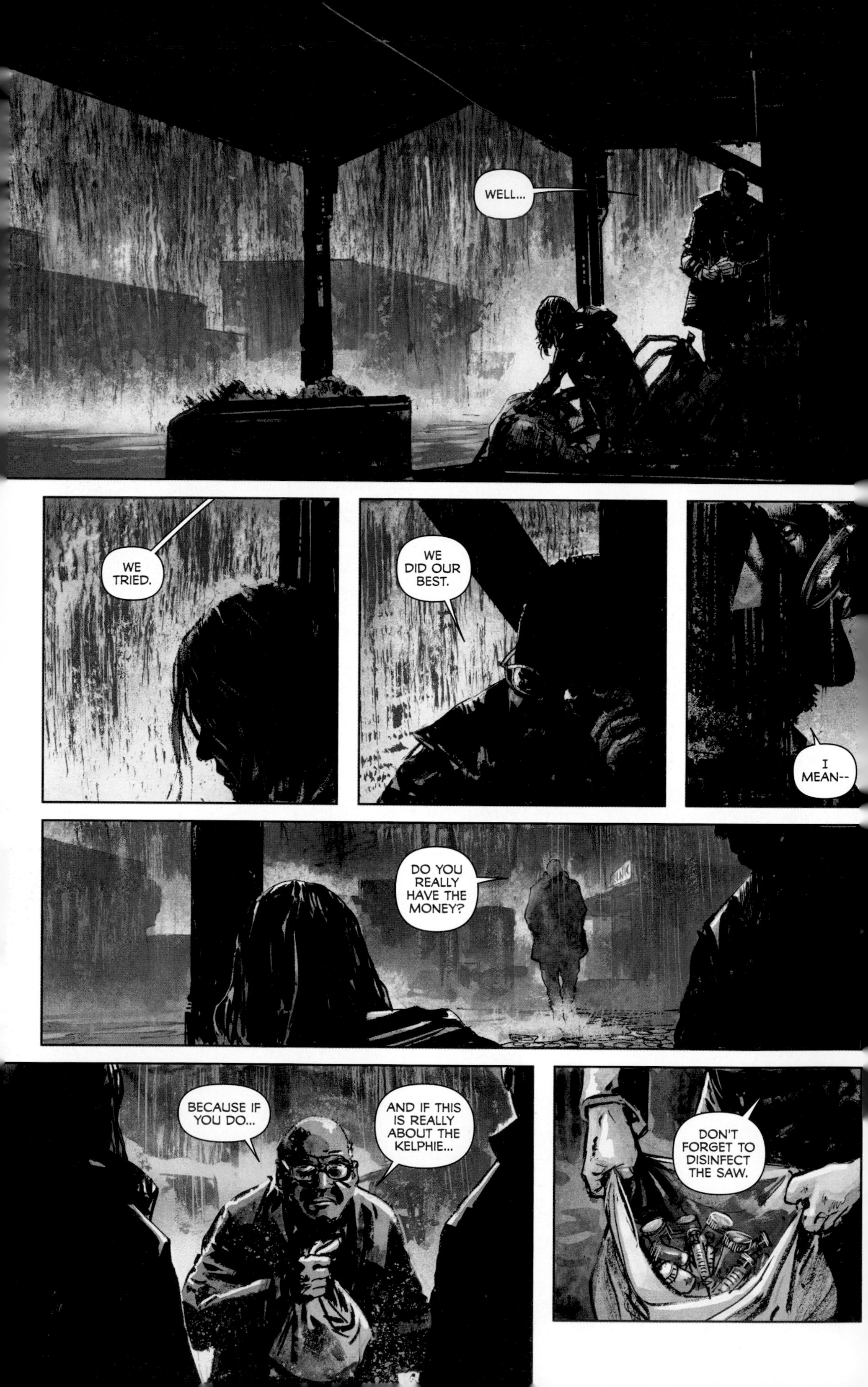
WELL...
WE TRIED.
WE DID OUR BEST.
I MEAN--
DO YOU REALLY HAVE THE MONEY?
BECAUSE IF YOU DO...
AND IF THIS IS REALLY ABOUT THE KELPHIE...
DON'T FORGET TO DISINFECT THE SAW.

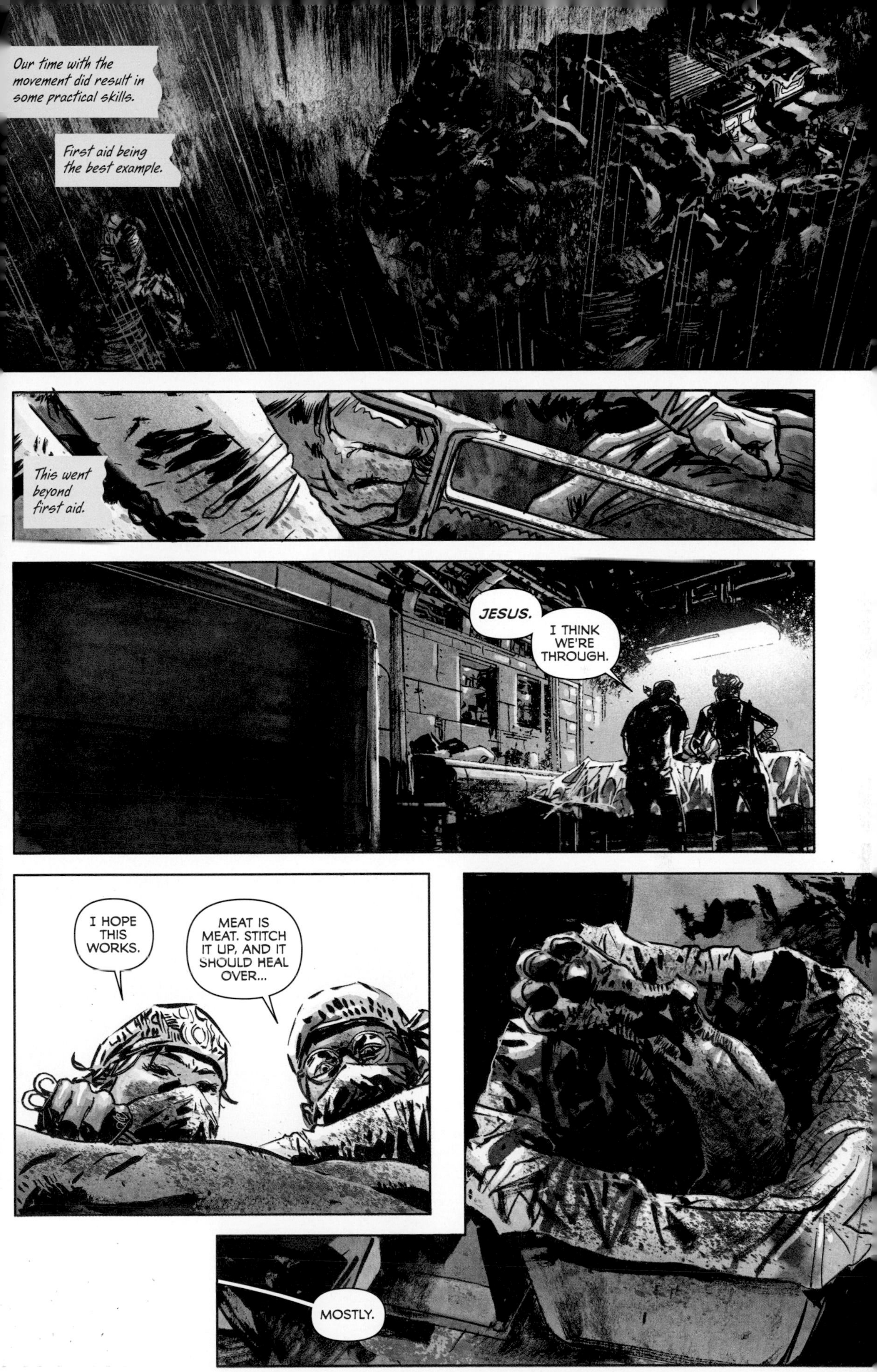
Our time with the movement did result in some practical skills.
First aid being the best example.
This went beyond first aid.
JESUS.
I THINK WE'RE THROUGH.
I HOPE THIS WORKS.
MEAT IS MEAT. STITCH IT UP, AND IT SHOULD HEAL OVER...
MOSTLY.

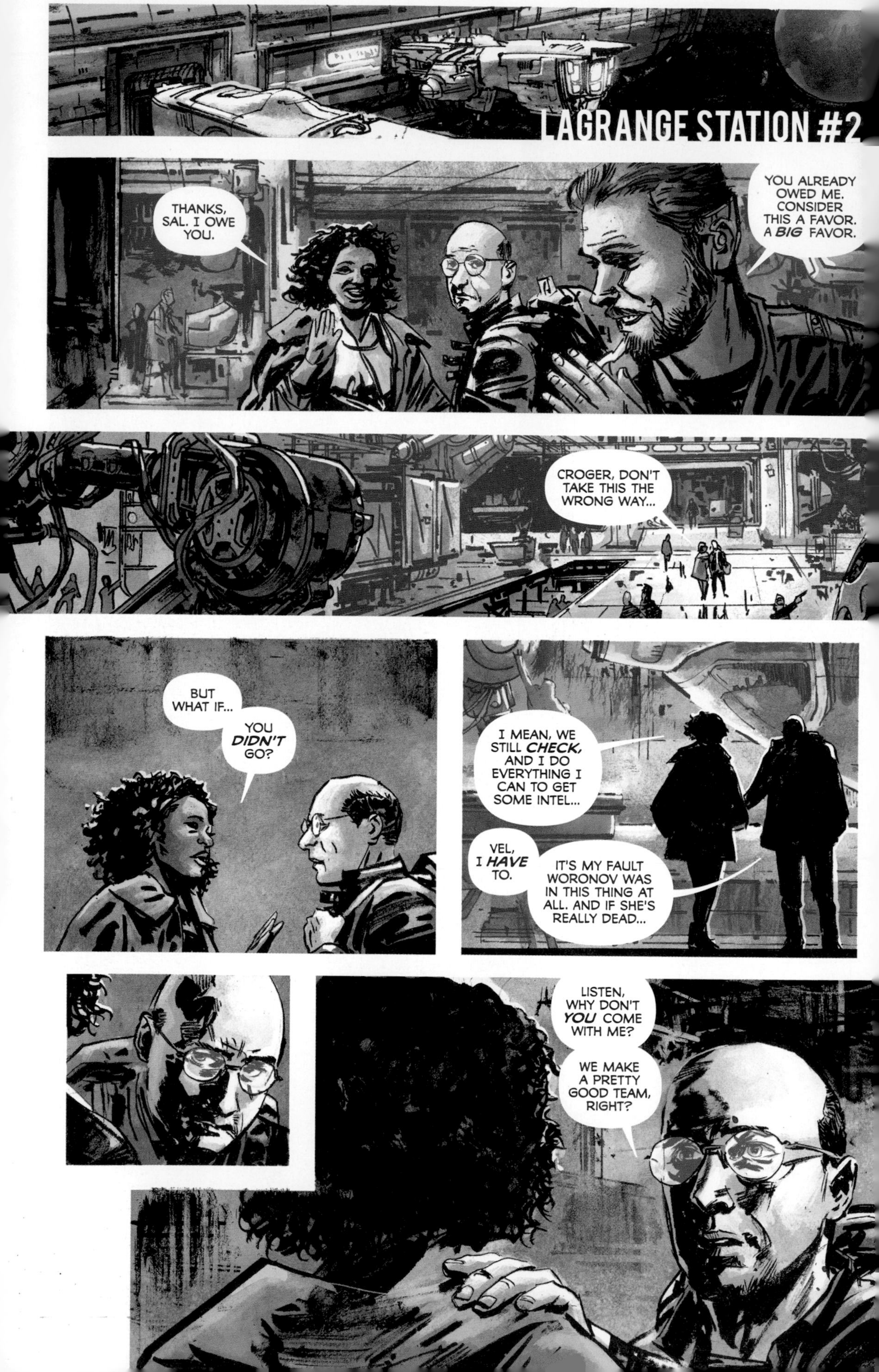
LAGRANGE STATION #2
THANKS, SAL. I OWE YOU.
YOU ALREADY OWED ME. CONSIDER THIS A FAVOR. A BIG FAVOR.
CROGER, DON'T TAKE THIS THE WRONG WAY...
BUT WHAT IF...
YOU DIDN'T GO?
I MEAN, WE STILL CHECK, AND I DO EVERYTHING I CAN TO GET SOME INTEL...
VEL, I HAVE TO.
IT'S MY FAULT WORONOV WAS IN THIS THING AT ALL. AND IF SHE'S REALLY DEAD...
LISTEN, WHY DON'T YOU COME WITH ME?
WE MAKE A PRETTY GOOD TEAM, RIGHT?

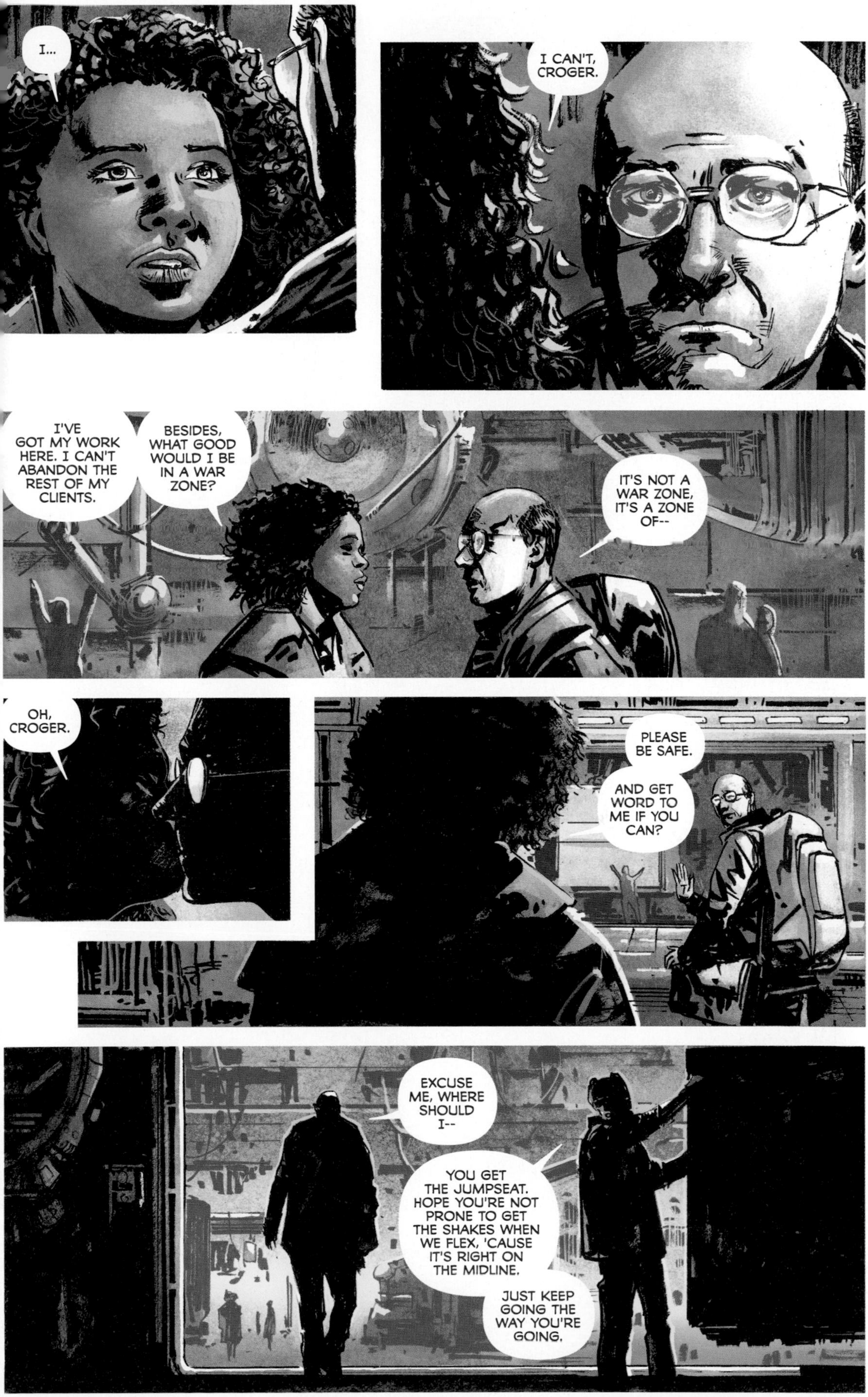
I...
I CAN'T, CROGER.
I'VE GOT MY WORK HERE. I CAN'T ABANDON THE REST OF MY CLIENTS.
BESIDES, WHAT GOOD WOULD I BE IN A WAR ZONE?
IT'S NOT A WAR ZONE, IT'S A ZONE OF--
OH, CROGER.
PLEASE BE SAFE.
AND GET WORD TO ME IF YOU CAN?
EXCUSE ME, WHERE SHOULD I--
YOU GET THE JUMPSEAT. HOPE YOU'RE NOT PRONE TO GET THE SHAKES WHEN WE FLEX, 'CAUSE IT'S RIGHT ON THE MIDLINE.
JUST KEEP GOING THE WAY YOU'RE GOING.

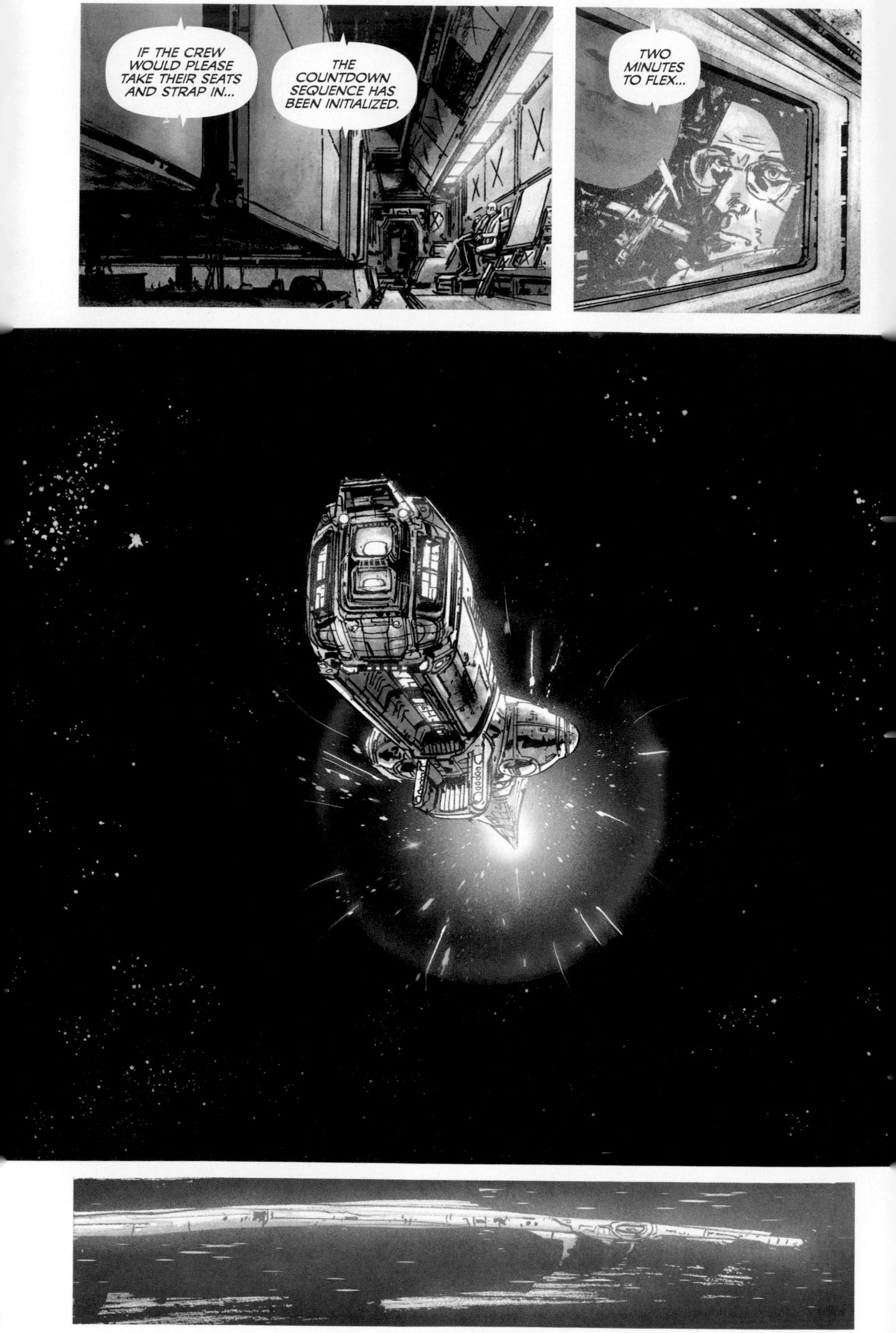
IF THE CREW WOULD PLEASE TAKE THEIR SEATS AND STRAP IN...
THE COUNTDOWN SEQUENCE HAS BEEN INITIALIZED.
TWO MINUTES TO FLEX...

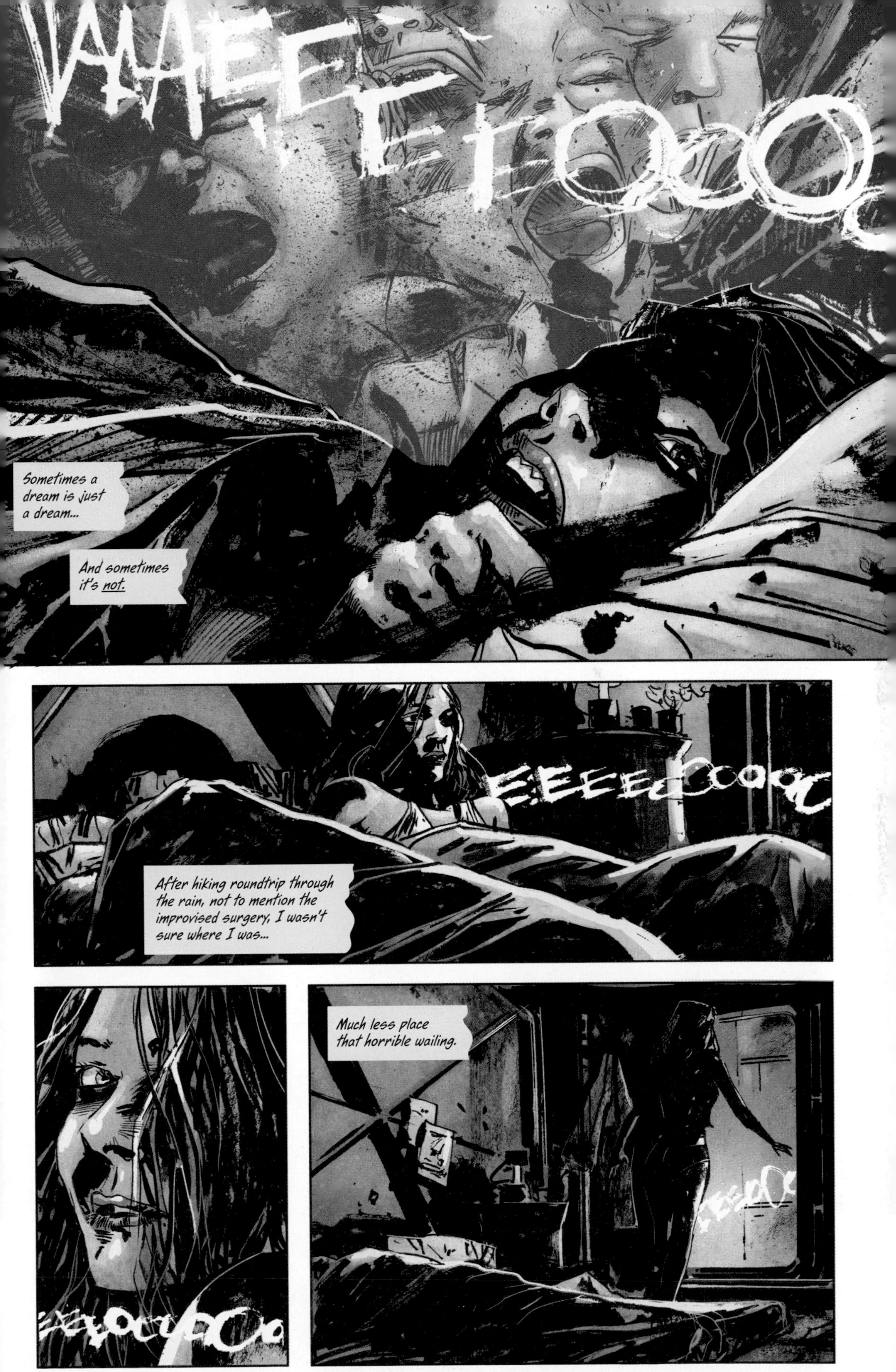
Sometimes a dream is just a dream...
And sometimes it's not.
After hiking roundtrip through the rain, not to mention the improvised surgery, I wasn't sure where I was...
Much less place that horrible wailing.

OH, NO.

THE DRUGS WERE SUPPOSED TO KNOCK YOU OUT FOR THE NIGHT.

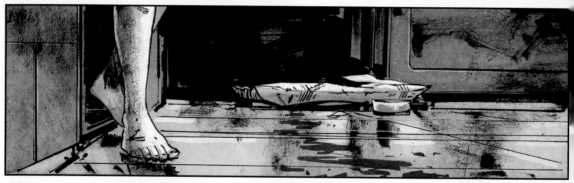

THERE YOU ARE! COME BACK WHERE IT'S WARMER AND LET ME CLEAN YOU UP.

COME ON, BABY...

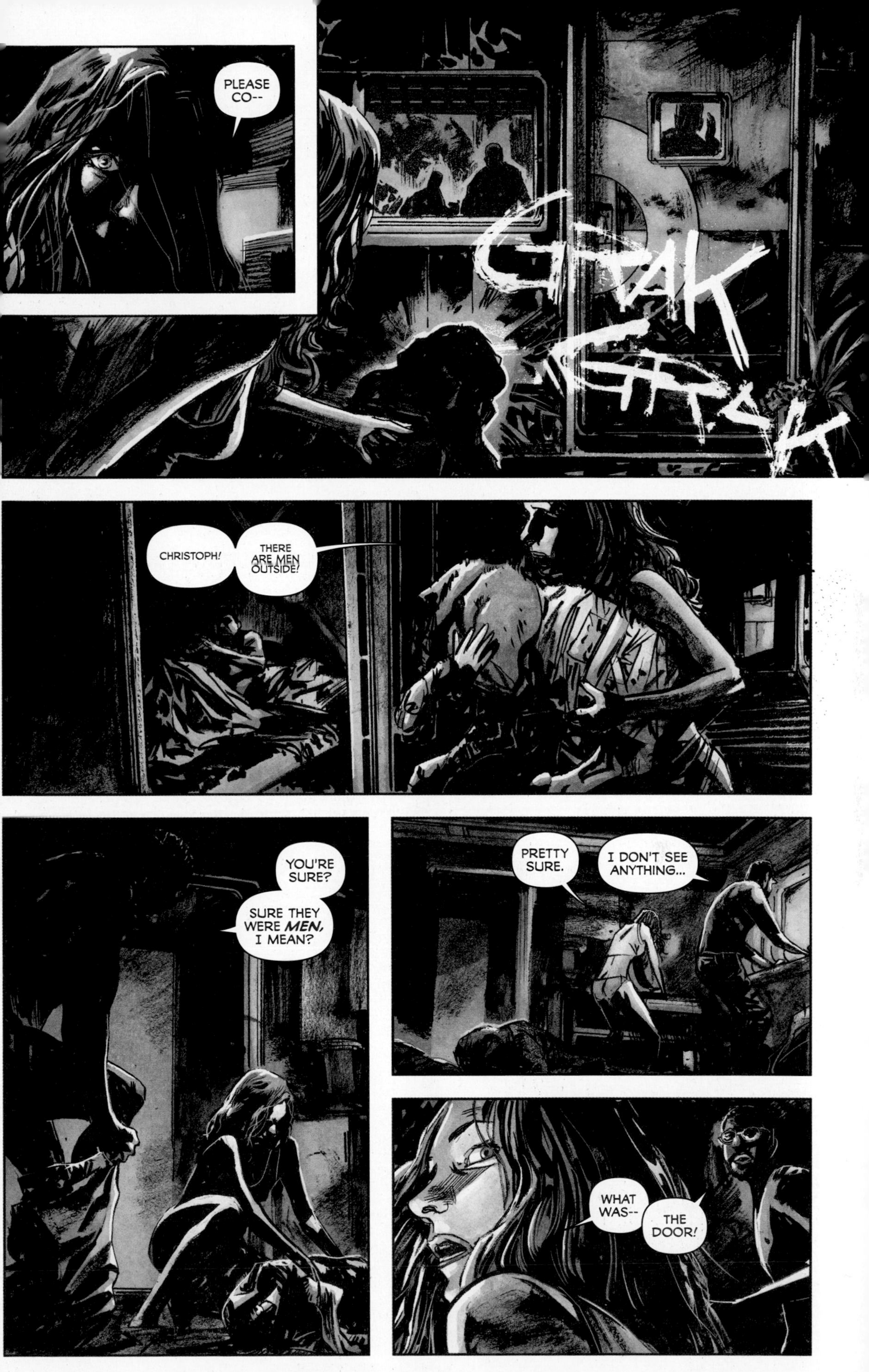
PLEASE CO--
CHRISTOPH!
THERE ARE MEN OUTSIDE!
YOU'RE SURE?
SURE THEY WERE *MEN,* I MEAN?
PRETTY SURE.
I DON'T SEE ANYTHING...
WHAT WAS--
THE DOOR!

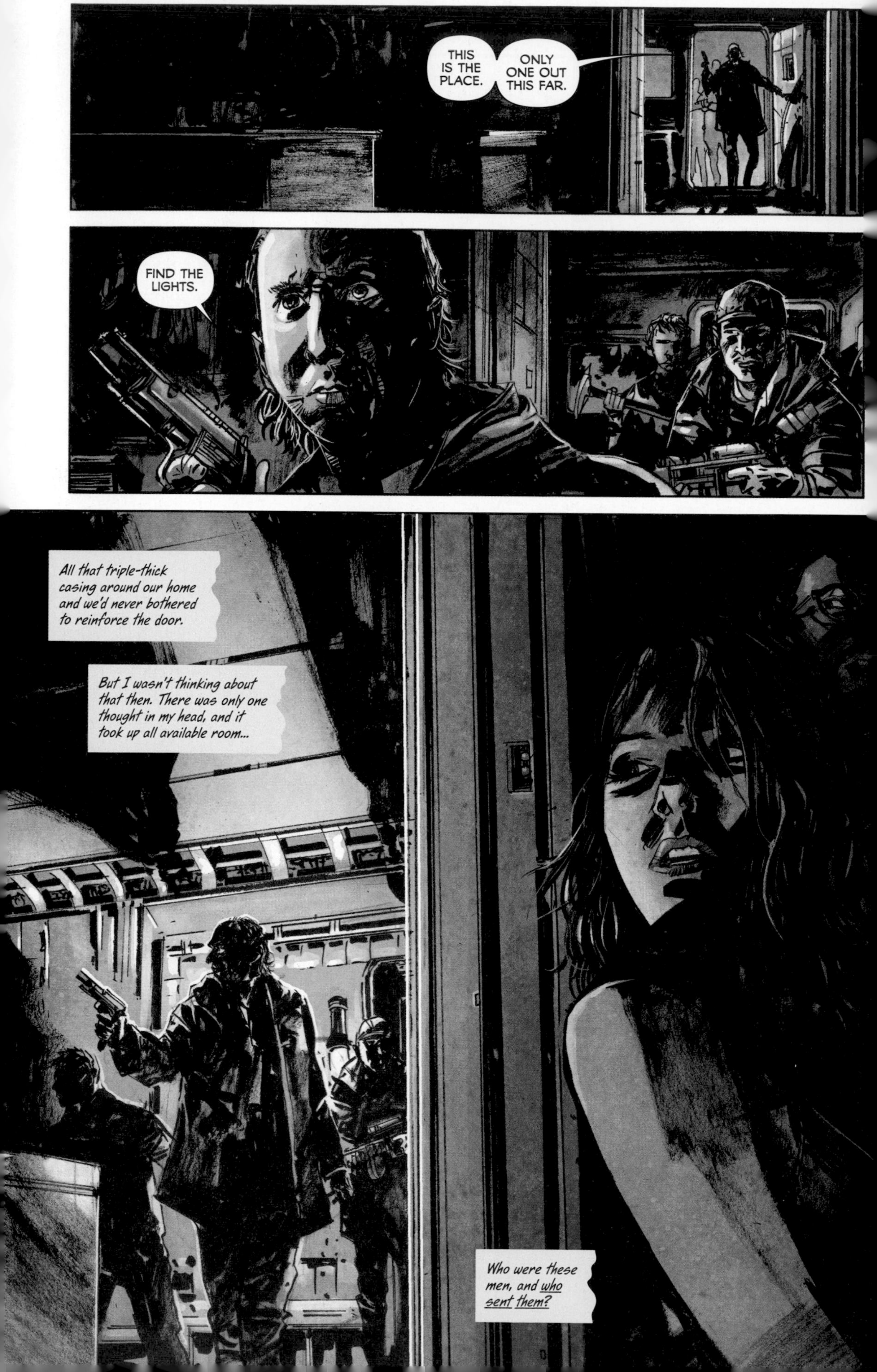
THIS IS THE PLACE.
ONLY ONE OUT THIS FAR.
FIND THE LIGHTS.
All that triple-thick casing around our home and we'd never bothered to reinforce the door.
But I wasn't thinking about that then. There was only one thought in my head, and it took up all available room...
Who were these men, and who sent them?

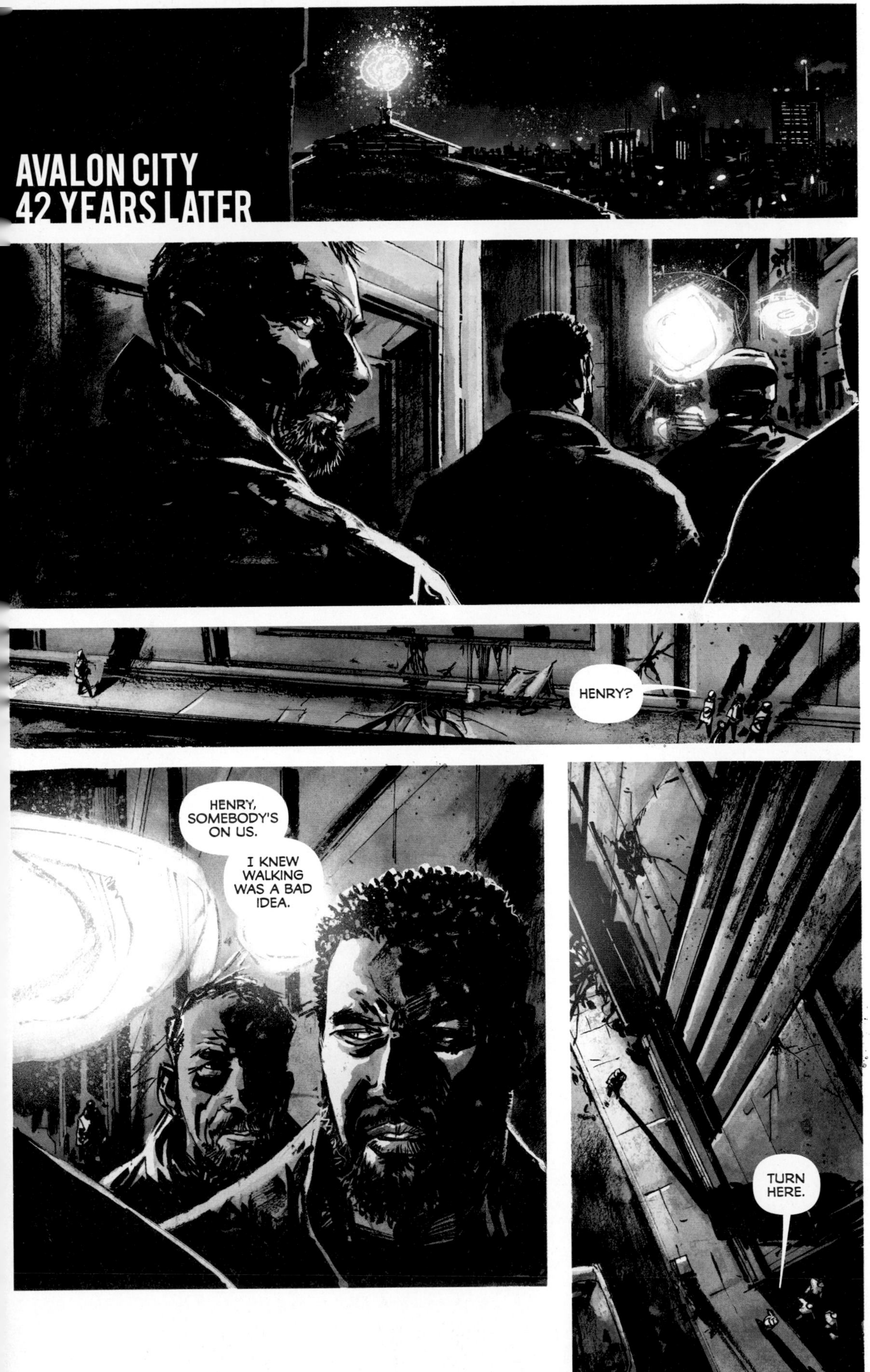
AVALON CITY
42 YEARS LATER
HENRY?
HENRY, SOMEBODY'S ON US.
I KNEW WALKING WAS A BAD IDEA.
TURN HERE.

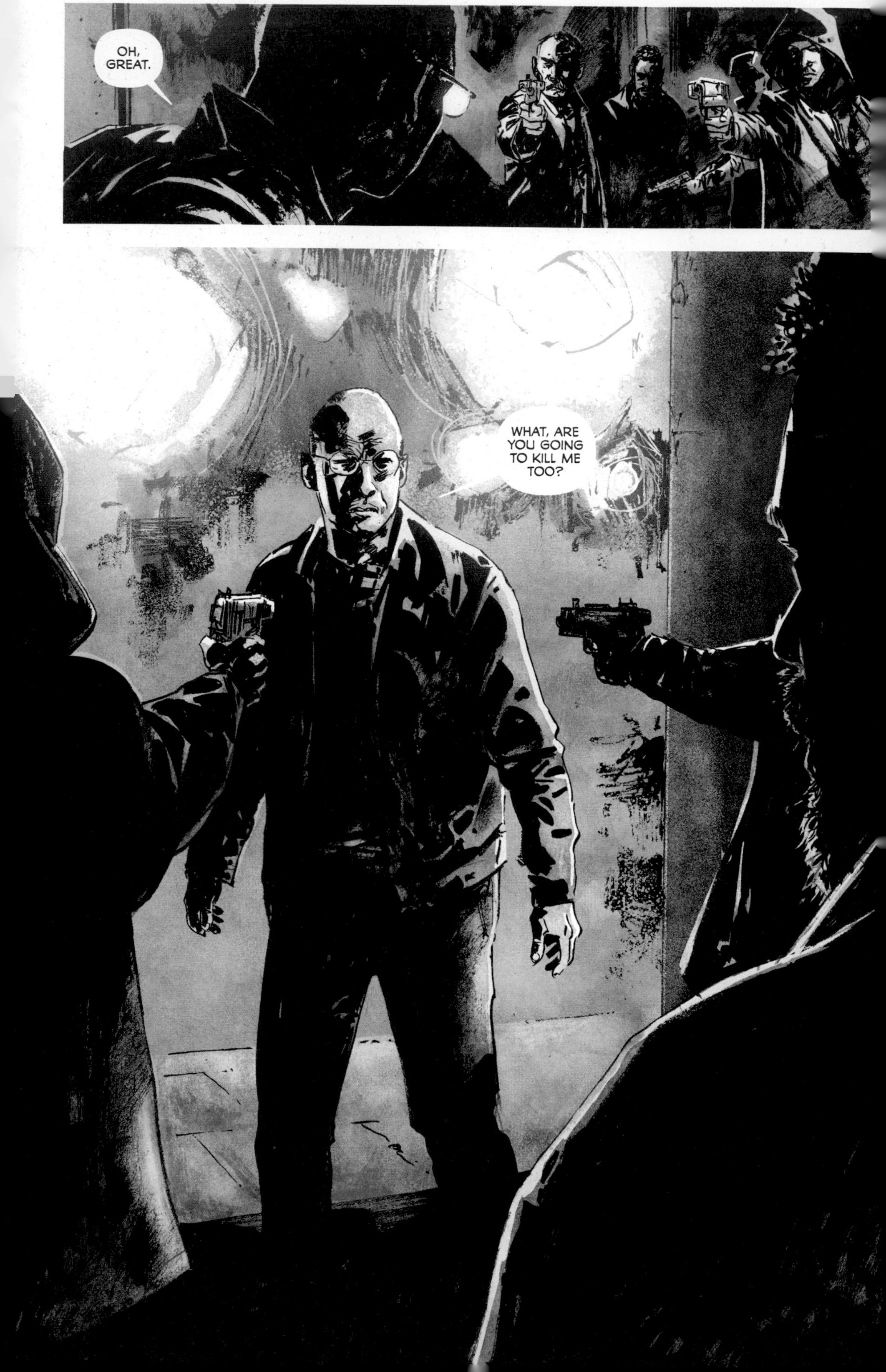
OH, GREAT.
WHAT, ARE YOU GOING TO KILL ME TOO?

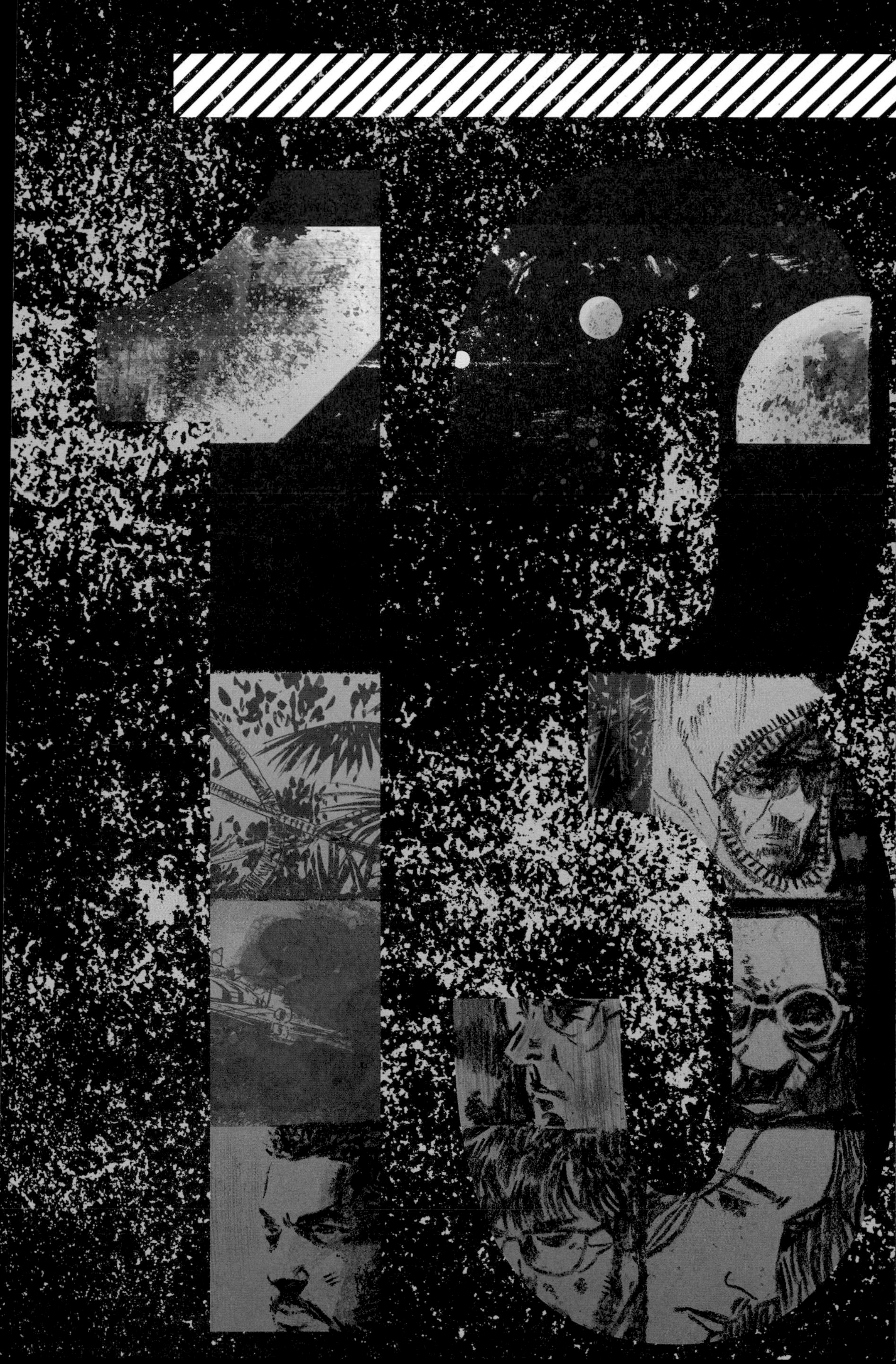

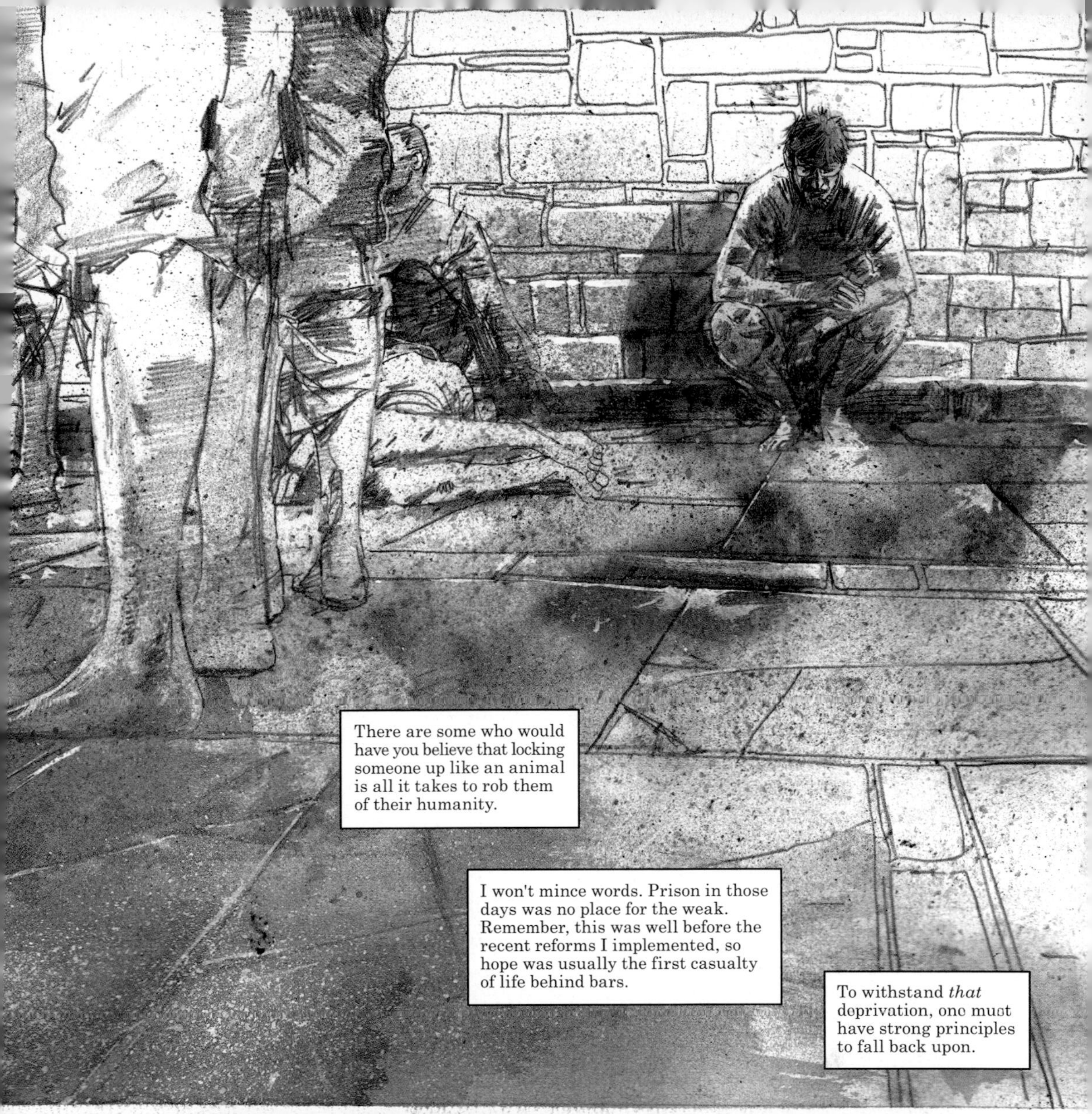
There are some who would have you believe that locking someone up like an animal is all it takes to rob them of their humanity.
I won't mince words. Prison in those days was no place for the weak. Remember, this was well before the recent reforms I implemented, so hope was usually the first casualty of life behind bars.
To withstand *that* deprivation, one must have strong principles to fall back upon.

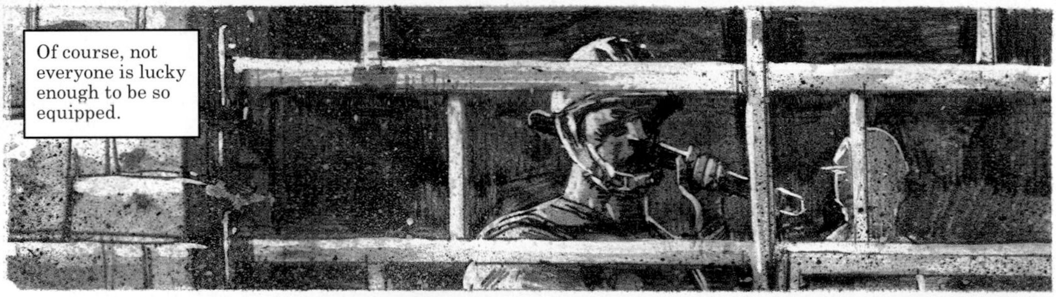
Of course, not everyone is lucky enough to be so equipped.

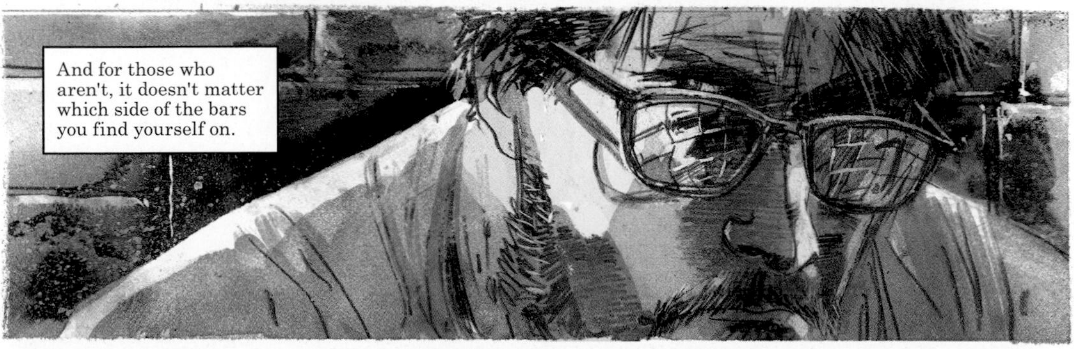
And for those who aren't, it doesn't matter which side of the bars you find yourself on.

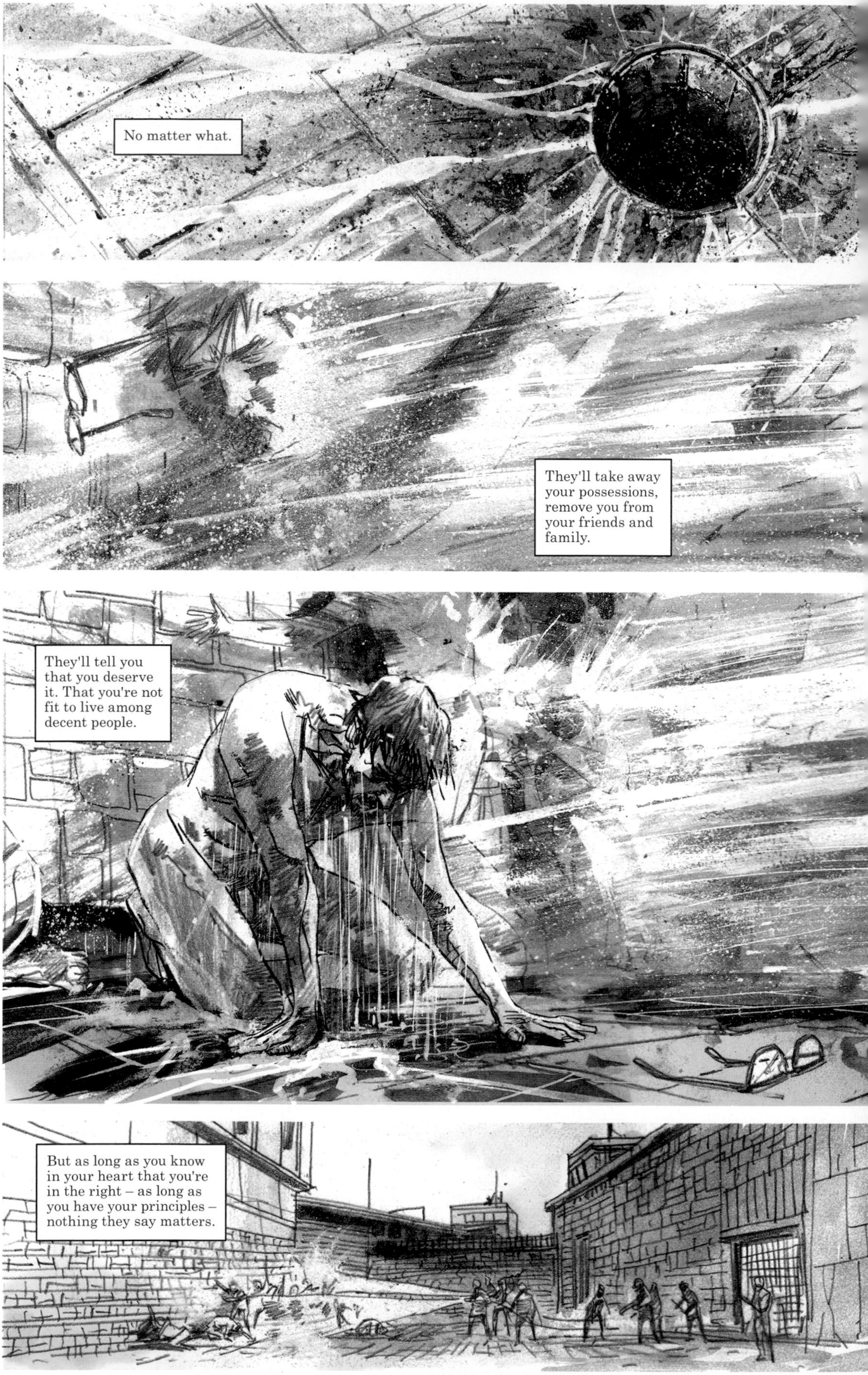
No matter what.
They'll take away your possessions, remove you from your friends and family.
They'll tell you that you deserve it. That you're not fit to live among decent people.
But as long as you know in your heart that you're in the right – as long as you have your principles – nothing they say matters.

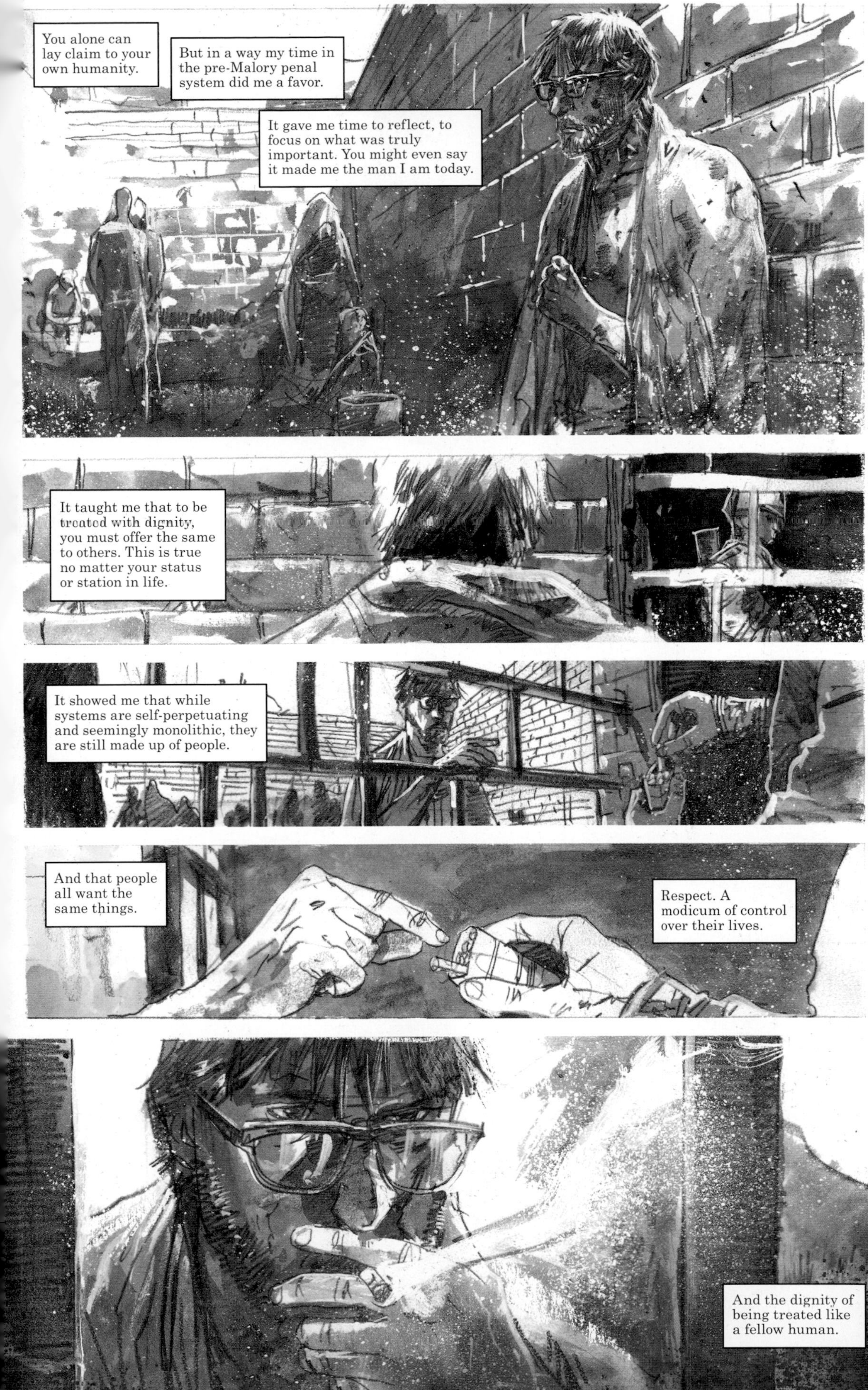
You alone can lay claim to your own humanity.
But in a way my time in the pre-Malory penal system did me a favor.
It gave me time to reflect, to focus on what was truly important. You might even say it made me the man I am today.
It taught me that to be treated with dignity, you must offer the same to others. This is true no matter your status or station in life.
It showed me that while systems are self-perpetuating and seemingly monolithic, they are still made up of people.
And that people all want the same things.
Respect. A modicum of control over their lives.
And the dignity of being treated like a fellow human.

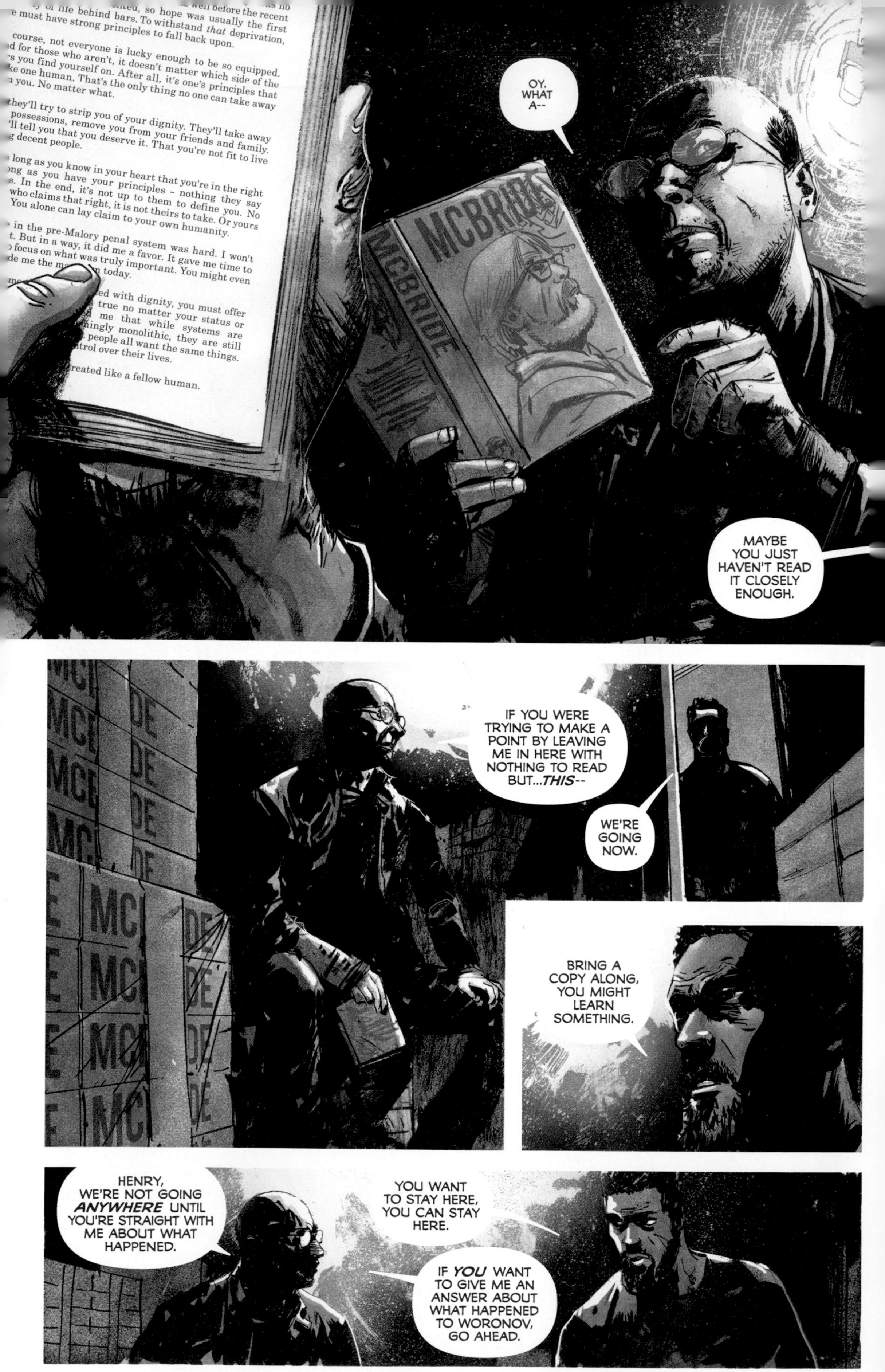

life behind bars, so hope was usually the first
must have strong principles to fall back upon.
course, not everyone is lucky enough to be so equipped.
for those who aren't, it doesn't matter which side of the
you find yourself on. After all, it's one's principles that
one human. That's the only thing no one can take away
you. No matter what.
they'll try to strip you of your dignity. They'll take away
possessions, remove you from your friends and family.
tell you that you deserve it. That you're not fit to live
decent people.
long as you know in your heart that you're in the right
as you have your principles – nothing they say
In the end, it's not up to them to define you. No
who claims that right, it is not theirs to take. Or yours
You alone can lay claim to your own humanity.
in the pre-Malory penal system was hard. I won't
But in a way, it did me a favor. It gave me time to
focus on what was truly important. You might even
me the today.
with dignity, you must offer
true no matter your status or
me that while systems are
monolithic, they are still
people all want the same things.
over their lives.
like a fellow human.
MCBRIDE
MCBRIDE
OY. WHAT A--
MAYBE YOU JUST HAVEN'T READ IT CLOSELY ENOUGH.
IF YOU WERE TRYING TO MAKE A POINT BY LEAVING ME IN HERE WITH NOTHING TO READ BUT...*THIS*--
WE'RE GOING NOW.
BRING A COPY ALONG, YOU MIGHT LEARN SOMETHING.
HENRY, WE'RE NOT GOING *ANYWHERE* UNTIL YOU'RE STRAIGHT WITH ME ABOUT WHAT HAPPENED.
YOU WANT TO STAY HERE, YOU CAN STAY HERE.
IF *YOU* WANT TO GIVE ME AN ANSWER ABOUT WHAT HAPPENED TO WORONOV, GO AHEAD.

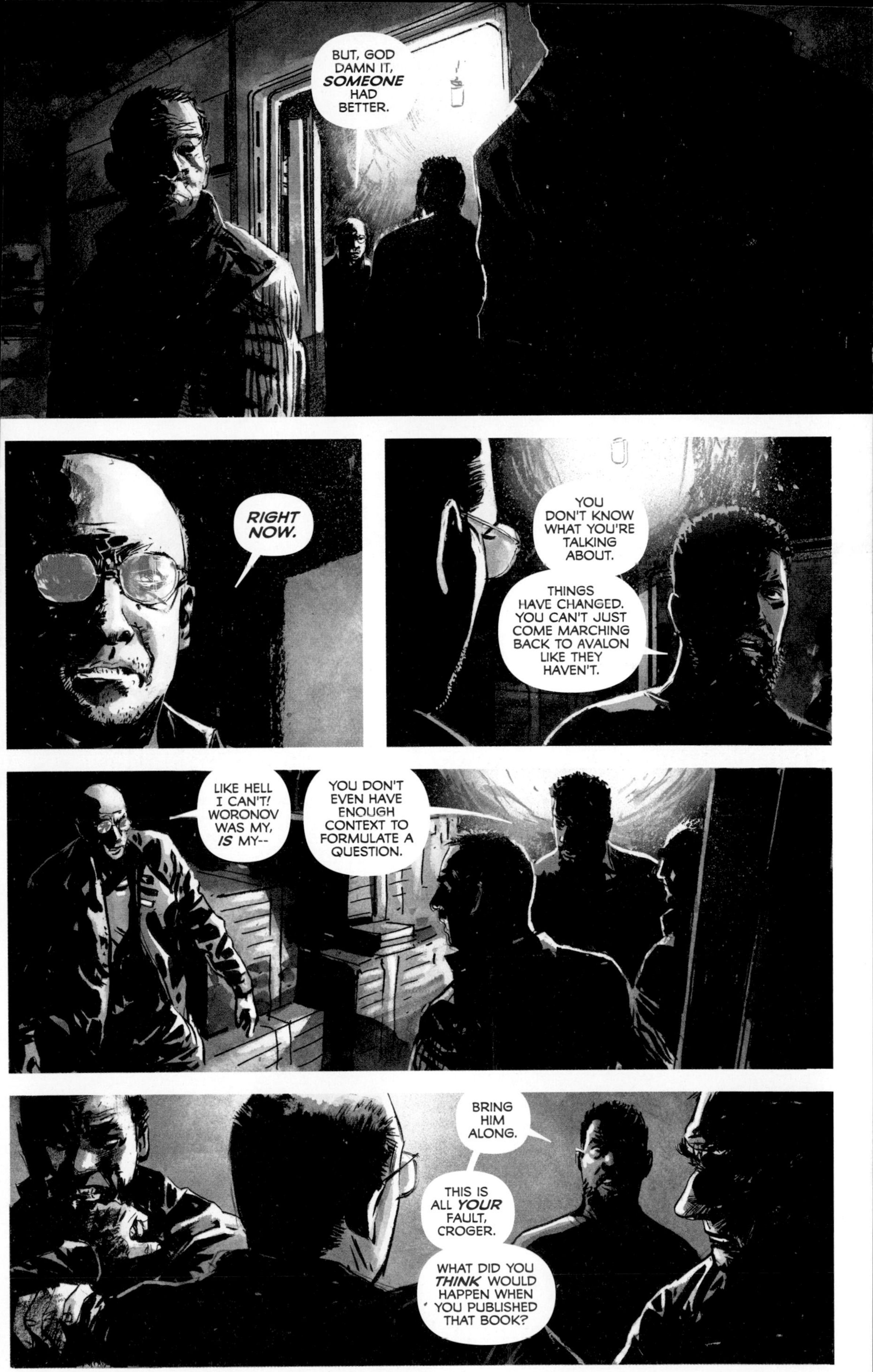
BUT, GOD DAMN IT, *SOMEONE* HAD BETTER.
RIGHT NOW.
YOU DON'T KNOW WHAT YOU'RE TALKING ABOUT.
THINGS HAVE CHANGED. YOU CAN'T JUST COME MARCHING BACK TO AVALON LIKE THEY HAVEN'T.
LIKE HELL I CAN'T! WORONOV WAS MY, *IS* MY--
YOU DON'T EVEN HAVE ENOUGH CONTEXT TO FORMULATE A QUESTION.
BRING HIM ALONG.
THIS IS ALL *YOUR* FAULT, CROGER.
WHAT DID YOU *THINK* WOULD HAPPEN WHEN YOU PUBLISHED THAT BOOK?

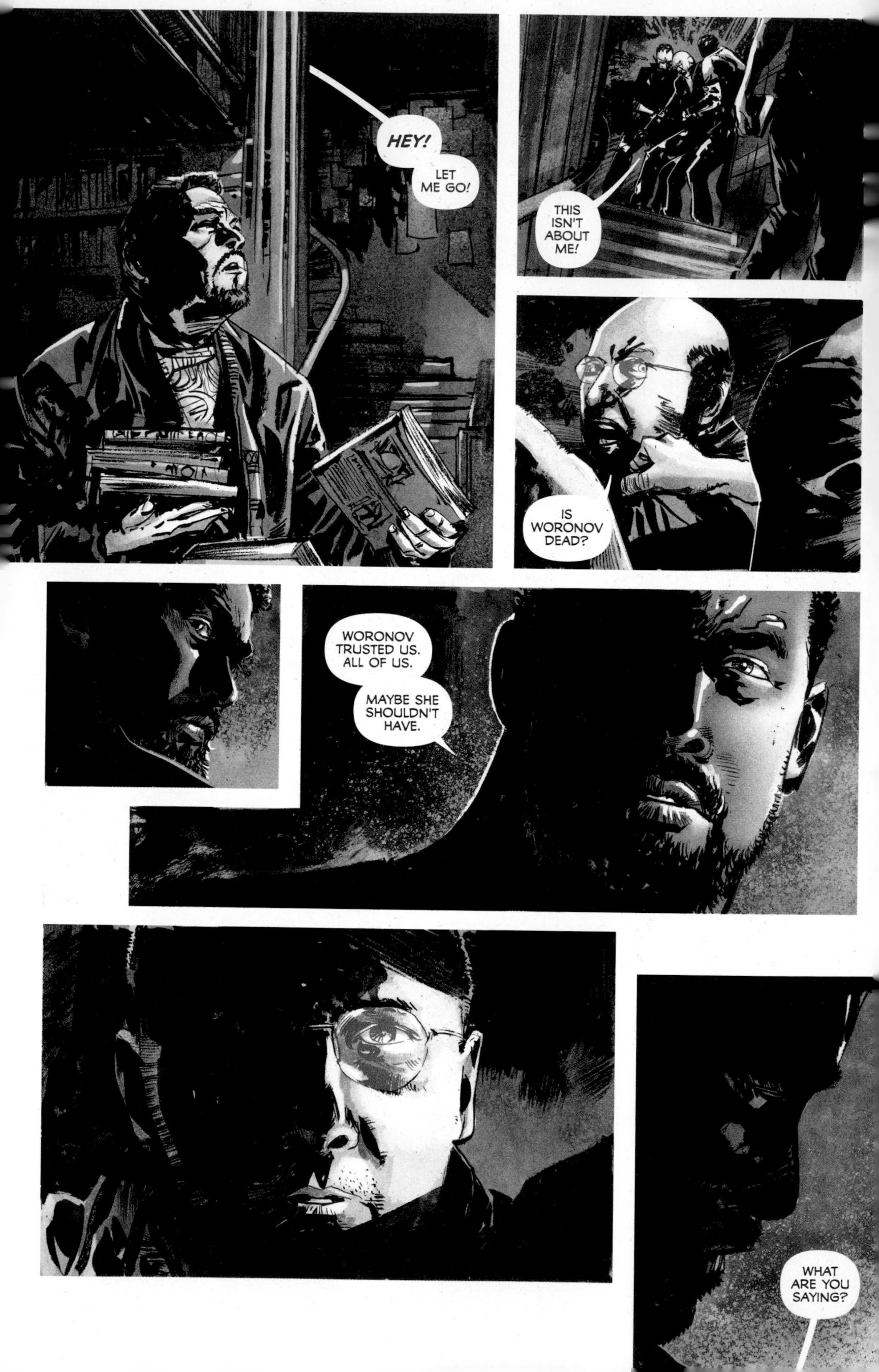
HEY!
LET ME GO!
THIS ISN'T ABOUT ME!
IS WORONOV DEAD?
WORONOV TRUSTED US. ALL OF US.
MAYBE SHE SHOULDN'T HAVE.
WHAT ARE YOU SAYING?

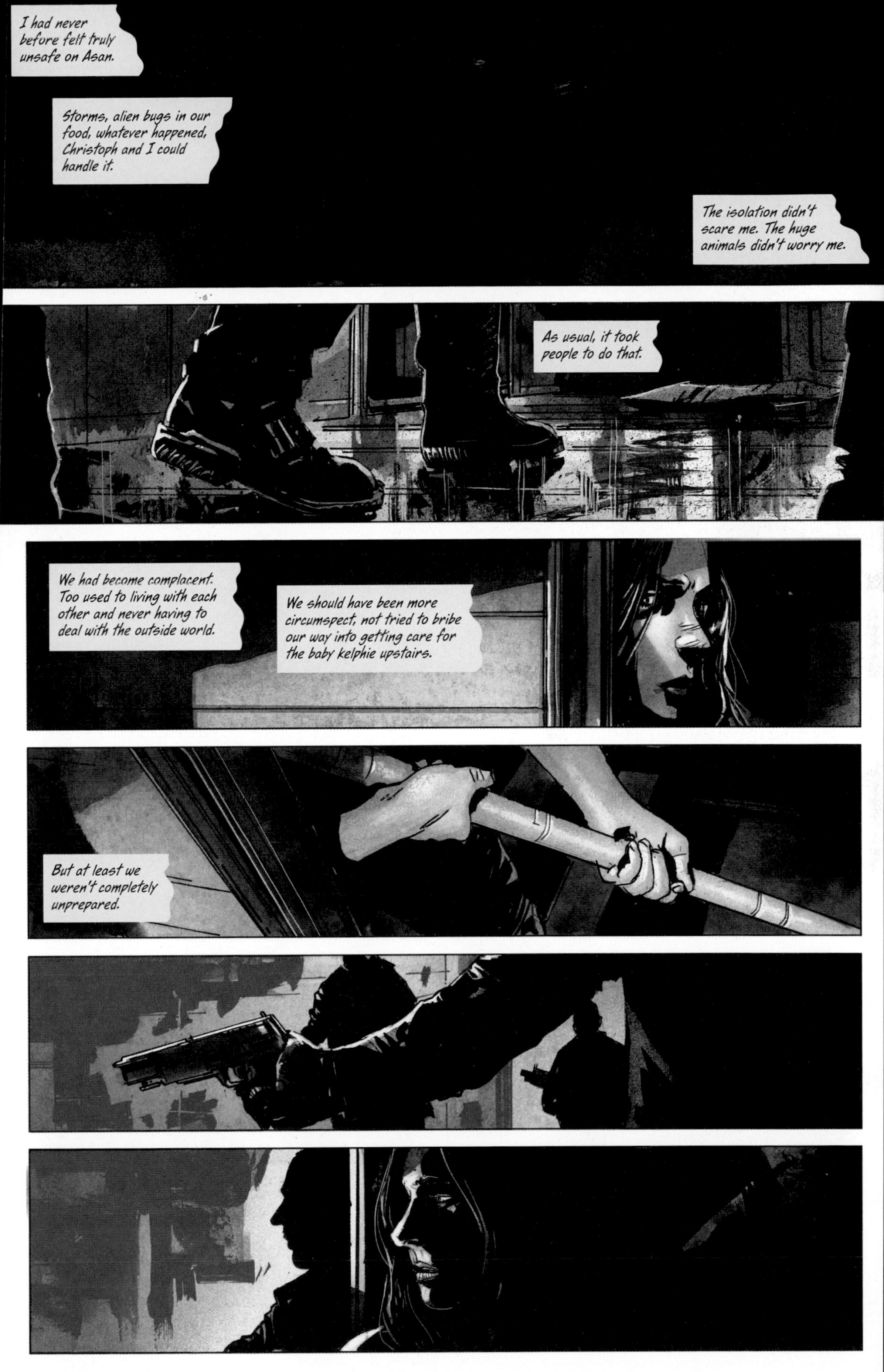
I had never before felt truly unsafe on Asan.
Storms, alien bugs in our food, whatever happened, Christoph and I could handle it.
The isolation didn't scare me. The huge animals didn't worry me.
As usual, it took people to do that.
We had become complacent. Too used to living with each other and never having to deal with the outside world.
We should have been more circumspect, not tried to bribe our way into getting care for the baby kelphie upstairs.
But at least we weren't completely unprepared.

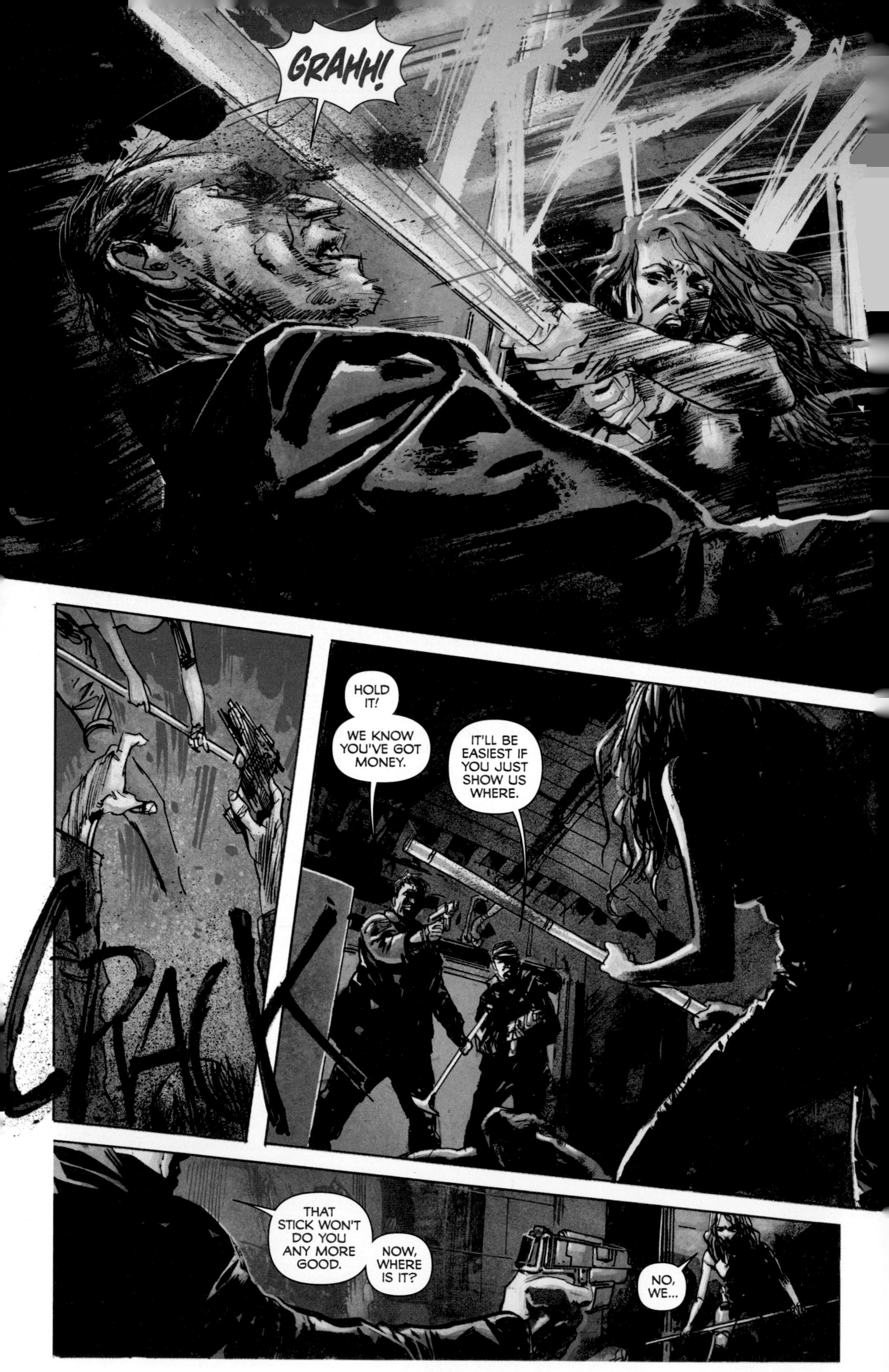
GRAHH!
CRACK
HOLD IT!
WE KNOW YOU'VE GOT MONEY.
IT'LL BE EASIEST IF YOU JUST SHOW US WHERE.
THAT STICK WON'T DO YOU ANY MORE GOOD.
NOW, WHERE IS IT?
NO, WE...

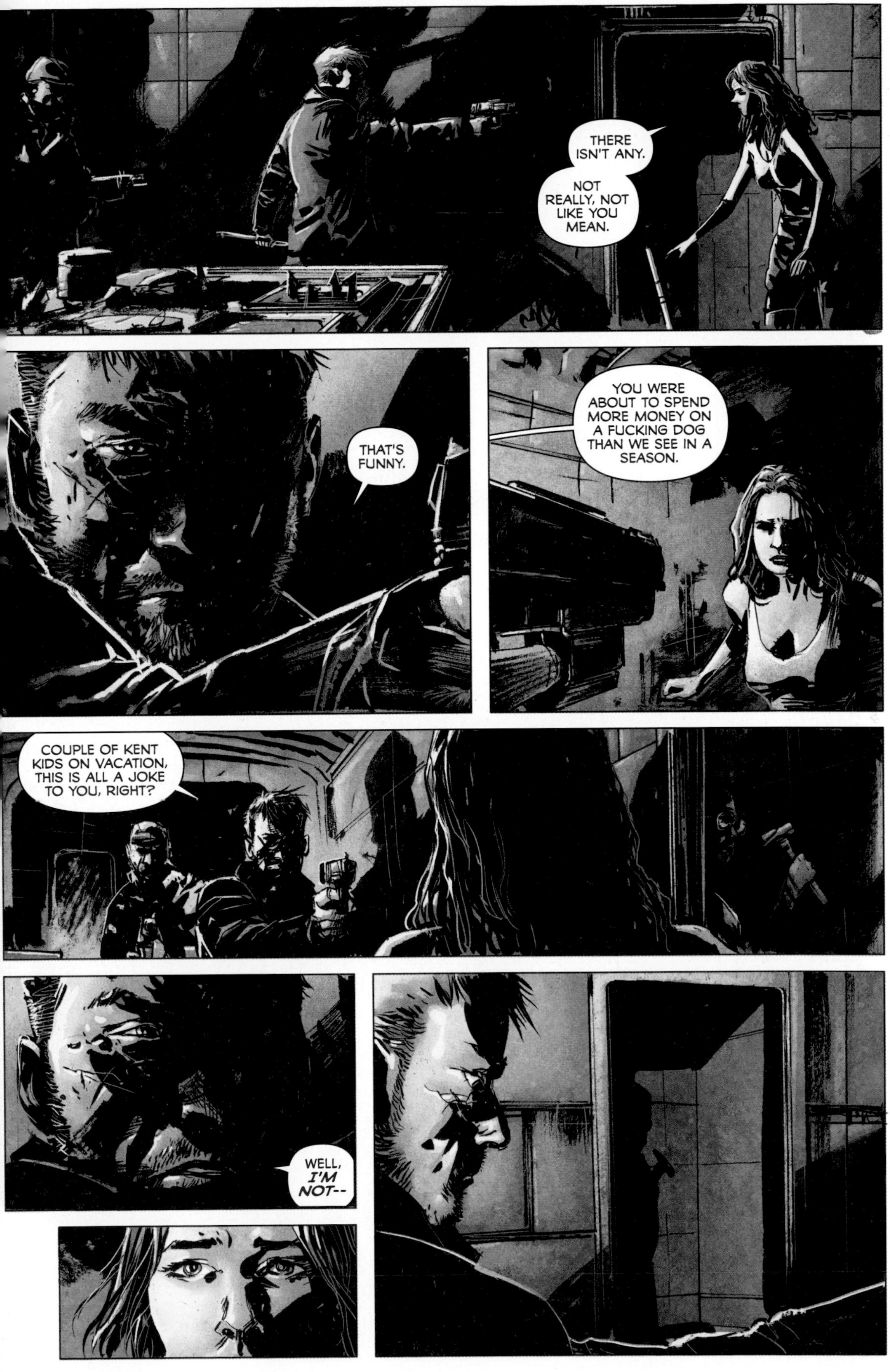
THERE ISN'T ANY.
NOT REALLY, NOT LIKE YOU MEAN.
THAT'S FUNNY.
YOU WERE ABOUT TO SPEND MORE MONEY ON A FUCKING DOG THAN WE SEE IN A SEASON.
COUPLE OF KENT KIDS ON VACATION, THIS IS ALL A JOKE TO YOU, RIGHT?
WELL, *I'M NOT*--

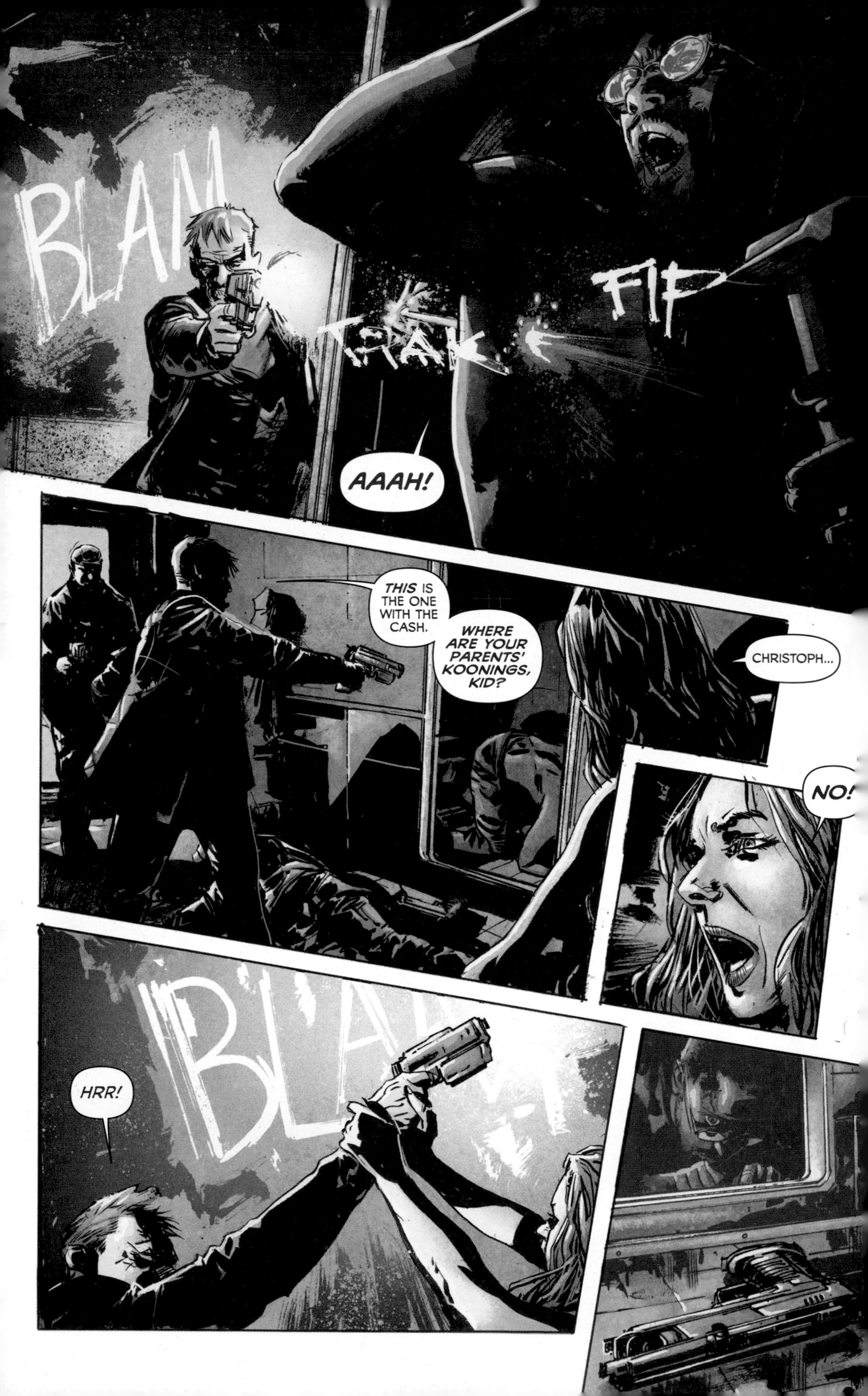
BLAM
TRAK
FIP
AAAH!
THIS IS THE ONE WITH THE CASH.
WHERE ARE YOUR PARENTS' KOONINGS, KID?
CHRISTOPH...
NO!
BLAM
HRR!

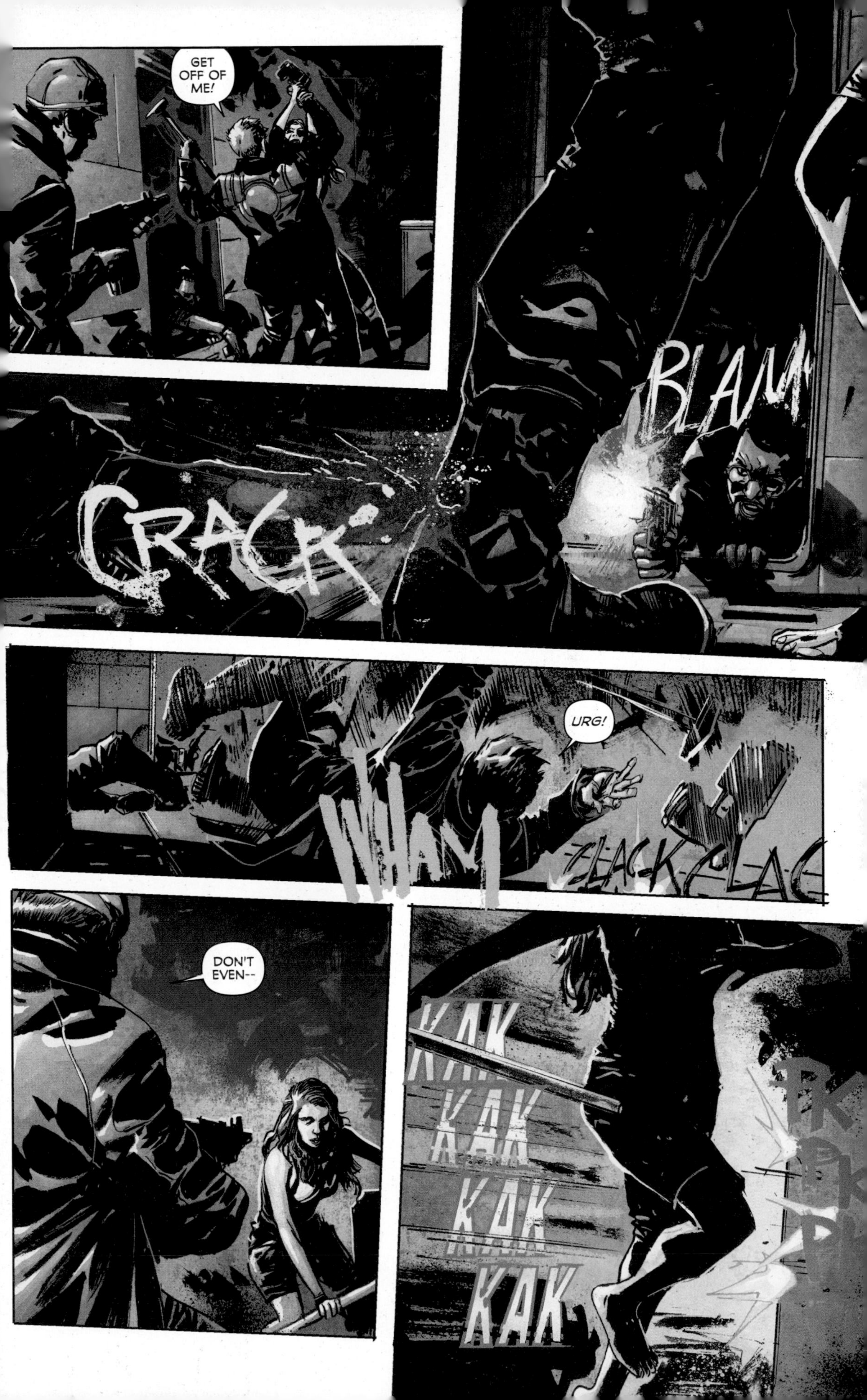
GET OFF OF ME!
BLAM
CRACK
URG!
WHAM
CLACK-CLAC
DON'T EVEN--
KAK
KAK
KAK
KAK

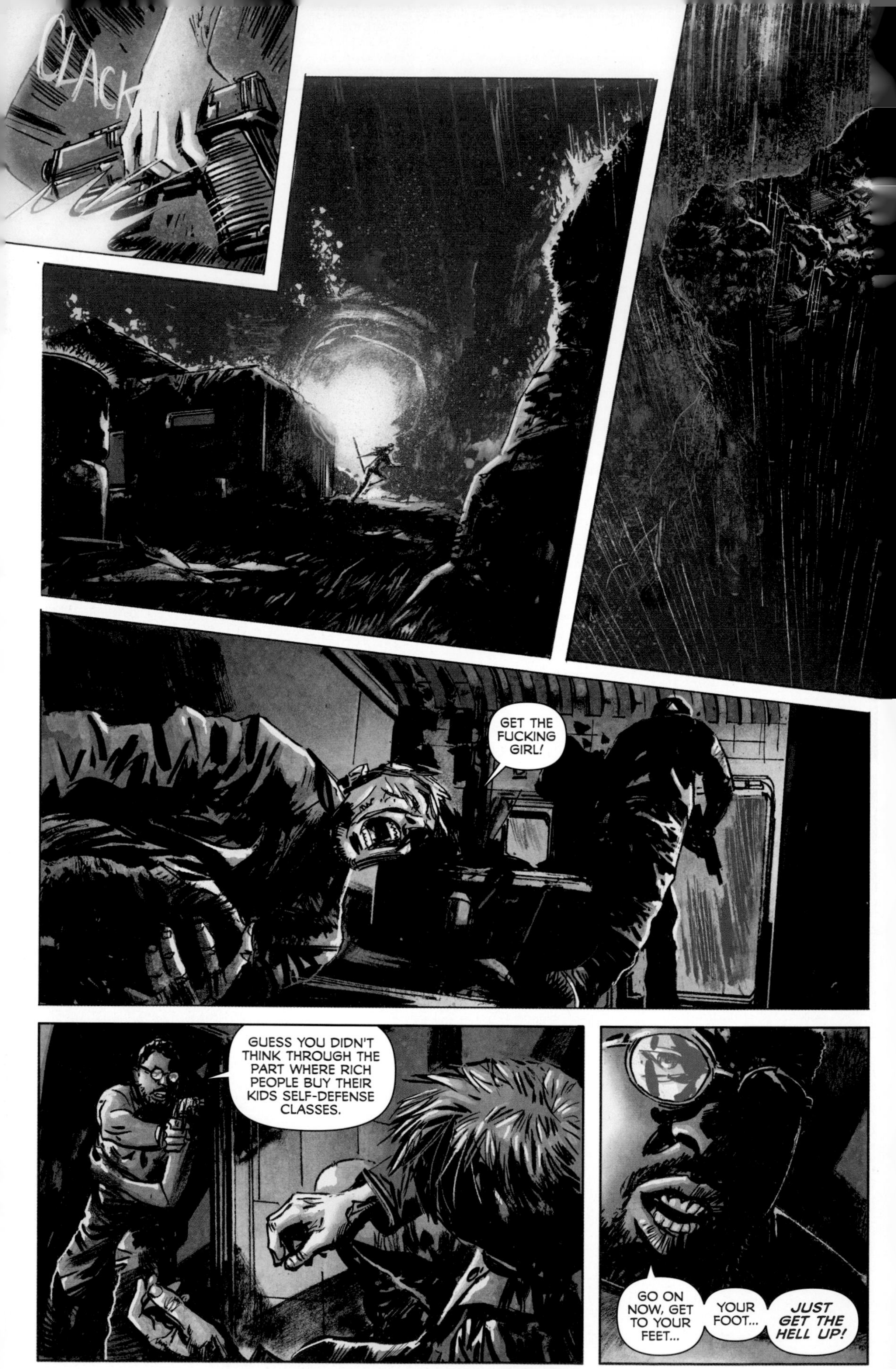
CLACK
GET THE FUCKING GIRL!
GUESS YOU DIDN'T THINK THROUGH THE PART WHERE RICH PEOPLE BUY THEIR KIDS SELF-DEFENSE CLASSES.
GO ON NOW, GET TO YOUR FEET...
YOUR FOOT...
JUST GET THE HELL UP!

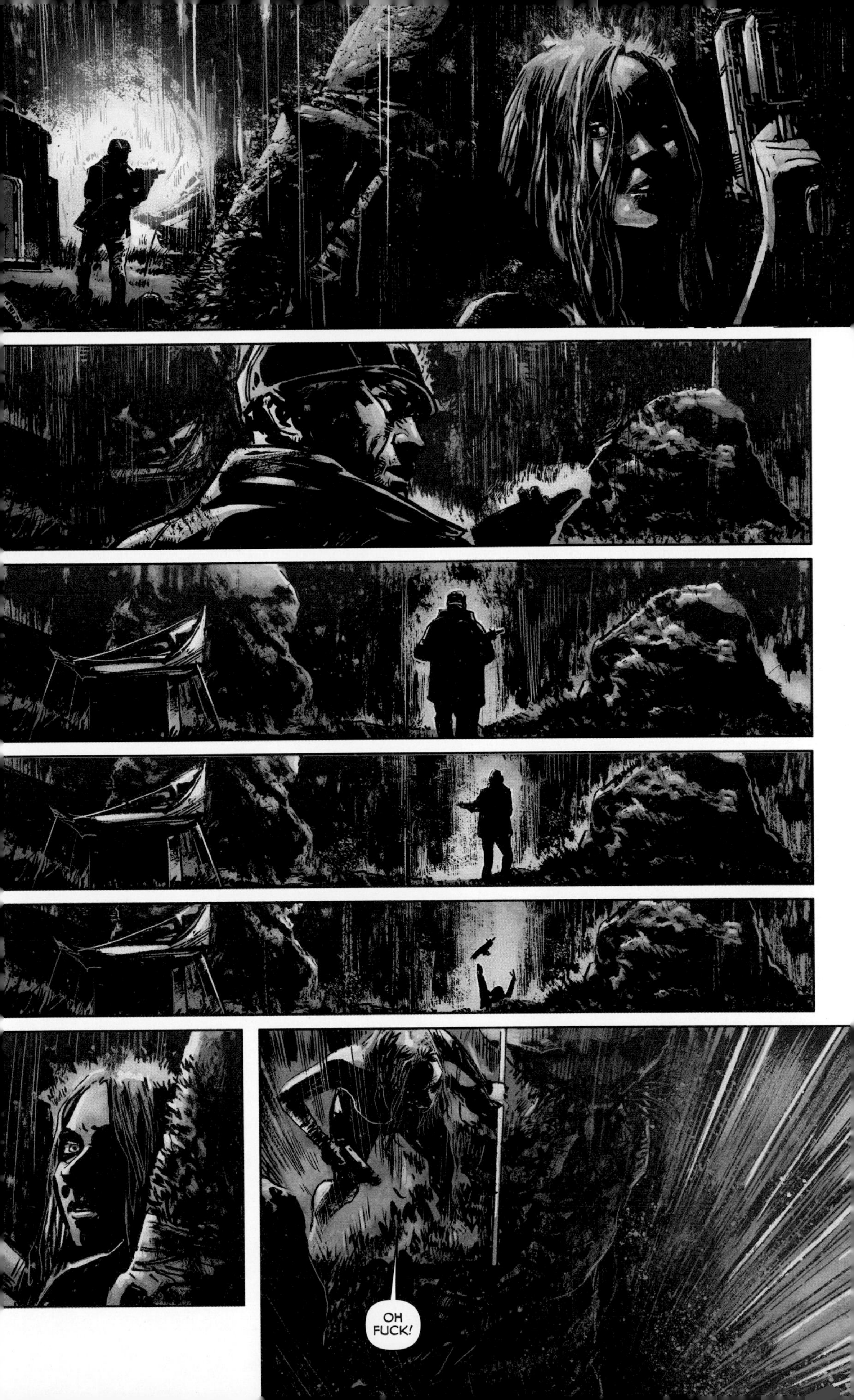
OH FUCK!

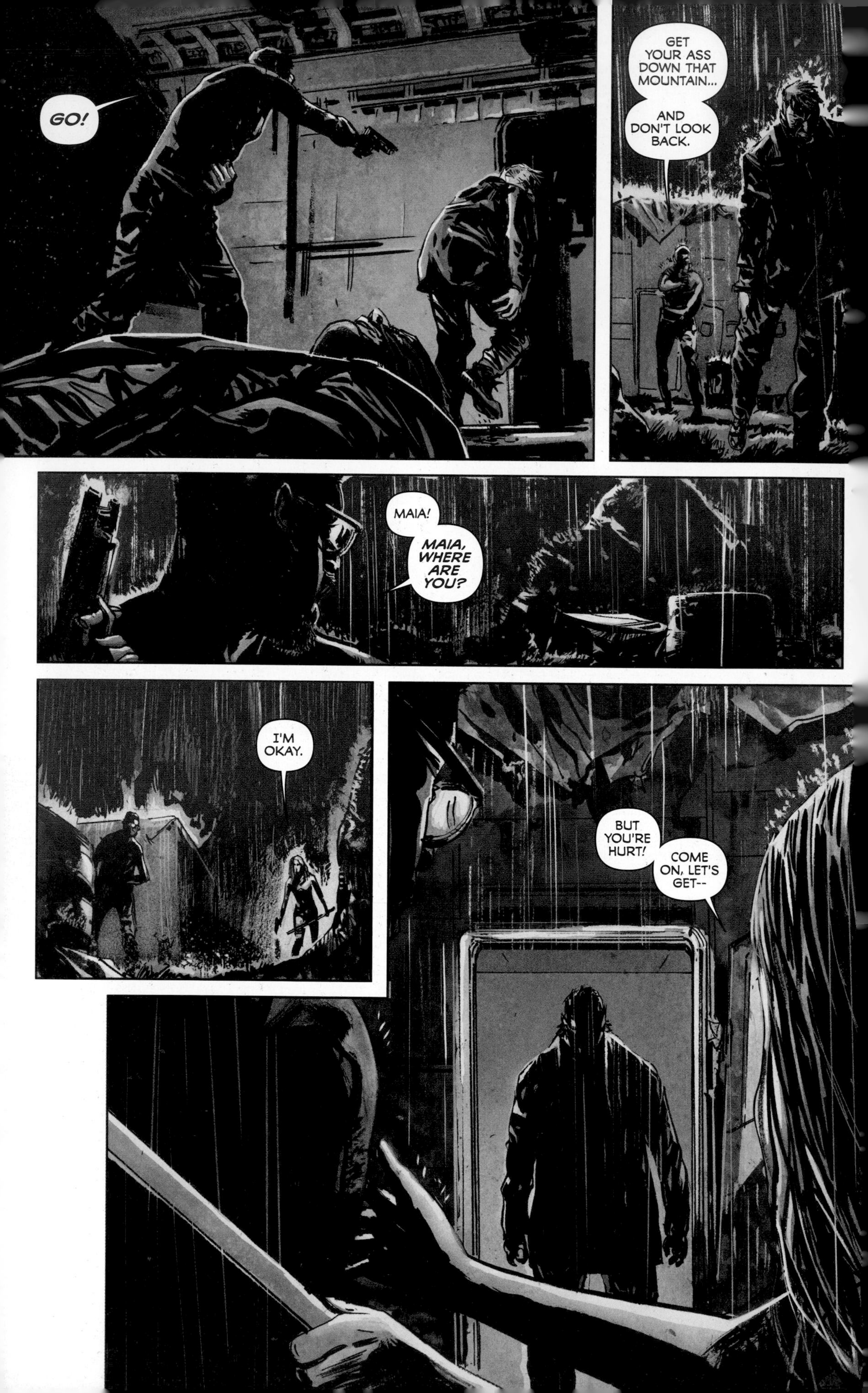
GO!
GET YOUR ASS DOWN THAT MOUNTAIN...
AND DON'T LOOK BACK.
MAIA!
MAIA, WHERE ARE YOU?
I'M OKAY.
BUT YOU'RE HURT!
COME ON, LET'S GET--

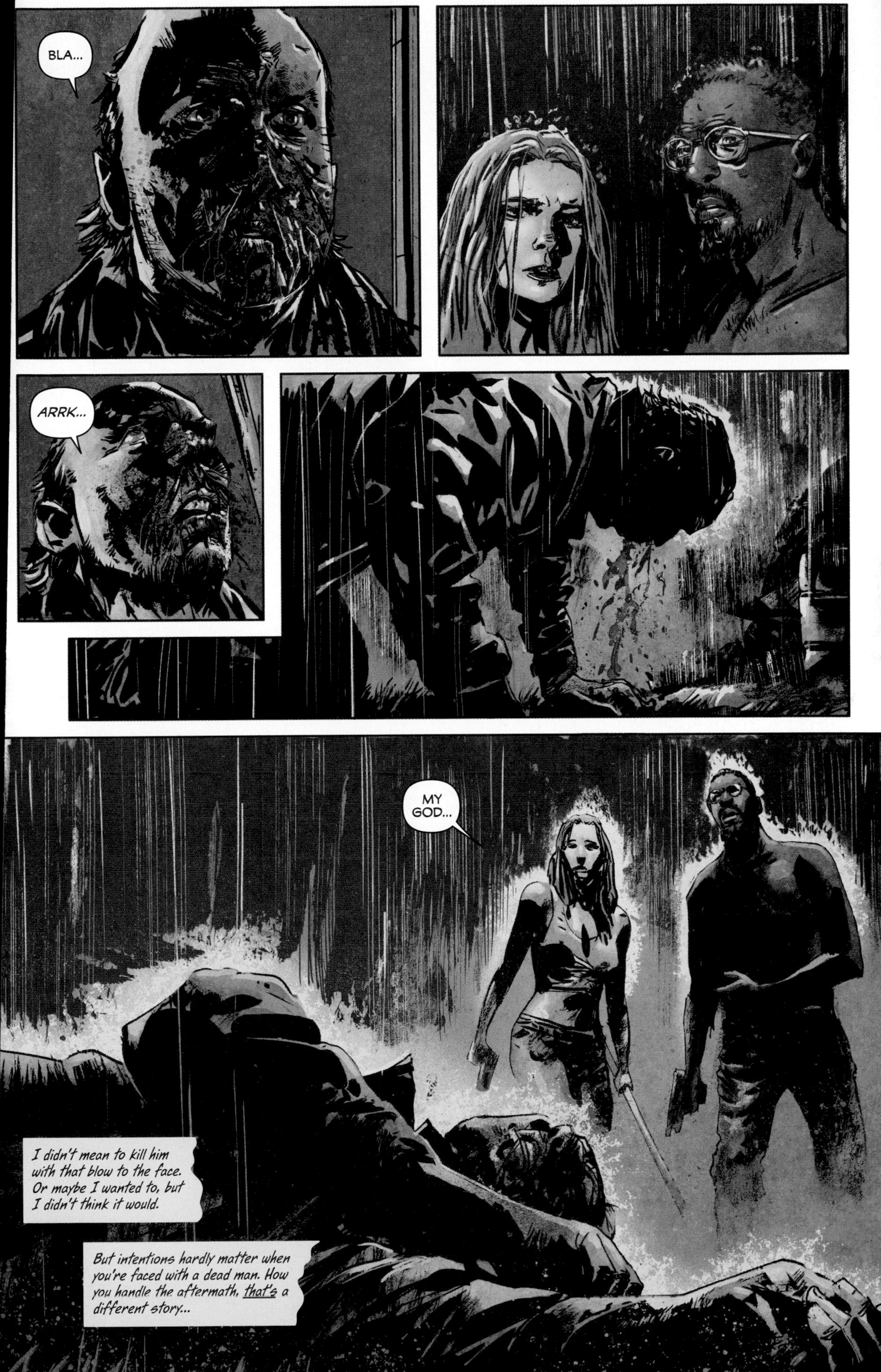
BLA...
ARRK...
MY GOD...
I didn't mean to kill him with that blow to the face. Or maybe I wanted to, but I didn't think it would.
But intentions hardly matter when you're faced with a dead man. How you handle the aftermath, that's a different story...

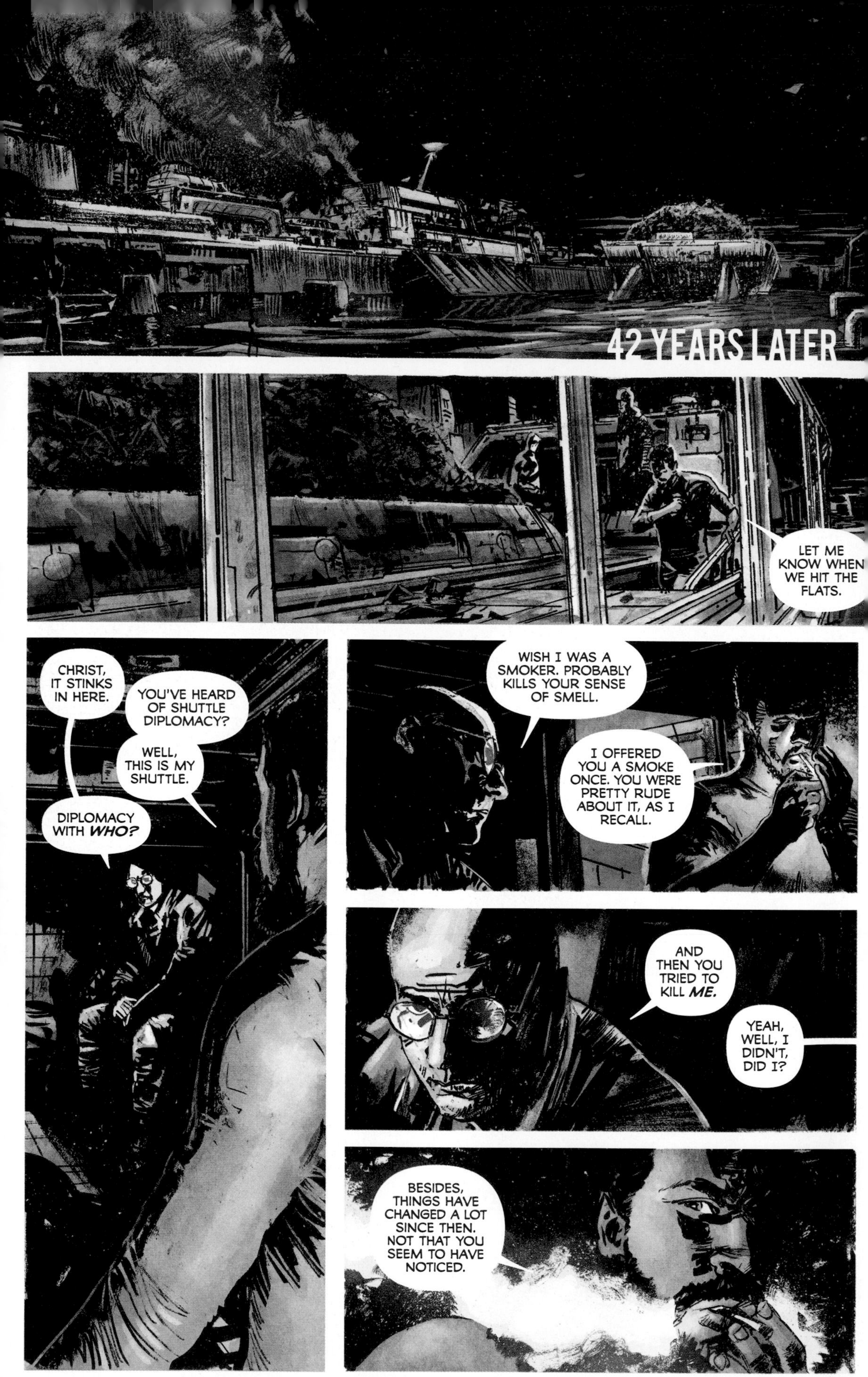
42 YEARS LATER
LET ME KNOW WHEN WE HIT THE FLATS.
CHRIST, IT STINKS IN HERE.
YOU'VE HEARD OF SHUTTLE DIPLOMACY?
WELL, THIS IS MY SHUTTLE.
DIPLOMACY WITH *WHO?*
WISH I WAS A SMOKER. PROBABLY KILLS YOUR SENSE OF SMELL.
I OFFERED YOU A SMOKE ONCE. YOU WERE PRETTY RUDE ABOUT IT, AS I RECALL.
AND THEN YOU TRIED TO KILL *ME.*
YEAH, WELL, I DIDN'T, DID I?
BESIDES, THINGS HAVE CHANGED A LOT SINCE THEN. NOT THAT YOU SEEM TO HAVE NOTICED.

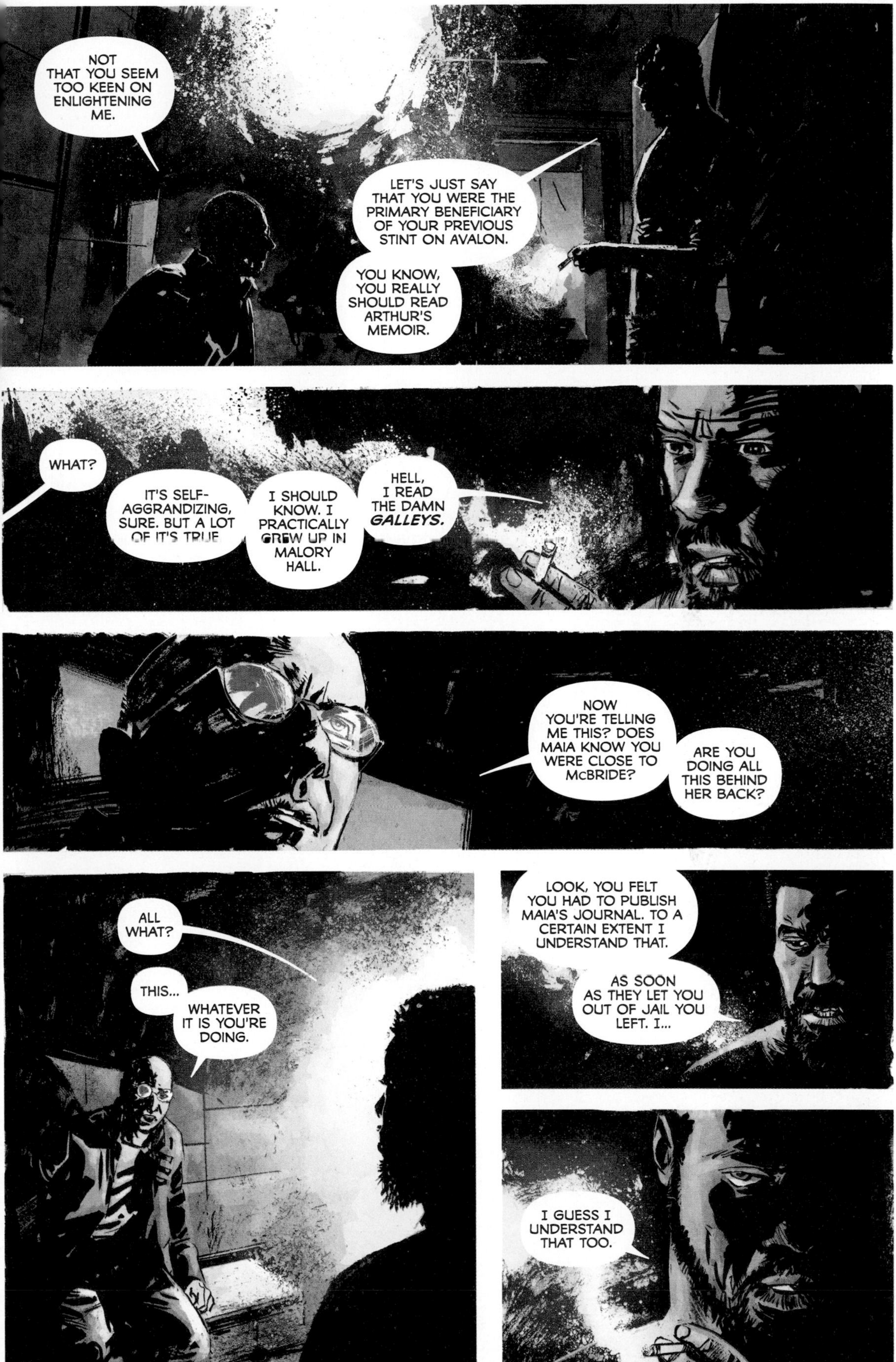
NOT THAT YOU SEEM TOO KEEN ON ENLIGHTENING ME.
LET'S JUST SAY THAT YOU WERE THE PRIMARY BENEFICIARY OF YOUR PREVIOUS STINT ON AVALON.
YOU KNOW, YOU REALLY SHOULD READ ARTHUR'S MEMOIR.
WHAT?
IT'S SELF-AGGRANDIZING, SURE. BUT A LOT OF IT'S TRUE.
I SHOULD KNOW. I PRACTICALLY GREW UP IN MALORY HALL.
HELL, I READ THE DAMN *GALLEYS.*
NOW YOU'RE TELLING ME THIS? DOES MAIA KNOW YOU WERE CLOSE TO McBRIDE?
ARE YOU DOING ALL THIS BEHIND HER BACK?
ALL WHAT?
THIS...
WHATEVER IT IS YOU'RE DOING.
LOOK, YOU FELT YOU HAD TO PUBLISH MAIA'S JOURNAL. TO A CERTAIN EXTENT I UNDERSTAND THAT.
AS SOON AS THEY LET YOU OUT OF JAIL YOU LEFT. I...
I GUESS I UNDERSTAND THAT TOO.

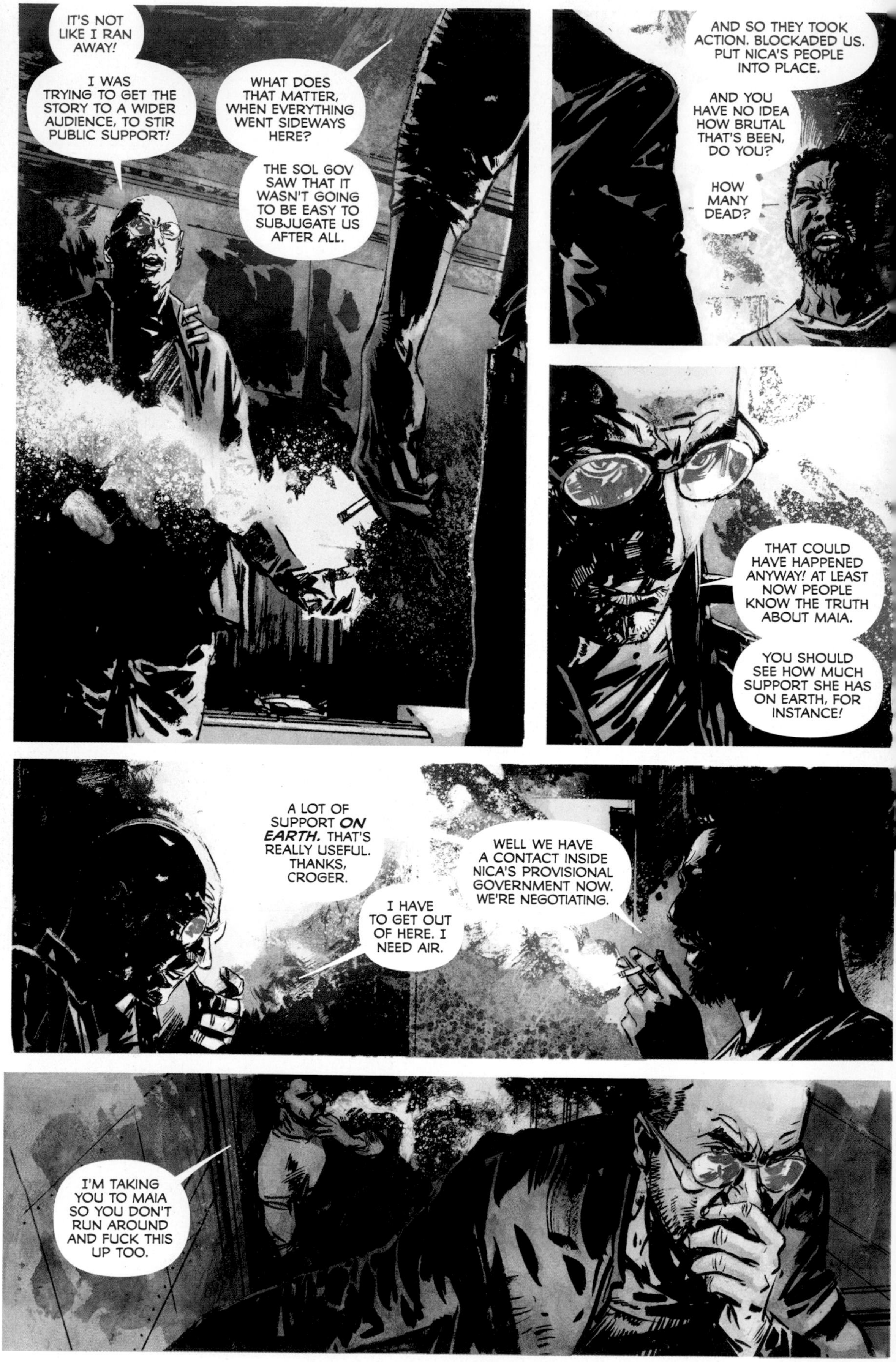
IT'S NOT LIKE I RAN AWAY!
I WAS TRYING TO GET THE STORY TO A WIDER AUDIENCE, TO STIR PUBLIC SUPPORT!
WHAT DOES THAT MATTER, WHEN EVERYTHING WENT SIDEWAYS HERE?
THE SOL GOV SAW THAT IT WASN'T GOING TO BE EASY TO SUBJUGATE US AFTER ALL.
AND SO THEY TOOK ACTION. BLOCKADED US. PUT NICA'S PEOPLE INTO PLACE.
AND YOU HAVE NO IDEA HOW BRUTAL THAT'S BEEN, DO YOU?
HOW MANY DEAD?
THAT COULD HAVE HAPPENED ANYWAY! AT LEAST NOW PEOPLE KNOW THE TRUTH ABOUT MAIA.
YOU SHOULD SEE HOW MUCH SUPPORT SHE HAS ON EARTH, FOR INSTANCE!
A LOT OF SUPPORT *ON EARTH.* THAT'S REALLY USEFUL. THANKS, CROGER.
I HAVE TO GET OUT OF HERE. I NEED AIR.
WELL WE HAVE A CONTACT INSIDE NICA'S PROVISIONAL GOVERNMENT NOW. WE'RE NEGOTIATING.
I'M TAKING YOU TO MAIA SO YOU DON'T RUN AROUND AND FUCK THIS UP TOO.

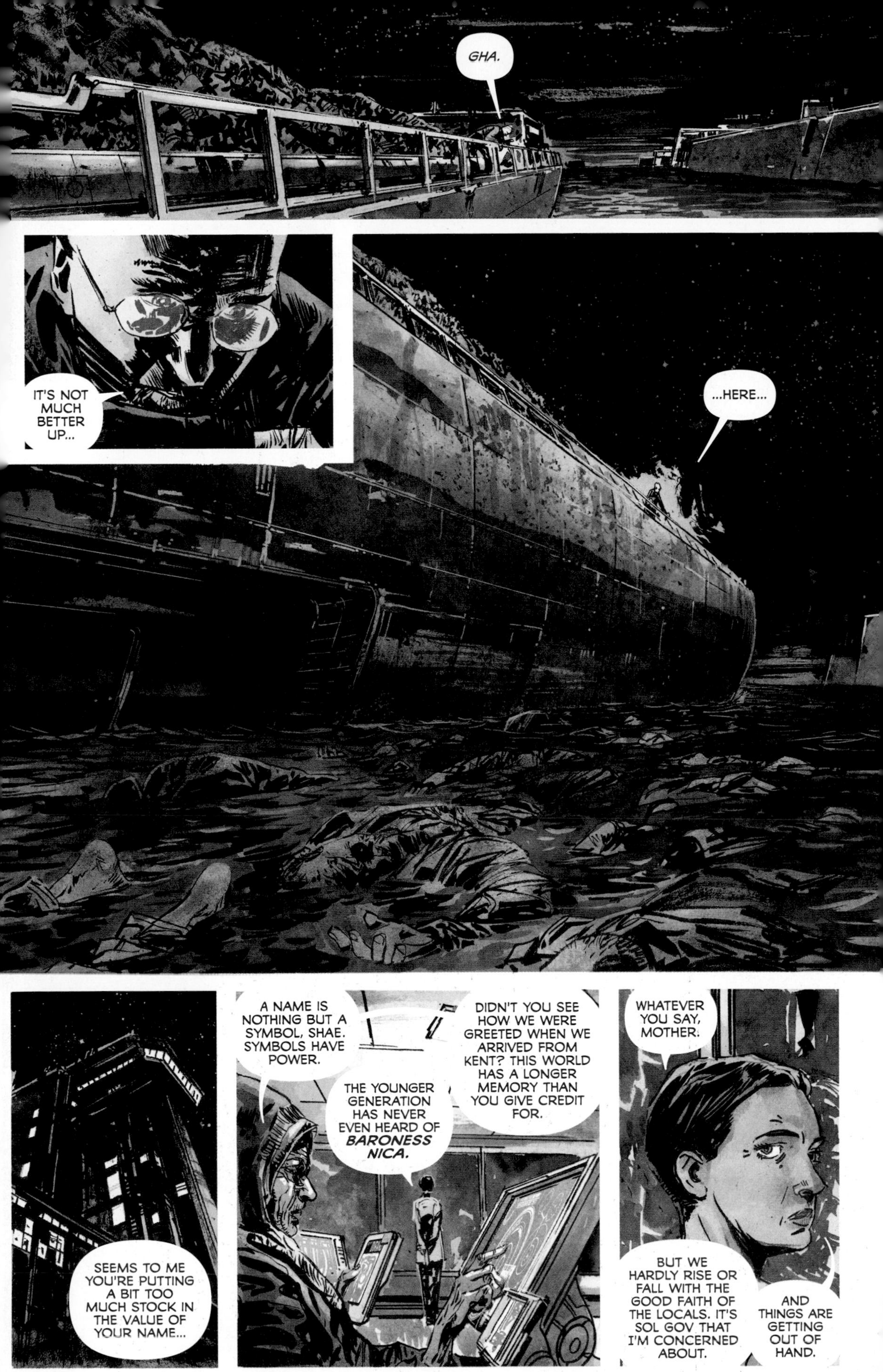
GHA.
IT'S NOT MUCH BETTER UP...
...HERE...
SEEMS TO ME YOU'RE PUTTING A BIT TOO MUCH STOCK IN THE VALUE OF YOUR NAME...
A NAME IS NOTHING BUT A SYMBOL, SHAE. SYMBOLS HAVE POWER.
THE YOUNGER GENERATION HAS NEVER EVEN HEARD OF *BARONESS NICA.*
DIDN'T YOU SEE HOW WE WERE GREETED WHEN WE ARRIVED FROM KENT? THIS WORLD HAS A LONGER MEMORY THAN YOU GIVE CREDIT FOR.
WHATEVER YOU SAY, MOTHER.
BUT WE HARDLY RISE OR FALL WITH THE GOOD FAITH OF THE LOCALS. IT'S SOL GOV THAT I'M CONCERNED ABOUT.
AND THINGS ARE GETTING OUT OF HAND.

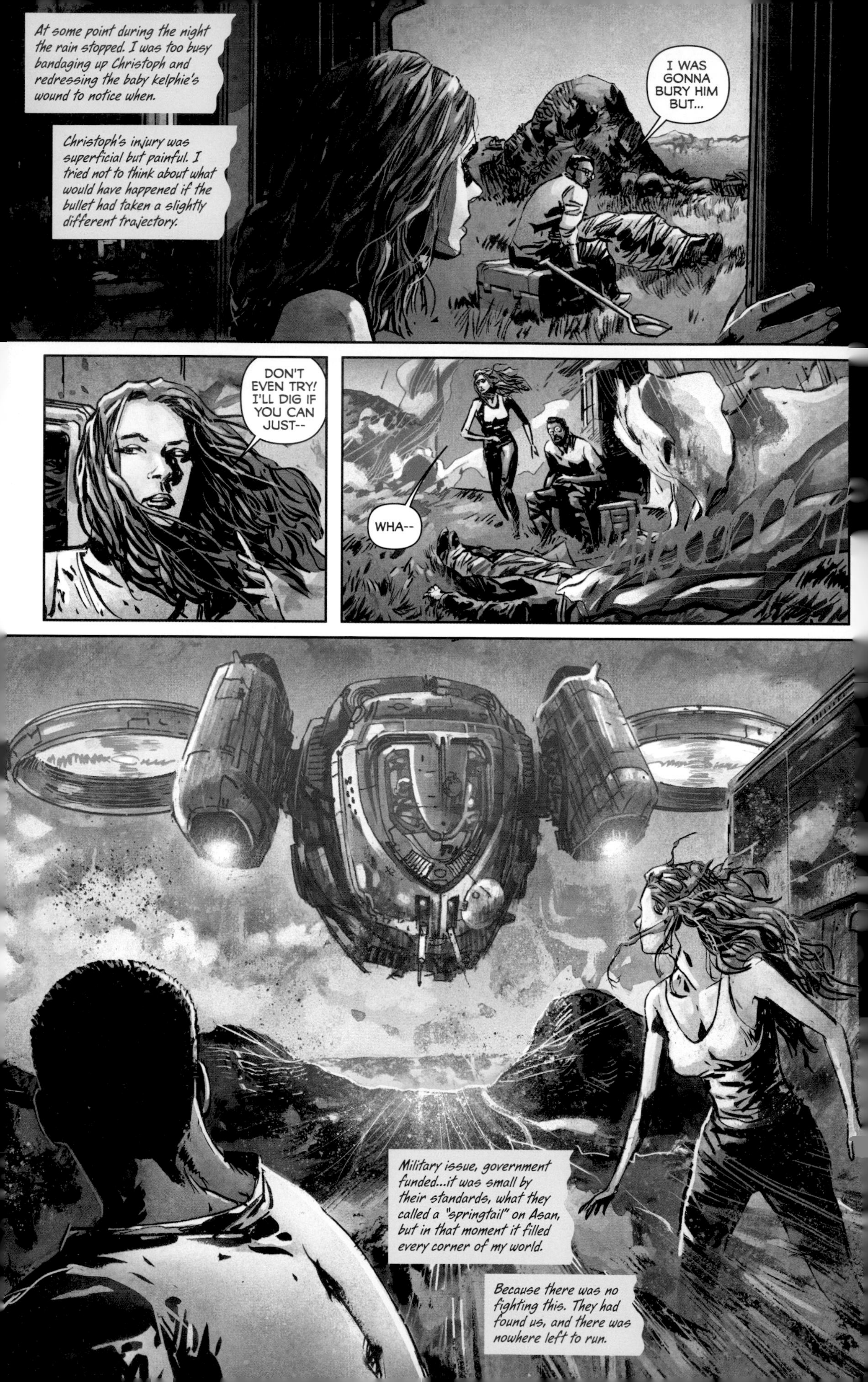
At some point during the night the rain stopped. I was too busy bandaging up Christoph and redressing the baby kelphie's wound to notice when.
Christoph's injury was superficial but painful. I tried not to think about what would have happened if the bullet had taken a slightly different trajectory.
I WAS GONNA BURY HIM BUT...
DON'T EVEN TRY! I'LL DIG IF YOU CAN JUST--
WHA--
Military issue, government funded...it was small by their standards, what they called a "springtail" on Asan, but in that moment it filled every corner of my world.
Because there was no fighting this. They had found us, and there was nowhere left to run.

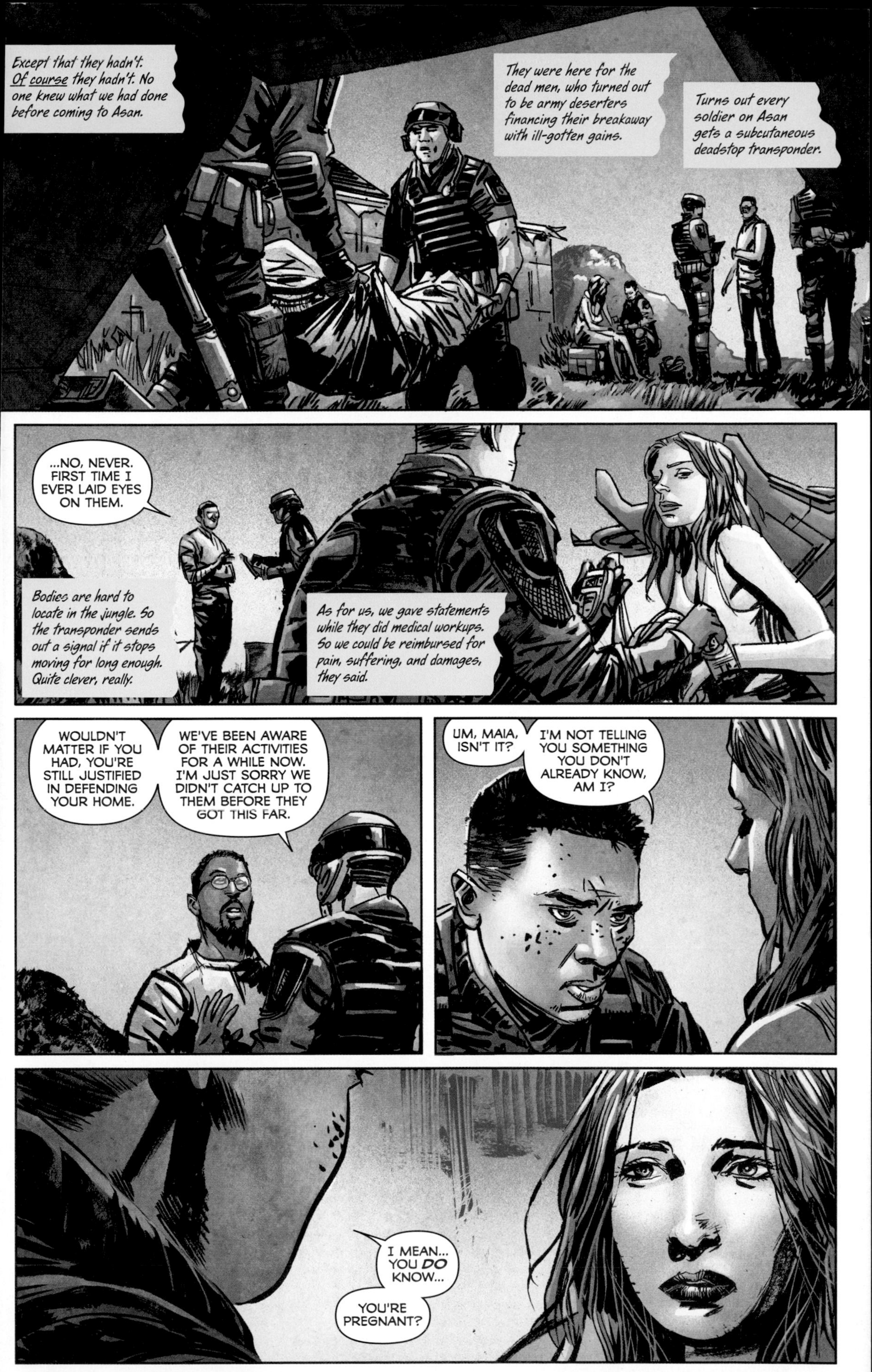
Except that they hadn't. Of course they hadn't. No one knew what we had done before coming to Asan.
They were here for the dead men, who turned out to be army deserters financing their breakaway with ill-gotten gains.
Turns out every soldier on Asan gets a subcutaneous deadstop transponder.
...NO, NEVER. FIRST TIME I EVER LAID EYES ON THEM.
Bodies are hard to locate in the jungle. So the transponder sends out a signal if it stops moving for long enough. Quite clever, really.
As for us, we gave statements while they did medical workups. So we could be reimbursed for pain, suffering, and damages, they said.
WOULDN'T MATTER IF YOU HAD, YOU'RE STILL JUSTIFIED IN DEFENDING YOUR HOME.
WE'VE BEEN AWARE OF THEIR ACTIVITIES FOR A WHILE NOW. I'M JUST SORRY WE DIDN'T CATCH UP TO THEM BEFORE THEY GOT THIS FAR.
UM, MAIA, ISN'T IT?
I'M NOT TELLING YOU SOMETHING YOU DON'T ALREADY KNOW, AM I?
I MEAN... YOU DO KNOW...
YOU'RE PREGNANT?

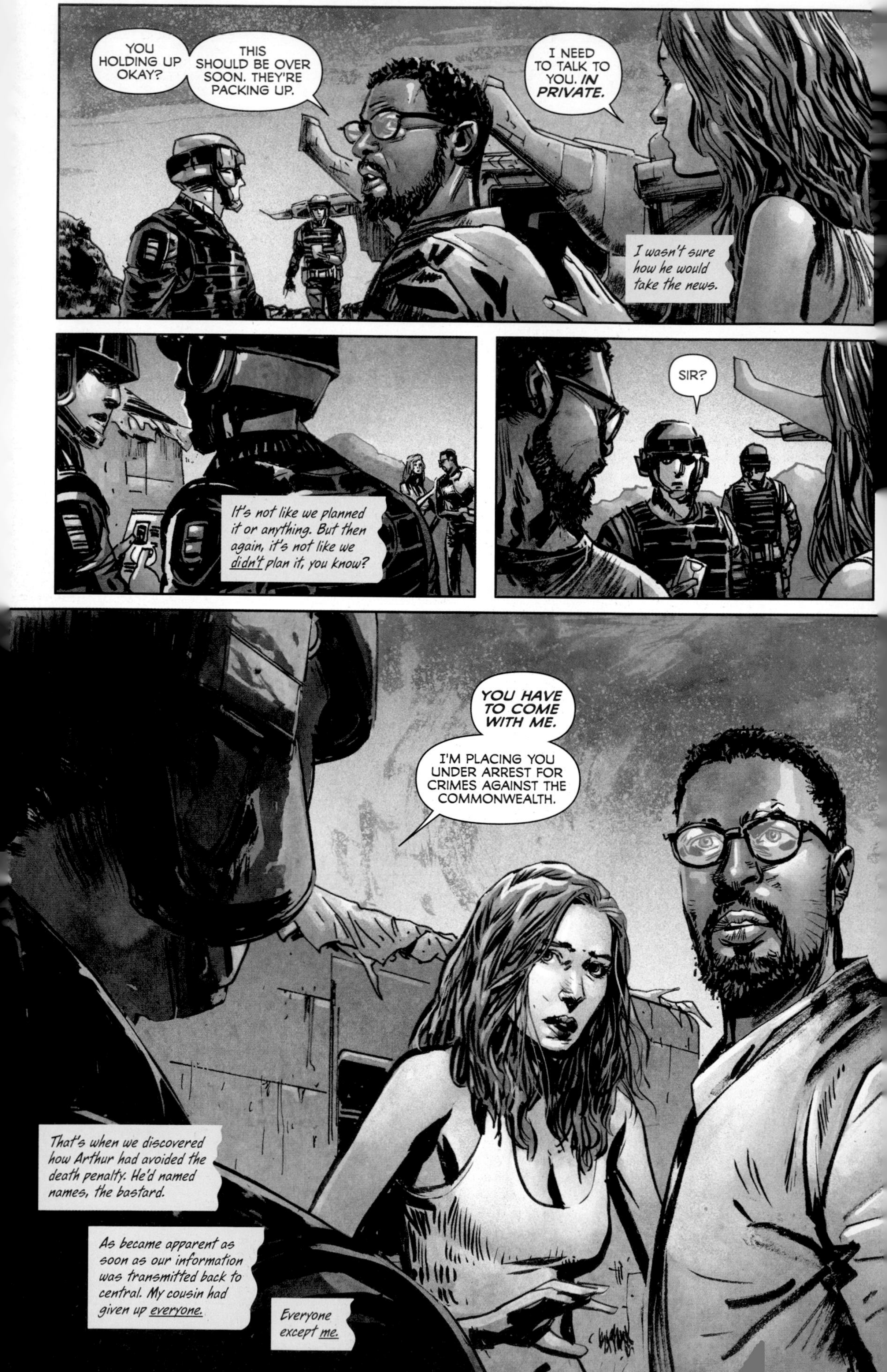
YOU HOLDING UP OKAY?
THIS SHOULD BE OVER SOON. THEY'RE PACKING UP.
I NEED TO TALK TO YOU. *IN PRIVATE.*
I wasn't sure how he would take the news.
It's not like we planned it or anything. But then again, it's not like we didn't plan it, you know?
SIR?
YOU HAVE TO COME WITH ME.
I'M PLACING YOU UNDER ARREST FOR CRIMES AGAINST THE COMMONWEALTH.
That's when we discovered how Arthur had avoided the death penalty. He'd named names, the bastard.
As became apparent as soon as our information was transmitted back to central. My cousin had given up everyone.
Everyone except me.

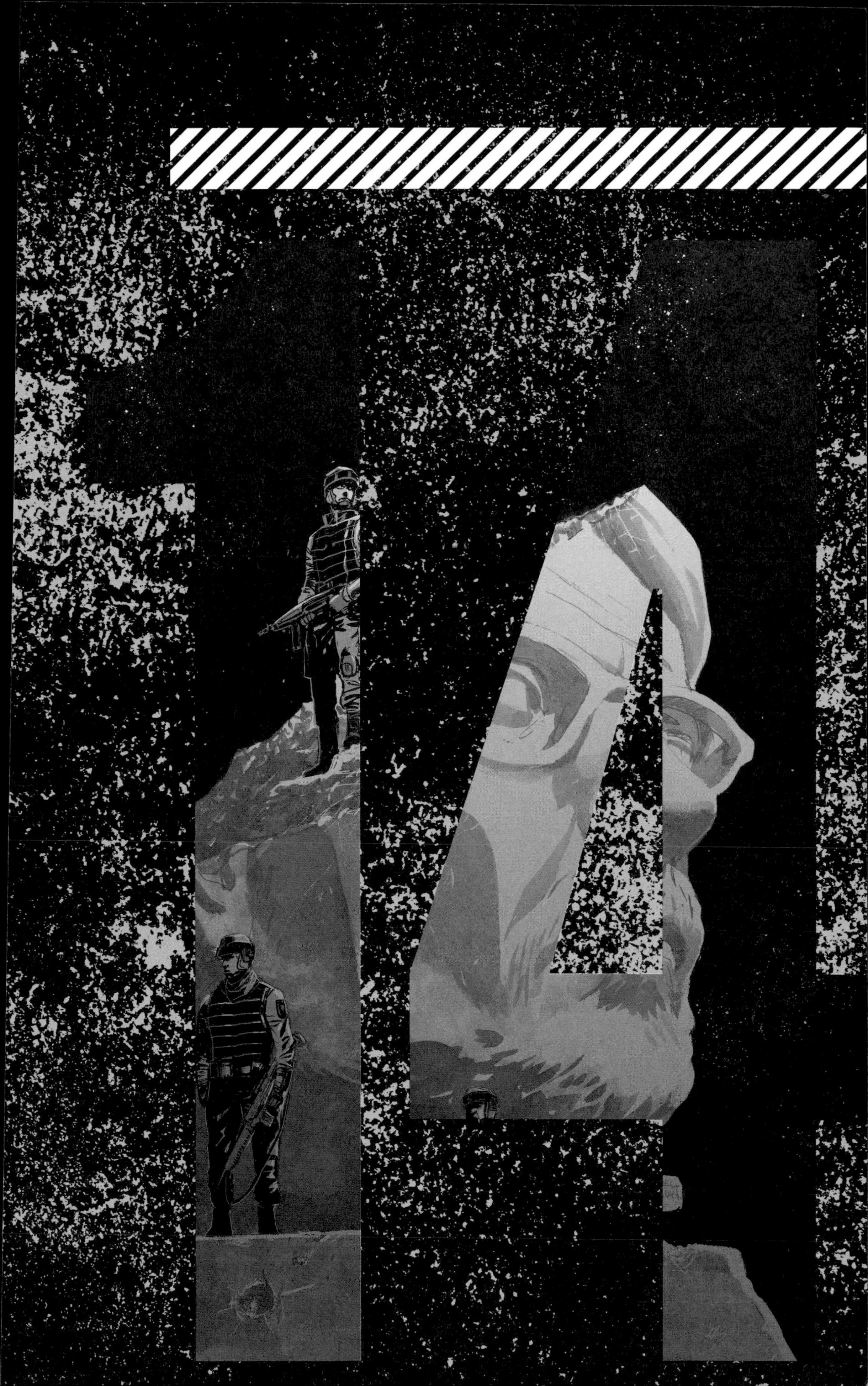

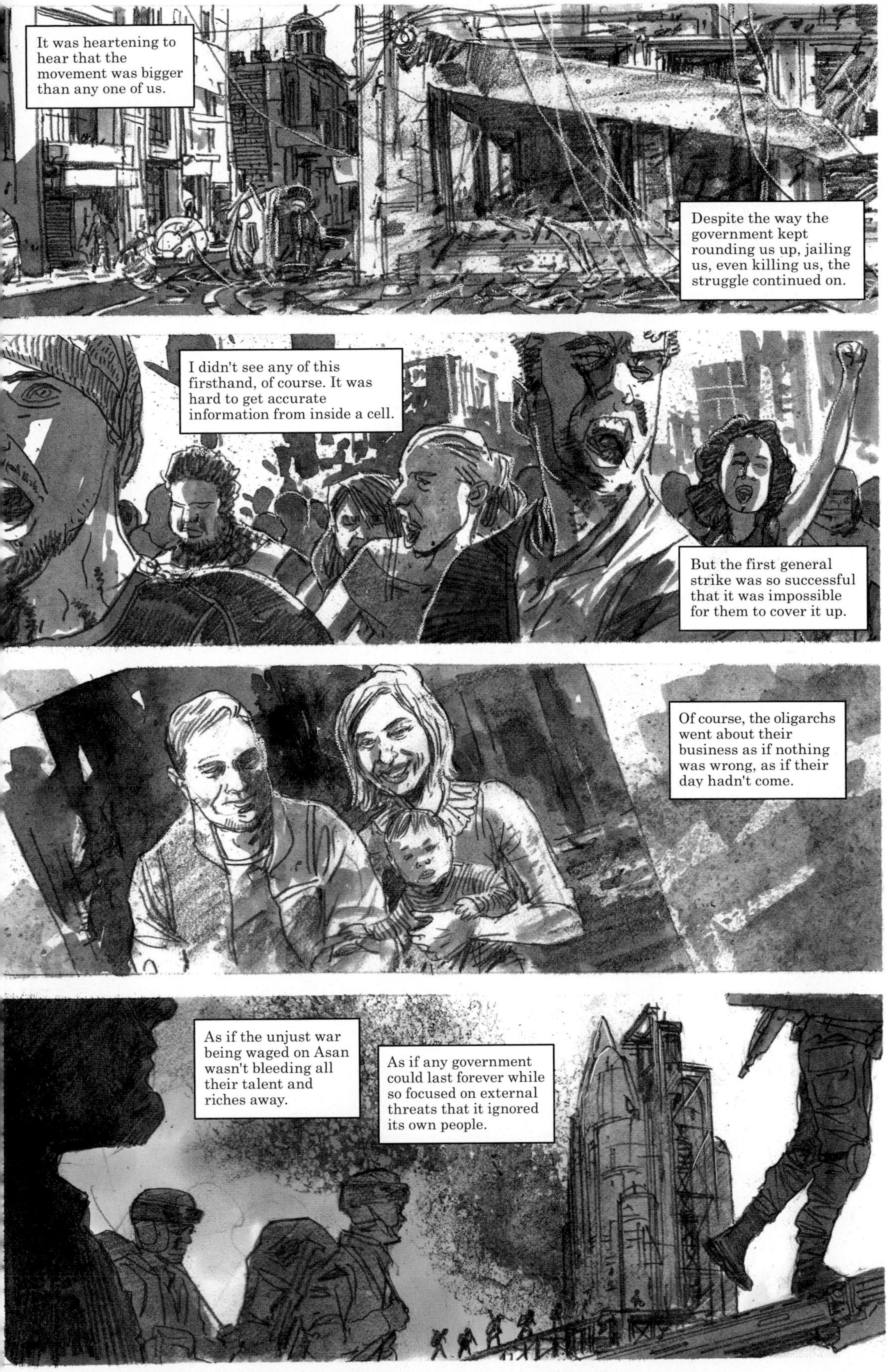
It was heartening to hear that the movement was bigger than any one of us.
Despite the way the government kept rounding us up, jailing us, even killing us, the struggle continued on.
I didn't see any of this firsthand, of course. It was hard to get accurate information from inside a cell.
But the first general strike was so successful that it was impossible for them to cover it up.
Of course, the oligarchs went about their business as if nothing was wrong, as if their day hadn't come.
As if the unjust war being waged on Asan wasn't bleeding all their talent and riches away.
As if any government could last forever while so focused on external threats that it ignored its own people.

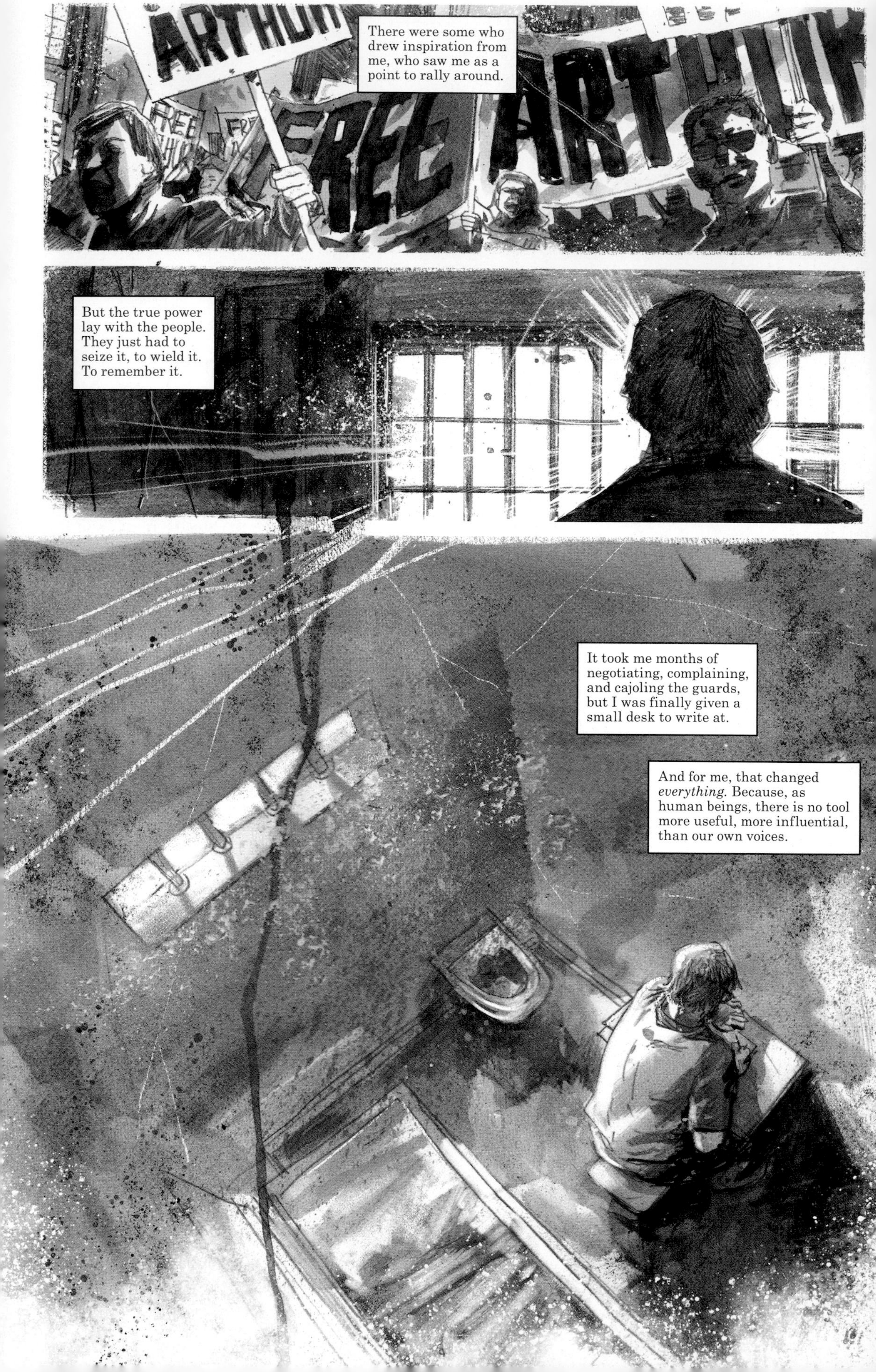
There were some who drew inspiration from me, who saw me as a point to rally around.
But the true power lay with the people. They just had to seize it, to wield it. To remember it.
It took me months of negotiating, complaining, and cajoling the guards, but I was finally given a small desk to write at.
And for me, that changed *everything.* Because, as human beings, there is no tool more useful, more influential, than our own voices.

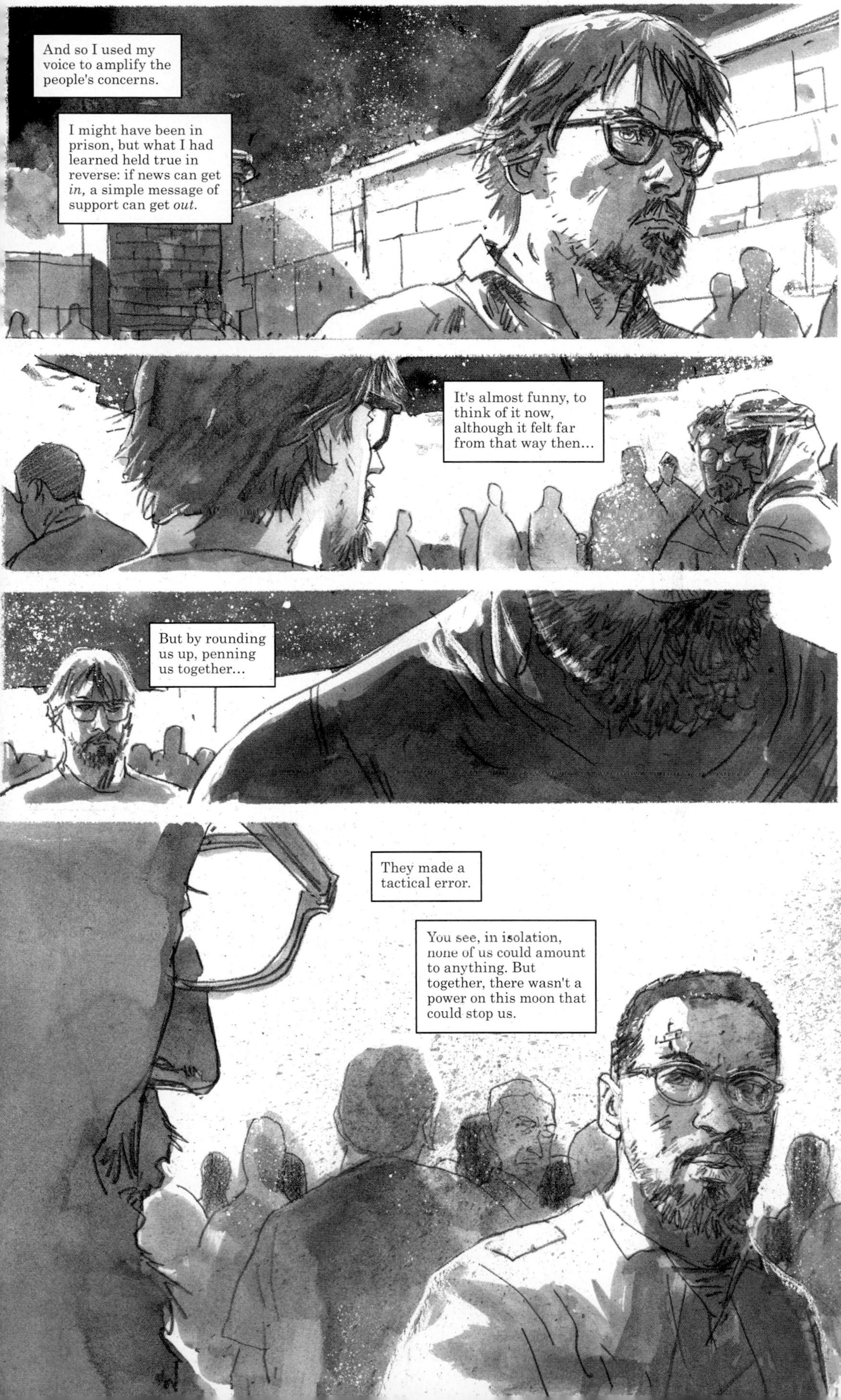
And so I used my voice to amplify the people's concerns.
I might have been in prison, but what I had learned held true in reverse: if news can get *in,* a simple message of support can get *out*.
It's almost funny, to think of it now, although it felt far from that way then...
But by rounding us up, penning us together...
They made a tactical error.
You see, in isolation, none of us could amount to anything. But together, there wasn't a power on this moon that could stop us.

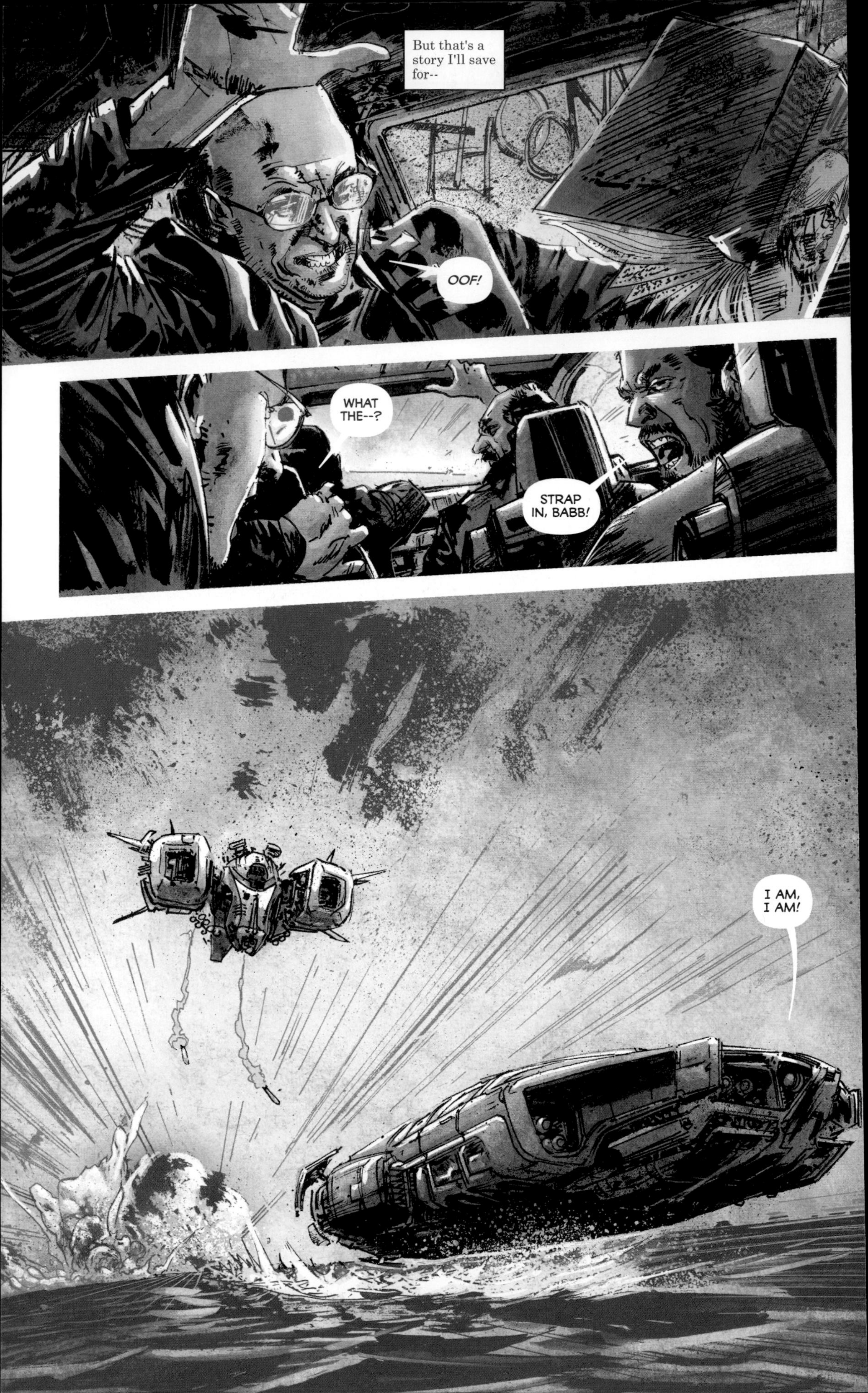
But that's a story I'll save for--
THOOM
OOF!
WHAT THE--?
STRAP IN, BABB!
I AM, I AM!

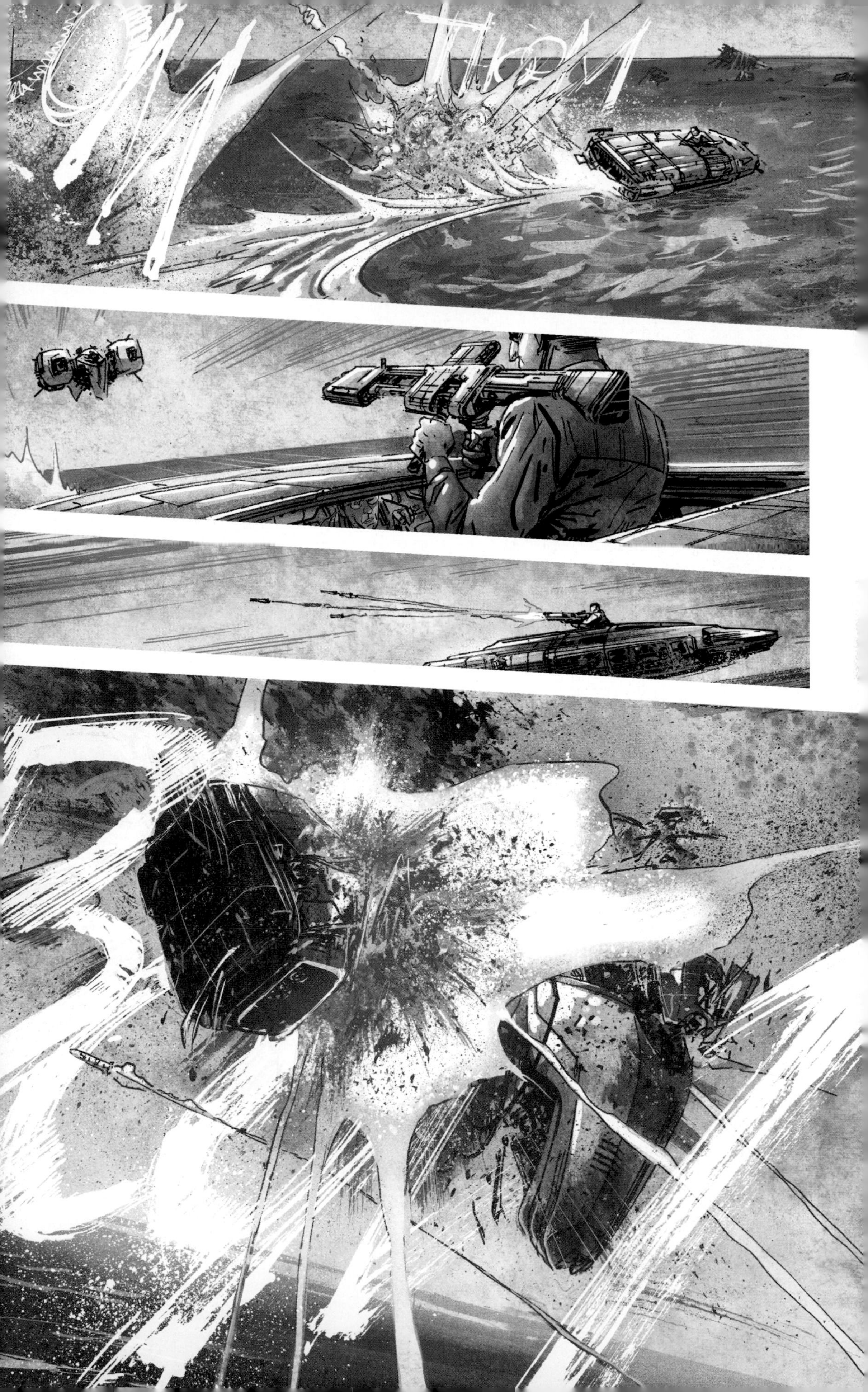
THOM

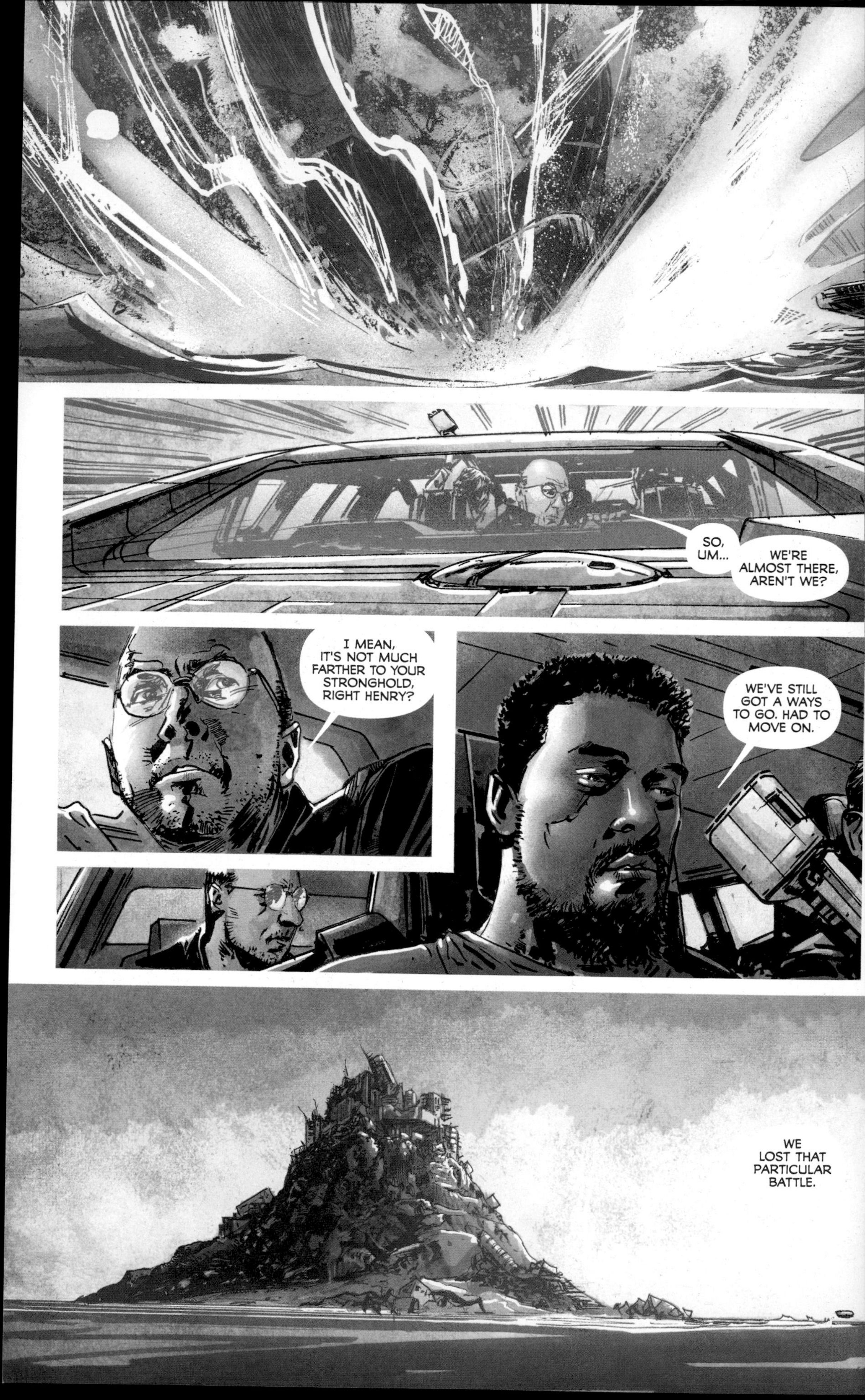
SO,
UM...
WE'RE ALMOST THERE, AREN'T WE?
I MEAN, IT'S NOT MUCH FARTHER TO YOUR STRONGHOLD, RIGHT HENRY?
WE'VE STILL GOT A WAYS TO GO. HAD TO MOVE ON.
WE LOST THAT PARTICULAR BATTLE.

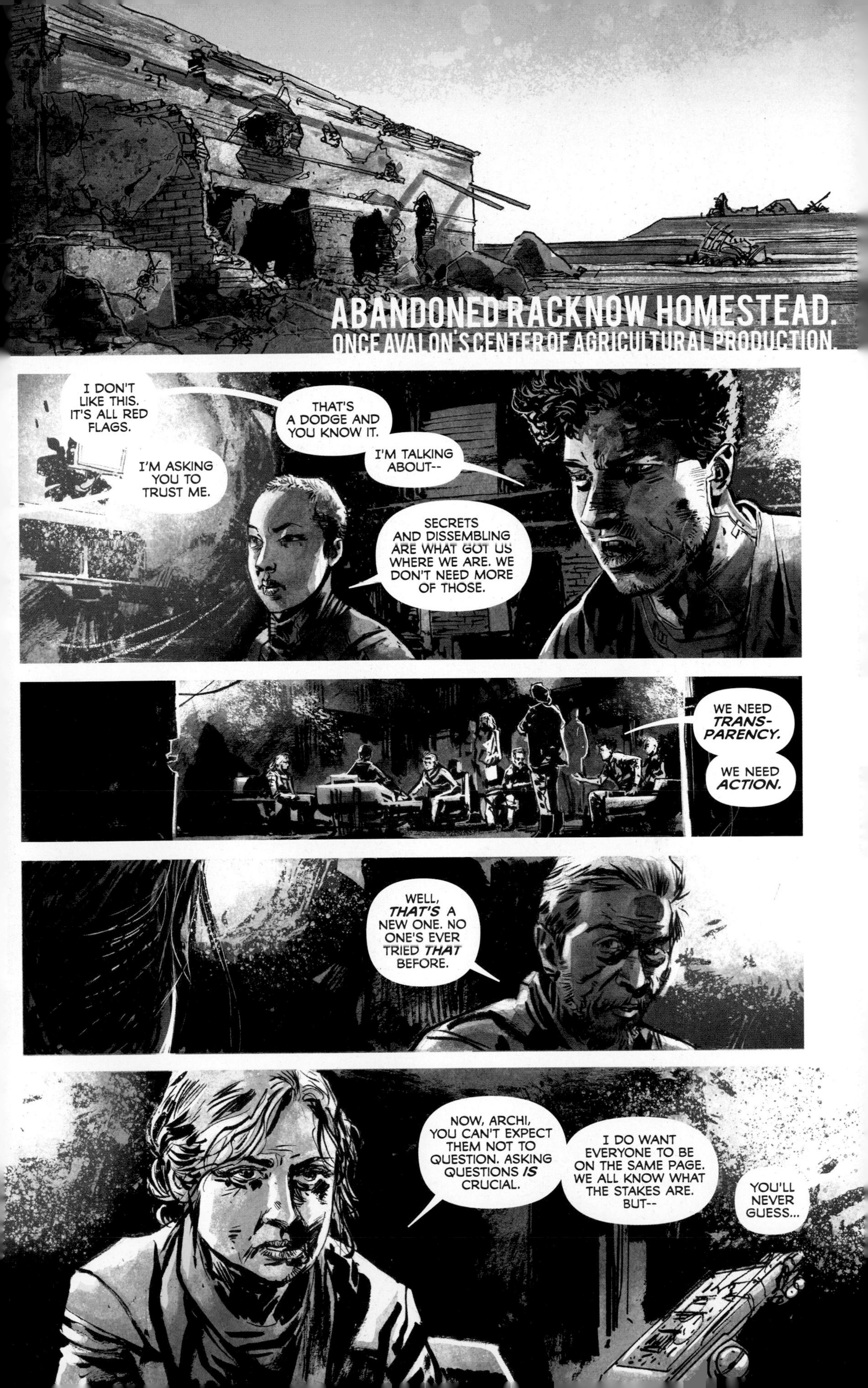
ABANDONED RACKNOW HOMESTEAD.
ONCE AVALON'S CENTER OF AGRICULTURAL PRODUCTION.
I DON'T LIKE THIS. IT'S ALL RED FLAGS.
THAT'S A DODGE AND YOU KNOW IT.
I'M ASKING YOU TO TRUST ME.
I'M TALKING ABOUT--
SECRETS AND DISSEMBLING ARE WHAT GOT US WHERE WE ARE. WE DON'T NEED MORE OF THOSE.
WE NEED TRANS-PARENCY.
WE NEED ACTION.
WELL, THAT'S A NEW ONE. NO ONE'S EVER TRIED THAT BEFORE.
NOW, ARCHI, YOU CAN'T EXPECT THEM NOT TO QUESTION. ASKING QUESTIONS IS CRUCIAL.
I DO WANT EVERYONE TO BE ON THE SAME PAGE. WE ALL KNOW WHAT THE STAKES ARE. BUT--
YOU'LL NEVER GUESS...

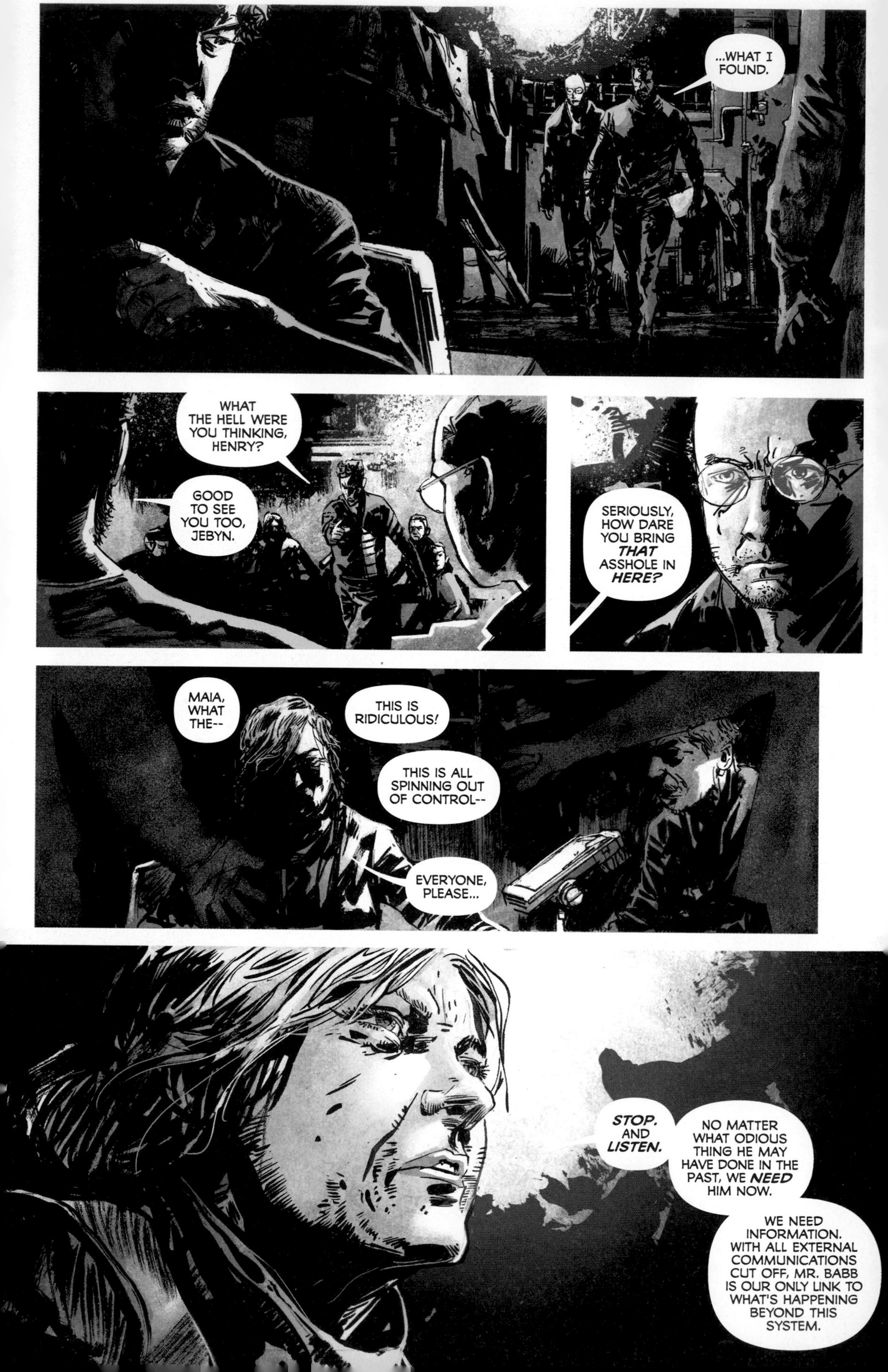
...WHAT I FOUND.
WHAT THE HELL WERE YOU THINKING, HENRY?
GOOD TO SEE YOU TOO, JEBYN.
SERIOUSLY, HOW DARE YOU BRING *THAT* ASSHOLE IN *HERE?*
MAIA, WHAT THE--
THIS IS RIDICULOUS!
THIS IS ALL SPINNING OUT OF CONTROL--
EVERYONE, PLEASE...
STOP. AND *LISTEN.*
NO MATTER WHAT ODIOUS THING HE MAY HAVE DONE IN THE PAST, WE *NEED* HIM NOW.
WE NEED INFORMATION. WITH ALL EXTERNAL COMMUNICATIONS CUT OFF, MR. BABB IS OUR ONLY LINK TO WHAT'S HAPPENING BEYOND THIS SYSTEM.

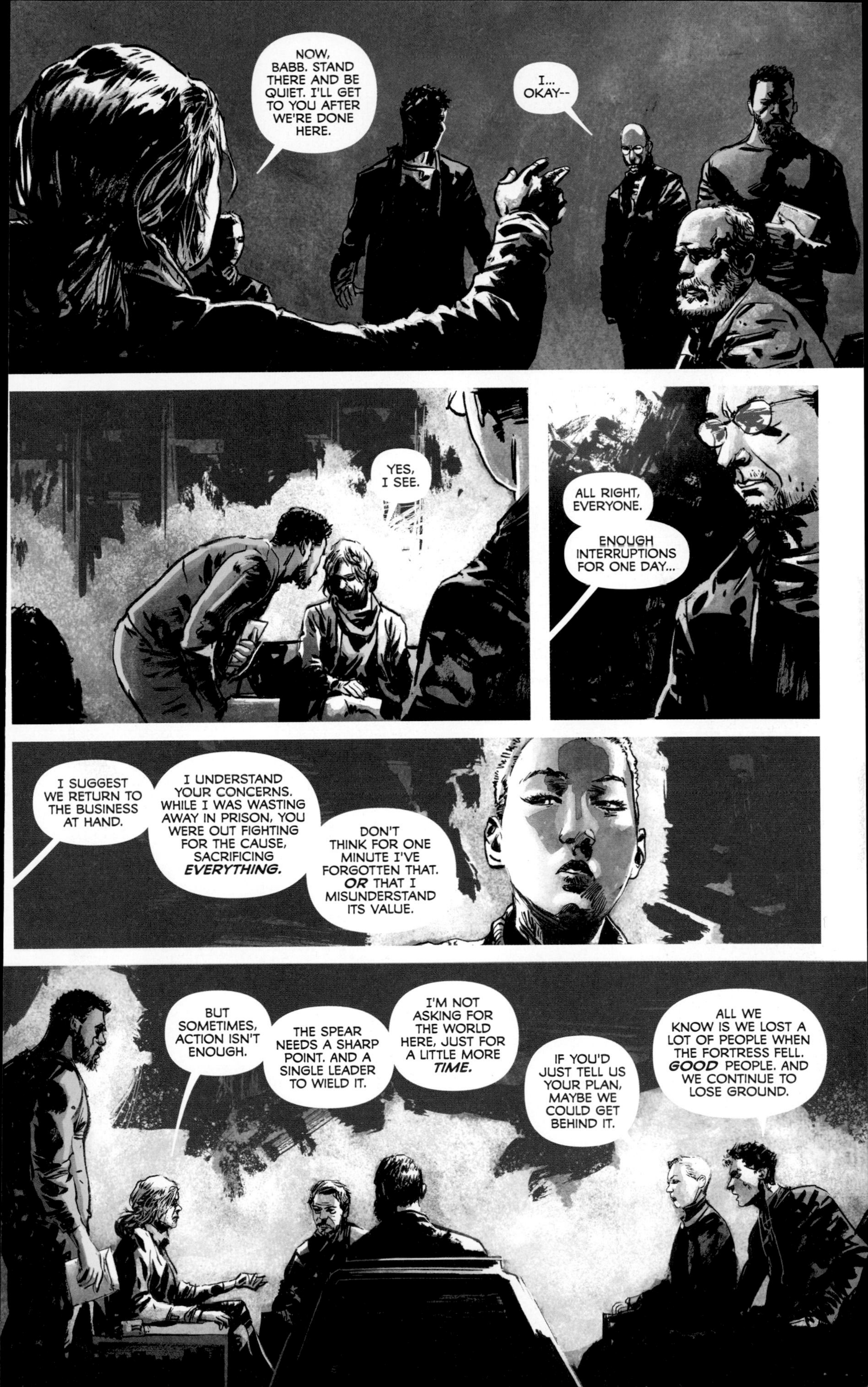
NOW, BABB. STAND THERE AND BE QUIET. I'LL GET TO YOU AFTER WE'RE DONE HERE.
I... OKAY--
YES, I SEE.
ALL RIGHT, EVERYONE.
ENOUGH INTERRUPTIONS FOR ONE DAY...
I SUGGEST WE RETURN TO THE BUSINESS AT HAND.
I UNDERSTAND YOUR CONCERNS. WHILE I WAS WASTING AWAY IN PRISON, YOU WERE OUT FIGHTING FOR THE CAUSE, SACRIFICING *EVERYTHING.*
DON'T THINK FOR ONE MINUTE I'VE FORGOTTEN THAT. *OR* THAT I MISUNDERSTAND ITS VALUE.
BUT SOMETIMES, ACTION ISN'T ENOUGH.
THE SPEAR NEEDS A SHARP POINT. AND A SINGLE LEADER TO WIELD IT.
I'M NOT ASKING FOR THE WORLD HERE, JUST FOR A LITTLE MORE *TIME.*
IF YOU'D JUST TELL US YOUR PLAN, MAYBE WE COULD GET BEHIND IT.
ALL WE KNOW IS WE LOST A LOT OF PEOPLE WHEN THE FORTRESS FELL. *GOOD* PEOPLE. AND WE CONTINUE TO LOSE GROUND.

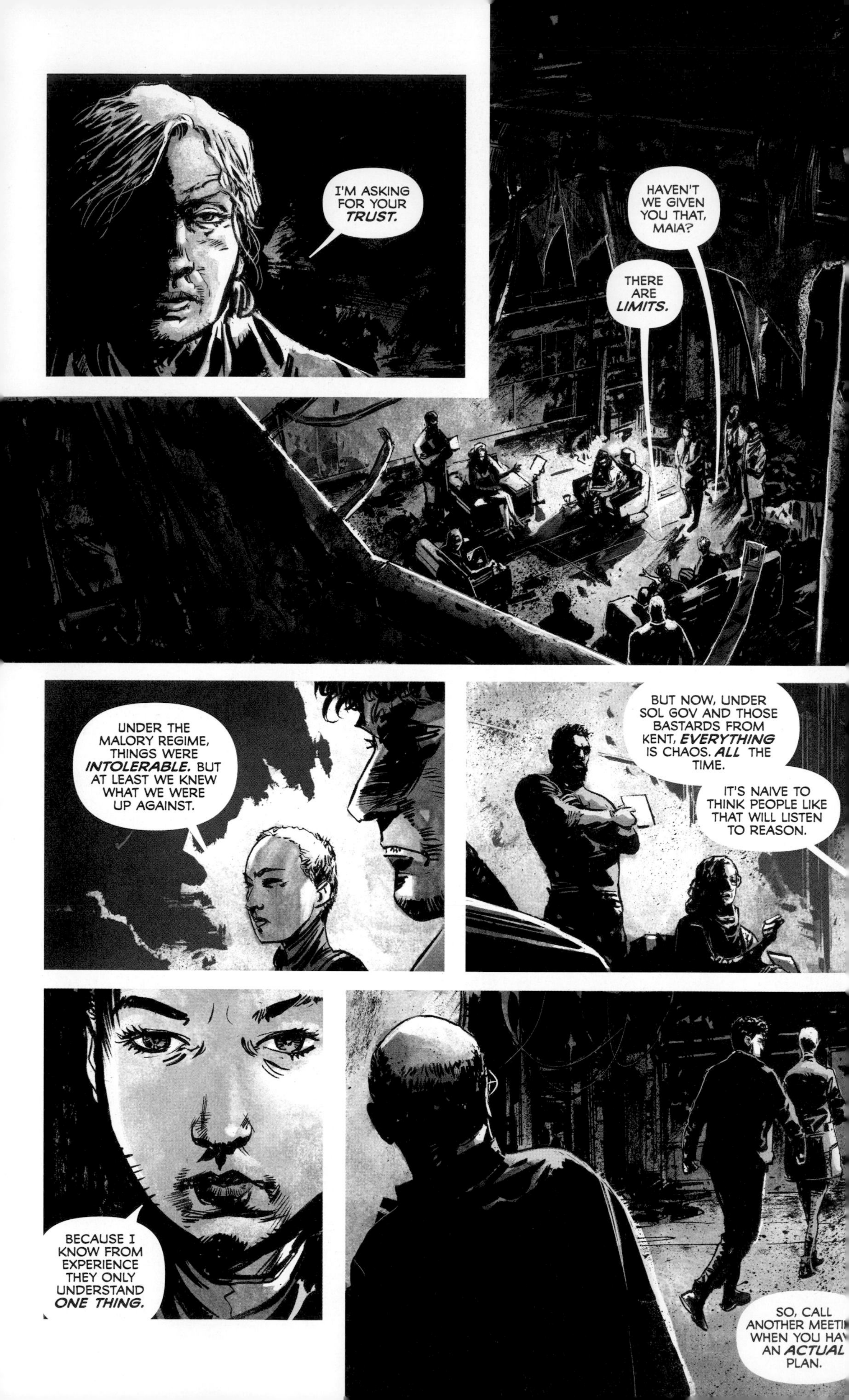
I'M ASKING FOR YOUR *TRUST.*
HAVEN'T WE GIVEN YOU THAT, MAIA?
THERE ARE *LIMITS.*
UNDER THE MALORY REGIME, THINGS WERE *INTOLERABLE.* BUT AT LEAST WE KNEW WHAT WE WERE UP AGAINST.
BUT NOW, UNDER SOL GOV AND THOSE BASTARDS FROM KENT, *EVERYTHING* IS CHAOS. *ALL* THE TIME.
IT'S NAIVE TO THINK PEOPLE LIKE THAT WILL LISTEN TO REASON.
BECAUSE I KNOW FROM EXPERIENCE THEY ONLY UNDERSTAND *ONE THING.*
SO, CALL ANOTHER MEETI WHEN YOU HAV AN *ACTUAL* PLAN.

WELL, THAT WAS ENTERTAINING.

BUT IF YOU'RE DONE BICKERING, I HAVE ACTUAL QUESTIONS THAT NEED ANSWERS.

WHERE'S WORONOV?

BABB, YOU'RE JUST GOING TO HAVE TO WAIT YOUR TURN.

NOW, ABOUT THE--

NO. *NOW*, MAIA.

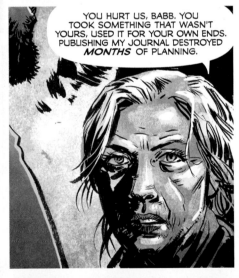

YOU HURT US, BABB. YOU TOOK SOMETHING THAT WASN'T YOURS, USED IT FOR YOUR OWN ENDS. PUBLISHING MY JOURNAL DESTROYED *MONTHS* OF PLANNING.

WE'RE STILL PICKING UP THE PIECES.

I WILL ADMIT, SOME GOOD CAME OUT OF IT TOO. BUT DON'T KID YOURSELF. YOU DIDN'T DO US ANY FAVORS.

I DON'T CARE. I JUST WANT TO KNOW WHAT HAPPENED TO MY COLLEAGUE.

WHAT DID YOU DO TO HER?

THE ANSWER TO THAT...

...IS IN *HERE*.

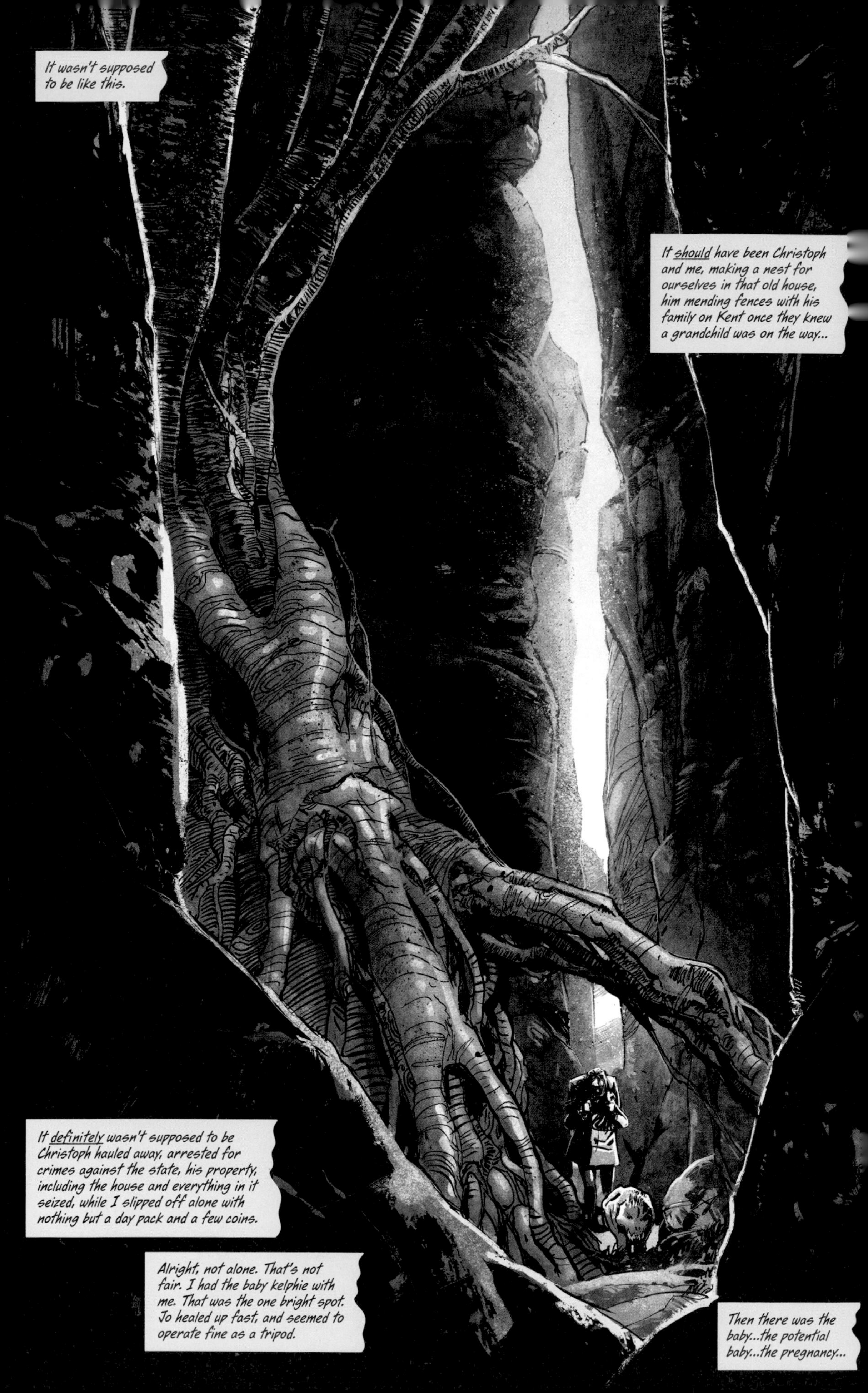
It wasn't supposed to be like this.
It should have been Christoph and me, making a nest for ourselves in that old house, him mending fences with his family on Kent once they knew a grandchild was on the way...
It definitely wasn't supposed to be Christoph hauled away, arrested for crimes against the state, his property, including the house and everything in it seized, while I slipped off alone with nothing but a day pack and a few coins.
Alright, not alone. That's not fair. I had the baby kelphie with me. That was the one bright spot. Jo healed up fast, and seemed to operate fine as a tripod.
Then there was the baby...the potential baby...the pregnancy...

If we hadn't been walking through a war zone, it might not have been so bad, at that. Fortunately, we saw very few people.

Jo was good company, seldom leaving my side.

If Christoph had been with me, it would have been an adventure. As it was, trying *not* to think about that took up most of my time.

Yet it was impossible to think of anything else.

Things that normally didn't hurt suddenly hurt. I wondered constantly, is this caused by the baby? Am I hurting it? Is it hurting me?

To escape, I turned to an ancient reader I had found in the house just before our world turned sideways.

There were a lot of corrupted files on it, and only one complete novel. So now you know why I can quote almost any passage from Allende's House of Spirits.

There were also some old political pamphlets, a book of household hints, and, happily, an Asanian field guide.

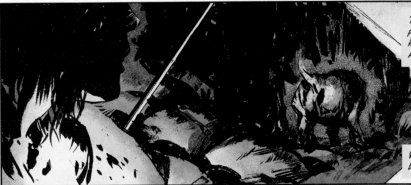

It didn't tell me much about Jo's species, but it did make me feel a lot more secure when Jo barked at unseen dangers.

Where kelphies are concerned, it's best to have them on your side...

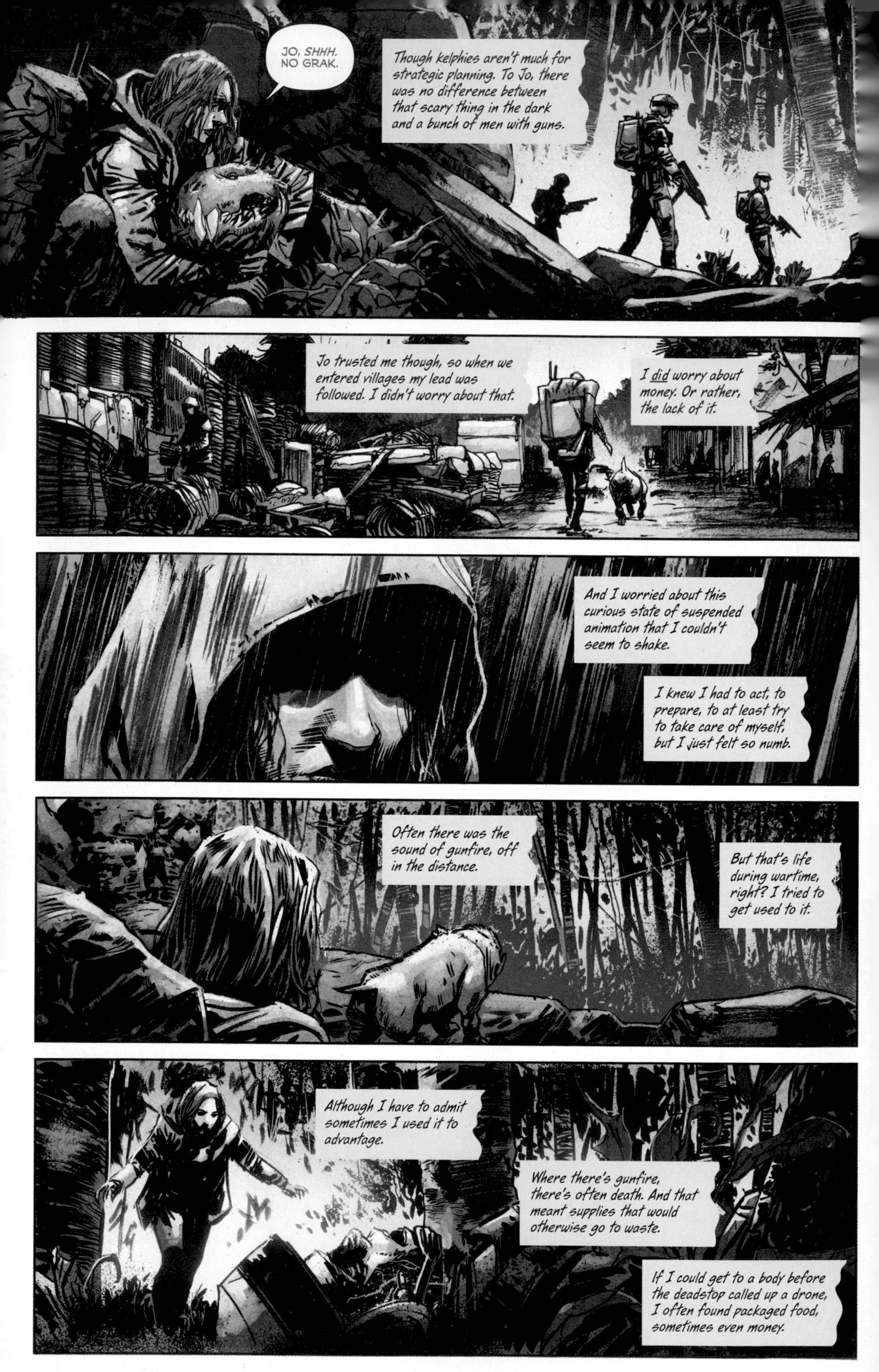

JO, *SHHH.* NO GRAK.
Though kelphies aren't much for strategic planning. To Jo, there was no difference between that scary thing in the dark and a bunch of men with guns.
Jo trusted me though, so when we entered villages my lead was followed. I didn't worry about that.
I did worry about money. Or rather, the lack of it.
And I worried about this curious state of suspended animation that I couldn't seem to shake.
I knew I had to act, to prepare, to at least try to take care of myself, but I just felt so numb.
Often there was the sound of gunfire, off in the distance.
But that's life during wartime, right? I tried to get used to it.
Although I have to admit sometimes I used it to advantage.
Where there's gunfire, there's often death. And that meant supplies that would otherwise go to waste.
If I could get to a body before the deadstop called up a drone, I often found packaged food, sometimes even money.

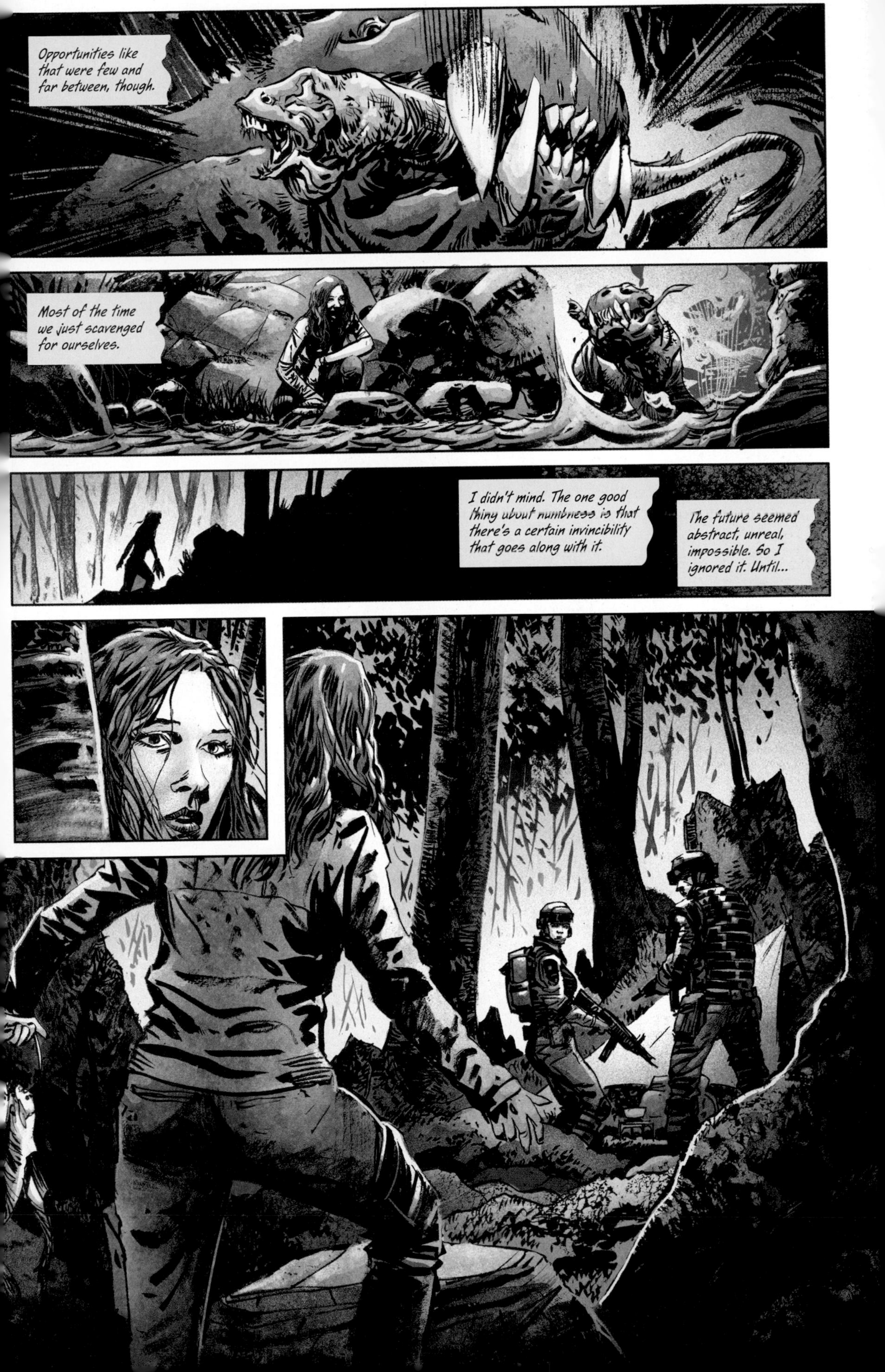
Opportunities like that were few and far between, though.
Most of the time we just scavenged for ourselves.
I didn't mind. The one good thing about numbness is that there's a certain invincibility that goes along with it.
The future seemed abstract, unreal, impossible. So I ignored it. Until...

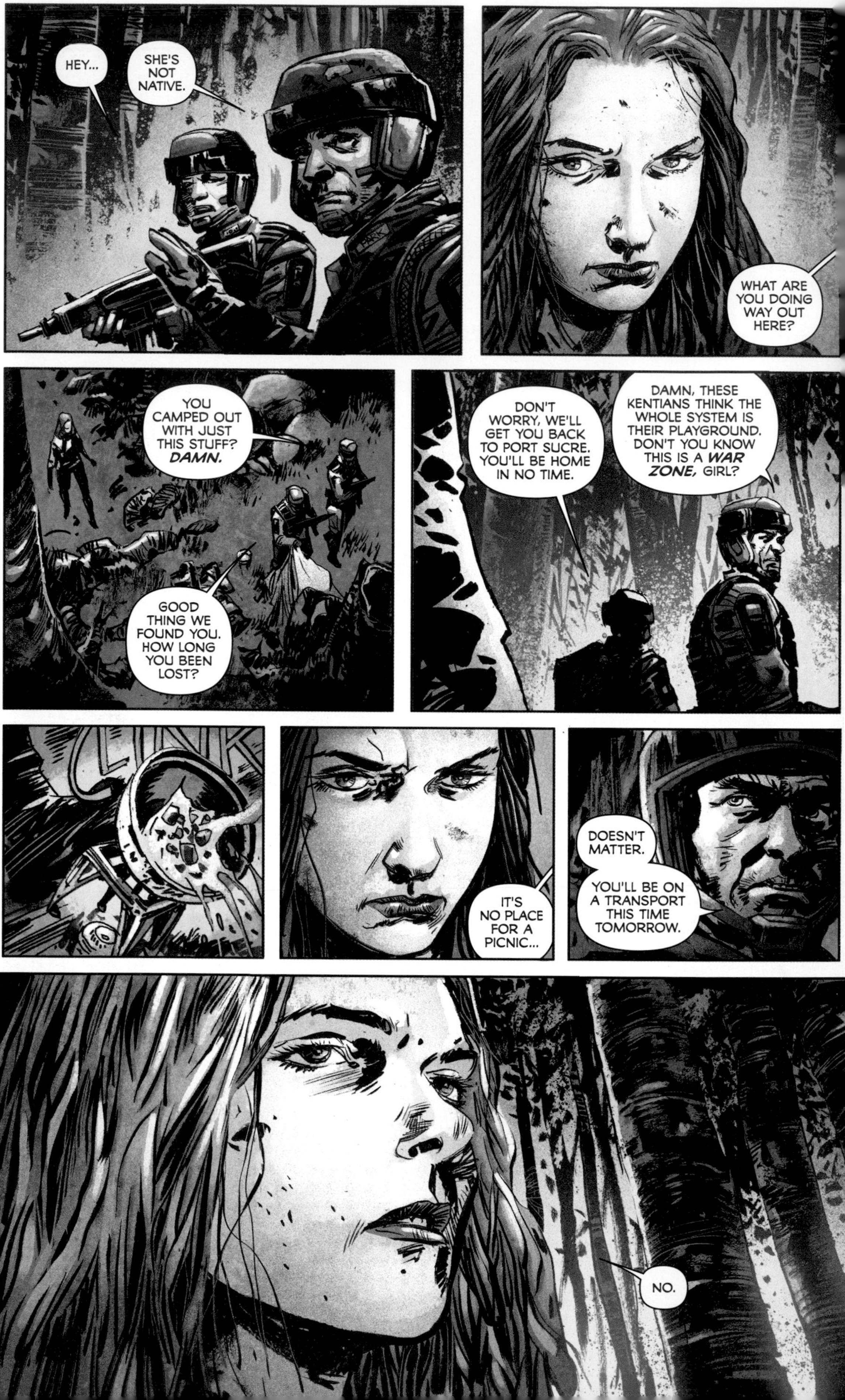
HEY...
SHE'S NOT NATIVE.
WHAT ARE YOU DOING WAY OUT HERE?
YOU CAMPED OUT WITH JUST THIS STUFF? *DAMN.*
GOOD THING WE FOUND YOU. HOW LONG YOU BEEN LOST?
DON'T WORRY, WE'LL GET YOU BACK TO PORT SUCRE. YOU'LL BE HOME IN NO TIME.
DAMN, THESE KENTIANS THINK THE WHOLE SYSTEM IS THEIR PLAYGROUND. DON'T YOU KNOW THIS IS A *WAR ZONE,* GIRL?
IT'S NO PLACE FOR A PICNIC...
DOESN'T MATTER.
YOU'LL BE ON A TRANSPORT THIS TIME TOMORROW.
NO.

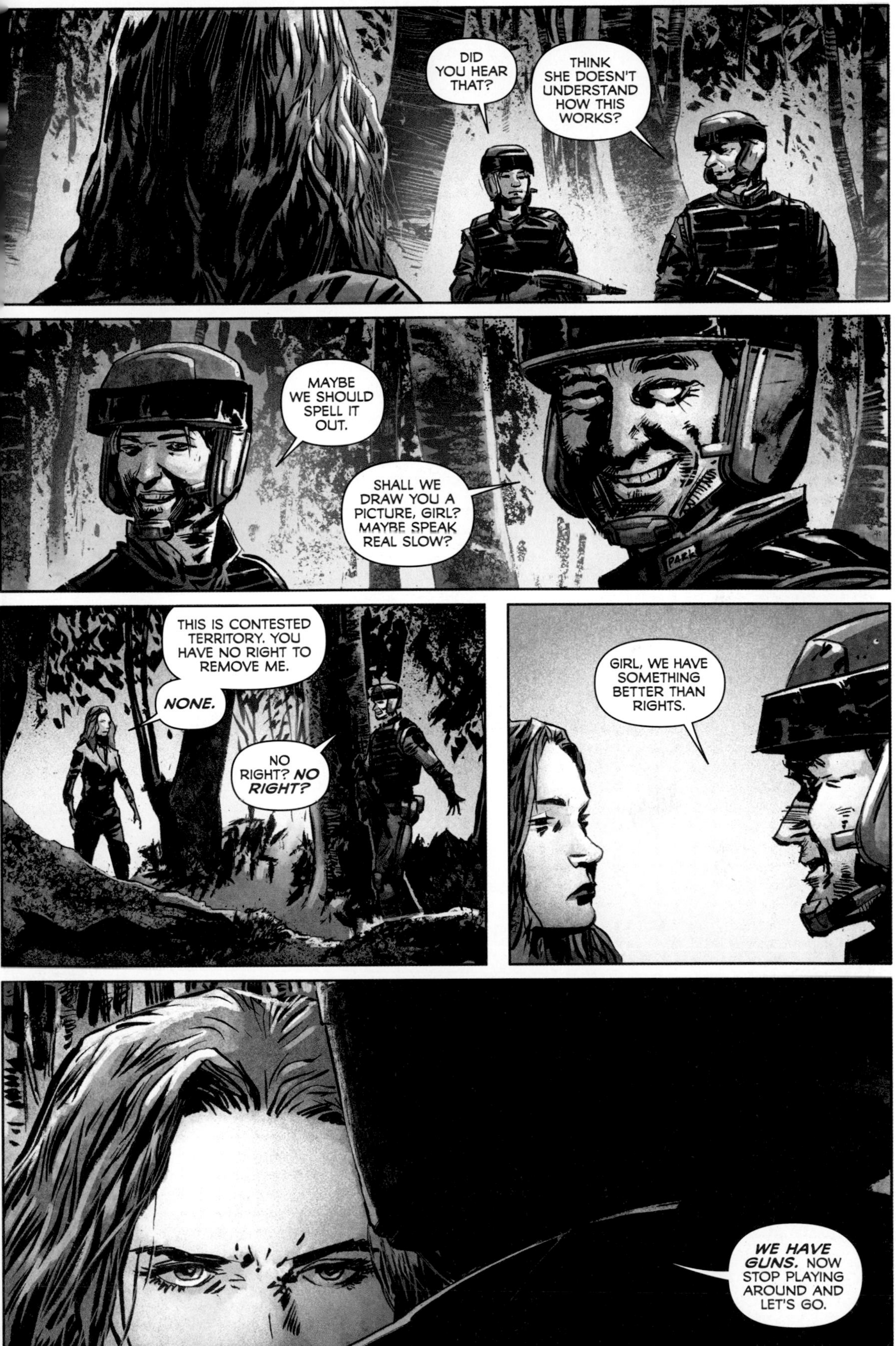

DID YOU HEAR THAT?
THINK SHE DOESN'T UNDERSTAND HOW THIS WORKS?
MAYBE WE SHOULD SPELL IT OUT.
SHALL WE DRAW YOU A PICTURE, GIRL? MAYBE SPEAK REAL SLOW?
PARK
THIS IS CONTESTED TERRITORY. YOU HAVE NO RIGHT TO REMOVE ME.
NONE.
NO RIGHT? NO RIGHT?
GIRL, WE HAVE SOMETHING BETTER THAN RIGHTS.
WE HAVE GUNS. NOW STOP PLAYING AROUND AND LET'S GO.

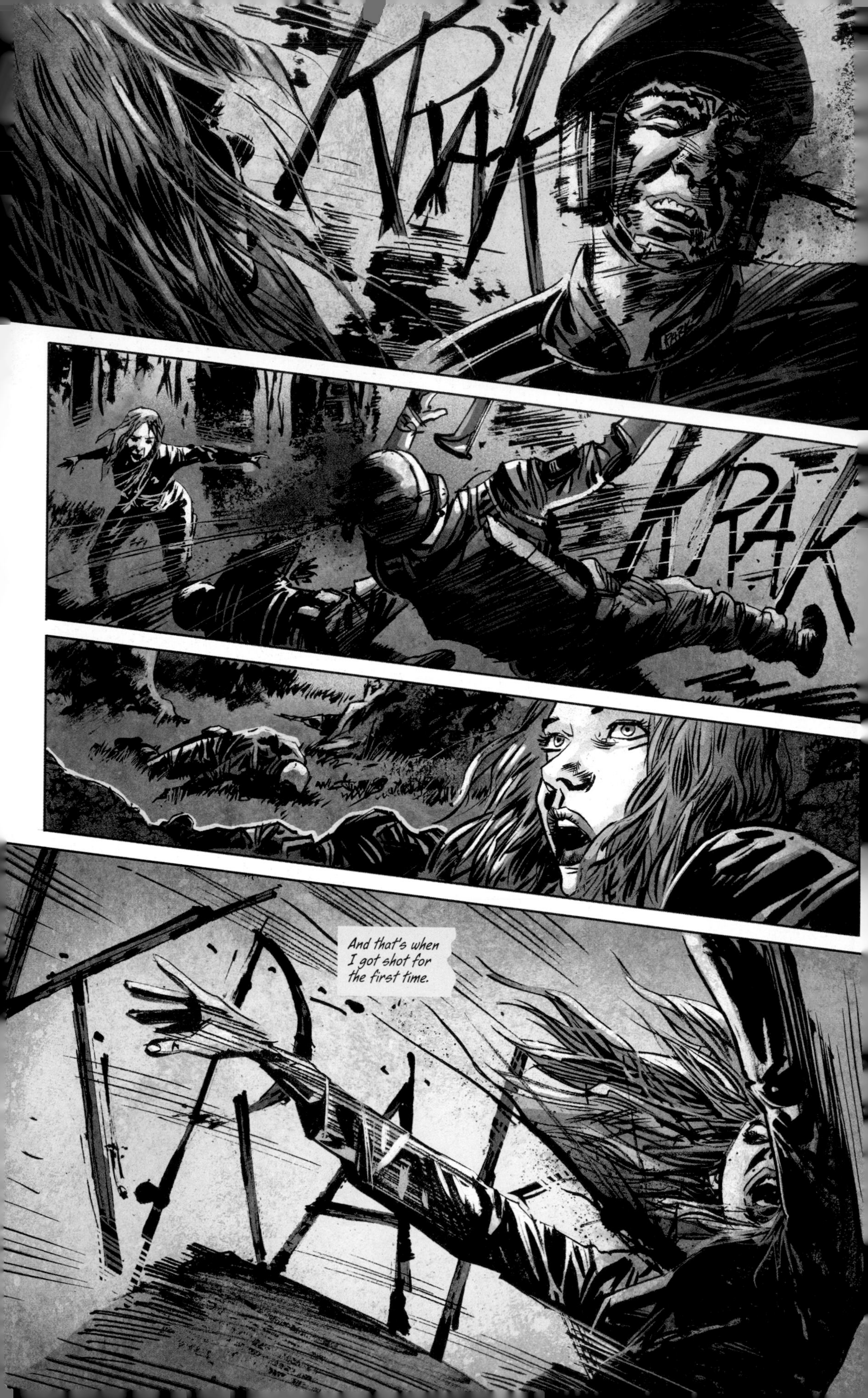
KRAK
KRAK
And that's when I got shot for the first time.

I WON'T LIE TO YOU, BABB.

WORONOV *IS* DEAD.

SHE WAS A GOOD WOMAN, A TRUSTED ADVISOR AFTER SHE VOLUNTEERED TO HELP US, AND TO MY SORROW, HER DEATH *WAS* MY FAULT.

12 YEARS LATER

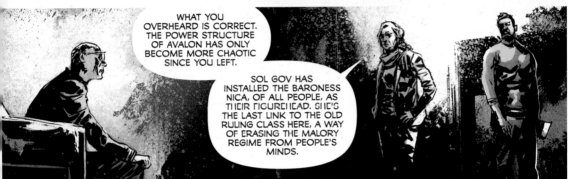

WHAT YOU OVERHEARD IS CORRECT. THE POWER STRUCTURE OF AVALON HAS ONLY BECOME MORE CHAOTIC SINCE YOU LEFT.

SOL GOV HAS INSTALLED THE BARONESS NICA, OF ALL PEOPLE, AS THEIR FIGUREHEAD. SHE'S THE LAST LINK TO THE OLD RULING CLASS HERE, A WAY OF ERASING THE MALORY REGIME FROM PEOPLE'S MINDS.

SHE'S BARELY A PUPPET, BUT HER DESIRE TO RECAPTURE HER FAMILY'S INFLUENCE IS UNDERMINING OUR EFFORTS TO FORM A WORKABLE ALTERNATIVE TO SOL RULE.

STILL, HER DAUGHTER SEEMS TO BE A PRAGMATIST.

WE'VE LEARNED THAT SHE'S NERVOUS ABOUT THE REPERCUSSIONS OF SUCH A CLOSE ALLIANCE WITH SOL GOV.

THAT'S THE WORK THAT HENRY HAS BEEN CARRYING ON.

IT WASN'T EASY TO GET TO THIS POINT. IT'S STILL HARD.

I SENT WORONOV INTO A DANGEROUS SITUATION, AND SHE PAID WITH HER LIFE.

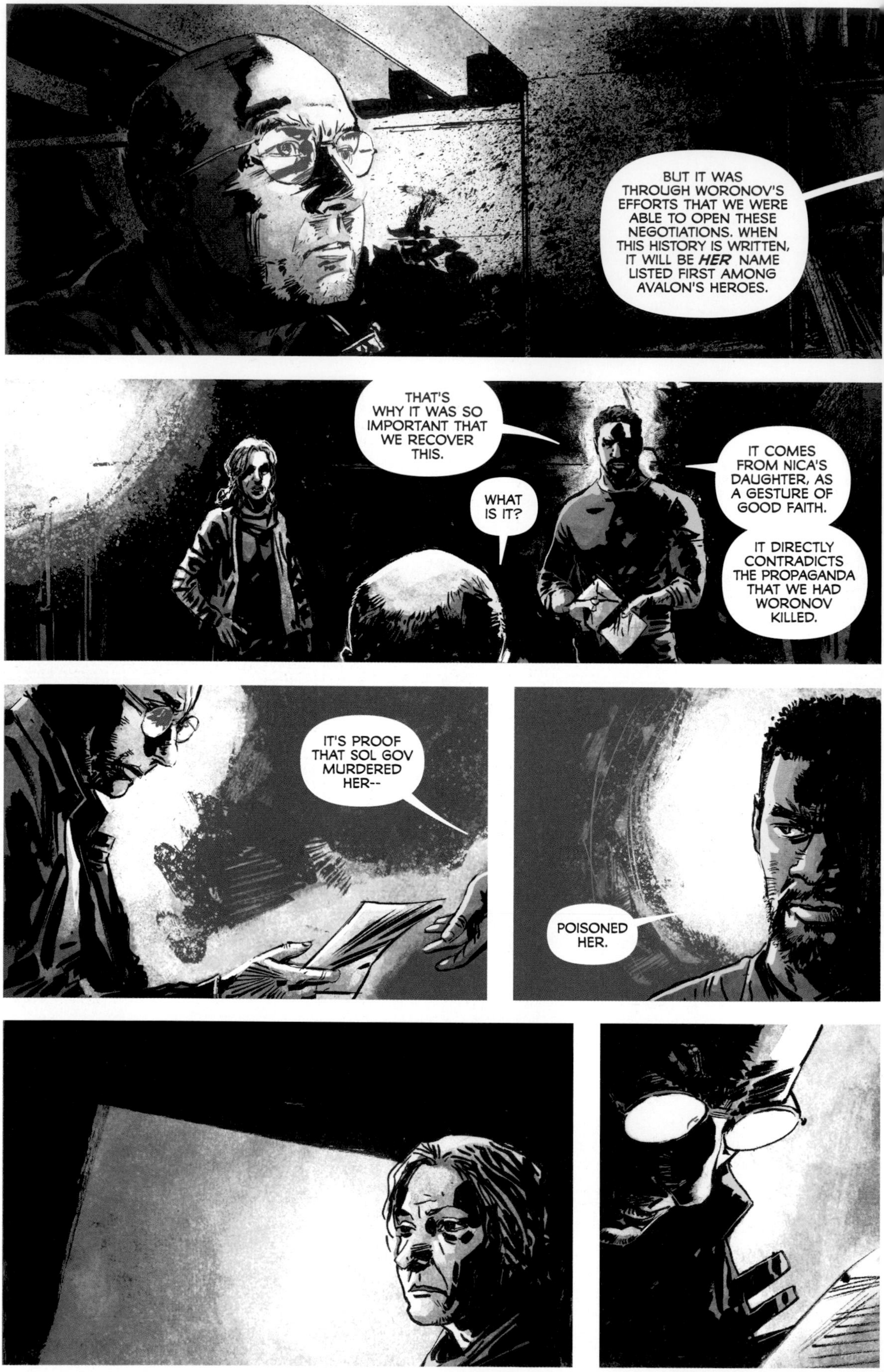
BUT IT WAS THROUGH WORONOV'S EFFORTS THAT WE WERE ABLE TO OPEN THESE NEGOTIATIONS. WHEN THIS HISTORY IS WRITTEN, IT WILL BE *HER* NAME LISTED FIRST AMONG AVALON'S HEROES.
THAT'S WHY IT WAS SO IMPORTANT THAT WE RECOVER THIS.
WHAT IS IT?
IT COMES FROM NICA'S DAUGHTER, AS A GESTURE OF GOOD FAITH.
IT DIRECTLY CONTRADICTS THE PROPAGANDA THAT WE HAD WORONOV KILLED.
IT'S PROOF THAT SOL GOV MURDERED HER--
POISONED HER.

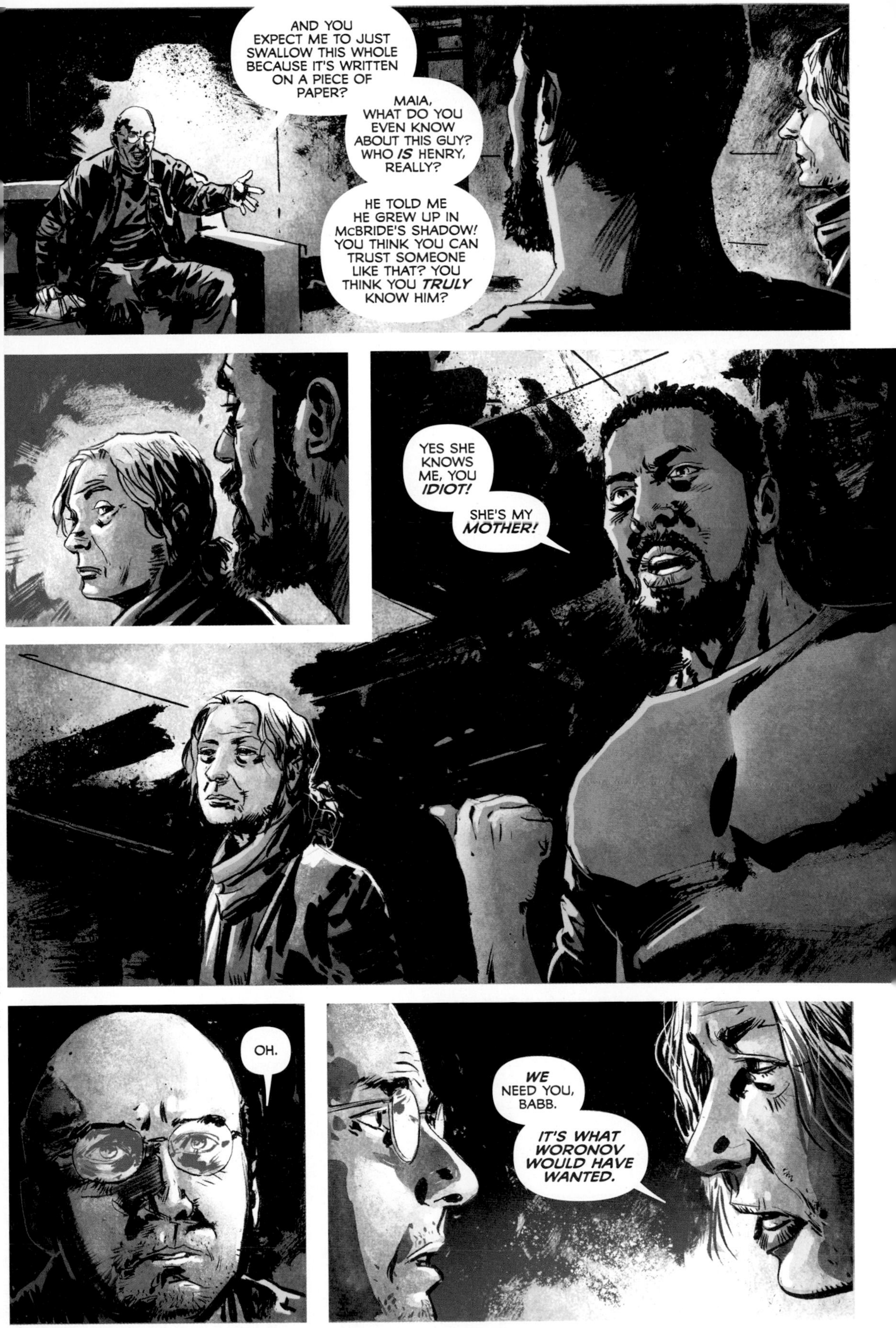
AND YOU EXPECT ME TO JUST SWALLOW THIS WHOLE BECAUSE IT'S WRITTEN ON A PIECE OF PAPER?
MAIA, WHAT DO YOU EVEN KNOW ABOUT THIS GUY? WHO *IS* HENRY, REALLY?
HE TOLD ME HE GREW UP IN McBRIDE'S SHADOW! YOU THINK YOU CAN TRUST SOMEONE LIKE THAT? YOU THINK YOU *TRULY* KNOW HIM?
YES SHE KNOWS ME, YOU *IDIOT!*
SHE'S MY *MOTHER!*
OH.
WE NEED YOU, BABB.
IT'S WHAT WORONOV WOULD HAVE WANTED.

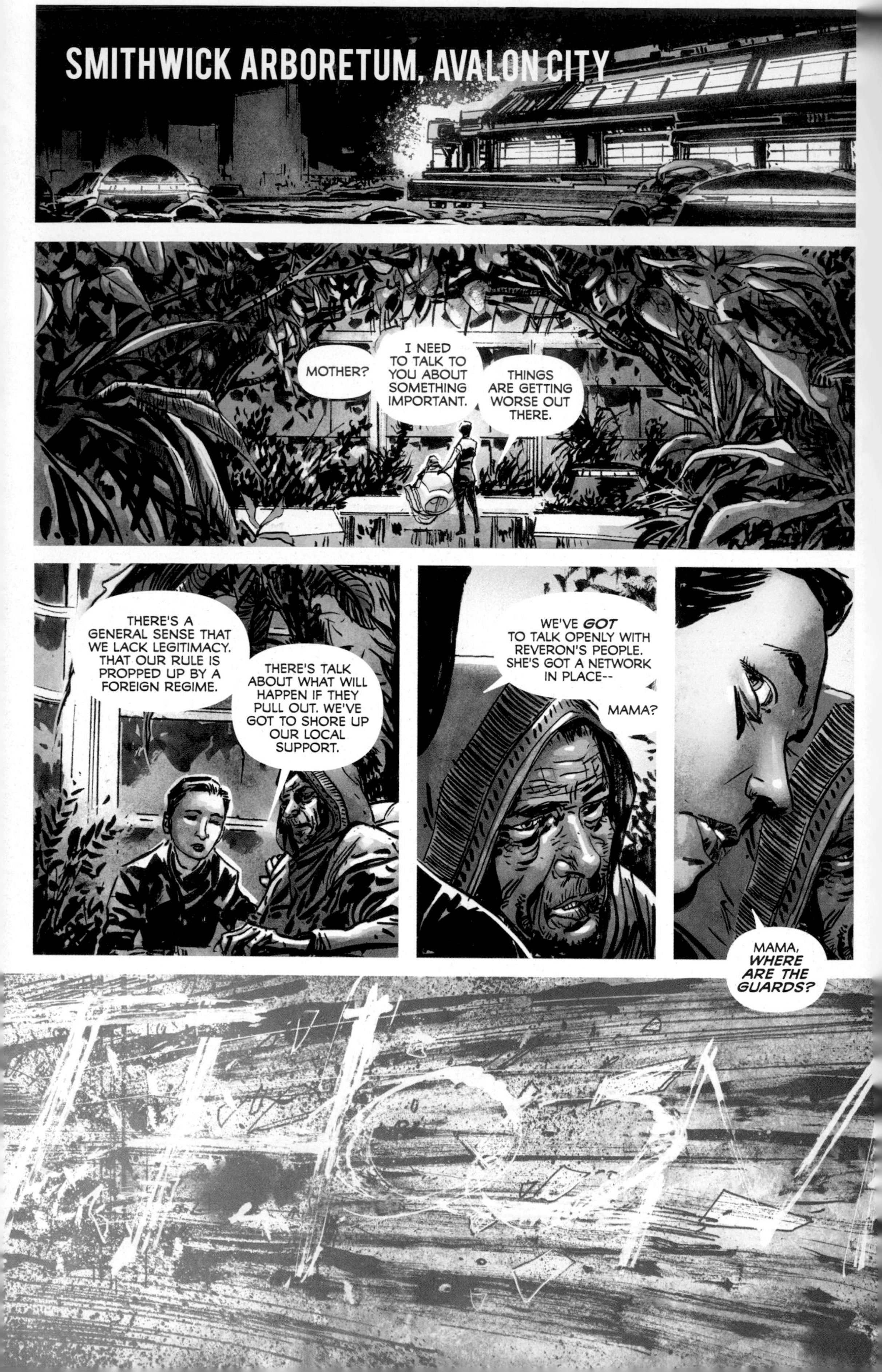
SMITHWICK ARBORETUM, AVALON CITY
MOTHER?
I NEED TO TALK TO YOU ABOUT SOMETHING IMPORTANT.
THINGS ARE GETTING WORSE OUT THERE.
THERE'S A GENERAL SENSE THAT WE LACK LEGITIMACY. THAT OUR RULE IS PROPPED UP BY A FOREIGN REGIME.
THERE'S TALK ABOUT WHAT WILL HAPPEN IF THEY PULL OUT. WE'VE GOT TO SHORE UP OUR LOCAL SUPPORT.
WE'VE *GOT* TO TALK OPENLY WITH REVERON'S PEOPLE. SHE'S GOT A NETWORK IN PLACE--
MAMA?
MAMA, *WHERE ARE THE GUARDS?*

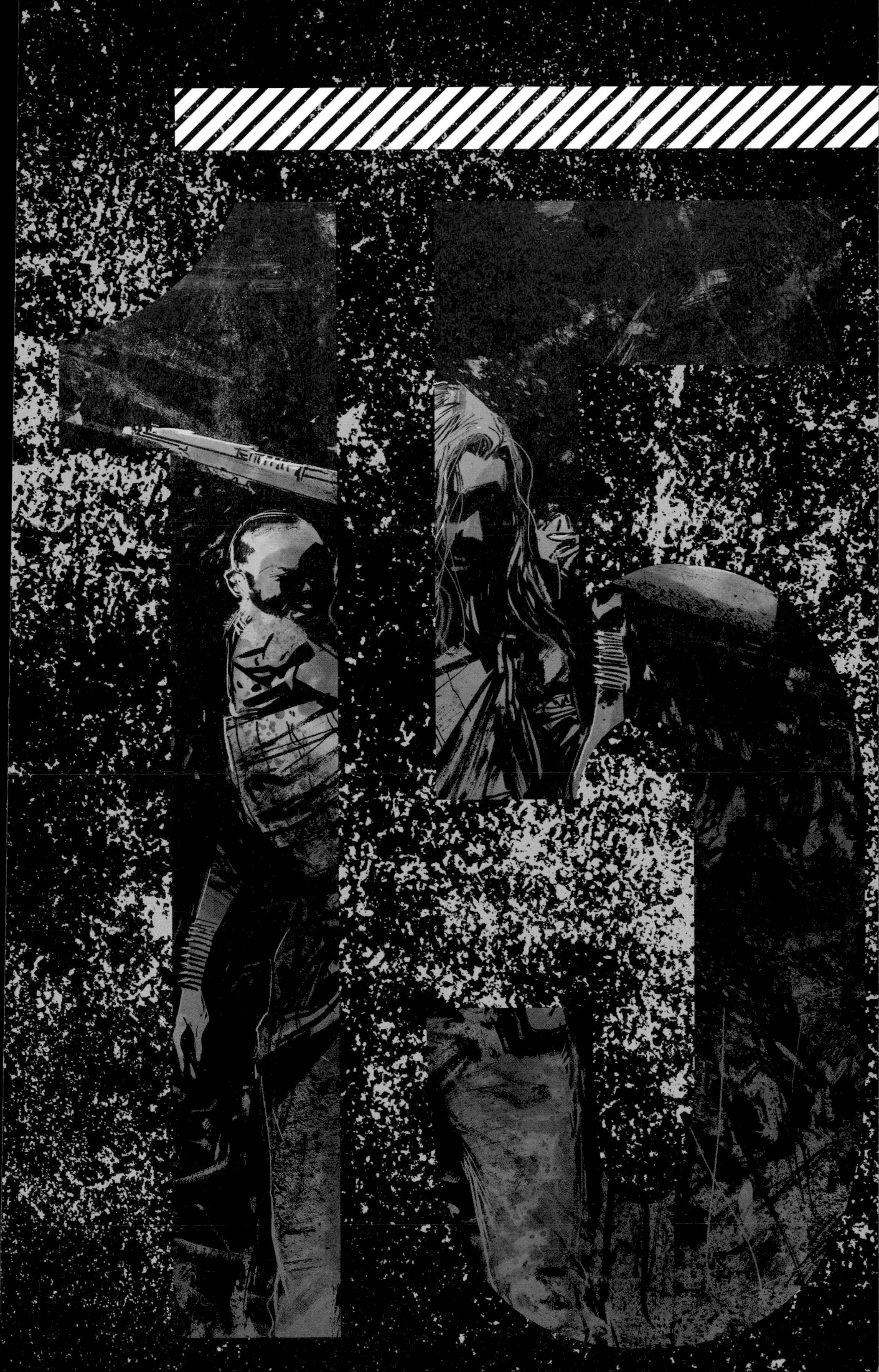

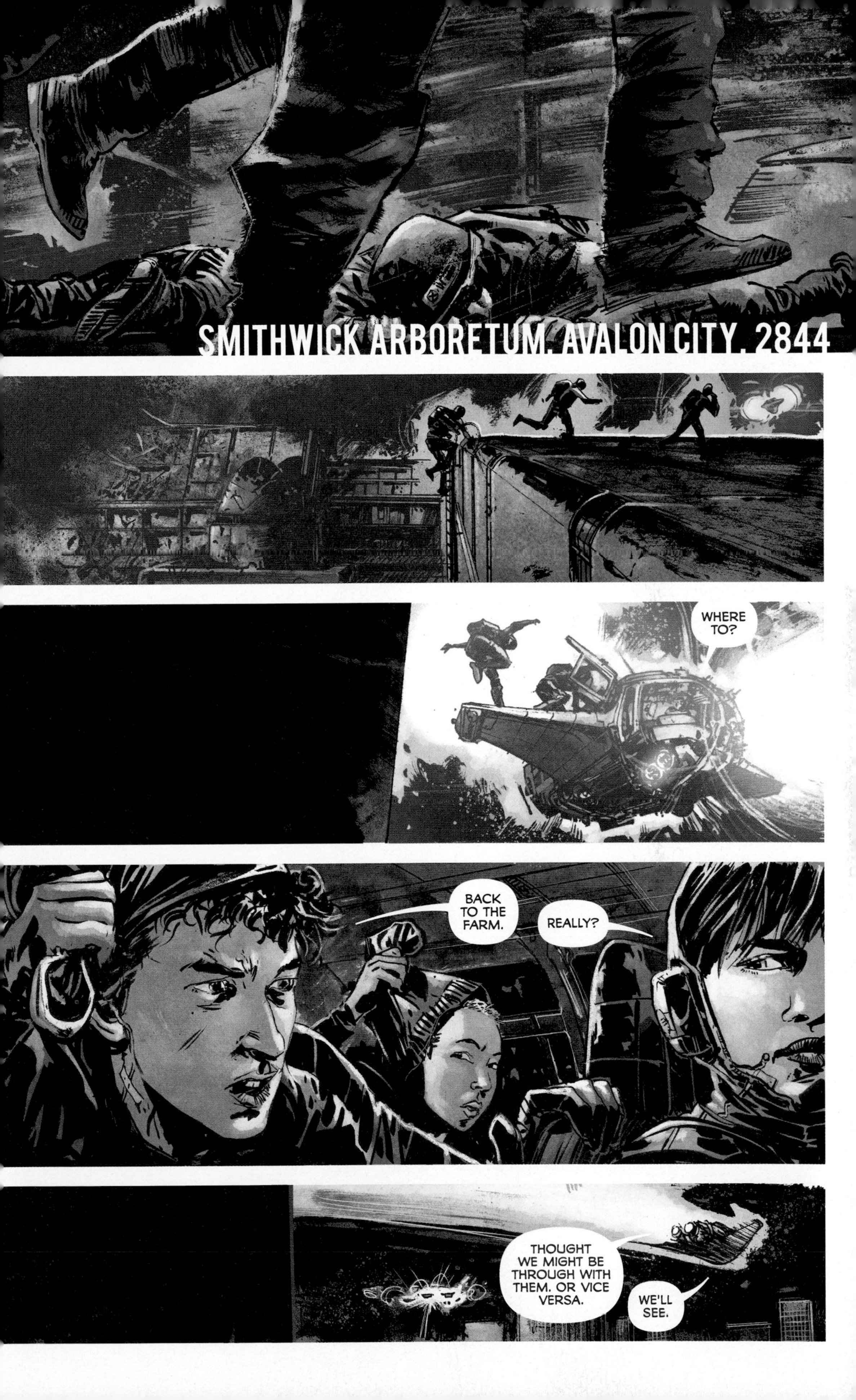
SMITHWICK ARBORETUM. AVALON CITY. 2844
WHERE TO?
BACK TO THE FARM.
REALLY?
THOUGHT WE MIGHT BE THROUGH WITH THEM. OR VICE VERSA.
WE'LL SEE.

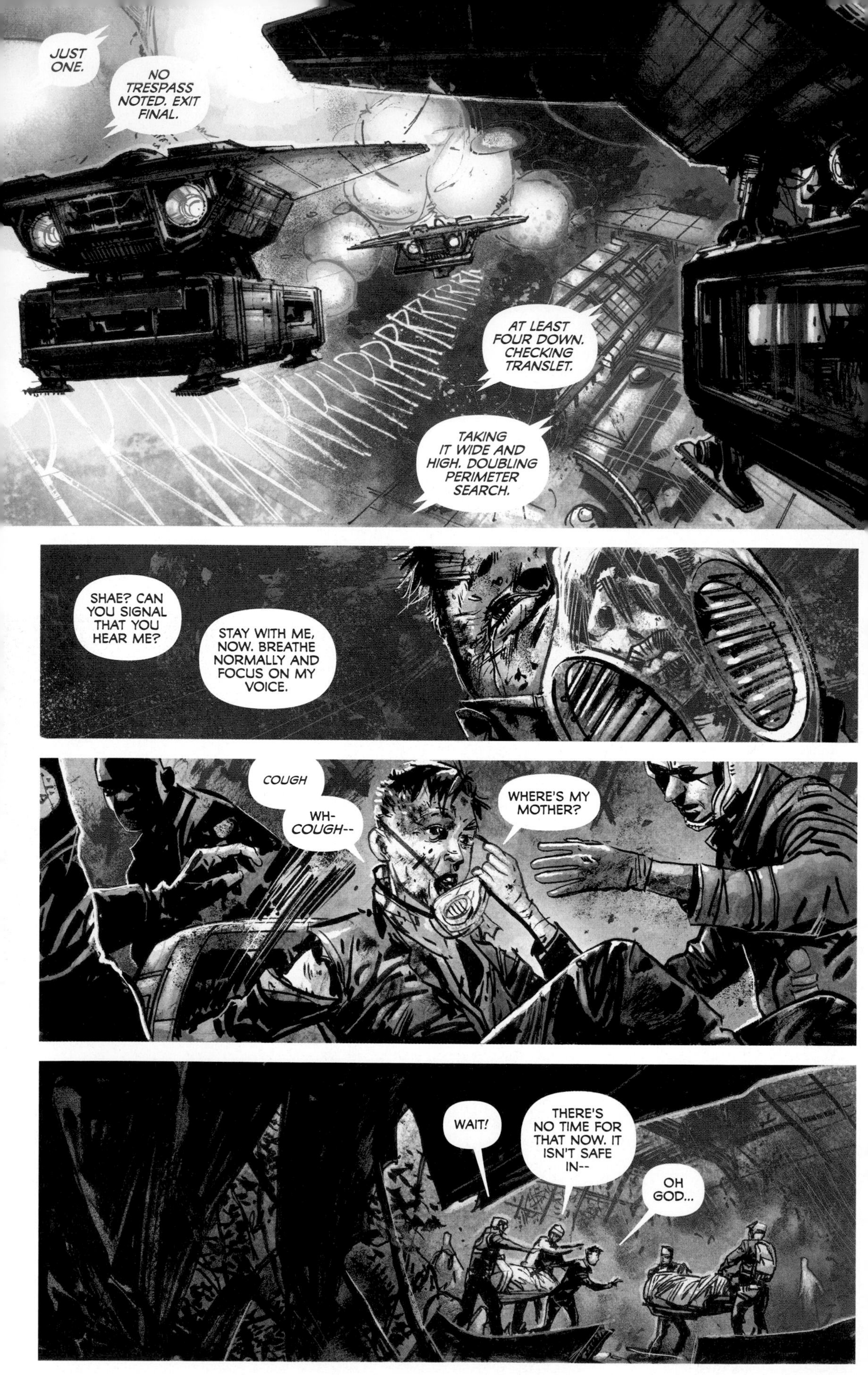
JUST ONE.
NO TRESPASS NOTED. EXIT FINAL.
AT LEAST FOUR DOWN. CHECKING TRANSLET.
TAKING IT WIDE AND HIGH. DOUBLING PERIMETER SEARCH.
SHAE? CAN YOU SIGNAL THAT YOU HEAR ME?
STAY WITH ME, NOW. BREATHE NORMALLY AND FOCUS ON MY VOICE.
COUGH
WH- COUGH--
WHERE'S MY MOTHER?
WAIT!
THERE'S NO TIME FOR THAT NOW. IT ISN'T SAFE IN--
OH GOD...

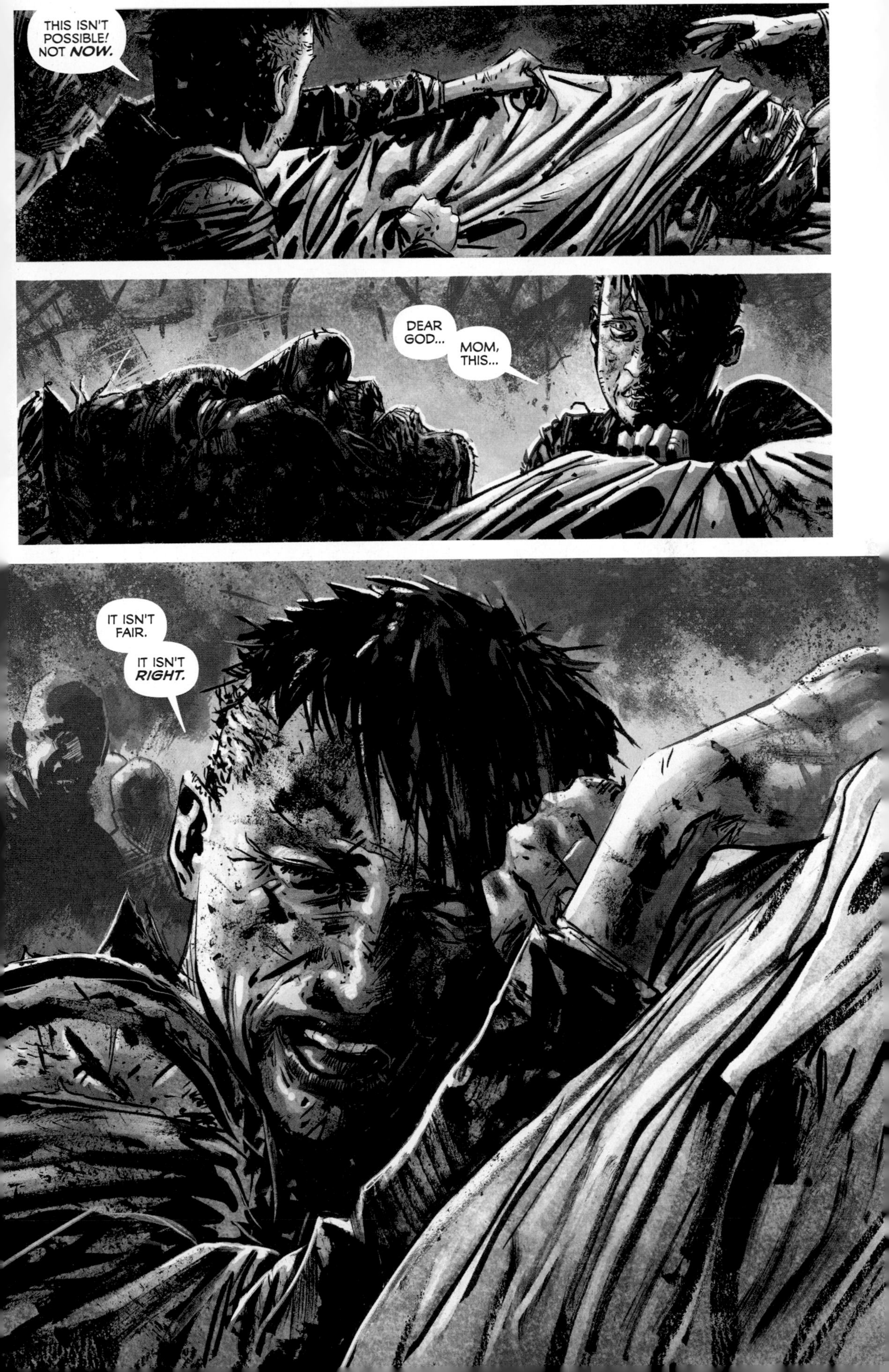
THIS ISN'T POSSIBLE! NOT *NOW.*
DEAR GOD...
MOM, THIS...
IT ISN'T FAIR.
IT ISN'T *RIGHT.*

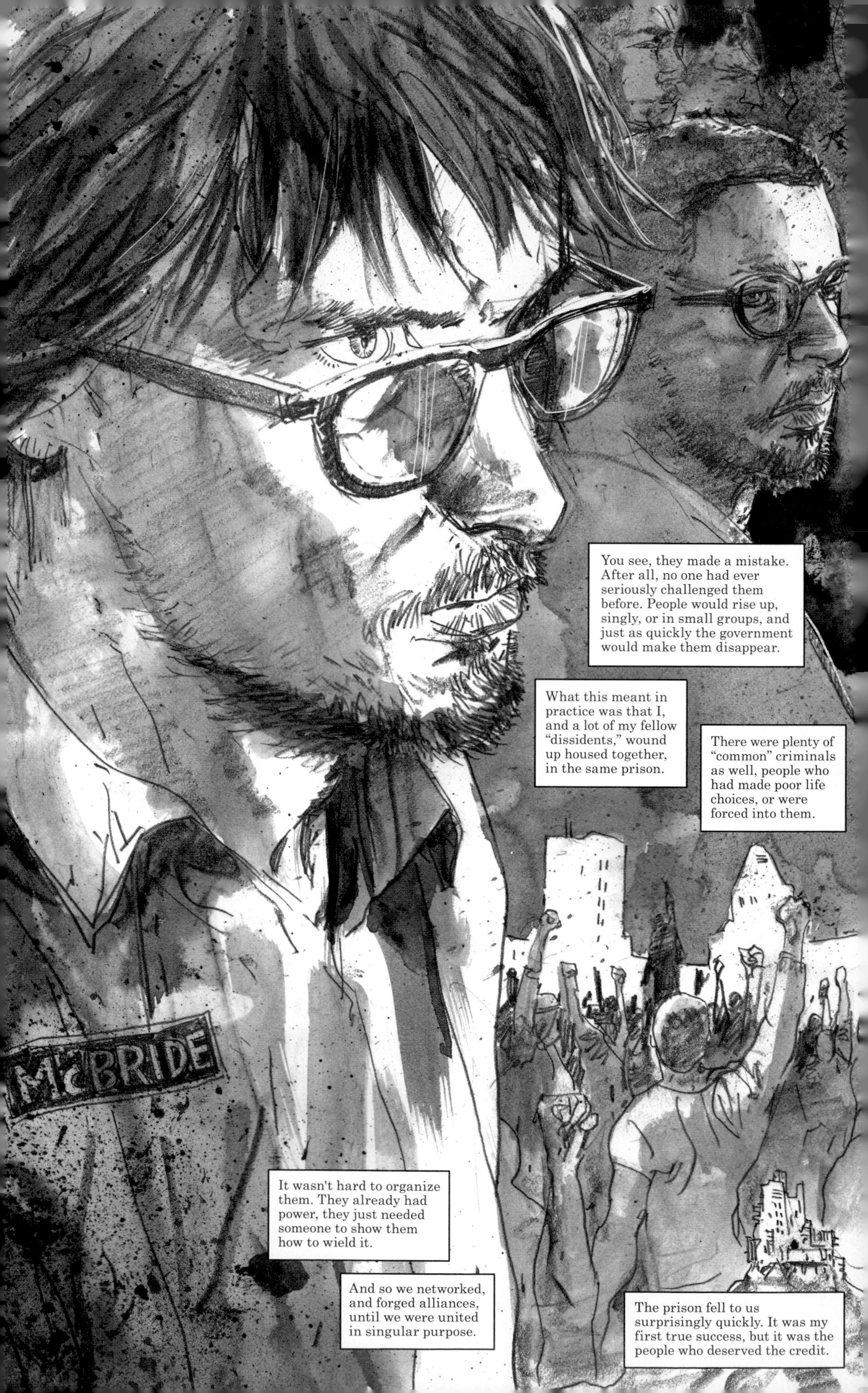
You see, they made a mistake. After all, no one had ever seriously challenged them before. People would rise up, singly, or in small groups, and just as quickly the government would make them disappear.
What this meant in practice was that I, and a lot of my fellow "dissidents," wound up housed together, in the same prison.
There were plenty of "common" criminals as well, people who had made poor life choices, or were forced into them.
McBRIDE
It wasn't hard to organize them. They already had power, they just needed someone to show them how to wield it.
And so we networked, and forged alliances, until we were united in singular purpose.
The prison fell to us surprisingly quickly. It was my first true success, but it was the people who deserved the credit.

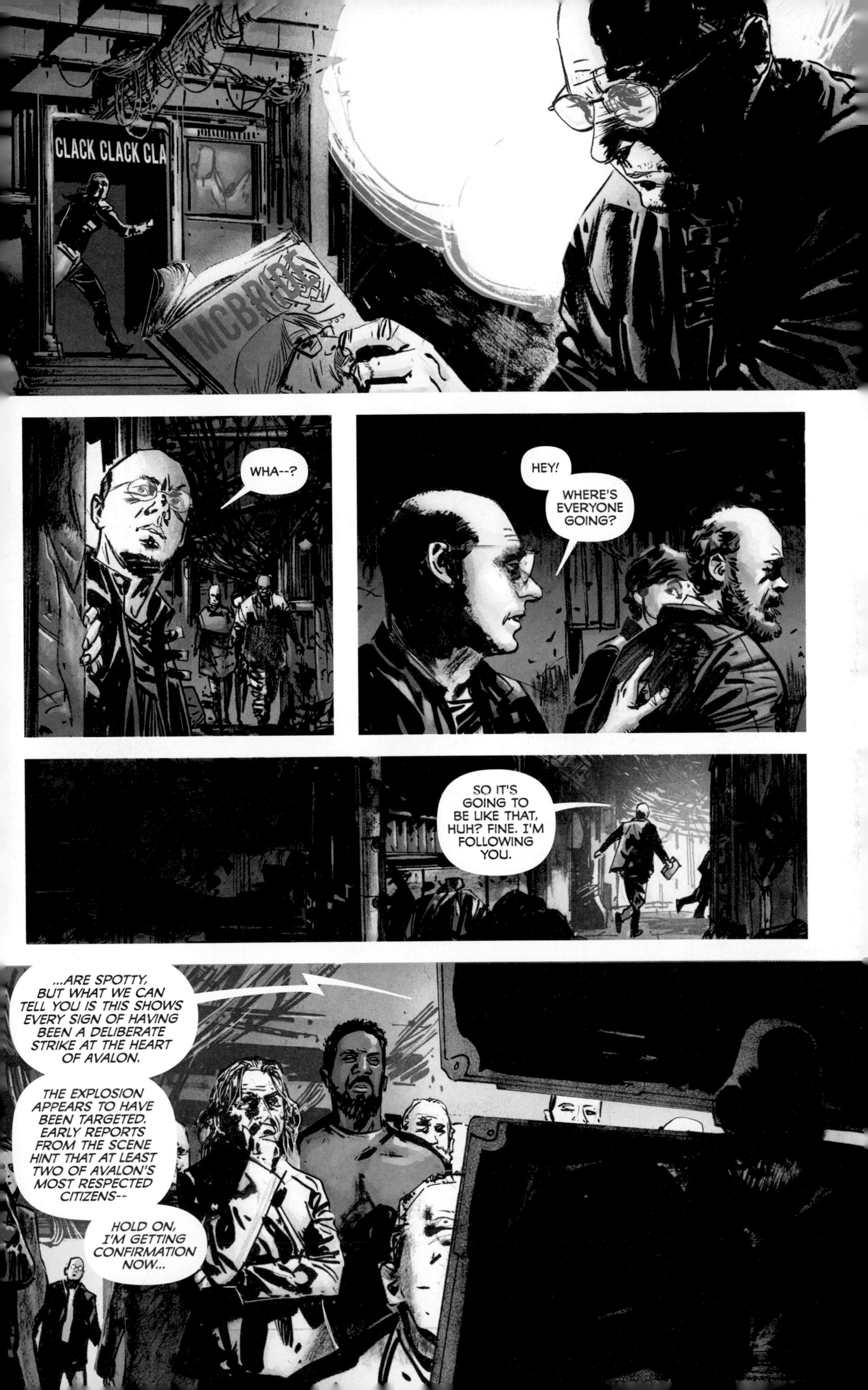
CLACK CLACK CLA
MCBRIDE
WHA--?
HEY!
WHERE'S EVERYONE GOING?
SO IT'S GOING TO BE LIKE THAT, HUH? FINE. I'M FOLLOWING YOU.
...ARE SPOTTY, BUT WHAT WE CAN TELL YOU IS THIS SHOWS EVERY SIGN OF HAVING BEEN A DELIBERATE STRIKE AT THE HEART OF AVALON.
THE EXPLOSION APPEARS TO HAVE BEEN TARGETED. EARLY REPORTS FROM THE SCENE HINT THAT AT LEAST TWO OF AVALON'S MOST RESPECTED CITIZENS--
HOLD ON, I'M GETTING CONFIRMATION NOW...

TRAGICALLY, THE LADY PANNONICA DE ROTHS, THE BARONESS OF KAPPA VALLEY, OFTEN REFERRED TO INFORMALLY AS NICA...

...HAS LOST HER LIFE IN THE ATTACK.

LADY PANNONICA WAS THE MATRIARCH OF ONE OF THE ASAN SYSTEM'S OLDEST AND WEALTHIEST FAMILIES.

9

8799900 ——SMITHWICK ARBORETUM——

ALTHOUGH EXILED TO KENT UNDER THE MALORY REGIME, NICA'S RECENT RETURN TO AVALON HAS BEEN WIDELY CELEBRATED AS A TURNING POINT IN OUR MOON'S FORTUNES.

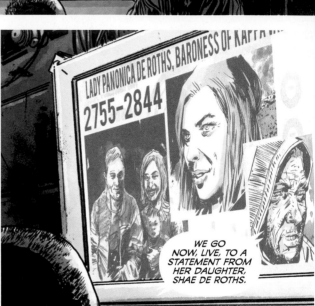

LADY PANONICA DE ROTHS, BARONESS OF KAPPA

2755-2844

WE GO NOW, LIVE, TO A STATEMENT FROM HER DAUGHTER, SHAE DE ROTHS.

THE ATTACK ON MY MOTHER AND ME WAS AN ASSAULT ON THE FRAGILE PEACE THAT WE, IN CONCERT WITH SOL GOV, HAVE BEEN ATTEMPTING TO BRING TO AVALON.

IT IS NOW CLEAR THERE CAN BE NO NEGOTIATION WITH FACTIONS THAT SEE VIOLENCE AS ITS OWN END. NO PEACE IS POSSIBLE FOR THOSE WHO LIVE BY THE SWORD.

AND SO, TO PRESERVE OUR WAY OF LIFE, WE WILL BE STEPPING UP PATROLS AND RE-INSTITUTING CURFEW IMMEDIATELY. THESE TERRORISTS WILL BE FOUND, AND DEALT WITH...

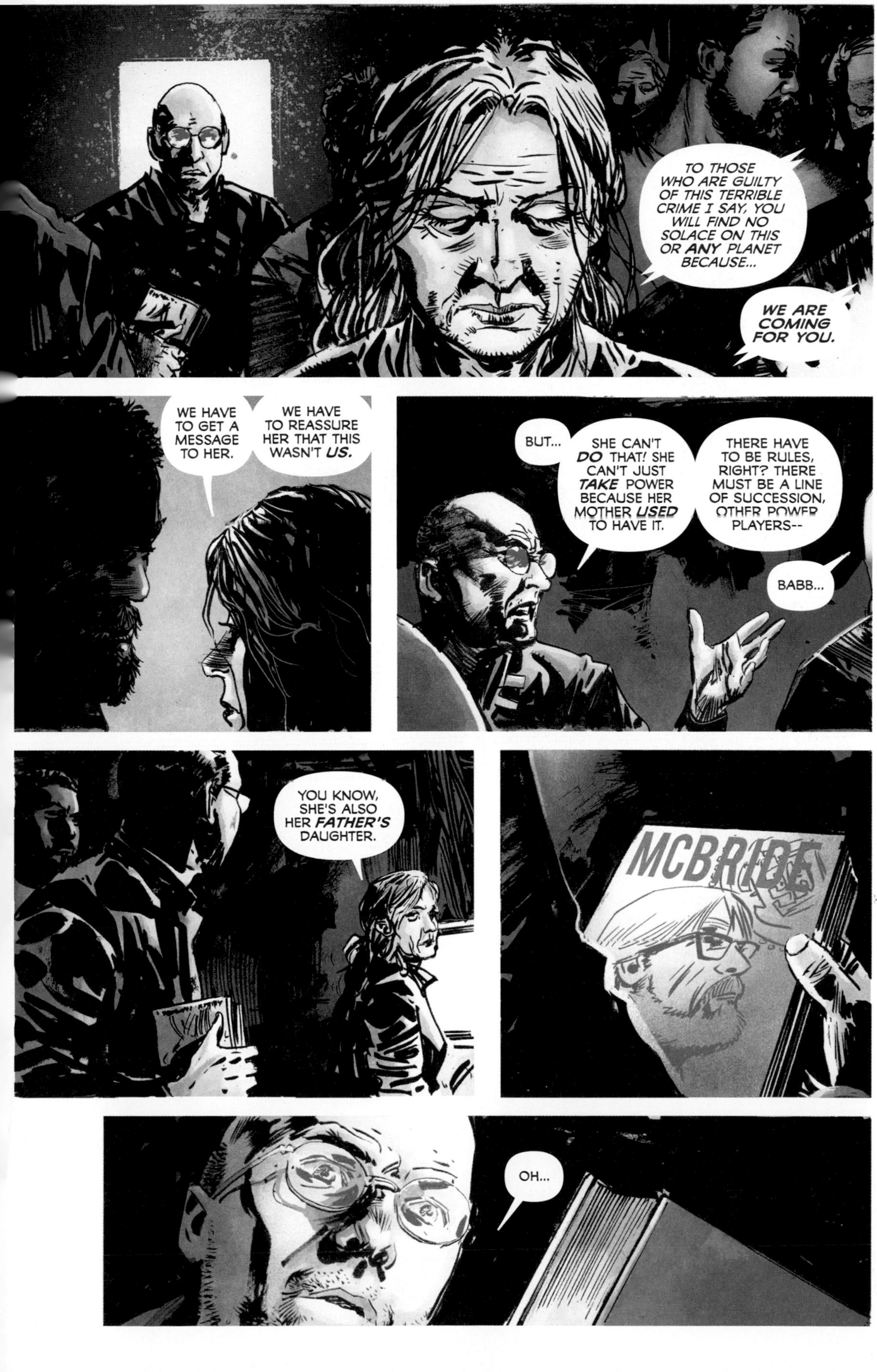
TO THOSE WHO ARE GUILTY OF THIS TERRIBLE CRIME I SAY, YOU WILL FIND NO SOLACE ON THIS OR ANY PLANET BECAUSE...
WE ARE COMING FOR YOU.
WE HAVE TO GET A MESSAGE TO HER.
WE HAVE TO REASSURE HER THAT THIS WASN'T US.
BUT...
SHE CAN'T DO THAT! SHE CAN'T JUST TAKE POWER BECAUSE HER MOTHER USED TO HAVE IT.
THERE HAVE TO BE RULES, RIGHT? THERE MUST BE A LINE OF SUCCESSION, OTHER POWER PLAYERS--
BABB...
YOU KNOW, SHE'S ALSO HER FATHER'S DAUGHTER.
MCBRIDE
OH...

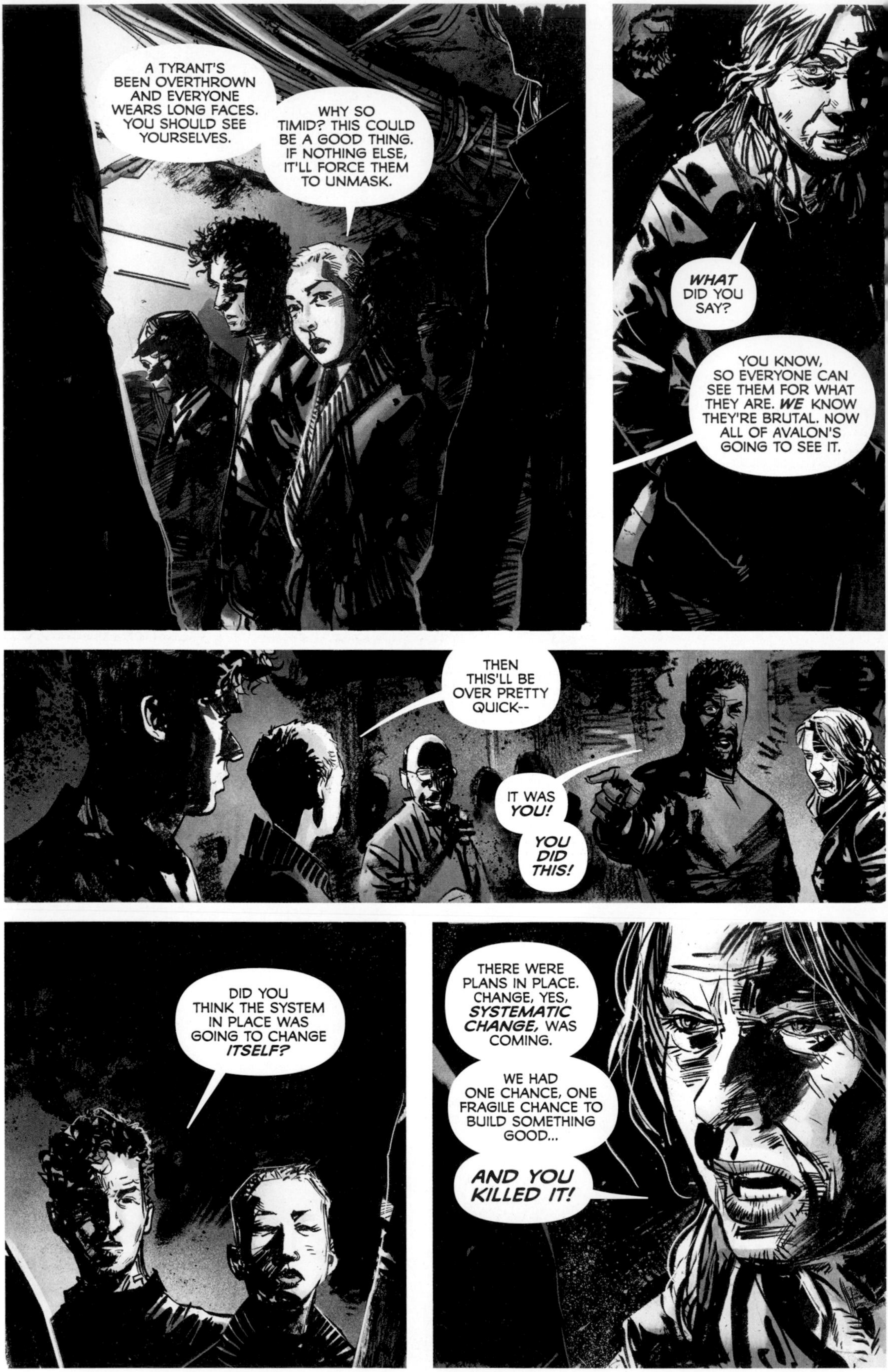
A TYRANT'S BEEN OVERTHROWN AND EVERYONE WEARS LONG FACES. YOU SHOULD SEE YOURSELVES.
WHY SO TIMID? THIS COULD BE A GOOD THING. IF NOTHING ELSE, IT'LL FORCE THEM TO UNMASK.
WHAT DID YOU SAY?
YOU KNOW, SO EVERYONE CAN SEE THEM FOR WHAT THEY ARE. *WE* KNOW THEY'RE BRUTAL. NOW ALL OF AVALON'S GOING TO SEE IT.
THEN THIS'LL BE OVER PRETTY QUICK--
IT WAS *YOU!*
YOU DID THIS!
DID YOU THINK THE SYSTEM IN PLACE WAS GOING TO CHANGE *ITSELF?*
THERE WERE PLANS IN PLACE. CHANGE, YES, *SYSTEMATIC CHANGE,* WAS COMING.
WE HAD ONE CHANCE, ONE FRAGILE CHANCE TO BUILD SOMETHING GOOD...
AND YOU KILLED IT!

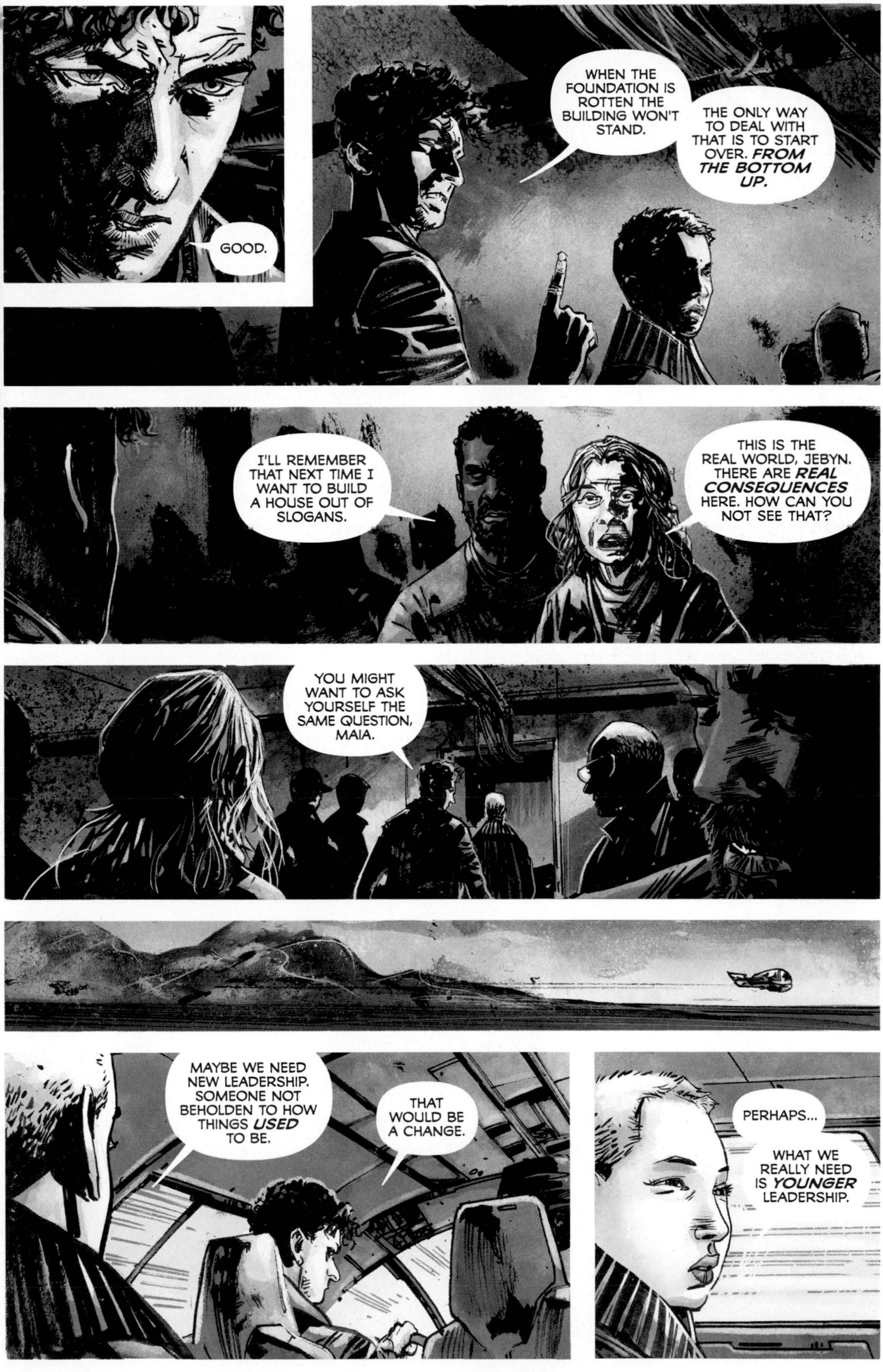
GOOD.
WHEN THE FOUNDATION IS ROTTEN THE BUILDING WON'T STAND.
THE ONLY WAY TO DEAL WITH THAT IS TO START OVER. FROM THE BOTTOM UP.
I'LL REMEMBER THAT NEXT TIME I WANT TO BUILD A HOUSE OUT OF SLOGANS.
THIS IS THE REAL WORLD, JEBYN. THERE ARE REAL CONSEQUENCES HERE. HOW CAN YOU NOT SEE THAT?
YOU MIGHT WANT TO ASK YOURSELF THE SAME QUESTION, MAIA.
MAYBE WE NEED NEW LEADERSHIP. SOMEONE NOT BEHOLDEN TO HOW THINGS USED TO BE.
THAT WOULD BE A CHANGE.
PERHAPS...
WHAT WE REALLY NEED IS YOUNGER LEADERSHIP.

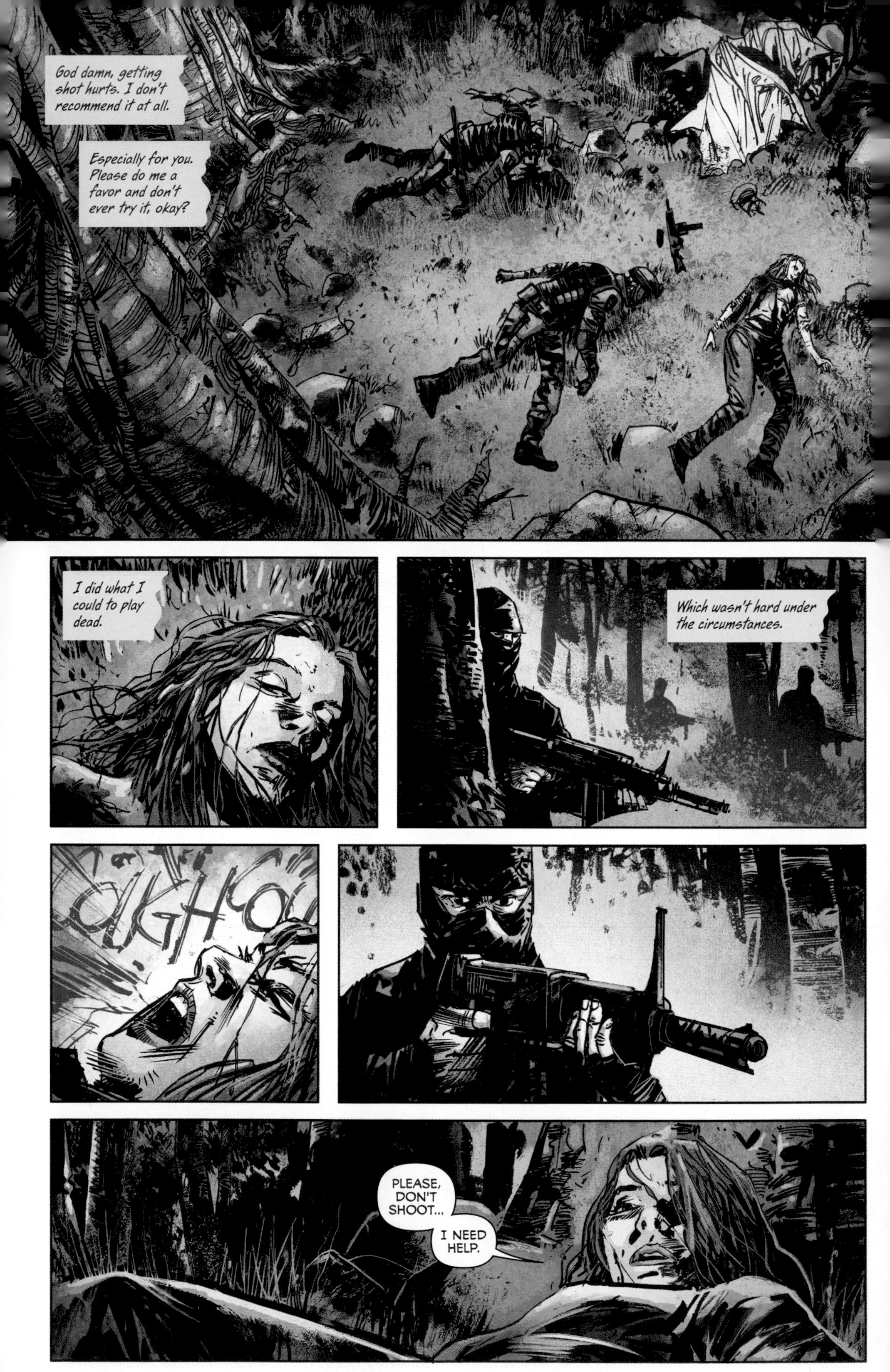
God damn, getting shot hurts. I don't recommend it at all.
Especially for you. Please do me a favor and don't ever try it, okay?
I did what I could to play dead.
Which wasn't hard under the circumstances.
PLEASE, DON'T SHOOT...
I NEED HELP.

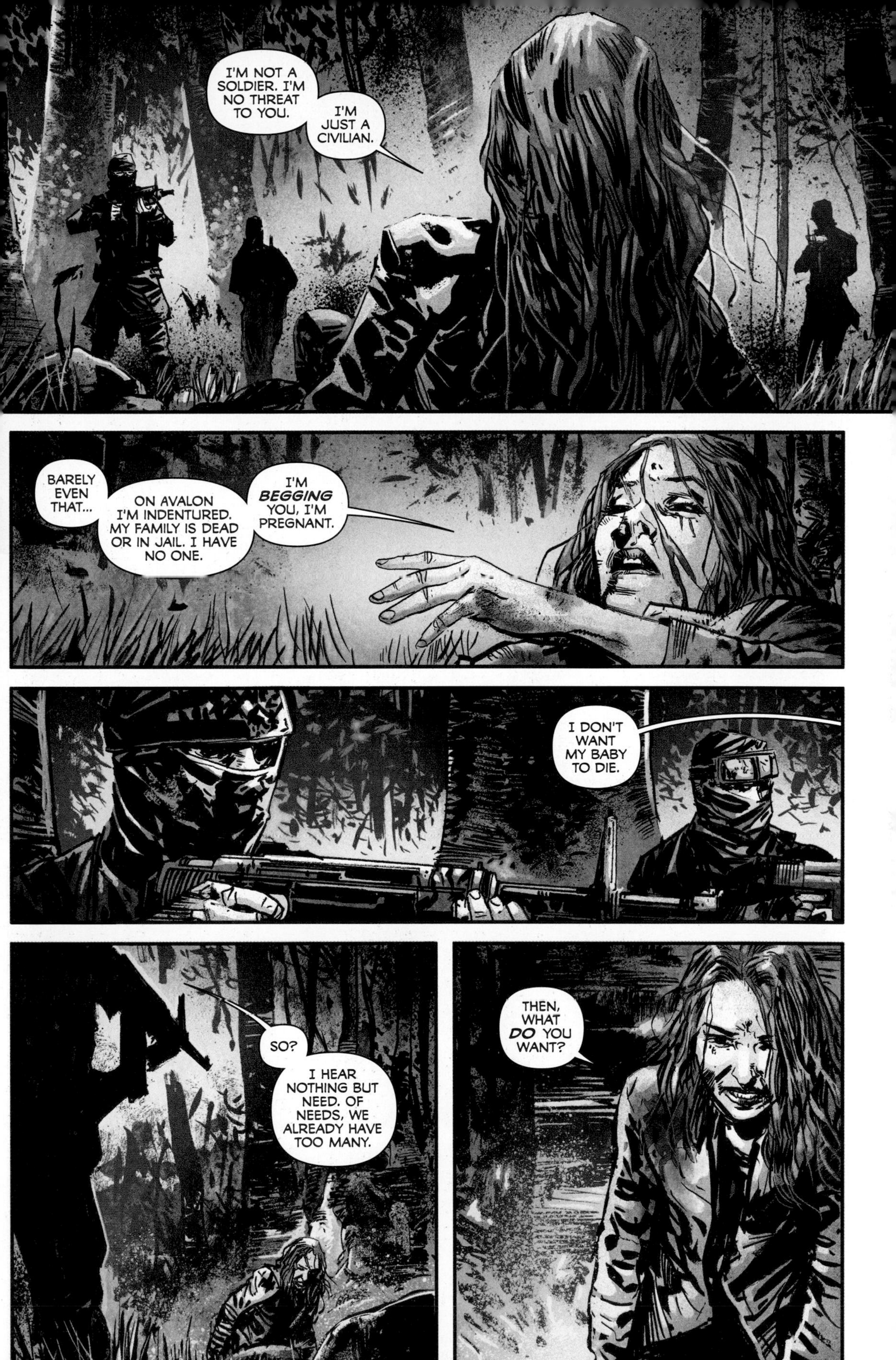
I'M NOT A SOLDIER. I'M NO THREAT TO YOU.
I'M JUST A CIVILIAN.
BARELY EVEN THAT...
ON AVALON I'M INDENTURED. MY FAMILY IS DEAD OR IN JAIL. I HAVE NO ONE.
I'M *BEGGING* YOU, I'M PREGNANT.
I DON'T WANT MY BABY TO DIE.
SO?
I HEAR NOTHING BUT NEED. OF NEEDS, WE ALREADY HAVE TOO MANY.
THEN, WHAT *DO* YOU WANT?

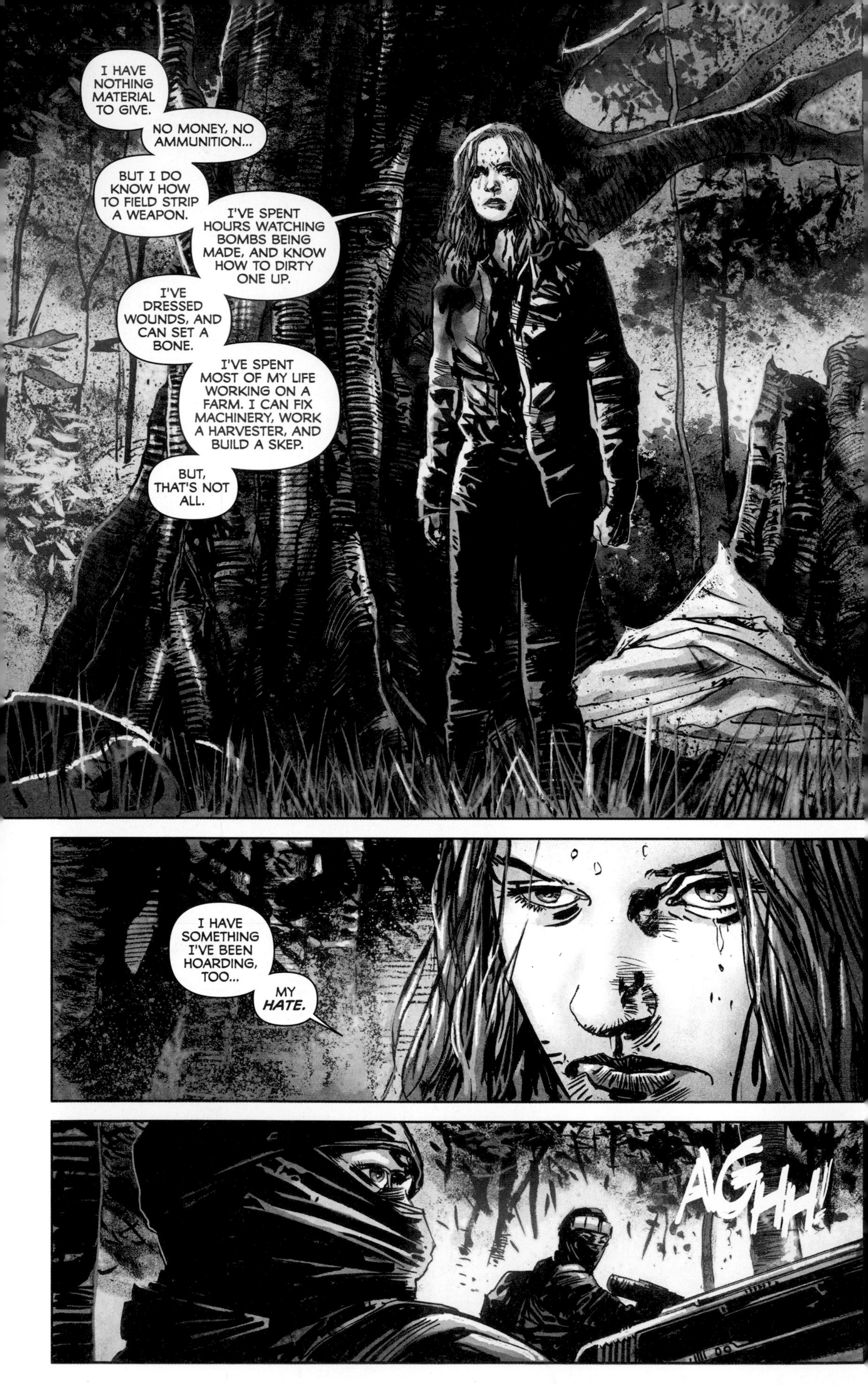
I HAVE NOTHING MATERIAL TO GIVE.
NO MONEY, NO AMMUNITION...
BUT I DO KNOW HOW TO FIELD STRIP A WEAPON.
I'VE SPENT HOURS WATCHING BOMBS BEING MADE, AND KNOW HOW TO DIRTY ONE UP.
I'VE DRESSED WOUNDS, AND CAN SET A BONE.
I'VE SPENT MOST OF MY LIFE WORKING ON A FARM. I CAN FIX MACHINERY, WORK A HARVESTER, AND BUILD A SKEP.
BUT, THAT'S NOT ALL.
I HAVE SOMETHING I'VE BEEN HOARDING, TOO...
MY *HATE.*
AGHH!

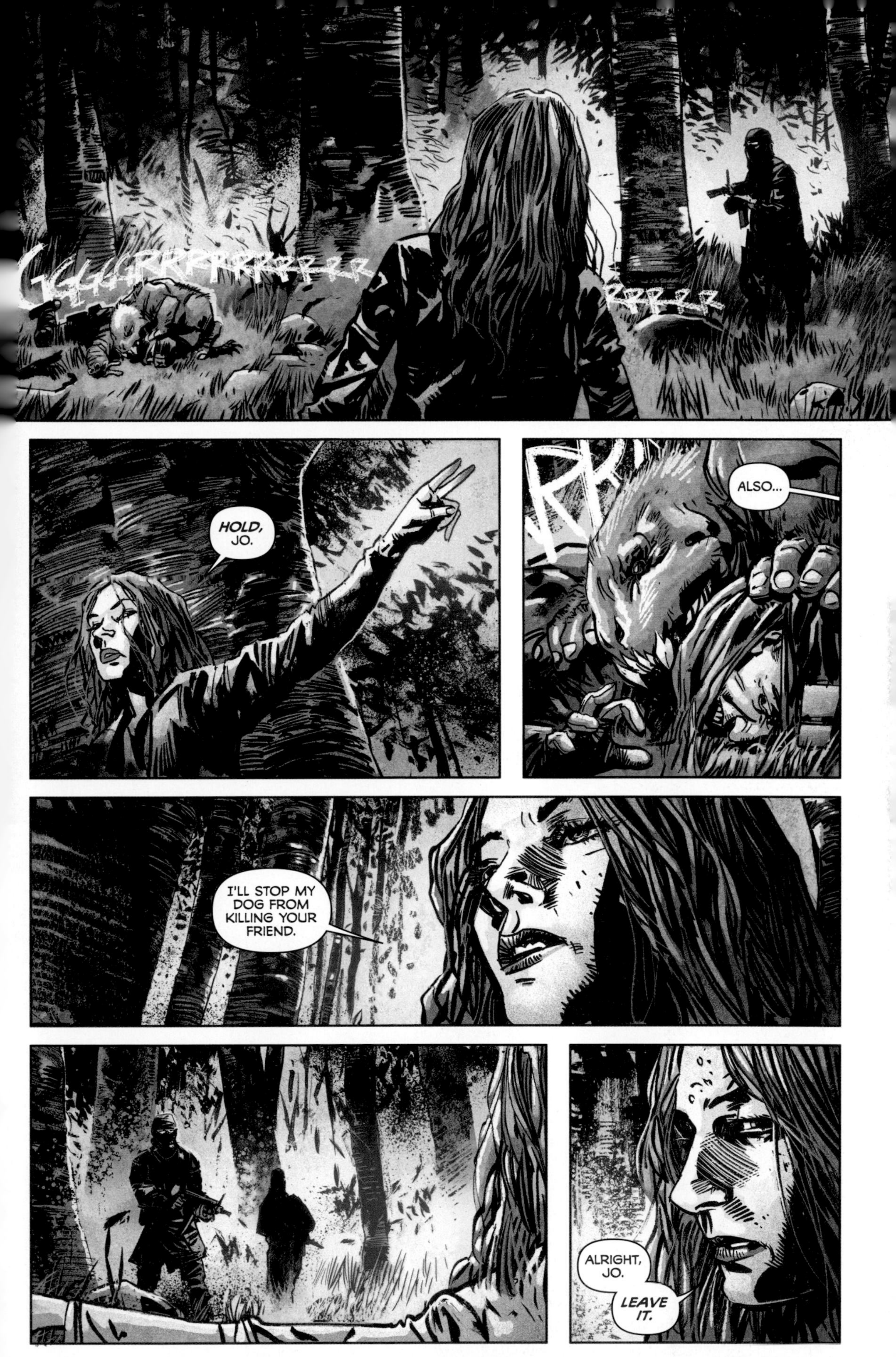
HOLD, JO.
ALSO...
I'LL STOP MY DOG FROM KILLING YOUR FRIEND.
ALRIGHT, JO.
LEAVE IT.

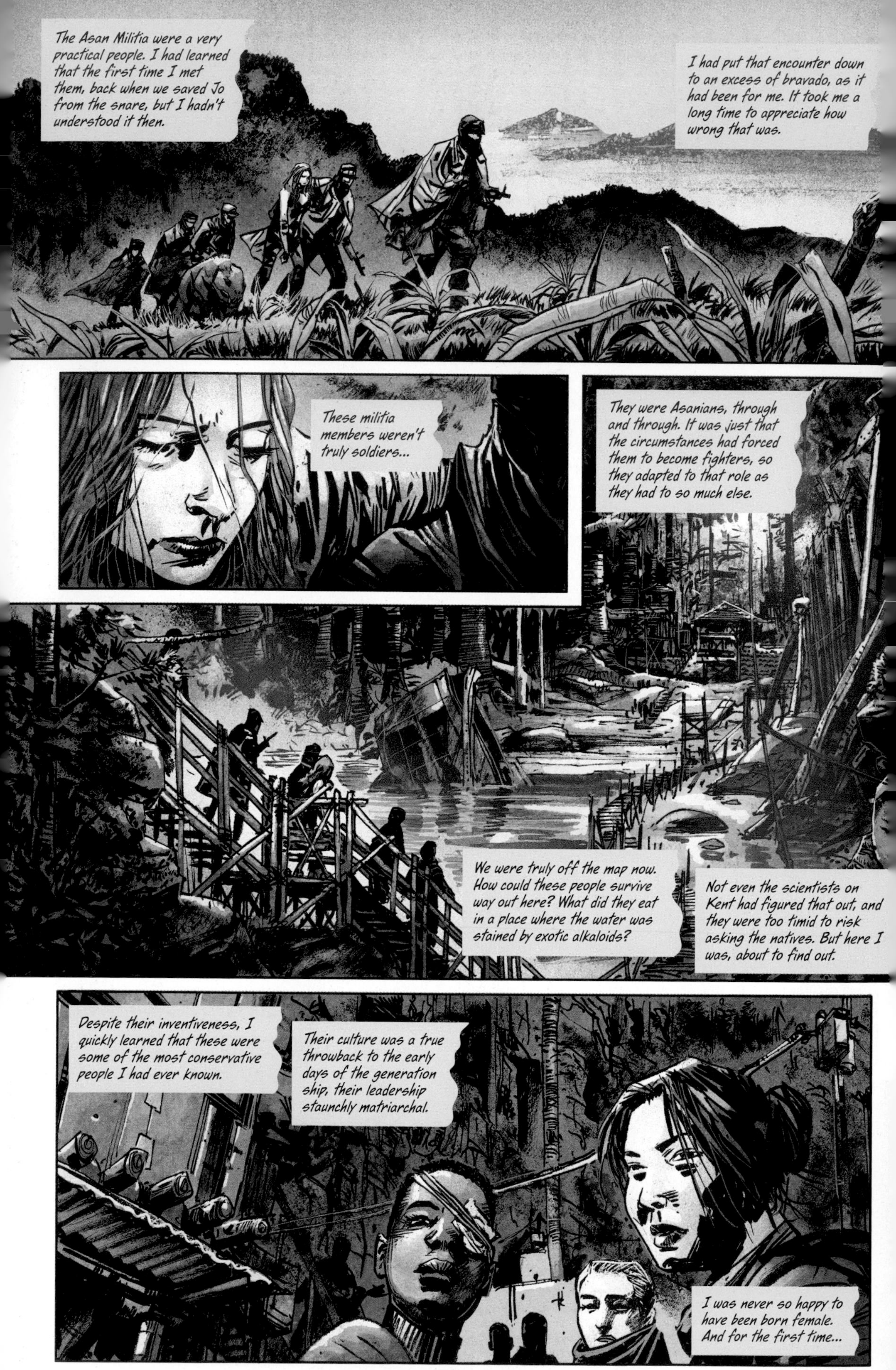
The Asan Militia were a very practical people. I had learned that the first time I met them, back when we saved Jo from the snare, but I hadn't understood it then.
I had put that encounter down to an excess of bravado, as it had been for me. It took me a long time to appreciate how wrong that was.
These militia members weren't truly soldiers...
They were Asanians, through and through. It was just that the circumstances had forced them to become fighters, so they adapted to that role as they had to so much else.
We were truly off the map now. How could these people survive way out here? What did they eat in a place where the water was stained by exotic alkaloids?
Not even the scientists on Kent had figured that out, and they were too timid to risk asking the natives. But here I was, about to find out.
Despite their inventiveness, I quickly learned that these were some of the most conservative people I had ever known.
Their culture was a true throwback to the early days of the generation ship, their leadership staunchly matriarchal.
I was never so happy to have been born female. And for the first time...

...I wondered about the gender of my baby.

My arm was slow to heal, slower than my pregnancy progressed, anyway.

But I wasn't given much chance to dwell on it. Long before I was completely recovered, I was put to work.

The extensive first aid training I'd received while part of the cell came in the most useful.

Injuries among the Asanians were frequent and varied, usually sustained in battle, but sometimes both mysterious and vicious.

As a female member of the community I took frequent turns cleaning and prepping weapons too.

There was prestige in such jobs, but I would have preferred working in one of the small gardens.

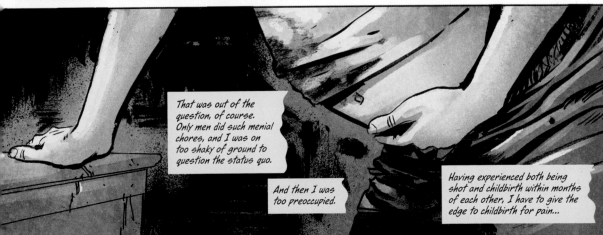

That was out of the question, of course. Only men did such menial chores, and I was on too shaky of ground to question the status quo.

And then I was too preoccupied.

Having experienced both being shot and childbirth within months of each other, I have to give the edge to childbirth for pain...

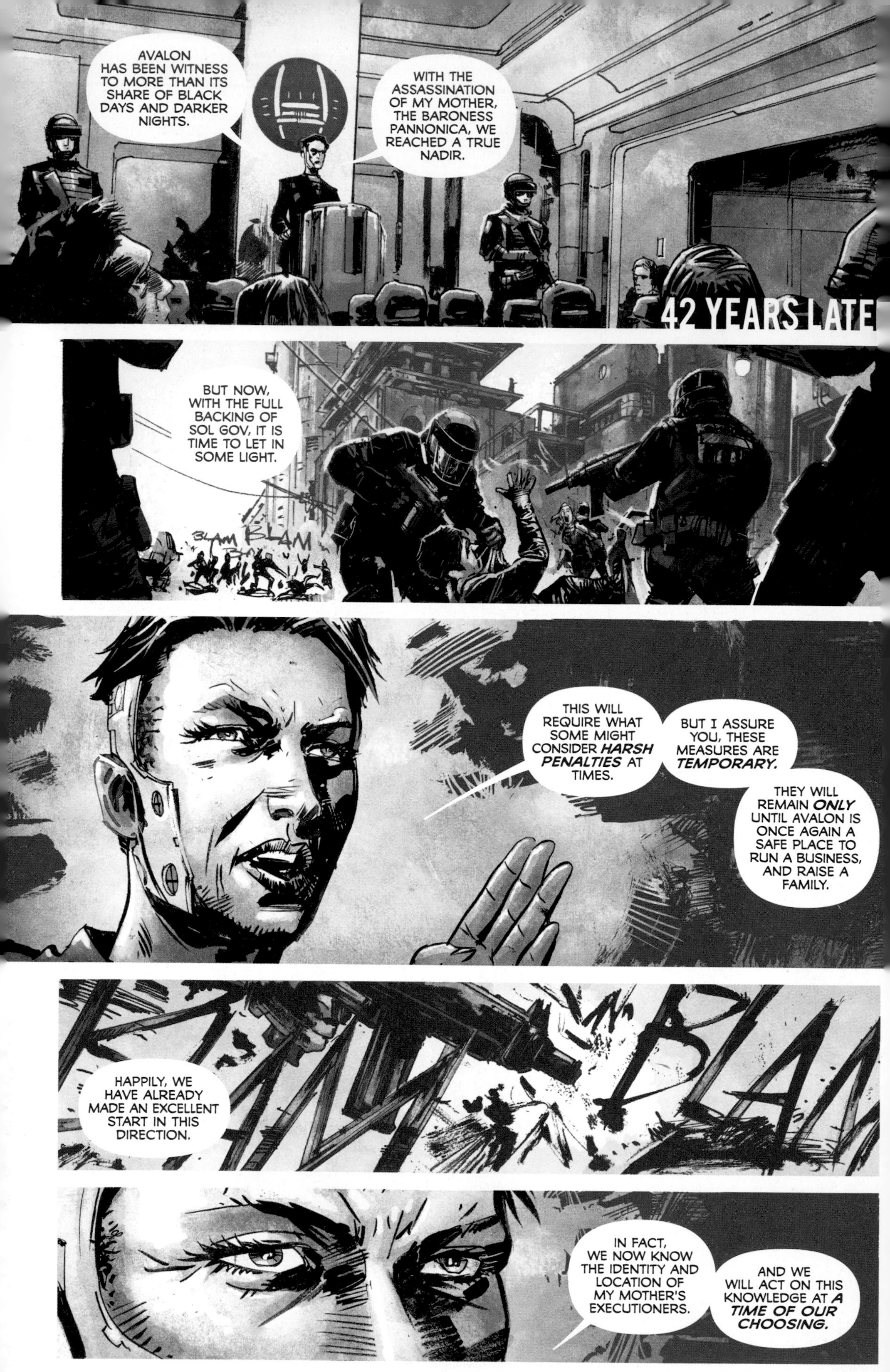
AVALON HAS BEEN WITNESS TO MORE THAN ITS SHARE OF BLACK DAYS AND DARKER NIGHTS.
WITH THE ASSASSINATION OF MY MOTHER, THE BARONESS PANNONICA, WE REACHED A TRUE NADIR.
42 YEARS LATE
BUT NOW, WITH THE FULL BACKING OF SOL GOV, IT IS TIME TO LET IN SOME LIGHT.
BLAM BLAM
THIS WILL REQUIRE WHAT SOME MIGHT CONSIDER **HARSH PENALTIES** AT TIMES.
BUT I ASSURE YOU, THESE MEASURES ARE **TEMPORARY.**
THEY WILL REMAIN **ONLY** UNTIL AVALON IS ONCE AGAIN A SAFE PLACE TO RUN A BUSINESS, AND RAISE A FAMILY.
HAPPILY, WE HAVE ALREADY MADE AN EXCELLENT START IN THIS DIRECTION.
BLAM
IN FACT, WE NOW KNOW THE IDENTITY AND LOCATION OF MY MOTHER'S EXECUTIONERS.
AND WE WILL ACT ON THIS KNOWLEDGE AT ***A TIME OF OUR CHOOSING.***

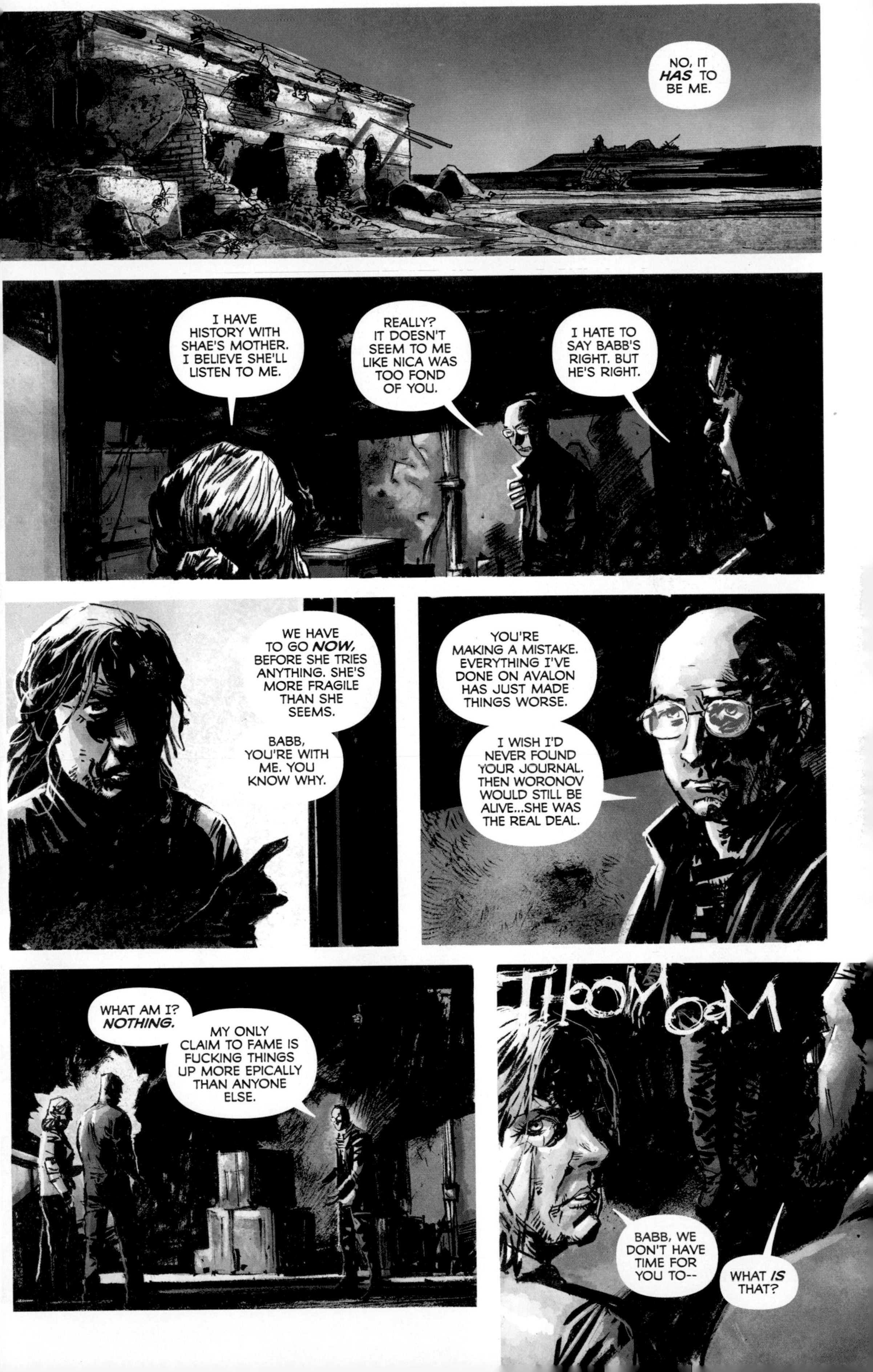
NO, IT *HAS* TO BE ME.
I HAVE HISTORY WITH SHAE'S MOTHER. I BELIEVE SHE'LL LISTEN TO ME.
REALLY? IT DOESN'T SEEM TO ME LIKE NICA WAS TOO FOND OF YOU.
I HATE TO SAY BABB'S RIGHT. BUT HE'S RIGHT.
WE HAVE TO GO *NOW,* BEFORE SHE TRIES ANYTHING. SHE'S MORE FRAGILE THAN SHE SEEMS.
BABB, YOU'RE WITH ME. YOU KNOW WHY.
YOU'RE MAKING A MISTAKE. EVERYTHING I'VE DONE ON AVALON HAS JUST MADE THINGS WORSE.
I WISH I'D NEVER FOUND YOUR JOURNAL. THEN WORONOV WOULD STILL BE ALIVE...SHE WAS THE REAL DEAL.
WHAT AM I? ***NOTHING.***
MY ONLY CLAIM TO FAME IS FUCKING THINGS UP MORE EPICALLY THAN ANYONE ELSE.
THOOM OOM
BABB, WE DON'T HAVE TIME FOR YOU TO--
WHAT *IS* THAT?

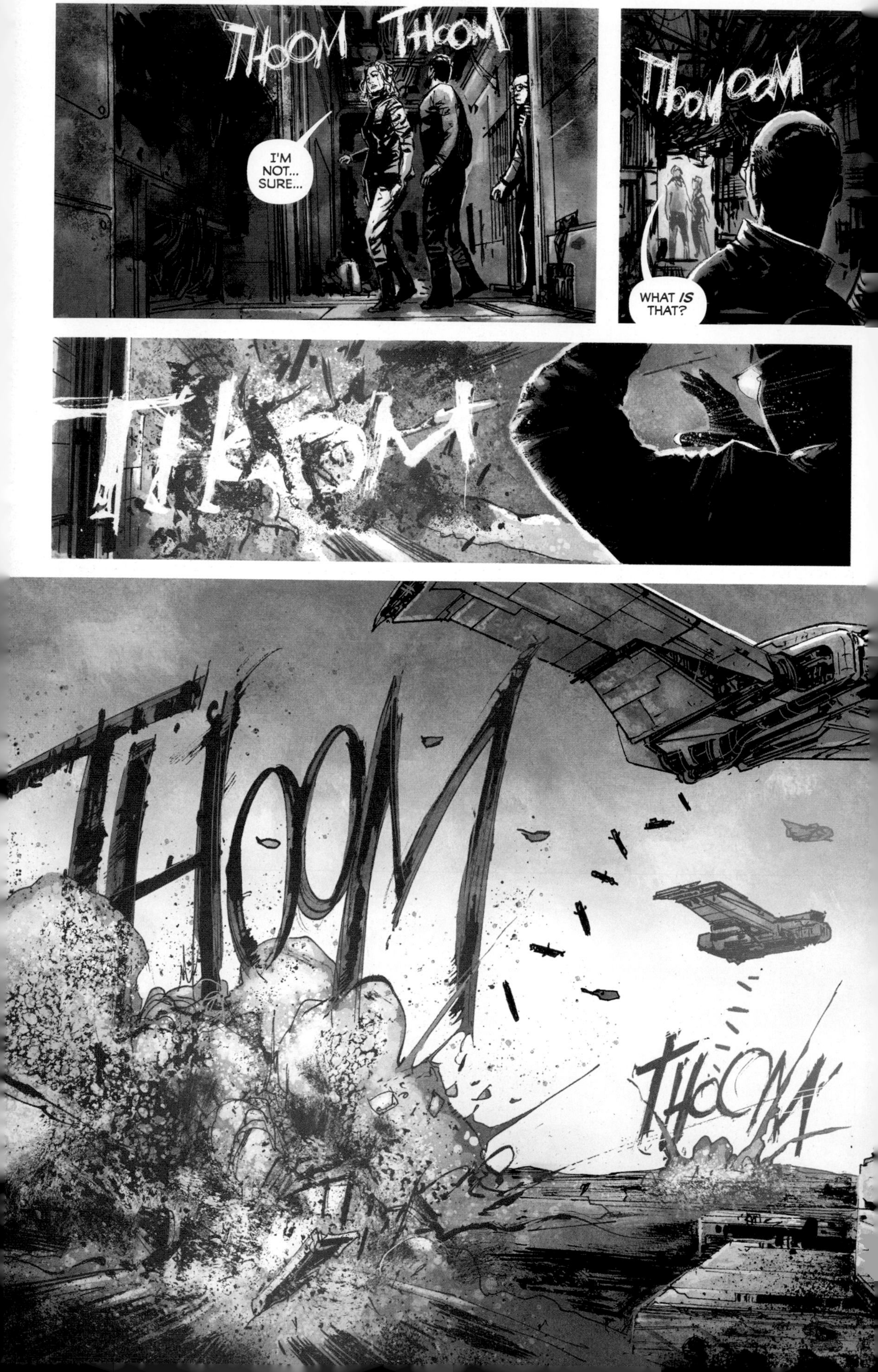
THOOM THOOM
I'M NOT... SURE...
THOOMOOM
WHAT IS THAT?
THOOM
THOOM
THOOM

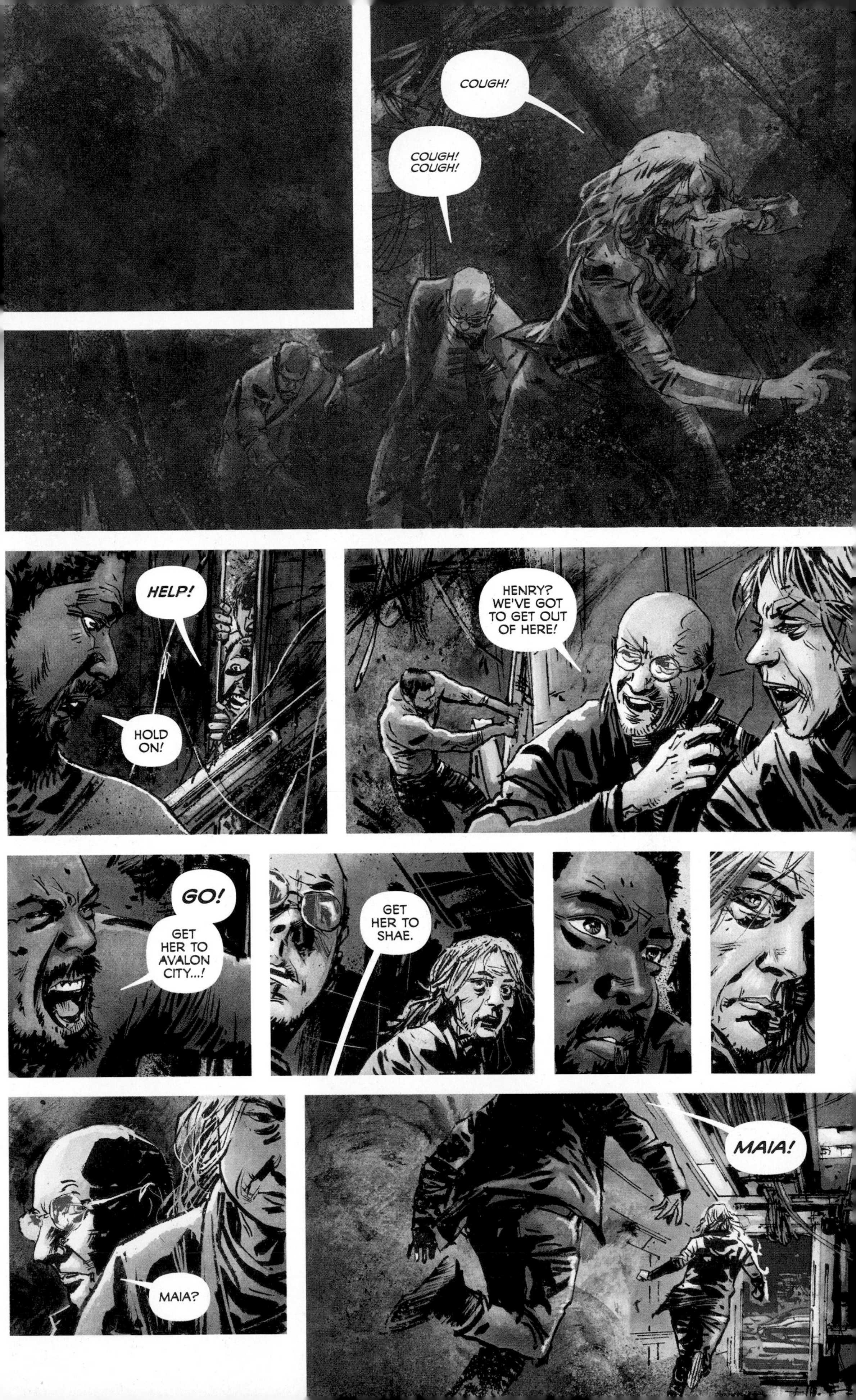
COUGH!
COUGH! COUGH!
HELP!
HOLD ON!
HENRY? WE'VE GOT TO GET OUT OF HERE!
GO!
GET HER TO AVALON CITY...!
GET HER TO SHAE.
MAIA?
MAIA!

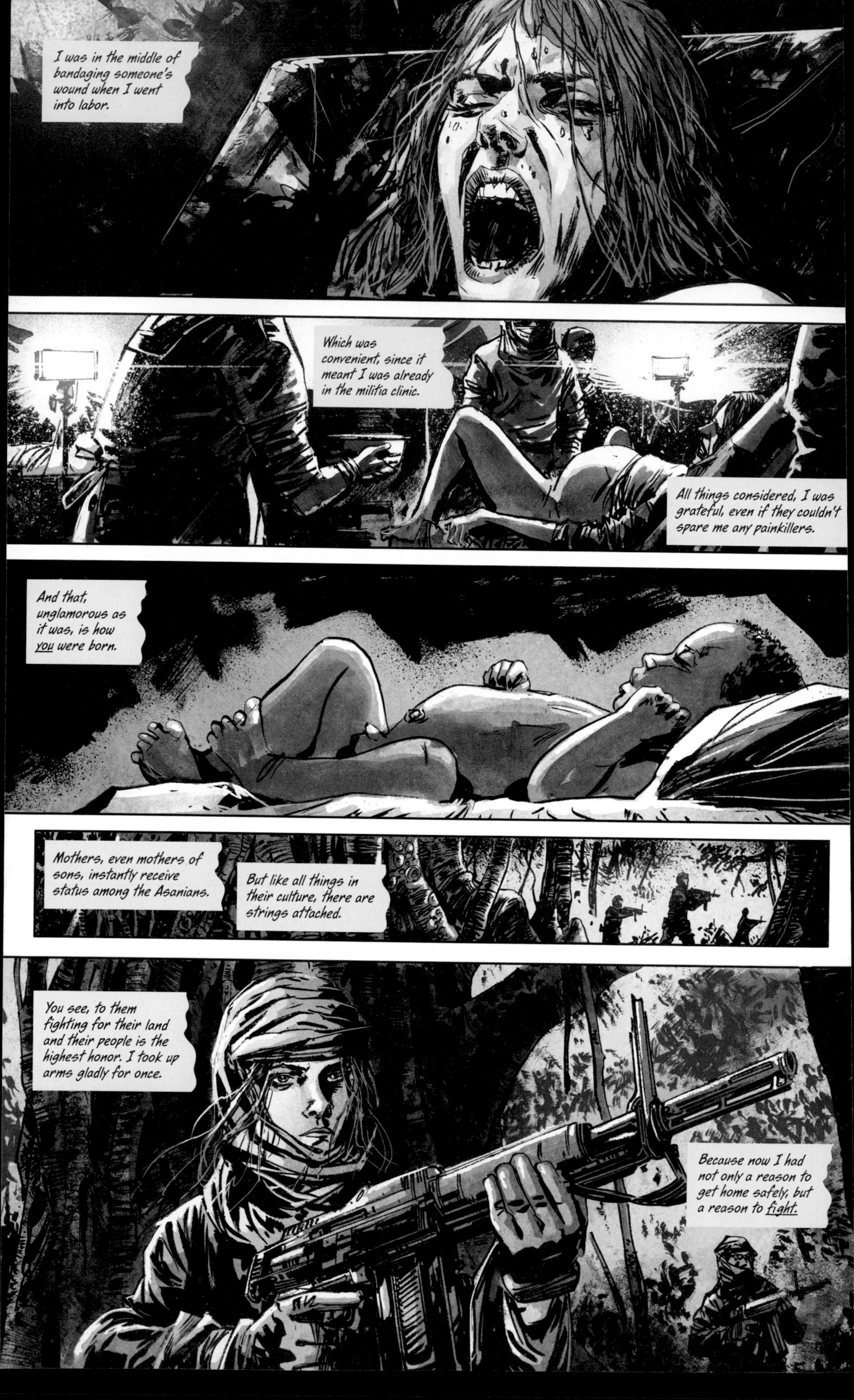
I was in the middle of bandaging someone's wound when I went into labor.
Which was convenient, since it meant I was already in the militia clinic.
All things considered, I was grateful, even if they couldn't spare me any painkillers.
And that, unglamorous as it was, is how you were born.
Mothers, even mothers of sons, instantly receive status among the Asanians.
But like all things in their culture, there are strings attached.
You see, to them fighting for their land and their people is the highest honor. I took up arms gladly for once.
Because now I had not only a reason to get home safely, but a reason to fight.

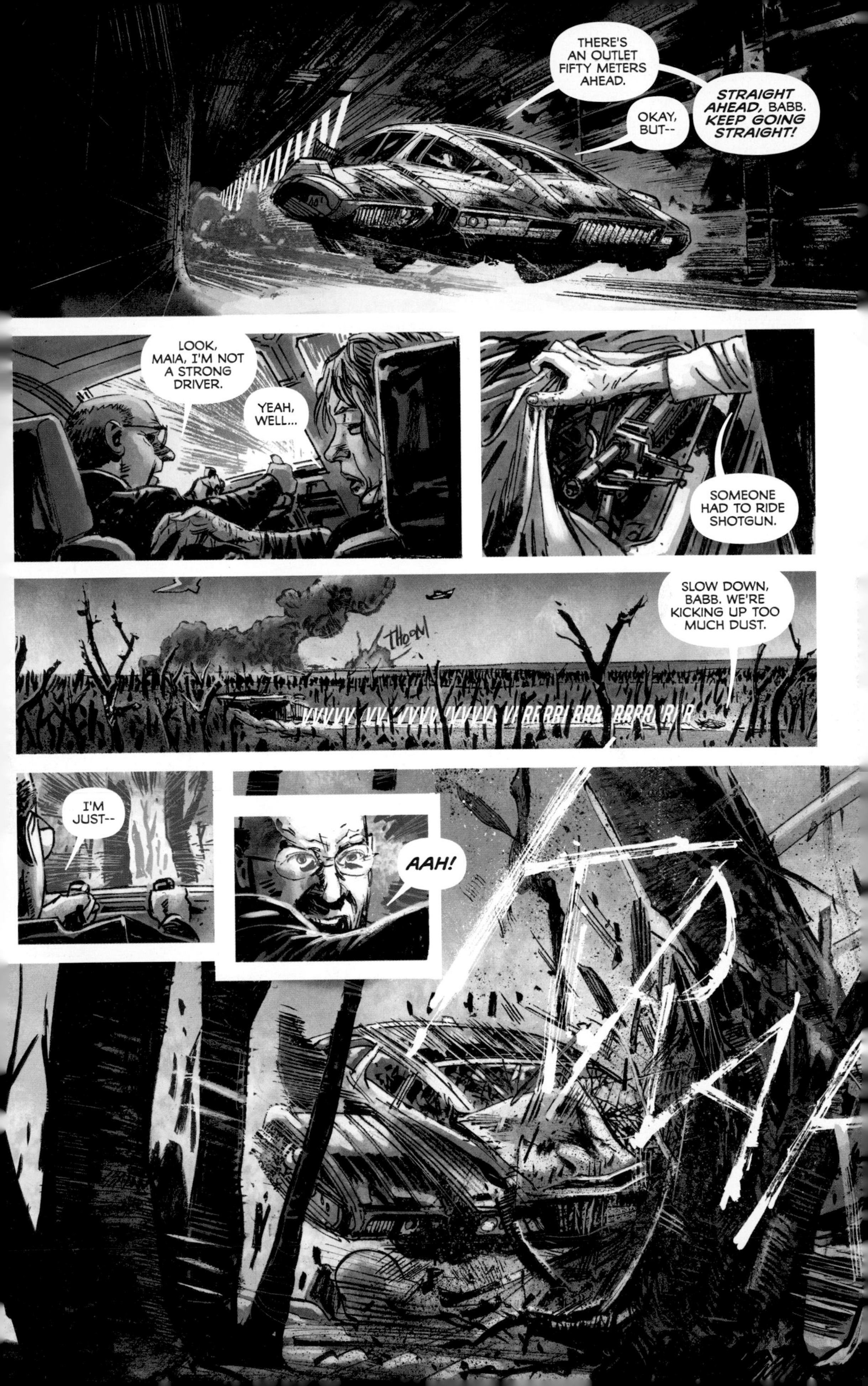
THERE'S AN OUTLET FIFTY METERS AHEAD.
OKAY, BUT--
STRAIGHT AHEAD,* BABB. *KEEP GOING STRAIGHT!
LOOK, MAIA, I'M NOT A STRONG DRIVER.
YEAH, WELL...
SOMEONE HAD TO RIDE SHOTGUN.
THOOM
SLOW DOWN, BABB. WE'RE KICKING UP TOO MUCH DUST.
I'M JUST--
AAH!

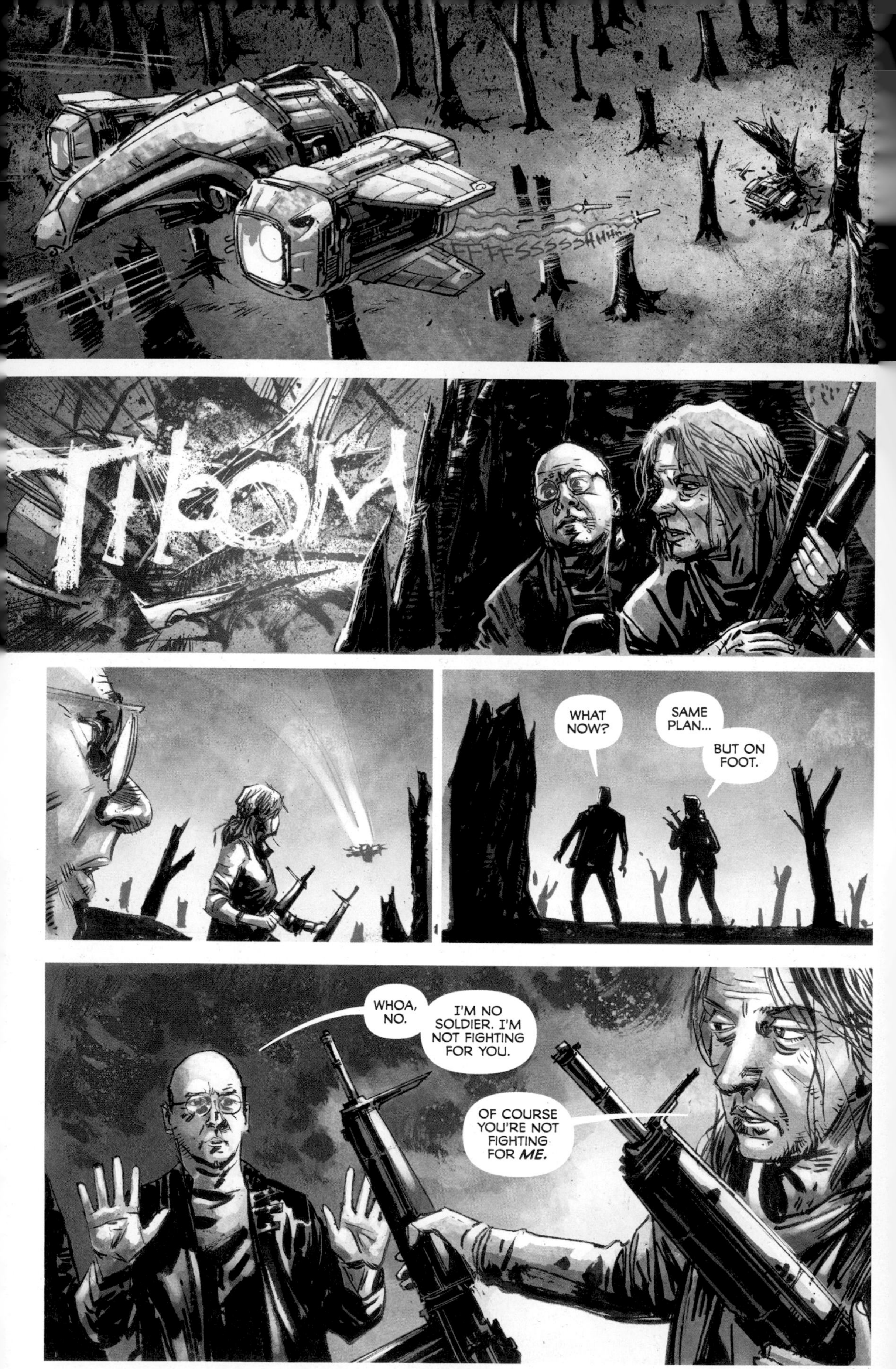
FFFFFSSSSSSHHHH
THOOM
WHAT NOW?
SAME PLAN...
BUT ON FOOT.
WHOA, NO.
I'M NO SOLDIER. I'M NOT FIGHTING FOR YOU.
OF COURSE YOU'RE NOT FIGHTING FOR *ME.*

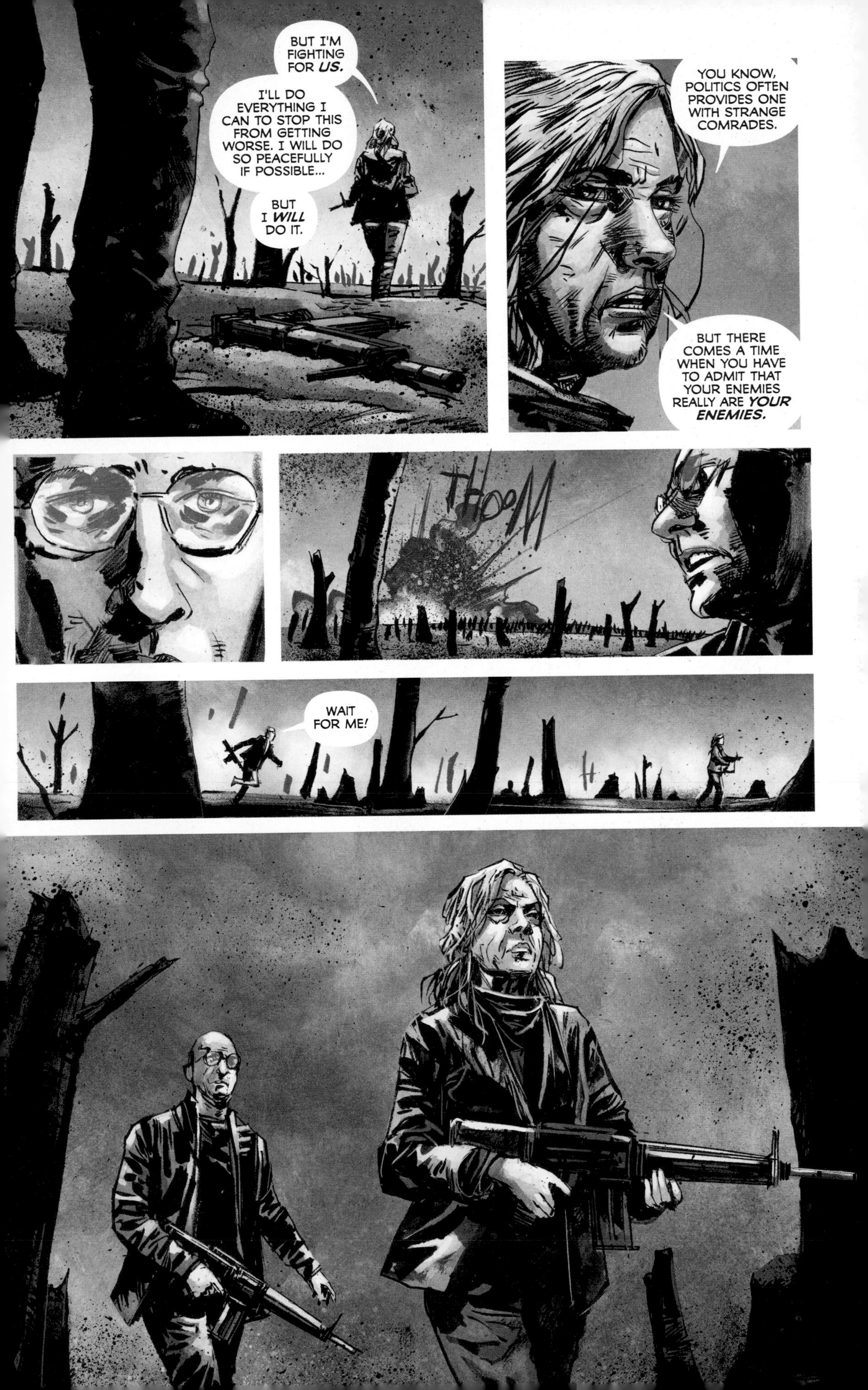
BUT I'M FIGHTING FOR US.
I'LL DO EVERYTHING I CAN TO STOP THIS FROM GETTING WORSE. I WILL DO SO PEACEFULLY IF POSSIBLE...
BUT I WILL DO IT.
YOU KNOW, POLITICS OFTEN PROVIDES ONE WITH STRANGE COMRADES.
BUT THERE COMES A TIME WHEN YOU HAVE TO ADMIT THAT YOUR ENEMIES REALLY ARE YOUR ENEMIES.
WAIT FOR ME!

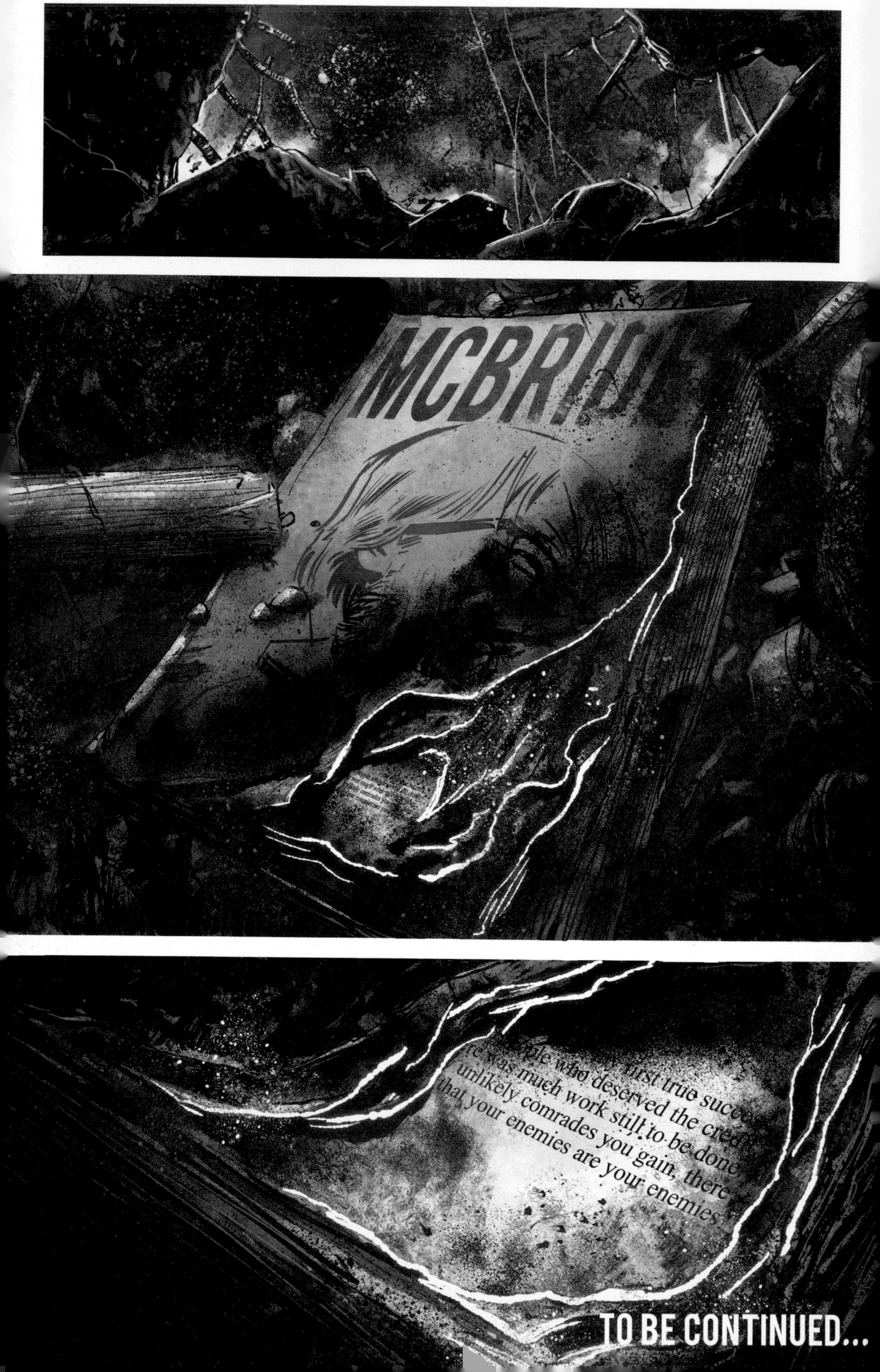
MCBRI
ple who deserved the cre
re was much work still to be done
unlikely comrades you gain, there
that your enemies are your enemies
TO BE CONTINUED...

END OF
CHAPTER
03

WELCOME TO ASAN

Whether this is your first trip to Asan or your twentieth, there's always something new to see. No sooner have you focused on the huge jumping insect to your right than your attention is drawn to a scaly creature crawling through the underbrush on your left. But wait, did that snake-like plant just move opposite the direction the wind is blowing?

Take a deep breath and relax. The first thing to realize about Asan is that you will never see all of it, or even most of it, no matter how often you visit. Despite the generations that have passed since humans first colonized this planet there are sights still unseen by human eyes, and virgin areas untouched by human hands. The average traveler won't be ambitious enough to break any truly new ground, but that doesn't mean the thrill of discovery isn't available on even the shortest trips to the largest towns.

So grab some raingear, slip this book in your pocket, and get ready for adventure! But please, always tell someone where you plan to hike and when you plan to be back. There are dangers on Asan unknown on Kent or Avalon, and it is the wise traveler who plans for the best while taking precautions to avoid the worst.

For ease of identification all names in this guide appear as they are known locally. The scientific names are still contested in most cases due to the paucity of communication with Earth (a problem that will no doubt be corrected in future editions of this book), but since this is a detail usually unappreciated by the general reader, we have decided to leave them out at this time. HAPPY WILDLIFE SPOTTING!

ELES

For many seekers of adventure, a trip to Asan that doesn't include an eles sighting is a trip wasted. It's easy to see why, as these creatures are both impressive and interesting. Despite their size, finding them is not easily done as they favor deep jungle and are shy of human habitations. You will have no problem identifying their favorite feeding grounds though, as these animals are indiscriminate about tearing apart trees and trampling undergrowth while questing for their preferred meals. These often include the hearts of older growth and fruiting bodies that grow high above the forest floor, resulting in large areas that look as if they have been flattened by a storm. This vegetal mayhem may seem alarming, but it has been hypothesized that without it the forests of Asan's southern hemisphere would be much less richly supplied with species as the eles break apart old trees, allowing young ones to take root in their stead.

Little is known about the intricacies of the eles' family life. Groups of related animals often travel together, and may persist for years as a cohesive unit, but the fact that some individuals seem to prefer a solitary existence points to a complex social structure that begs for further study. This difference in lifestyle was initially thought to be a product of gender roles, and you may still hear solo eles referred to as "bachelors." This conclusion was based on the false idea that animals on Asan would have only two genders, as Earth life usually does. We now know that life on Asan follows rules of its own, which have only recently begun to be unraveled.

KELPHIE

Often referred to simply as "dogs," this is one animal that even the most casual wildlife observer is likely to notice. Not only are they robustly sized and prone to a loud, gravelly, penetrating bark, they are also among the few animals on Asan that have developed a taste for living around people. Indeed, some smaller towns have developed packs so large that they are considered a nuisance by locals, but to the visitor from Kent or Avalon watching them can be a delight, especially when they have pups in tow.

A word of caution is warranted here: while kelphies often live around human habitation without incident, scavenging on refuse and whatever they can hunt in the transitional jungle close to town, they are quite capable of inflicting serious bites. Don't underestimate their loyalty to their pack mates, as more than one visitor has learned to their sorrow while attempting to interact with a young or injured individual.

Like many Asanian animals, the social life of a kelphie is rich and complex. Gender seems to be unfixed, although some researchers have noted that we may simply lack an organizing principle beyond our own male/female dichotomy. Regardless, we do know that any given individual is capable of producing offspring, but in practice they never do so in more than one season running and never in packs comprised of less than four members.

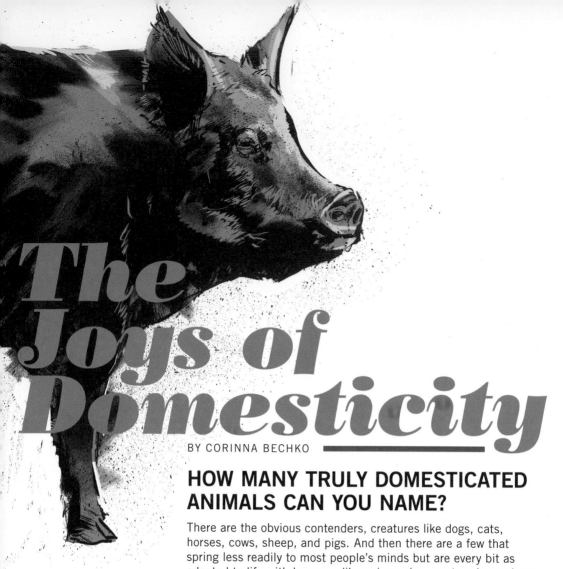

The Joys of Domesticity

BY CORINNA BECHKO

HOW MANY TRULY DOMESTICATED ANIMALS CAN YOU NAME?

There are the obvious contenders, creatures like dogs, cats, horses, cows, sheep, and pigs. And then there are a few that spring less readily to most people's minds but are every bit as adapted to life with humans, like guinea pigs, western honey bees, pigeons, yaks, and koi. If you think about it for a while, you'll probably come up with a list that numbers around 40. But why is this? Out of the millions of species that exist on our planet, why do we have to scour the globe to find a paltry couple of dozen that will consent to live alongside us in a communal relationship? Compared to the impact that humanity has had on most other aspects of our world, this number seems surprisingly low.

Of course, if you expand your search beyond the animals that have changed to fit our needs, your count will be much higher. Axolotls, snakes, gerbils, geckos, parrots, mink, and even alligators are common in captivity. We value them for companionship, eat their meat, harvest their fur, and sell their offspring. But none of these fits the narrow definition of being truly domesticated, which is to say that they have not changed significantly through selective breeding so that they differ much from their wild counterparts. In fact, the most substantive changes in these populations are usually cosmetic, as when a breeder produces a new color morph of corn snake. The hatchling may be quite pretty, but no one expects that it will behave much differently from a corn snake captured from the wild. Comparatively, wolves and dogs are worlds apart, even when they happen to look similar. So, are we just not trying hard enough with these other guys, or what?

In truth, most animals can be tamed to some extent. Zoo animals often become quite attached to their keepers. Parrots form strong bonds with their humans too, and some fish even learn to recognize their caregivers. But that doesn't mean that the species as a whole would be a good fit for domestication. The reasons are complex, but Dr. Jared Diamond, an expert on evolutionary physiology, narrows it down to six essential criteria. It's not hard to find animals that fulfill one or two, but it is the rare beast that tics every box.

The first and maybe most important attribute is adaptability of diet. Picky eaters don't last long around humans in lean times. Dogs are great at this. They're happy to scarf down whatever they find, as are goats. Even notoriously finicky domestic felines will readily switch between hunting for themselves, chowing down on table scraps, and scavenging on the street.

Second, and closely related to diet, is the willingness to reproduce in captivity. Animals that require elaborate courtship displays or that become overly territorial when mating are hard for humans to provide for.

Third, they must mature quickly. This is most true of animals used for meat, but it's also a requirement for any species that we hope to influence through selective breeding (or at least it was before the advent of new technologies that work directly on DNA in a lab). This is one of the biggest reasons that Asian elephants aren't considered domesticated despite their long history of laboring for humankind. There is, of course, a further reason that Asian elephants and not African elephants are drafted for this purpose, but we'll get to that in a moment.

Fourth, humans aren't very big or very strong compared to many of the animals that live in our general proximity. For that reason we prefer to work with creatures that are already docile by nature. Just think of the difference between a horse and a zebra, or better yet, ask a zoo professional. Zebras are notoriously unpredictable and prone to biting. Horses retain many of the same behaviors, but are much more "trustworthy." Interestingly, while this difference in personality has certainly been enhanced by breeding, it was probably innate to their separate lineages before humans came on the scene. The same is true for African and Asian elephants, the former displaying more aggression in captive situations.

Fifth, and closely related to docility, is the absence of a strong startle or panic response.

Imagine two herds, one of gazelles and one of sheep. Startle the gazelles and they bounce off in all directions, heedless of fences or obstacles. Startle the sheep and they nervously flock together, a behavior that lends itself quite easily to being herded. Cats are a strange outlier here, since wild cats, particularly the smaller varieties, are prone to vigilance and a fear of novel stimuli. It's worth noting, then, that some studies have shown that the part of the brain that ramps up this response is smaller in domestic cats than in any of their wild counterparts.

Lastly, a pre-existing social hierarchy is key in allowing a wild species to make the jump to domesticity. In other words, the animal has to have a slot into which it can fit a human, otherwise it simply will never recognize us as part of its in-group. Cats may seem to not fit this criterion either, but here fact and fiction collide. It is true that most kinds of cats maintain territories, but think of the lion's ability to form them communally. There is now good evidence that our feline companions are descended not from a lone hunter, but from a species that held similar communal territories too. Feral cats certainly can form large colonies in which unrelated cats regard each other as family members, which is how our cats seem to respond to us too.

With these specifications in mind, could we conceivably tame and domesticate alien life forms too, should we ever find any? The answer is probably yes, as long as the creatures have the capacity to recognize us as a fellow being and respond accordingly. As it turns out, the path to domestication isn't one imposed by humanity upon other species, but is instead a partnership that has benefits for both creatures despite any abuses that may result. Human willpower alone isn't enough to make it work. Our animal companions must always meet us half way.

Superh

By CORINNA BECHKO

WHERE LIFE IS CONCERNED, OUR PLANET HIT THE JACKPOT.

There's life everywhere here, from the driest desert to the deepest ocean trench. It exists high in the atmosphere, deep below ground, even on top of other life. But when we search elsewhere in our solar system, we come up with a big fat goose egg. Oh sure, there are tantalizing glimpses of maybe. A meteor with what could be microfossils from Mars, a couple of chemical signatures that could denote something going on in the oceans of other moons. But so far, life on Earth is all we've got. So surely we're the gold standard of what makes a planet habitable, right?

Perhaps not. There are a lot of things about our world that make our continued existence a bit of a crapshoot. We're barely in the "goldilocks zone" for one thing. That's the ring around any star where water can be liquid, a prerequisite for life as we know it. Get too close, the water boils away. Too far, and it's all locked up as ice. There are ways around this, of course, but that's the general idea. "In the zone" conditions are just right for rivers, lakes, and oceans. But Mars is placed even better than we are, and look what happened there. We still don't know quite what went wrong, or why our neighbor was once flush with water where now it's drier than any bone. Clearly there's more to habitability than just location.

From our own experience, we can conjecture about what some of these things are. A magnetic field is a must, for one thing. Without it, we'd be prey to all sorts of space "weather" bombarding us with energetic, deadly particles in addition to the solar wind. The particles are bad enough, but it's the wind that would do the real damage as it slowly stripped our atmosphere and spread it into space, leaving behind a barren, dry rock. Not unlike Mars, now that you mention it, with its incredibly thin atmospheric shell. It's worth noting that Mars once had a magnetic field of its own that dissipated billions of years ago.

So obviously an atmosphere is the next thing necessary, since it provides not only shielding from space but life-giving chemistry as well. It's hard for a small world to hold on to one of these, as exemplified by our moon, which doesn't have one at all. And, counter-intuitively, it might be enhanced by plate tectonics, hothouse like Venus where it's difficult to imagine any life thriving. But what if we had more atmosphere, not because it was thicker, but because the Earth was bigger? Recent studies suggest that "super-Earths," rocky planets two or three times the size of our own, might have an easier time holding onto an atmosphere and protecting life. Such planets would still have plate tectonics, but theirs might be slower and less locally destructive.

Another factor to consider is time. Since the "goldilocks zone" changes with the

ibitable

the very cause of so much misery and death. Volcanoes and earthquakes aren't healthy for anyone living within their impact zone, but they do create vents and cracks in the Earth's surface that allow gasses to escape. The moon has quakes too, but without any water to literally dampen them down, they continue for up to an hour. That's far too long for comfort on an inhabited world, which means there's something like a feedback loop going on down here that allows the crust to move but prevents quakes of such deadly duration.

Putting all of these factors together, it's clear that the Earth is prime real estate for life. But is it the best there is? Is this a mansion with a pool and tennis court, or are we packed into a rental with old shag carpeting and a view of the freeway? It's impossible to know from our sample of one, but there's good evidence that other places could be better.

We're fairly certain that any habitable world would have a magnetic field and atmosphere, but what about the parameters? Would a more robust magnetic field be better? The jury's out on that one, since some theories predict that mutations caused by occasional cosmic ray bombardment help drive faster evolutionary rates, resulting in more biodiversity. Likewise, a thicker atmosphere might result in a hellish

heat and size of its host star, some very old, very stable stars might have very, very old planets in orbit around them. A longer history means more time for life to form, diversify, and even change the planet to suit itself. If such a planet were larger than the Earth, there would be more space for life to spread out and more localized pockets to harbor it, too.

And then there's water, the one substance we always return to. The Earth is blessed with deep, mysterious oceans covering 70% of its surface, but living things are fairly widely distributed in a lot of that volume. If the same amount were spread over a much larger area, but more shallowly, it might well be more productive. It's easy to imagine such a scenario on a super-Earth orbiting a quiet orange dwarf (a type of star just a little less massive, and a lot longer-lived, than our own).

The question of finding such a treasure-trove of life is an open one given the advances being made in planet hunting, but the dream of traveling to one remains a fantasy for now. All things considered, the Earth isn't such a bad place, shag carpeting not withstanding. It might not be the richest jackpot imaginable, but it's a lot more comfortable than any place else we've been. Considering the alternatives, that's worth protecting.

Gardens Both Human and In

BY CORINNA BECHKO

HUMANS ARE VERY GOOD AT MODIFYING ECOSYSTEMS. Sometimes the adjustments are small, as when we plant a garden or mow a lawn. Sometimes they are vast, as when we tip the chemical composition of the atmosphere so out of natural balance that even the weather is affected. The point is, everything we do has some sort of impact, even breathing and eating. To live, it seems, is to change the world, often without even meaning to.

We aren't the only ones who do this, of course. Beavers build dams that force rivers into new courses, tapirs open trails through thick jungle undergrowth, and elephants turn savannah into grassland by uprooting trees. Even insects leave their mark. Take, for instance, leaf-cutter ants. Although individually tiny, their huge colonies are responsible for processing nearly 20 percent of all leaf growth in the New World tropics.

If you've ever been to Central or South America, you've probably witnessed the leaf-cutters in action. Comprised of around 40 distinct species, these ants share a propensity for harvesting small pieces (well, small to us—they often dwarf the ant) of green leaves from trees and bushes, then marching their bounty back to their nests. The resulting "ant highways" are hard to miss, as they stretch as far as 30 meters (100 feet) into the surrounding jungle, both horizontally across the forest floor and vertically up into the canopy. Despite their voracious appetites, they don't pillage the surrounding foliage indiscriminately. Careful analysis shows that only 10 percent of available plant species are affected, and that woody species are chosen over herbaceous ones. Introduced species are also preferred over native varieties, probably because they haven't evolved defenses against the ants' sharp jaws.

Why are the ants so picky? It turns out that they aren't actually eating the leaves (although they do ingest some of the sap as a ready and quick energy supply) but are mulching it to spread on fungal "gardens" cultivated deep within their enormous nests. And since the fungus is finicky, the ants have to be too. It takes a lot of hard work, but the resulting rich food supply can sustain a colony of up to 10 million members.

human

It's worth pointing out that not all ants are created equal. Each has a job, or caste, into which they are hatched. Any given ant colony has a queen, soldiers, and workers, but leaf-cutters take this division of labor to an extreme. There are ants that forage, ants that cut leaves, ants that clean the leaves of dirt and pathogens that could infect the fungus, soldier ants, gardener ants, ants that process the mulch, ants that keep the queen cleaned and fed, and of course the queen herself who may live up to 20 years. But each and every one of them is dependent upon the fungal garden. If anything should happen to it, the colony dies too.

All of which brings up an interesting question. Why would any animal specialize to such an extent that it becomes dependent upon just one food source, much less one that has basically become domesticated to the point that it does poorly on its own in the wild? Isn't that a risky venture, given that a plague or environmental change could wipe out the entire species? The answer is, in many ways, momentum. Obviously the leaf-cutters are fruitful. And the more successful their egg production, fed on a steady diet of nutritious fungus became, the more pressure there was, evolutionarily speaking, to continue down the same path. In this way ants are much like us. We too subsist largely on domesticated foodstuffs, and have for about 12,000 years. And like the ants, a drastic shift in our environment would kill most of our agricultural production, rendering us helpless in the face of mass starvation even if some of us could switch to other sources of nutrition. It's just that the ants have been doing it for about 50,000 years longer and so are that much more set in their narrow ways. But both social insects and social humans live within a complex web of supply and demand that necessitates constant upkeep and modification of the local environment in order for the next generation to survive. And so both must have a healthy ecosystem in order to thrive.

Researchers love to point to parallels between ants and humans, but there's a glaring difference too. The jury is still out on the question of insect consciousness and learning ability, but ants in particular are very much trapped in their lifestyle. Each has a role to play, and play it they must or else die. They can't change caste any more than they can exist alone outside of their colony. Humans, too, do poorly by themselves. And yet, we have the ability to learn from our mistakes, to change our way of life, and to make active decisions that benefit our communities and the world at large in ways that ants could never dream. Of course, this means that we have the ability to be selfish too, something that no ant can ever be.

And so, given that we can and must change our environment no matter what, just by existing, how do we make decisions beyond that? If leaf-cutter ants ceased to exist, a huge source of soil nutrients would be lost, the ratio of plant species in tropical rainforests would be different, and many other species would be affected. If something as small as an ant can have such a huge impact, what should our own role be? There's no easy answer to that, but there's power in the simple fact that we can make choices that other species can't. Beavers must build dams. Elephants must uproot trees. And leaf-cutter ants must cut leaves. Humans must draw breath, but beyond that our constraints are relatively few. The choices may be hard, but if we are conscious of them the ways in which we change the world can bear fruit in the future, not merely the present.

Want to plant your own garden that benefits generations of creatures who can't plant their own? Check out these resources:

- **THE AUDUBON NATIVE PLANT DATABASE**
- **THE XERCES SOCIETY POLLINATOR-FRIENDLY PLANT LIST**
- **THE USDA FOREST SERVICE GUIDE TO NATIVE GARDENING** (FOR THOSE IN THE US)

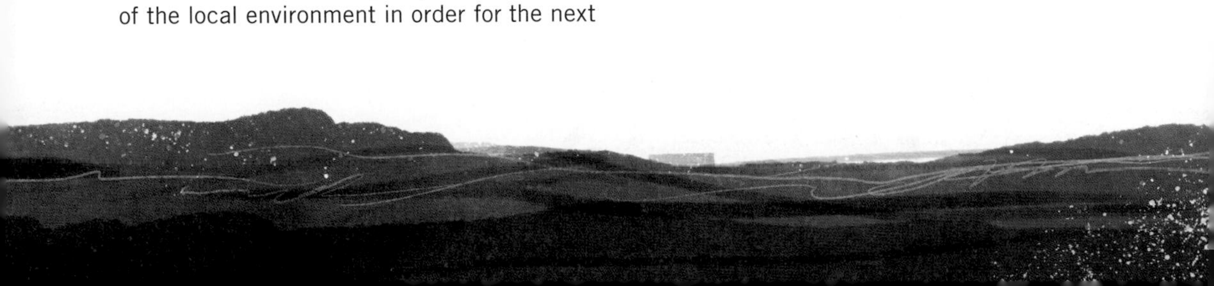

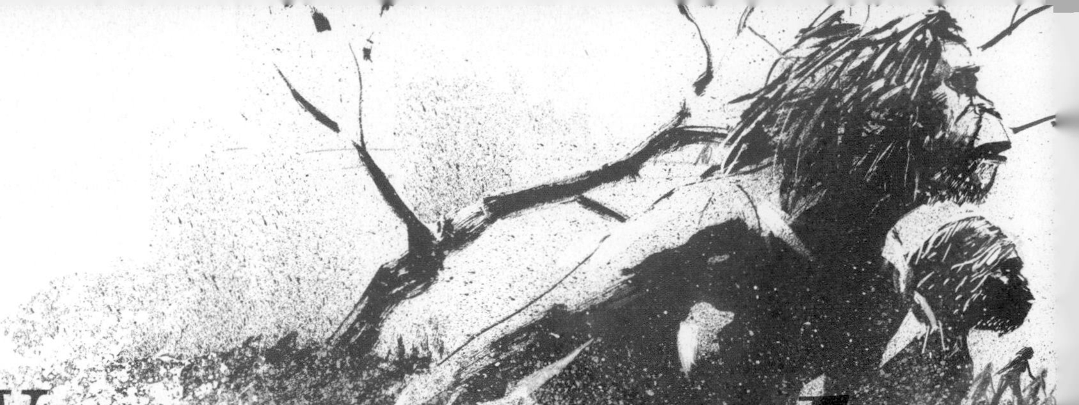

Women and Children First

BY CORINNA BECHKO

HISTORY IS RIFE WITH BRAVE EXPLORERS AND INTREPID MIGRATIONS. There are even some schools of thought that claim this as the defining trait that makes us human, the single imperative that ensured our survival when every other similar species died out. It's what moved us out of Africa, across continents, and to such far-flung and remote shores as Hawaii and Easter Island.

Of course, not every human enjoys a peripatetic lifestyle, but enough of us do that we have remained a single species despite our now worldwide distribution. We move around so much that, even before the advent of modern travel, we interbred at a surprising rate. Certainly, people from different areas of the world have unique attributes. But such differences really are skin deep. When the genetic variation of two humans from two different continents is compared it diverges less than that of two chimpanzees from opposite sides of their range. This astonishing fact becomes even more surprising when one considers populations of, say, Galapagos finches, of which there are 13 species, all descended from a common ancestor a few million years ago. Humans have remained one species because, unlike finches, we like to roam.

Early on, when the first migrations were taking place and humanity was spreading beyond its birthplace, it was probably family groups and small mixed bands that were doing the exploring, slowly, on foot, with women sometimes leading the way. Later, as humans became established all over the world, agriculture took hold, and cultures diverged. At this time it was probably specialized exploratory parties that took to the seas in small boats to conquer islands and other areas unreachable by land. As human populations grew and recorded history evolved, it was usually men who would organize such trips, deeming them too dangerous for the women who had to stay home and tend to babies anyway. Thus was born our idea of what an explorer looks and sounds like, along with names, all male, that betoken excitement and an indomitable spirit.

But now, as we careen into the modern era, there is no livable place left on Earth unexplored. That leaves only space to conquer, and we already know that nowhere near enough to reach within a few years is habitable. Unlike Columbus' journey to the "New World" or Marco Polo's Eastern sojourn, it will take much more than a lifetime to reach the nearest potential Earth-like world. Which means that to do so, we must build and inhabit ships space-worthy enough to last for generations, bringing us full circle to the original small family bands that moved across continents tens of thousands of years ago. Nor will it be men who take the lead here, as the first generation is likely to be comprised only of women, or at least of far more women than men, equipped with a supply of fertilized eggs that need only be nourished inside a mother to form the second generation.

Will we someday expand our range so much that we inhabit other solar systems? The history of humanity would seem to argue yes. And there's a good chance that we will do it just as our ancestors did, with women and children going first.

COVERS

BY GABRIEL HARDMAN

ISSUE ELEVEN

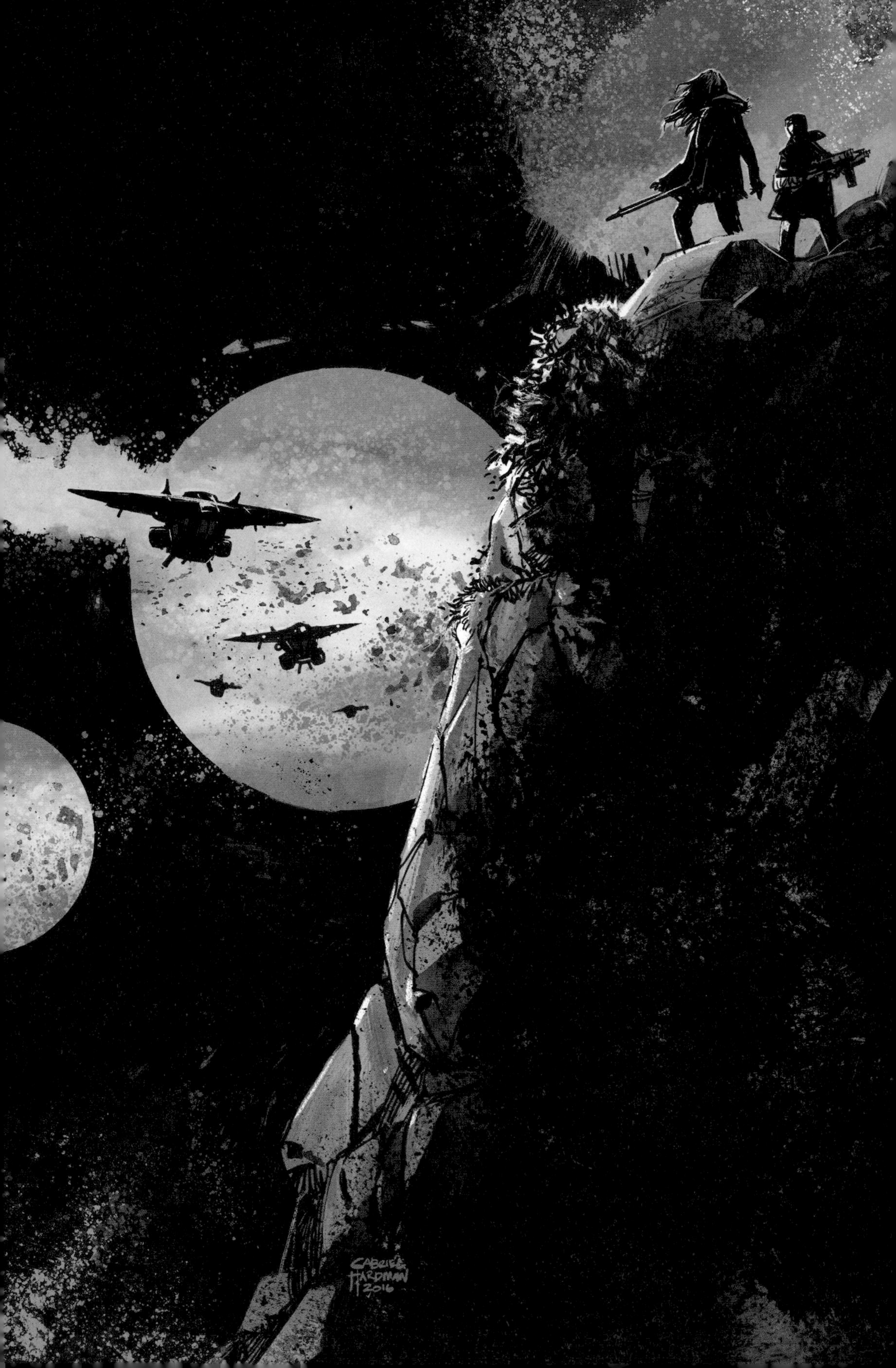
GABRIEL
HARDMAN
2016

ISSUE TWELVE

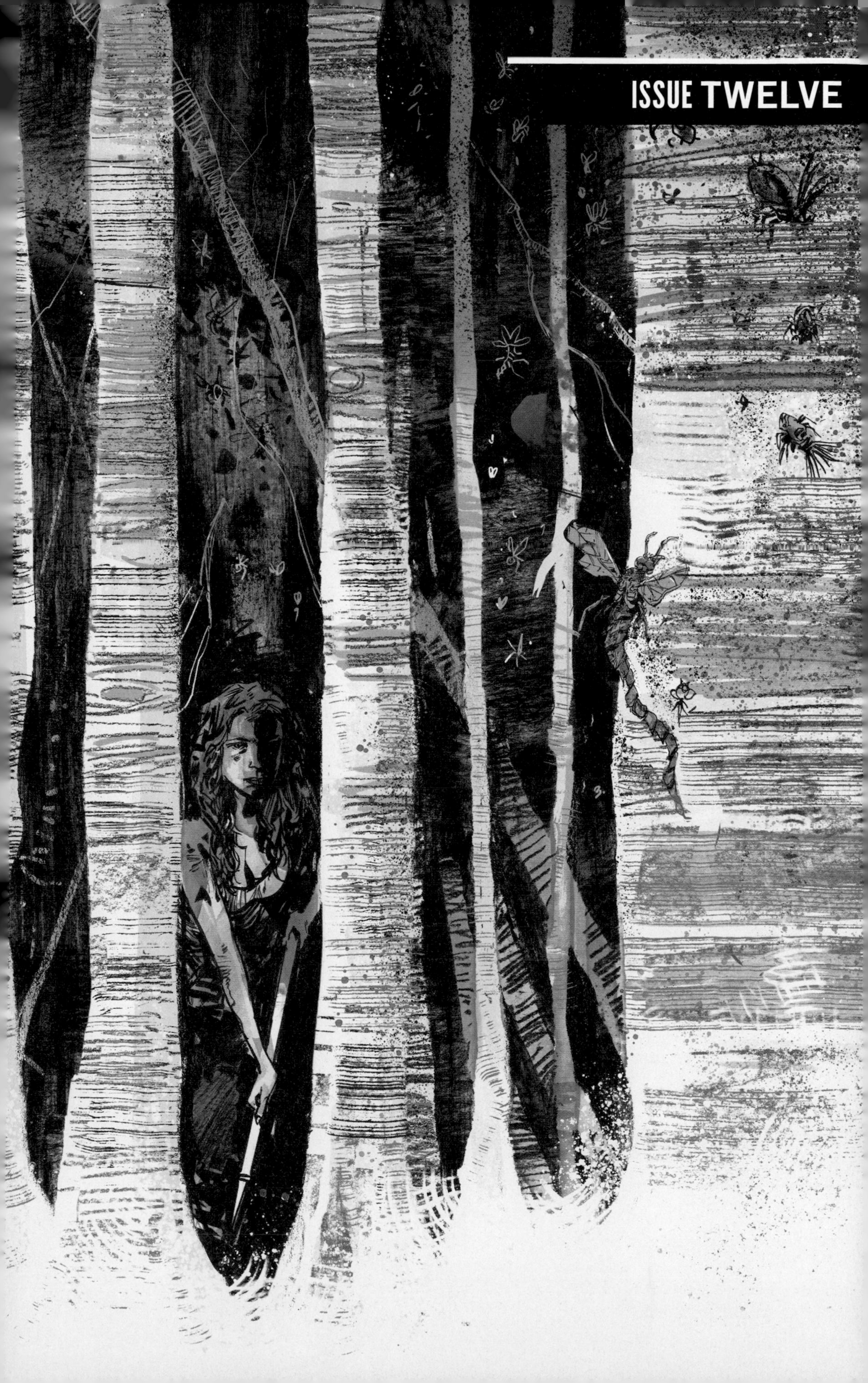

ISSUE THIRTEEN

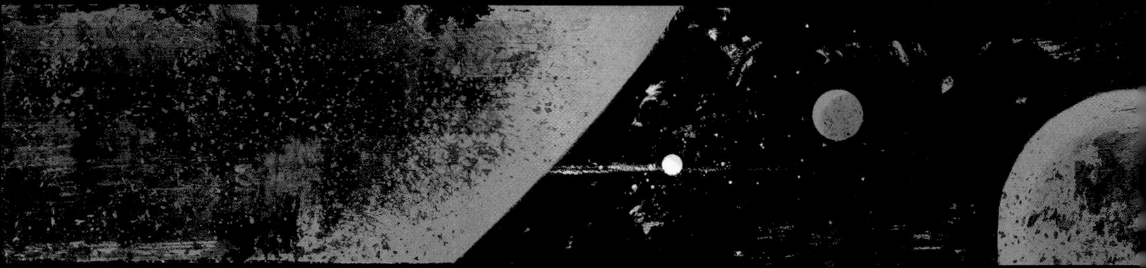

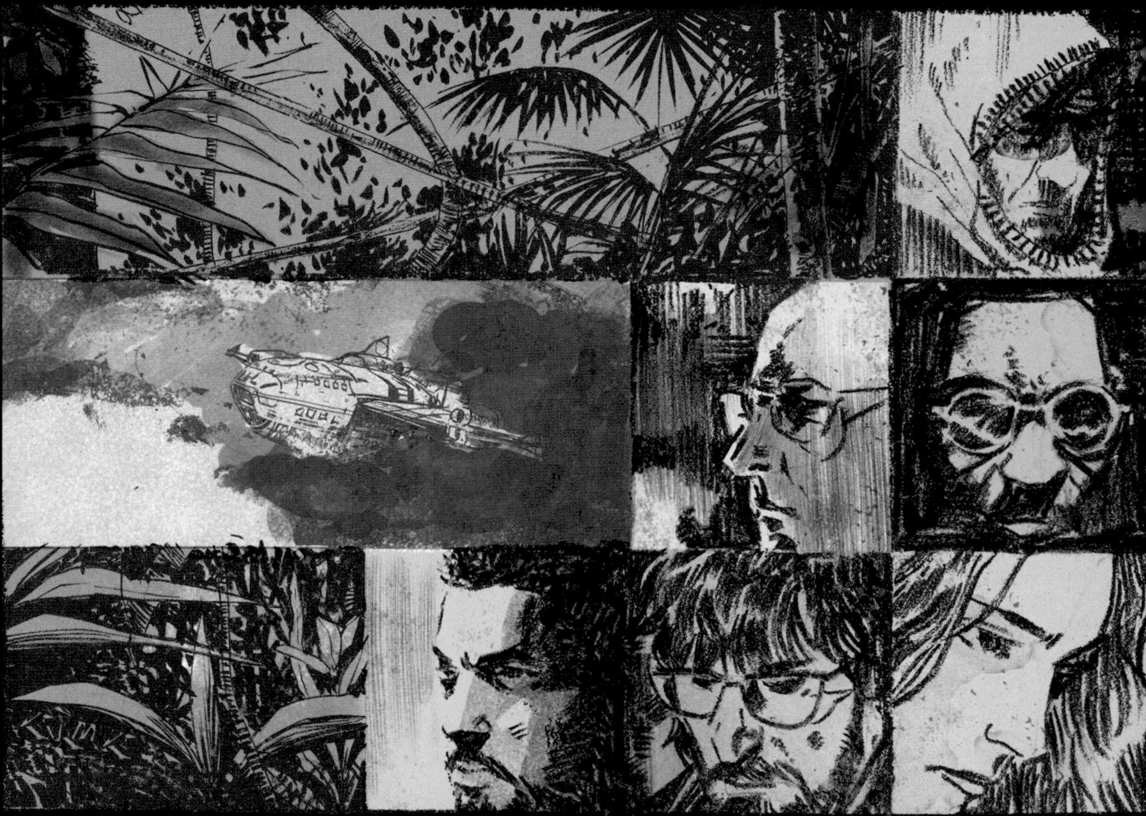

ISSUE FOURTEEN

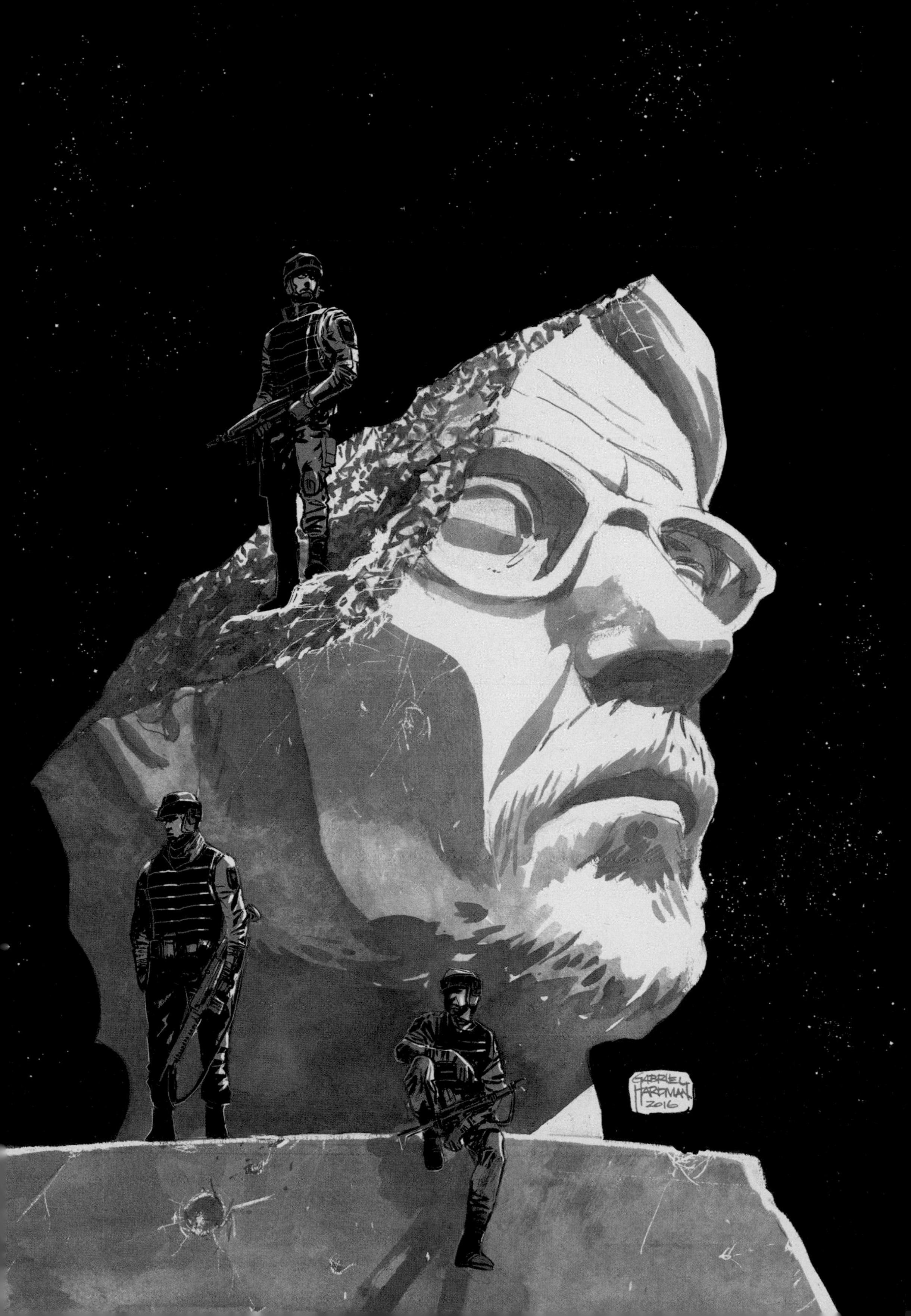
GABRIEL HARDMAN 2016

ISSUE FOURTEEN
UNUSED

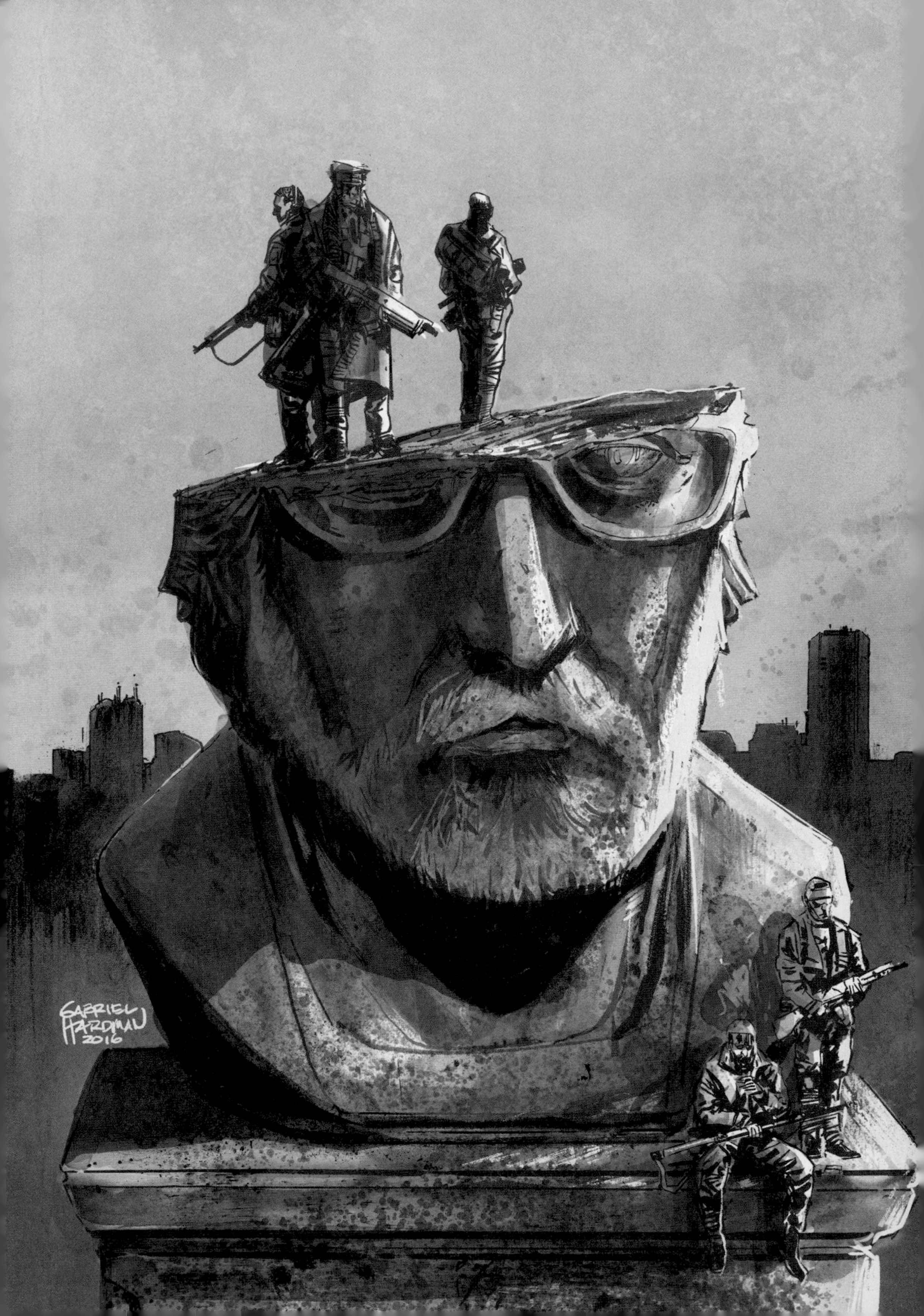
GABRIEL HARDMAN 2016

ISSUE FIFTEEN

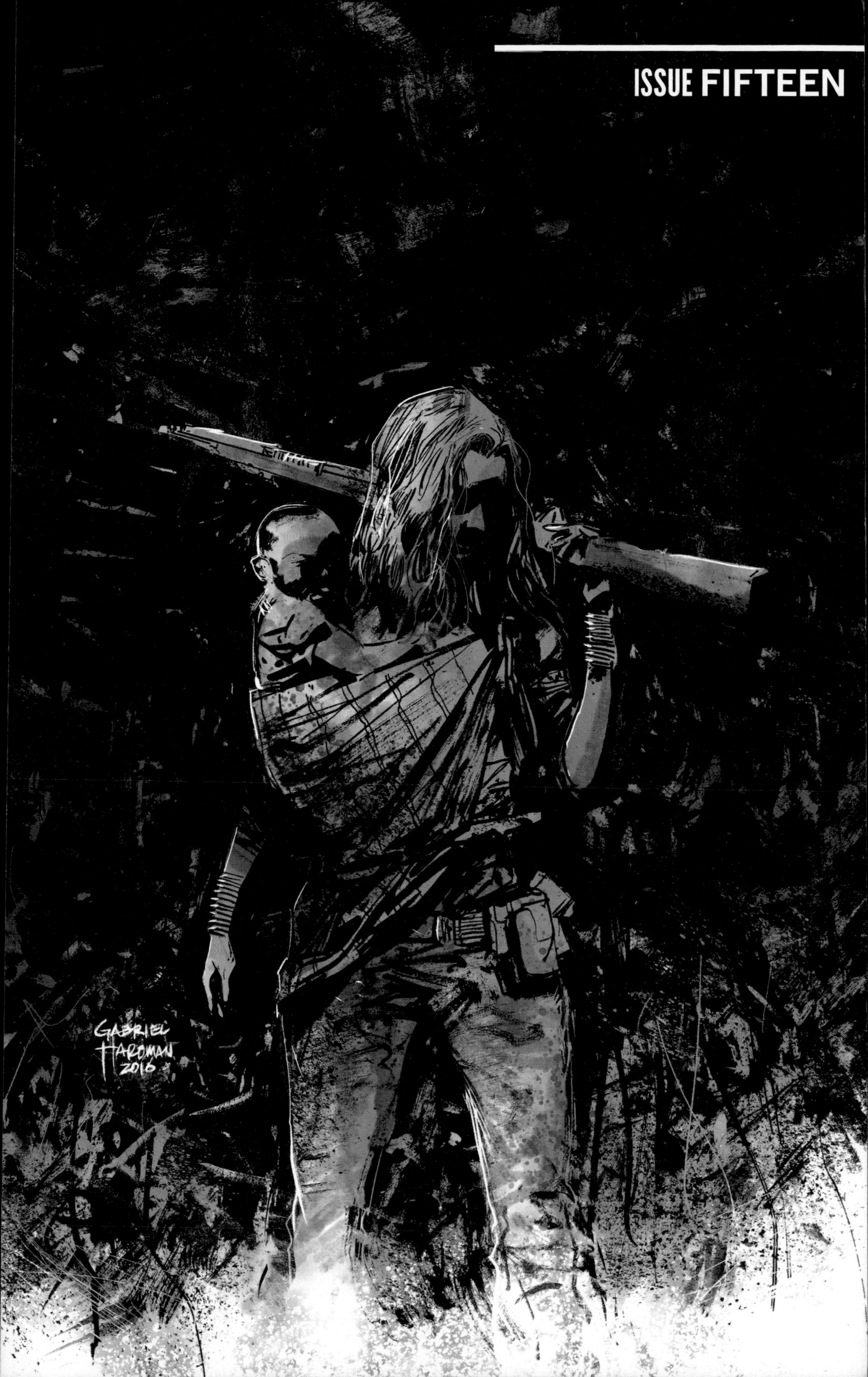
GABRIEL
HARDMAN
2016

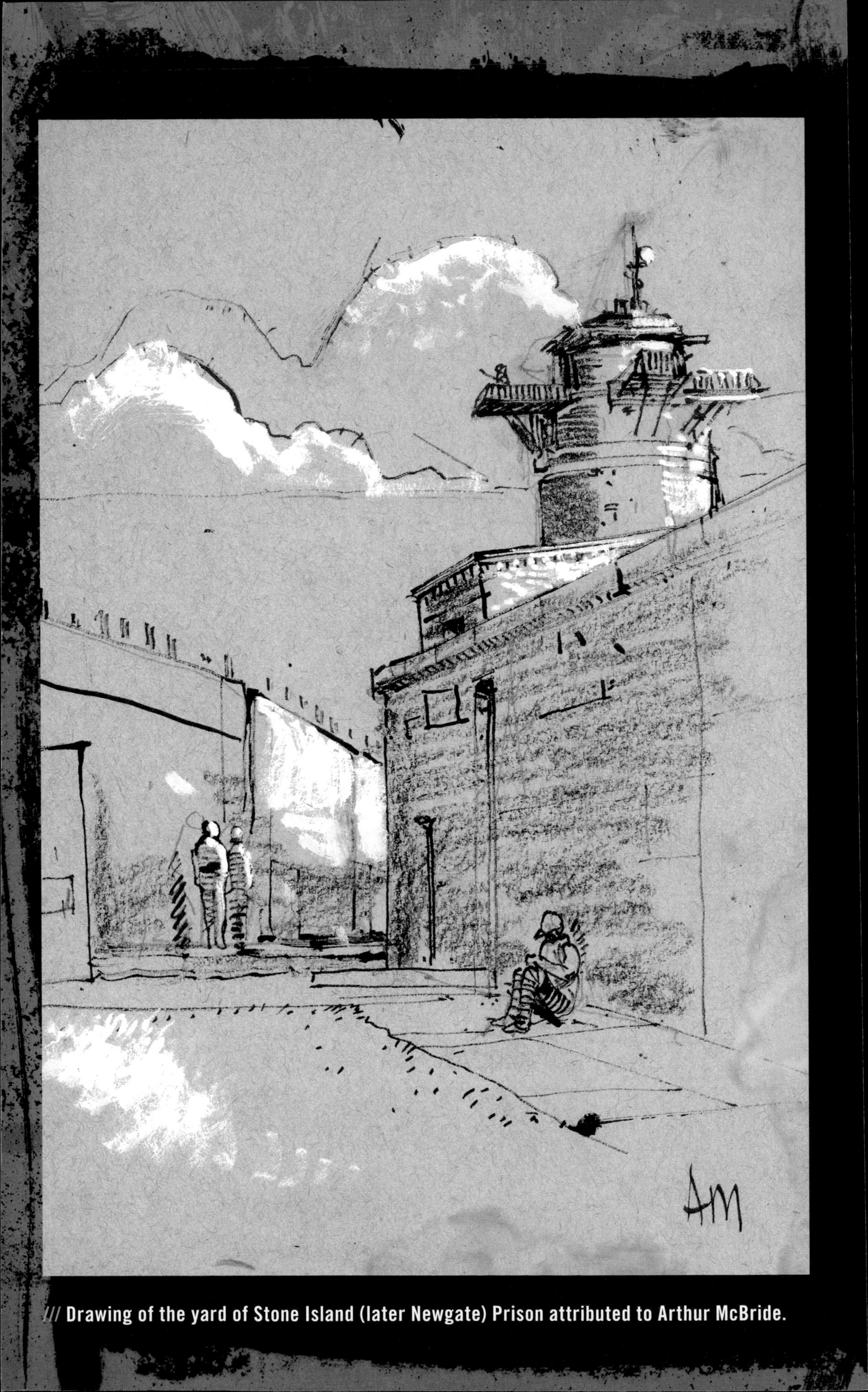
AM

/// Drawing of the yard of Stone Island (later Newgate) Prison attributed to Arthur McBride.

GABRIEL HARDMAN
is the writer/artist of *Kinski*, published digitally by Monkeybrain Comics and collected in print by Image Comics. He also co-wrote (with Corinna Bechko) and drew *Savage Hulk* for Marvel Comics, *Sensation Comics* for DC Comics, *Star Wars: Legacy* for Dark Horse Comics, and *Planet Of The Apes* for Boom! Studios. He has drawn *Hulk*, *Secret Avengers* and *Agents of Atlas* for Marvel as well as the OGN *Heathentown* for Image/Shadowline. He's worked as a storyboard artist on movies such as *Interstellar*, *Inception*, *Tropic Thunder* and *X2*. He lives with his wife, writer Corinna Bechko, in Los Angeles.

gabrielhardman.tumblr.com   @gabrielhardman

CORINNA BECHKO
has been writing comics since her horror graphic novel *Heathentown* was published by Image/Shadowline in 2009. Since then she has worked for numerous publishers including Marvel, DC, Boom!, Dynamite and Dark Horse on titles that include *Aliens/Vampirella* and *Lara Croft and the Frozen Omen*, as well as co-writing *Star Wars: Legacy Volume II*, *Savage Hulk* and *Sensation Comics* featuring Wonder Woman. She is a zoologist by training and shares her home with co-creator/husband Gabriel Hardman, three cats, a lovebird, a farm dog, and a fancy street rabbit.

corinnabechko.tumblr.com   @corinnabechko

JORDAN BOYD

Despite nearly flunking kindergarten for his exclusive use of black crayons, Jordan has moved on to become an increasingly prolific comic book colorist. Some of his most recent credits include *Planet Hulk* and *Ant-Man* for Marvel, and *Deadly Class* for Image. He and his family reside in Norman, OK.

boydcolors.tumblr.com   @jordantboyd

DYLAN TODD
is an art director and graphic designer. You might have seen his work on comics like *Sacrifice*, *Five Ghosts*, *Edison Rex*, *POP*, or *Avengers A.I.* Sometimes he writes comics and sometimes he writes about comics. Despite the fact that they don't show up in pictures, he actually does have eyebrows. His life's ambition is to meet an actual ewok.

bigredrobot.net   @bigredrobot

ALSO BY THE AUTHORS

HEATHENTOWN
WRITTEN BY CORINNA BECHKO
ART BY GABRIEL HARDMAN

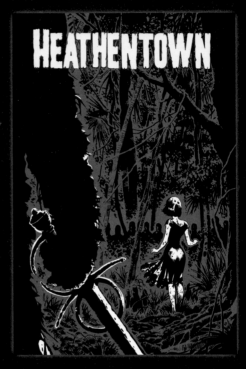

When Anna travels deep within the Florida Everglades to attend her closest friend's funeral, she finds herself in an eerie small town where death might not be the end. To discover the truth, she unearths a coffin, starting a chain reaction and bringing an ancient malevolence into the town bent on Anna's destruction!

"An unorthodox horror story, equal parts hidden worlds, lost love and mammoths, *Heathentown* is that rarest of things—a genuinely unusual take on the undead... Bechko and Hardman are a perfectly matched team as Hardman's beautiful, highly cinematic art captures the excitement and complex emotions of Bechko's memorable and nuanced story." –Publishers Weekly

FROM IMAGE COMICS/SHADOWLINE

KINSKI
WRITTEN AND DRAWN BY GABRIEL HARDMAN

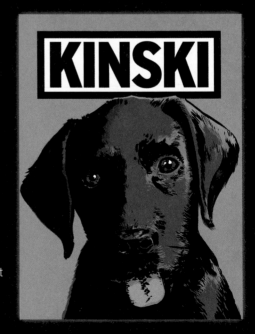

Kinski. The story of a boy and his dog. Only the boy is a traveling salesman and the dog doesn't belong to him.

Joe's self-styled mission to save a puppy from its neglectful owners escalates into a righteous crusade in this quirky crime thriller written and drawn by Gabriel Hardman (*Hulk, Heathentown, Planet of the Apes*).

"Hardman...creates a tense atmosphere that makes *Kinski* the *Breaking Bad* of dognapping tales." –A.V. Club

"[Gabriel] Hardman doesn't waste one line here, and the work is strong, iconic, and just plain awesome...This one is a true winner. You need this comic."–Bag and Board

FROM IMAGE COMICS